Best of luck.
HWCoyle

HAROLD COYLE

SWORD POINT

A NOVEL

VIKING

VIKING

Published by the Penguin Group
27 Wrights Lane, London W8 5TZ, England
Viking Penguin Inc., 40 West 23rd Street, New York, New York 10010, USA
Penguin Books Australia Ltd, Ringwood, Victoria, Australia
Penguin Books Canada Ltd, 2801 John Street, Markham, Ontario, Canada L3R 1B4
Penguin Books (NZ) Ltd, 182–190 Wairau Road, Auckland 10, New Zealand

Penguin Books Ltd, Registered Offices: Harmondsworth, Middlesex, England

First published in the USA by Simon and Schuster, New York 1988
First published in Great Britain by Viking 1989
1 3 5 7 9 10 8 6 4 2

Printed and bound by
Richard Clay Ltd, Bungay, Suffolk

A CIP catalogue record for this book is available from the British Library

ISBN 0-670-82570-0

To A. A. Stovall: "When do I get to meet the company commander?"

and

Tony L. McLain: "Thanks, Dad."

Wars may be fought by weapons, but they are won by men. It is the spirit of the men who follow and of the man who leads that gains the victory.
— GEORGE S. PATTON

Weapons are an important factor in war, but not the decisive one; it is the man and not the materials that counts.
— MAO TSE-TUNG

Contents

Foreword

War is the realm of chance. No other human activity gives it greater scope; no other has such incessant and varied dealings with this intruder. Chance makes everything more uncertain and interferes with the whole course of events.

—KARL VON CLAUSEWITZ

This is a story about a war and the people fighting it. The time and place of the war are unimportant. What is important are the people, their roles and their experiences.

It is easy for modern man to focus on the technical aspects of war and seek solutions and resolution through science and technology. Science, after all, is logical and predictable. Technology is understandable and controllable. The Soviets, comfortable with science and technology, approach warfare and combat in a scientific manner. The ideal military system, from the Soviet viewpoint, is one that can deliver predictable results by using proper force ratios and other such definable inputs. Hence they establish norms and place high value on conformity and discipline so that actions in battle are a predictable constant, not an unknown. Doctrine in the Red Army has the same weight as regulations, and orders to subordinates are detailed and restrictive.

The United States, on the other hand, places its trust in the ability of the individual soldier and his leaders. A great deal of freedom and discretion is afforded the American small-unit leader. Doctrine is often viewed as a guide. Initiative on the part of the commander at all levels is expected, allowing commanders to issue what are referred to as mission-type orders, orders that leave the details for the subordinate commander to figure out.

Both systems of doing business have their merits and are based on the national character of the military that uses them. More important, properly used, both systems will work in war. Many examples from past wars support this. The Soviet Union, the victor of the greatest land war ever waged, proved time and again in 1944–45 that its system worked. The United States also can point to its campaigns in that war and subsequent wars and state that its system works. The interesting question is, What would happen if these two systems were pitted against each other? The answer would be determined not by the weapons and not by the cause for which they were being employed. It would be the people, not the system or the weapons, that determined the outcome. Though weapons and tactics are important, they have the same thing in common: people. It is therefore the people that this story concerns itself with.

The war discussed in this novel takes place in the Islamic Republic of Iran. An invasion of that country by the Soviets is not out of the question, since they have already "intervened" militarily in Iran twice—once in August 1941 and once in March 1946. Today, securing its southern border, squashing the spread of Islamic fundamentalism before it overflows into the USSR, preventing any military alliance between the Gulf states, and controlling the Strait of Hormuz, through which much of the West's oil flows, are very real national objectives for the USSR, especially if it is unable to turn that region into a neutral zone— that is, one free of Western influence. At the same time, containing the Soviet Union and keeping the Strait of Hormuz open are part of the United States's national policy. The concept of a limited confrontation in Iran is therefore far more realistic today than that of a general war in Western Europe.

This book is neither a textbook nor an attempt to predict the future. The doctrine, tactics, plans and policies discussed do not reflect current or planned U.S. Army doctrine, tactics, plans and policy. Nor are the characters in the story based on any people, living or dead. Any similarity between the characters in this book and real people is purely coincidental. Many people will find fault with some of the actions and decisions of the characters. Some of the weapons effects and employment are equally open to criticism. This is, however, a novel, and the author uses his literary license, often.

Politics and strategic and operational plans and decisions are not discussed in detail except where they are important to the story and its characters. The reader should find himself in the same situation, limited to the immediate and narrow world in which the characters of *Sword Point* live, lacking a full understanding of the "Big Picture."

Times used throughout the story are local times and Greenwich Mean Time (GMT); Iranian time is three and a half hours ahead of GMT, accounting for the unusual differences between time zones reflected in this book. All events are sequential.

All unit designations in the novel are fictitious, but their organizations and equipment allowances are, in general, in accordance with current tables of organization. All information on weapons effects and characteristics as well as information on Iran are from open source materials available to the general public. The author has never had access to contingency plans concerning operations in Southwest Asia or participated in simulations concerning Iran or the Gulf states. The scenario depicted here is pure fiction.

A Glossary of Military Terms will be found at the back of the book.

Characters

IN THE ORDER OF THEIR APPEARANCE

AMERICANS

DONALD DUNCAN—Sergeant First Class
Platoon Sergeant,
1st Platoon, B Company, 3rd Battalion,
503rd Infantry, 12th Division

FRANCIS WEIR—Lieutenant General
Commander,
10th U.S. Corps

JACK NESBITT—Master Sergeant
Operations Sergeant,
3rd Battalion, 4th Armor, 2nd Brigade,
25th Armored Division

SCOTT DIXON—Major
Operations Officer (S-3)
3rd Battalion, 4th Armor, 2nd Brigade,
25th Armored Division

EDWARD LEWIS—Major
Executive Officer,
2nd Battalion, 354th Infantry,
Tennessee National Guard

HAROLD R. GREEN—Lieutenant Colonel
Commander,
2nd Battalion, 354th Infantry,
Tennessee National Guard

AMANDA MATTHEWS—1st Lieutenant
Assistant Intelligence Officer (S-2)
2nd Brigade, 25th Armored Division

JOHN EVANS—Captain
Commander,
A Company, 2nd Battalion, 517th Airborne,
17th Airborne Division

ROBERT HORN—Lieutenant General
Deputy Chief of Staff for Operations,
U.S. Army

HAROLD CERRO—2nd Lieutenant
Platoon Leader,
2nd Platoon, A Company, 2nd Battalion,
517th Airborne, 17th Airborne Division

ED MARTAIN—Major, U.S. Air Force
Fighter-bomber pilot
401st Squadron, 59th Tactical Fighter Wing

RANDY CAPELL—1st Lieutenant
Scout Platoon leader,
3rd Battalion, 4th Armor, 2nd Brigade,
25th Armored Division

BRITISH

PERCY JONES—Major, British Army
Foreign Exchange Officer/Liaison Officer
U.S. 25th Armored Division/10th Corps

SOVIET

ANATOL VORISHNOV—Major
1st Officer,
3rd Battalion, 68th Tank Regiment,
33rd Tank Division

MIKHAIL KURPOV—Senior Lieutenant
Platoon Leader,
89th Reconnaissance Battalion,
89th Motorized Rifle Division

NIKOLAI ILVANICH—Junior Lieutenant
Platoon Leader,
3rd Company, 2nd Battalion,
285th Guards Airborne Regiment,
95th Guards Airborne Division

PYOTR SULVINA—Colonel
1st Officer,
28th Combined Arms Army

IVAN OVCHAROV—Colonel
Chief of Staff,
28th Combined Arms Army

VLADIMIR GUDKOV—Captain
Commander,
Oscar-class nuclear attack submarine *Iskra*

NEBOATOV—Captain
Commander,
2nd Company, 1st Battalion,
381st Motorized Rifle Regiment,
127th Motorized Rifle Division

LVOV—Captain
Commander,
3rd Company, 2nd Battalion,
285th Guards Airborne Regiment,
95th Guards Airborne Division

Chapter 1

To be prepared for war is one of the most effective means of preserving the peace.
—GEORGE WASHINGTON

Fort Campbell, Kentucky
1655 Hours, 24 May (2255 Hours, 24 May, GMT)

A casual glance would have revealed nothing out of the ordinary. The sandy track running east to west disappeared into a pine forest, where it was lost from sight as it made a sharp L turn to the north. The tall grass and the branches of the trees were motionless in the stillness of the late afternoon. The only sign of life was the occasional lazy buzz of an insect flitting about. Sergeant First Class Donald Duncan and the men of the 1st Platoon, B Company, 3rd Battalion, 503rd Infantry, had spent hours making sure that that was all anyone would see.

Only upon closer inspection of the tree line south of the track could the steel-blue barrels of several rifles and machine guns be seen protruding from concealed positions. Behind each weapon was a man, hunched down, his face distorted by camouflage paint, his battle-dress uniform, or BDUs, soaked in his own sweat. They lay there motionless, waiting for the signal to fire. That signal would come from one of two sources. The primary cue to fire was a booby trap on the trail. A smoke grenade with its pin removed had been placed back in its shipping tube in such a manner as to hold down the spoon that triggered it. A thin wire was attached to the grenade and stretched across the track six inches above the ground and tied to a tree on the other side.

Anyone walking down the track would be snarled in the wire, pulling the smoke grenade from its shipping tube and allowing the spoon to flip up and detonate the grenade. When that happened, everyone in the platoon would commence firing along his assigned sector of responsibility. If, for some unseen reason, the opposing force, or OPFOR, did not trip the booby trap, the platoon leader would order the platoon to open fire.

The ensuing firefight would be short but bloodless. The men of both Duncan's platoon and the OPFOR—opposing force—were using MILES, short for "multiple integrated laser engagement system." Each weapon was tipped with a rectangular gray box which emitted a laser beam every time the weapon was fired. Every man, friendly or OPFOR, had laser detectors on his helmet and webb gear that would detect the laser beam from another weapon. When this happened, a buzzer, also attached to each man's gear, would go off, telling him and his buddies that he was "dead." The use of MILES ensured that there would be no doubt who won and who lost, a far cry from the days when most training exercises degenerated into screaming matches of "I shot you" and "No you didn't."

Duncan watched the track from his position. Beside him was his platoon leader, a young second lieutenant of twenty-two who had been with the unit less than three weeks. This was the first time the lieutenant had been out on tactical training, and, as a result, he was nervous and fidgety. Duncan, a veteran of nine years' service and numerous second lieutenants, was a patient teacher. He had tactfully explained to his lieutenant everything the platoon was supposed to do and had walked him around, showing him what to check and look for. The lieutenant, visibly chafing to "take charge," wisely accepted Duncan's advice and coaching, asking many questions and mentally noting whom Duncan left on his own and whom he micromanaged. In time he would be running the show. But not today.

Waiting to spring an ambush is, at best, tedious and nerveracking. The frenzied activity of preparing the ambush and the fighting positions was followed by hours of lying in dirt and grass. The young soldiers, used to ceaseless banter and ear-splitting music, were required to maintain a high state of vigilance in silence and almost total isolation. The same cover and concealment that protected them from the enemy separated the men of the 1st Platoon from one another and from their leaders. Each man in the platoon was alone except for the man in the fighting position with him and perhaps the men in the positions immediately to their left and right. The urge to talk and keep each other company was countered by the need to remain silent so that the platoon's position would not be given away. Those who craved a cigarette were discouraged from smoking, because the point element—advance party—of the OPFOR would be alert to the smell of cigarette smoke.

Each man's ordeal was made worse by the heat and the insects that populated the pine forest. Soaked from their exertions in preparing for the ambush and from the humidity, the soldiers had sweat rolling down them from every pore on their bodies. Even if there had been a breeze, it would have been unable to penetrate the pine forest. What sweat had evaporated left large white circles of encrusted-salt stains on everyone's BDUs. Sweat from their brows burned their eyes as it ran down and settled in their eye sockets. But uncomfortable as this was, it did not compare to the annoyance of the insects. Bugs of every description buzzed about freely or crawled on the soldiers, biting exposed skin as they worked their way into the clothing. Few of the men were able to fight the urge to swat and scratch—actions which, however, were mostly futile; efforts to kill or shoo the bugs seemed only to encourage them. These little annoyances did much to increase each man's desire for combat. At least when the OPFOR came, he would be able to lash out at someone, with tangible results.

Duncan's mind, wandering from one random thought to the next, was brought back to the problem at hand by a report from the platoon's forward security element, located one hundred meters down the trail. Using a sound-powered phone, they reported movement to their front. Duncan's only instructions to them were, "Stay alert and keep me posted." He glanced at his watch. It was 1658 hours. Those shit-for-brains idiots really took their time, Duncan thought before he turned to his platoon leader and whispered, "Show time, Lieutenant." Raising himself ever so slightly from his concealed position, Duncan signaled the squad leaders to get ready. There was a slight rustling as men readjusted their positions and prepared to engage the OPFOR. In a few seconds all was again still. They were ready.

The first sign that told them the OPFOR was near was the crunching of sand beneath boots and the sound of someone scurrying about in the grass and the bushes. It was the OPFOR's point element. Two men from the 2nd Platoon, the OPFOR for that day, were leapfrogging down the track in advance of their platoon's main body. Their job was to alert the rest to danger before the whole platoon became involved. The two-man point element worked its way slowly, in no hurry to "die." One man would overwatch, ready to cover by fire if necessary from one side of the track while the other dashed ten to twenty meters ahead to a new firing position in the bushes on the other side of the track. Both men would then scan the area, looking for signs of the enemy. When they were satisfied that all was clear, the man who had been overwatching would get up and dash down the trail to a new position past his partner, who would now be overwatching.

Duncan watched the progress of the point element. The call light on the sound-powered phone signaled an incoming call. Duncan picked it up and whispered, "Duncan." It was the security element reporting the passing of the 2nd Platoon's main body. Duncan didn't reply. He settled down next to his lieutenant and whispered, "Two more minutes and they're in the bag."

From the machine-gun position to his left, the sudden *beep-beep-beep* of a digital watch announced that it was 1700 hours. Duncan, his eyes as wide as saucers, turned to the source of the noise, then back to the OPFOR point element. They had gone to ground, only the swaying of branches to show where they had disappeared. Duncan looked about, noticing that the call light of the sound-powered phone was on. He picked up the phone and answered. The man on the other end announced that the 2nd Platoon was deploying on either side of the trail. The 1st Platoon's ambush had been blown. Further reports from the security element were cut short by the popping of small-arms fire.

Without hesitation, Duncan turned to his lieutenant and shouted, "We've blown the ambush!" then yelled to the squad leaders, "Break contact and move to the rally point, *now!*" Without waiting for a response or needing one, Duncan grabbed the phone, yanked the wires from it and shouted to his platoon leader, "Let's go, Lieutenant, time to get out of here."

Under the control of their squad leaders, the 1st Platoon began to move. The 2nd Platoon, however, was on top of them before they could make a clean getaway. A running gun battle resulted as the 1st Platoon attempted to get back to its rally point, where it would be picked up by helicopters. The 2nd Platoon tried to get around them and pin them. As they dashed from tree to tree,

Duncan grabbed the platoon leader and told him to take the 2nd and 3rd Squads while he tried to delay the 2nd Platoon with the 1st Squad. The platoon leader agreed, shouted out for the 2nd and 3rd Squads to continue to withdraw, and moved out. Duncan turned to look for Staff Sergeant Hernandez, the squad leader for 1st Squad. He didn't see him or the assistant squad leader. Seeing no alternative, Duncan attempted to regain control of the situation. From his position, he yelled, "First Squad, rally on me!"

That was a mistake. Command and control of the platoon had been long since lost. No one knew where anyone else was in the thick pine forest. Instead of serving to rally the 1st Squad, Duncan's order served only to draw attention in his direction. Assuming a crouch, he turned to move to a position from which to set up a hasty defense. Breaking out from between two trees, he suddenly found himself confronted by two men from the 2nd Platoon. Instinctively, all three of them leveled their M-16s and began to blast away. Although he was able to get one of his attackers, Duncan also was hit, which caused his MILES buzzer to begin squawking in his left ear. Disgusted, he straightened up to look about. The early-evening stillness of the pine forest was shattered by the squawk of dozens of MILES buzzers and the tapering off of small-arms fire. A shout from the controller signaled the end of a fruitless day's effort. The 1st Platoon had been wiped out in less than ten minutes.

The Armenian Soviet Socialist Republic
0230 Hours, 25 May (2230 Hours, 24 May, GMT)

The predawn darkness covered the tank column like a cloak as it moved off the dirt road into its assembly area. Traffic regulators from the regiment directed the tanks into their assigned positions. The move went like clockwork, with the lead company moving forward and occupying positions in a shallow arch facing west. The next company in line peeled off and occupied a similar arch facing to the south, with its far-right tank making contact with the far-left tank of the first company. The third company did likewise, facing north and completing the circle by linking itself with the first two tank companies. In this manner, the 3rd Battalion of the 68th Tank Regiment cleared the main road and deployed with nothing more than a few quick motions from the faint flashlights of the traffic regulators.

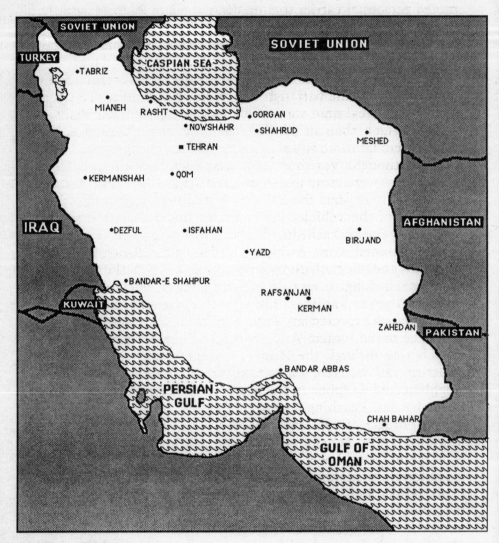

MAP 1: IRAN

Major Anatol Vorishnov brought his eight-wheeled BTR-60 armored personnel carrier to a halt in the lee of a huge boulder in the center of the circle created by the tanks. At a distance of fifty meters he could barely make out the image of the battalion commander's tank coming to a halt in a shallow depression. That pitiful attempt to seek cover served to remind Vorishnov just how vulnerable the battalion was in this bleak mountainous region that the regiment was traveling through; more vulnerable to sudden attack than in open steppes like those around Kiev—which were far more suitable for mechanized warfare. And there at least, thought Vorishnov, the dark earth and the lush green spring grass were more inviting and easier to live with.

As the driver shut the BTR down and the other staff officers piled out of the vehicle, Vorishnov mentally reviewed the upcoming operation, scheduled to commence in two hours. The 28th Combined Arms Army, consisting of three motorized rifle divisions and one tank division, the 33rd, to which the 68th Tank Regiment belonged, was to advance along a line from Jolia to Marand, then to Tabriz—a total distance of over 270 kilometers. While no one expected any serious resistance from the rabble that the once proud Iranian Army had become, the division's line of march was through the Zagros mountain range along narrow, twisting valleys. Here a handful of fanatics could stop the most sophisticated weapons in the world with a few rocket launchers and a barrier. Reaching Tabriz wouldn't be the end of their difficulties; in fact, it wouldn't even be the halfway point. Not until they were near Tehran, over six hundred kilometers from their start point, would the 28th Combined Arms Army have some open terrain to maneuver in.

As selfish and unprofessional as the thought was, Vorishnov was thankful that the 33rd Tank Division would be following the motorized rifle divisions. The thought of being trapped in a narrow valley by an ambush sprung by crazed Muslims trying to become martyrs was terrifying to him. Stories of such incidents in Afghanistan had been passed around by word of mouth from people who had been there. He glanced at his watch. Two more hours and it would all begin. With a little luck and a lot of help from Spetznetz commando teams, from the KGB, from Tudeh—the Iranian Communist Party—and from a couple of well-placed airborne assaults, the 28th Combined Arms Army would be overlooking the Strait of Hormuz in four weeks. Or, Vorishnov thought, that's what the plan is.

Aboard a U.S.A.F. liaison jet en route from Washington, D.C., to Fort Hood, Texas
1730 Hours, CST, 24 May (2330 Hours, 24 May, GMT)

Lieutenant General Francis Weir sat staring out the small window at the clouds below. Absentmindedly his fingers drummed upon the red-covered document labeled SECRET sitting on his lap. He still found it difficult to accept that he had just been ordered to move his entire corps from Fort Hood and Fort Polk to Iran and be prepared to conduct combat operations against Soviet forces now massing to invade that country. The 10th Corps was tagged to go to NATO, not Southwest Asia. They didn't have plans covering any such contingency. That was supposed to be someone else's job. Yet less than three hours ago he had been told to forget about Europe and prepare his corps for deployment to the Persian Gulf.

The corps commander turned to the order and opened it to the page with the mission statement and read it again:

> *10th Corps will mobilize and deploy from home station to designated ports of embarkation (see Annex E), for movement to the Persian Gulf. The U.S. Navy will transport 10th Corps to ports of debarkation (to be determined); 10th Corps will assemble and prepare to conduct combat operations against enemy forces in co-operation with other U.S. and allies' forces as directed.*

Weir turned to the list of annexes. Next to Annex E was: "To be Published." He closed the document and turned back to the window. Christ, he thought, not only can't they tell me yet where I'm leaving from or where I'm going to land, they don't even know who I'm supposed to fight. He turned to his operations officer. "Chris, did you get word back to Hood to have the corps orders group ready when we get back?"

"Yes, sir. I talked to the chief of staff. He indicated that most of the staff and all of the division commanders were still there. Of course, we might not be able to get General Allen from Fort Polk there, but the chief said he will try."

"Have you figured out what we're going to tell them when we get there?"

The operations officer thought for a moment. "Well, sir, other than what they told us in D.C., no, sir, I haven't."

The corps commander considered that response. "Well, Chris, neither have I. But don't worry, we still have another hour to pull something out of our ass that makes sense."

The operations officer didn't answer, watching as his commander turned back to the window and continued drumming on the order in his lap.

Fort Hood, Texas
1730 Hours, 24 May (2330 Hours, 24 May, GMT)

Without rising from his desk, Master Sergeant Jack Nesbitt covered the phone receiver and called out to his boss, the battalion S-3, "Major Dixon, the brigade three is on the line for you."

Dixon looked at his watch. He mumbled out loud to himself, "Shit! That's all I need. Doesn't he know this is Friday?" Then to Sergeant Nesbitt, "Tell him I'm not here, that I went home to play with my wife."

Nesbitt put the phone back to his ear and relayed the first part of the message, listened for a moment, then covered the receiver again. "No go, Major. He says it's very important."

Everything in the 25th Armored Division was important. The trick was to know what really was important. Dixon decided that Michaelski, the brigade S-3, wouldn't be calling this time of day on a Friday unless it really was important. He picked up the phone, "Dixon here. What's so hellfire important that it can't wait till Monday?"

"Tuesday, Scott. Don't forget this *was* going to be a three-day weekend."

"Yeah, I remember. And I intend to keep it a three-day weekend. So what is it you want?"

"I just got a call from Division that we are to stand by to receive a warning order. No one seems to know what it's about or when this warning will be given. I do know that anyone who is on leave is to be recalled and that the corps commander was called to D.C. and is currently en route back with some kind of order."

Dixon straightened up and began to consider what the brigade

S-3 was saying. "Are we having an emergency redeployment exercise?"

"No. I know that for sure. You're not due a redeployment exercise. But that's about all I know. Whatever it is, the division orders group is on alert to be prepared to assemble in fifteen minutes, and the Old Man wants the brigade orders group ready to go once Division is done with him."

"So, no one knows anything except that everyone is to stand by. Are we initiating a full recall?"

"No one has said as much yet, Scott, but I would strongly advise you that you hang on to your staff and company commanders until we know what's going on for sure."

There was a pause before Dixon replied, "OK, Ralph, wilco. Just keep me posted. Colonel Childress isn't going to be thrilled about sitting around on a Friday evening waiting for Division."

After hanging up the phone, Dixon walked out to Nesbitt's desk. "Sergeant Nesbitt, get hold of the company commanders and tell them not to leave for home until they get word from the CO. If they've left already, have the company CQs get them back in. Pass the same word around to the staff, including our people. I'll be in the colonel's office for a few minutes.

Without waiting for a response, Dixon headed down the hall toward the battalion commander's office, but stopped, turned and went back into his own office. He reached over his desk, picking up the phone receiver with one hand while hitting the preset button labeled HOME. The colonel could wait another minute. Dixon needed to tell his wife not to hold dinner for him.

Memphis, Tennessee
1745 Hours, 24 May (2345 Hours, 24 May, GMT)

As luck would have it, Ed Lewis had no sooner closed and locked the door than the phone rang. He stood there for a moment, hand on the doorknob, and half turned, debating whether to forget it and walk away or go back in and answer it. From the car, his wife called for him to leave it. Lewis looked at the car, loaded with kids, camping gear and food. Three days' camping with a visit to the Grand Ole Opry was waiting for him. But wait it would. He yelled to his wife to hang on a little longer while he answered the phone.

Put out by the untimely interruption, Lewis picked up the receiver and answered dejectedly with a simple "Hello."

"Ed, I'm glad I caught you." It was Colonel Franklin from State Headquarters. "I tried the armory, but no one was there. Is Hal still in town?" Hal was Harold R. Green, the commander of the 2nd Battalion, 354th Infantry (Mechanized), Tennessee National Guard.

"Yes, I believe he was going to stick around and catch up on some rest. They've been dogging him kinda hard down at City Hall. What's up?"

"Ed, you've been federalized."

Lewis stood there for a moment dumbfounded. "Federalized? Me? What in the hell for?"

"Not just you, the whole battalion. Actually, the order doesn't go into effect until midnight tonight."

"A Presidential order?"

"They're the best kind, aren't they?"

Lewis did not appreciate the colonel's poor attempt at humor. "Christ, sir, what's going on?"

"I don't know, Ed. As soon as I have something, I'll let you know. Until then, let's get the show on the road. Get your people moving and I'll start getting things ready from this end."

"Who do we work for, the state or the 25th Armored Division?"

"Don't know, Ed. The order didn't say. It looked like someone simply copied the format out of the reg and sent it out without any additional instructions. Like I said, as soon as I have something, I'll pass it on. I have to go now, the Adjutant General just walked in."

Ed went to the front door, yelled to his wife to get the kids out of the car and ran up the stairs to change into his BDUs.

After a dash through the city, through two stop signs, one red light and three near-misses, Lewis made it to the armory. He parked his car, still loaded with camping gear, in the slot marked "Battalion XO." Captain Tim Walters, the full-time training officer and assistant S-3 for the battalion, was already in his office, talking on the phone. Other people were also present, most still in civilian clothes. Lewis saw the operations NCO, Master Sergeant Kenneth Mayfree, and motioned for him to come over.

"Kenny, have we gotten hold of the Old Man yet?"

"No, sir. Tim tried his office, his home and City Hall. No one has seen him since midafternoon, and no one answers at home."

Lewis thought, Great, just great—the one time the stalwart of our community decides to slip out of town early for the weekend is the day someone decides to start World War Three. That last thought gave Lewis a sudden chill. Until that moment, he hadn't thought of war. His mind had been so busy trying to sort out what to do and whom to call that the reason for their being federalized wasn't given a second thought. He looked around at the people in the armory moving about, going in and out of offices or talking on phones. They were all familiar to Lewis. Not only had he been in the Guard with most of them for years, he had grown up with some of them and did business with many of them daily. At a glance, there seemed to be no difference from any night at the armory when the staff gathered for a short meeting or a weekend drill. But this was different. This wasn't going to be a short meeting or a drill. They were going to war.

That thought kept swimming around in his head as he went into his office and sat down at his desk. While millions of Americans were fleeing cities across the nation to enjoy the Memorial Day weekend, the 3rd Battalion, 354th Infantry, was going to war.

Moscow, USSR
0355 Hours, 25 May (0055 Hours, 25 May, GMT)

A small convoy of four long black Zil limousines raced through the deserted streets in the early-morning light. The General Secretary of the Communist Party and the Foreign Minister, both fresh from the military airfield, were riding in the third car today. They, as well as other selected Party officials, had been "out of place," visiting other countries or at locations other than their normal duty positions. The General Secretary, having completed a visit to Finland, had been en route to a meeting with the President of France when his aircraft was rerouted over East Germany back to Moscow. The Foreign Minister had been in Vienna, conferring with representatives of Israel on the matter of emigration of Soviet Jews. He had left the Soviet Embassy in Vienna without notice and been whisked away on a waiting Aeroflot liner. The two men had arrived at the military airfield outside Moscow within minutes of each other, satisfied that their part in the deception plan had been a success.

The General Secretary reclined in the backseat, his eyes closed but still awake. He was resting from his trip and preparing himself for the ordeal he knew they would all have to face shortly. It was important that he be able to portray the sincere, friendly image the Western news media had come to love, when he announced before the cameras that the Soviet Union had been forced to take military action to stabilize its southern borders. He knew that his story would not hold with those who knew the truth. It was not they whom he was interested in. It was the uninformed, the timid and those who favored "peace in our time," at any cost, that he wanted to sway. He had complete confidence that he could do so as he had done in the past.

Across from him, the Foreign Minister was less confident. He fidgeted with the hand loop hanging on the side of the limousine as he looked out the window with a blank stare. Hours of debate that had often degenerated into screaming matches had led to nought. The Foreign Minister knew they were making a serious error. Years of diplomacy were about to be washed away in an ill-conceived military adventure of dubious value. He still could not understand how stupid and blind the other members of the Politburo were. They were opening Pandora's box, and only he saw it.

The General Secretary opened his eyes slightly and looked at the Foreign Minister. "You still do not believe we can succeed, do you?"

The Foreign Minister turned his blank stare to the General Secretary. "Succeed? It all depends on what you consider to be a success. If we want to own a few thousand more square kilometers of sand and rock, we will succeed. If our goal is, as you say, to fulfill our national destiny and seize a warm-water port, we will succeed. If it is our goal to put a stranglehold on the West's oil supply, we will succeed. But I ask you, Comrade, will the price be worth it? Will we ever be able to gain the confidence of the West again? Even if no one lifts a finger to stop us, which I doubt, what kind of arms race will this start and where will it end?"

Without moving or changing expression, the General Secretary replied, "It would appear that I have selected a conservative for a

Foreign Minister. You have become, over these past few months, quite a spokesman for the 'loyal' opposition."

The emphasis on "loyal" caused the Foreign Secretary's face to flush with anger. "I am, and always will be, a loyal Party member. It is my duty to show you the reality of the world, even when it goes against the conventional wisdom of the rest of the pack."

Still showing no emotion, the General Secretary continued, "No one doubts your loyalty to the Party or me. You must, however, see that the time for debate is over. We are committed. You know as well as I that it is useless to have power and not use it. Our Party and our nation depend on the continuous and measured exercise of power. The world respects, and fears, our power. No one would respect a toothless bear. The day we become too timid to use it will be the end of the Soviet Union. We will decay from within and without. Besides, the West has a short memory. The securing of Eastern Europe was a matter of great concern in 1948 and an accepted fact by 1960. Afghanistan was seen as a threat to world peace in 1979 and forgotten by the time we signed the INF Treaty in 1987. No, I see great gains with little to lose."

The Foreign Secretary did not respond. He merely turned back to the window and looked at the buildings that raced by, buildings that held fellow countrymen unaware that in a matter of minutes they would be at war again.

West of Balam Qal'eh, Afghanistan
0425 Hours, 25 May (0100 Hours, 25 May, GMT)

The road that ran from Herat in Afghanistan to Mashhad in Iran really didn't deserve the title of "road." As he lay on the sand dune, peering through his binoculars, Senior Lieutenant Mikhail Kurpov considered the road for a moment. He had seen, and traveled, many bad roads in his three years as a member of the 89th Reconnaissance Battalion. This road, however, had to be the worst. While the tracked vehicles could travel it with no problems, he wondered how well the supply trucks would be able to hold up. Everything the 89th Motorized Rifle Division would need during the operation they were about to launch would have to travel down that road. No doubt, the road would claim many a truck.

Unfortunately, the road was better than what the division would eventually have to depend upon for a supply route. Once

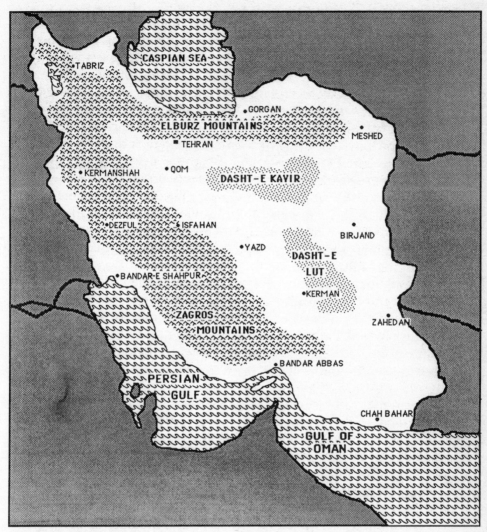

MAP 2: TERRAIN

into Iran, the 89th MRD would advance twenty kilometers to Kariz, then strike southwest for Birjand, 155 kilometers to the southwest across desert, with dirt roads and goat trails the division's only link with the rear. It was the job of Kurpov's scout-car platoon to find the best goat trails and mark them for the 208th Motorized Rifle Regiment that would follow him on the division's western axis. The other scout-car platoon of the company would do the same thing to the east, leading the 209th MRR. If at all possible, the division commander wanted to keep the division on two different axes of advance. Kurpov had his doubts as to whether they could do that. There just weren't that many decent roads or trails.

Movement to Kurpov's left interrupted his thoughts. He turned to watch three BMP infantry-fighting vehicles from the battalion's BMP company creep forward up the spine of a low ridge into firing positions. Four more square, squat BMPs sat just off the road, engines idling, in a wadi. The squeaking of sprockets and tracks and the rumble of the BMPs' engines cut through the predawn quiet. To Kurpov, the noise was enough to wake the dead.

He turned and looked at the Iranian border post again to see whether the guards had also heard the noise. The two Iranians who had been on duty for the last two hours were still there, in the same positions they had assumed when they relieved their comrades. One was leaning up against the side of the building, arms folded and rifle slung over his shoulder. The second was sitting in a chair at the pole barrier with his rifle across his lap and his head hanging. Kurpov was sure they were asleep. He looked up from his binoculars back to the BMPs moving into position. They were ready. A quick glance at his watch showed there were only two minutes left. He turned his body toward the BMPs in the wadi. With a red-filtered flashlight, Kurpov signaled to the commander of the BMPs—two short flashes, which meant that the Iranians did not appear to be alert. The commander waved back in acknowledgment.

His role finished for the moment, Kurpov looked beyond the BMPs in the wadi, toward the east. Although he couldn't see a thing, he knew that there were over twelve thousand men and thousands of tracked and wheeled vehicles hidden in wadis and behind sand dunes, ready to rush forward into enemy territory.

Just as the sun began to peek over the eastern horizon, the

chatter of three machine guns, followed by the boom of a BMP's 73mm. main gun, split the dawn silence. Kurpov swung back around and looked toward the border post in time to see the first 73mm. round hit the building. He put the binoculars up to his eyes and searched for the two border guards who had been on duty. A bright-red splotch was on the wall of the building where the one guard had been leaning. The guard who had been in the chair at the pole barrier had been knocked over backward and was sprawled across the road. Other Iranians began to rush out of the building, only to be cut down in a hail of machine-gun fire.

The four BMPs in the wadi revved their engine and rolled out onto either side of the road. Once on line, they began to fire their machine guns. Though not as accurate as the BMPs that were firing from the stationary positions, they appeared to be more threatening as they moved forward. Two more Iranians came out of the building—now enveloped in flames—with their hands up. But their gestures were ignored as all seven BMPs turned their machine guns on them.

Kurpov let his binoculars drop slowly. For a moment, he took in the whole scene before him. The BMPs were now passing the burning building. As they went by, the two nearest the building turned their turrets toward it and sprayed it with machine-gun fire. The bodies of a dozen Iranians lay strewn about, cut down before they had had a chance to fire a single round.

So, this is war. Kurpov held that thought as he scrambled down the sand dune to his BRDM reconnaissance vehicle.

Headquarters, 2nd Brigade, 25th Armored Division,
Fort Hood, Texas
0730 Hours, 25 May (1330 Hours, 25 May, GMT)

The conference room was slowly filling with commanders and staff officers of the St. Vith Brigade, so called because of the stand its heraldic predecessor had made at Saint-Vith, Belgium, against overwhelming odds during World War II. The brigade executive officer stood at the front of the room giving last-minute directions to the enlisted men setting up the room, while mentally taking note of who was still missing from the orders group.

As his eyes swept the room, they stopped when he came to the brigade assistant intelligence officer off to the side, going over briefing notes. The intelligence officer, or S-2, could not be contacted, off camping somewhere. Ordinarily this situation would have been chalked up to poor timing or bad luck and left to the assistant to handle. But both the brigade commander and the executive officer had serious reservations about the ability of this assistant S-2, First Lieutenant Matthews—who not only was new to the staff, recently transferred from the 10th Corps G-2 section, but was the first female officer to serve on the brigade staff.

Despite years of equal-opportunity training and the slow evolutionary change of the character of the U.S. Army, the XO was ill at ease having Lieutenant Matthews on the staff. At five foot seven, Amanda Matthews had a figure that looked good even in her baggy BDUs. Her short blond hair framed a face that could only be described as stunning. The XO thought how terribly out of place she seemed. In a few minutes they would be talking about war, a real war that was going on as they sat there. A war that they were preparing to join. One tour in the closing days of Vietnam had shown the XO what war could do to people, mentally as well as physically. In his mind, he could not picture Lieutenant Matthews in battle. At home, yes. Modeling on Madison Avenue, yes. Crawling along a ditch, under fire, in some Godforsaken country, no. Lieutenant Matthews looked up at that moment and met his eyes. The XO felt himself blush, then turned away to continue his check of who was still missing.

Lieutenant Matthews paused for a moment and continued to stare at the XO. She knew what was going on in his mind: Is *she* good enough to do the job? How well will *she* hold up when the shit really hits the fan? . . . Nothing changed. Every time she came into a unit, from her first day at West Point to her assignments at Fort Hood, she had had to fight the same attitude. At least in the past she had not been the first or the only female officer in the unit. This assignment, however, was different. Since coming down to the brigade, she had been treated with the respect due an officer but not the confidence or trust that was accorded to the other junior staff officers. She had been warned by friends of hers on the staff of the 25th Armored Division that the brigade commander and the S-2 had fought tool and nail against her assignment. They had even stated that it was better to leave the position open rather than put a female in a tactical headquarters that would operate as far forward as the brigade would. In the end, the division commander had told the brigade commander to shut up and accept her. This he did, but reluctantly and with barely concealed hostility. She had been warned it was not going to be easy. She felt, however, as if she were starting with two strikes against her.

Feeling rage slowly building, Lieutenant Matthews turned her thoughts away from her plight and to the notes she had for the briefing. She knew she was ready, having spent most of the previous night at corps G-2 reviewing every bit of information coming in on Soviet activities and Iranian reactions. She had rummaged through the files, dragging out every old intelligence report and study on the area that she could find. Her preparation even included a trip to the post library, where she had pulled everything she could find on Iran, from *National Geographic* articles to area study books. Maps of Iran were at a premium that day on Fort Hood. Everyone wanted one. That's where having friends in the right place paid off. The 2nd Brigade was probably the only brigade in the corps that had a full range of maps not only of Iran but of the Gulf states and the southern USSR.

With the XO's announcement "Gentlemen, the brigade commander," the briefing began. After being introduced by the XO, Lieutenant Matthews began her briefing with an overview of the topography and demographics of Iran.

"Iran lies on a large plateau bordered in the south by the Persian Gulf, in the north by the Caspian Sea and the Soviet Union, in the west by Turkey and Iraq, and in the east by Afghanistan and Pakistan. Major terrain features are the Zagros Mountains that start in the northwest and run southwest, parallel with the Iraqi border, to the Persian Gulf. The second major mountain range, the Elburz Mountains, also starts in the northwest but runs almost due east, where it ends just short of Afghanistan. In the center of the country, between the two mountain ranges, are two large deserts, the Dasht-e-Kavir, or Great Salt Desert, in the north and the Dasht-e-Lut to the south. *Dasht* is a word used for the gravel slopes that surround the *kavir*, a salt crust that covers marshes of black mud. As the crust is easily broken, many parts of these deserts remain unexplored. Iran's oil reserves are concentrated in the southwest near the Iraqi border, and offshore in the Persian Gulf.

"Less than fourteen percent of the country receives over fifty-two percent of the annual rainfall. This is mostly in the north-west, in the area that runs from Tehran to the Soviet and Turkish borders. Even though the land is quite mountainous, it is in this region, in the valleys, that the majority of the population and agriculture is located. Temperatures range from below the freezing point during the winter to a high of one hundred thirty-two degrees in the summer, but there are parts of the Elburz Mountains where snow never disappears."

Lieutenant Matthews stopped for a moment while her NCO changed maps to show population densities and divisions. She looked at both the brigade commander and the XO to see whether they were tracking the briefing. The XO gave her a nod of approval.

"Last estimates place the population at approximately thirty-five million. Because of the growth rate and the generally poor quality of the medical care, the population is an extremely young one, with a median age in the low twenties. While the majority of the population in the central region is Persian with Indo-European origins, there are several minorities. The most important of these are the Turkomans in the northwest, who are interrelated with other members of this group in both Turkey and the Soviet Union; the Kurds in the west, who are related to compatriots in Iraq; and the Baluchis in the southeast, who are related to the Baluchis in Pakistan. Ninety-eight percent of the population is Muslim. Iran is the only country in the world where the majority of the population is Shiite. Only among the Kurds, Baluchis, Turkomans and Arabs living in the country does the Sunni Muslim belief predominate."

She paused again while her NCO put up a new map, one showing the symbols of military units. The brigade commander was busily writing notes on small three-by-five cards. The XO, with a faint smile of approval, nodded for her to continue.

"The first impression that the current invasion by the Soviets is a bolt out of the blue is incorrect." She paused for a moment and watched the brigade commander noticeably straighten up with a quizzical look on his face.

"Are you trying to tell me, Lieutenant, that we knew about this?"

Without flinching, Matthews continued, "Apparently the Central Intelligence Agency, the National Security Agency and the

Defense Intelligence Agency each were collecting data on the modernization and buildup of Soviet forces in the area but passed it off as either routine modernization or preparation for the rotation or reinforcement of forces in Afghanistan. The Soviets have maintained a normal level of activities in all other areas of the world, especially in Europe, where they have already begun their semiannual rotation of recruits. As a result of this normality, there was an insufficient increase in intelligence indicators to warrant an increase in the Watchcon level." Again Lieutenant Matthews paused for a moment to let this last bit of information sink in before proceeding.

"The current Soviet offensive appears to be following the same basic plan as its 1941 invasion of Iran, with a few new twists, these primarily being amphibious landings along the Caspian Sea here at Bandar-e Anzali and Astaneh and airborne assaults reported at Khvoy, Tabriz and Rasht. Major ground forces in the northeast include one combined-arms army moving along an axis from Jolia to Tabriz through the Zagros Mountains and a second combined-arms army moving along the coastal plain of the Caspian Sea. A third army of unknown composition is in reserve south of Baku. In the northeast, a corps-sized element is moving west along an axis from Kizyl-Arvat to Gorgan, with a second corps-sized element moving south from Ashkabad to Quchan. Several other divisions are assembling farther inside the Soviet Union, here at Nebit-Dag and Mary. In the east a single motorized rifle division has been identified moving along an axis west from Herat in Afghanistan to, probably, Mashhad. Current intelligence gathered from several sources, including monitoring of official Iranian news agencies, indicates that the Soviet invasion came as a complete surprise to the Iranians. Only token resistance is being met by the Soviets. With the majority of Iran's forces involved in active fighting against the Iraqis, and in view of the country's lack of mobile reserves, the Soviets will meet little in the way of organized resistance for at least the next five to seven days, maybe longer." Lieutenant Matthews paused to allow the commander to study the map showing the activity she had just described. When he was comfortable with the information, he nodded for her to continue.

"A preliminary analysis brings out three major points. The first clearly indicates that Tehran is the offensive's initial objective. Seizure of the northwest, the coast of the Caspian Sea and Tehran will place the majority of the population, agriculture and industry of Iran under Soviet control. This would leave only two other worthwhile objectives: the oilfields in the southwest and control of the Strait of Hormuz in the south. The second point is that the USSR is using relatively small forces along established lines of communication. Although it does have a large number of forces in the Transcaucasus region, they are being held in place to serve either as a threat to Turkey or as a second echelon. There is insufficient information at this time to confirm either theory. This could also mean that the USSR's objectives are limited to the seizure of Tehran or that it is being careful not to shove more forces into the country than can be supplied.

"The final point, and perhaps the most important to us, is the fact that the Soviets have taken no other actions anywhere else in the world to increase their state of readiness. An intelligence summary released to 10th Corps earlier this morning from the DIA concluded that it appears to be the Soviets' intent to keep the conflict localized to Iran. In fact, Soviet ambassadors in all NATO countries had scheduled appointments with the heads of those countries within an hour of the invasion to present the Soviets' position and explanation."

At this point, the brigade commander interrupted. "It's going to take one hell of a line of BS to turn this stunt into a lily-white crusade to save humanity." For the first time there was laughter in the room. Turning to Lieutenant Matthews, he asked, "Amanda, do you have anything else?"

For a moment, Lieutenant Matthews was in shock. This was the first time since she had come to the brigade that the brigade commander had called her by her first name. She simply replied, "No, sir."

"That was a good briefing, thank you."

As she went to take her seat, the XO gave her a nod of approval. She was part of the team.

Daradiz Pass, Iran
1700 Hours, 25 May (1330 Hours, 25 May, GMT)

The captain finished making the rounds of the positions occupied by his paratroopers. All was in order. Brought in by helicopter in the predawn darkness, the airborne company had had no problem overwhelming the Iranians who were supposed to man the positions now filled by his men. Four months of training, rehearsals and preparation for this single operation had paid off. At the cost of one man wounded and a sprained ankle sustained during the debarkation from the helicopters, the airborne company had taken out forty-five Iranians. There were, of course, no prisoners. The plan did not allow for the holding of prisoners.

Standing on the edge of a cliff, the captain looked down at the unending column of tanks, armored personnel carriers and trucks of the 28th Combined Arms Army passing below him. With the seizure of the Daradiz Pass, no defenses or major obstacles stood between the 28th CAA and Marand. The 28th would easily make its initial objective on schedule. All was in order. Carefully, the captain limped back from the edge. With nothing more to do for a while, he finally had time to find a nice comfortable spot where he could sit down and tend to his sprained ankle.

Chapter 2

It is well that war is so terrible or we should grow too fond of it.

—ROBERT E. LEE

Fort Bragg, North Carolina
1940 Hours, 26 May (0040 Hours, 27 May, GMT)

Company A of the 2nd Battalion, 517th Airborne Regiment, was used to waiting. It wasn't unusual to get rigged for a jump, move out onto the ready line and then wind up waiting for hours as an unexpected weather front or increase in winds caused a delay. The men were no strangers to the Green Ramp either. At times it seemed to them that every time some head of state in an obscure country sneezed, the 17th Airborne Division was put on alert. And, of course, there were always the readiness tests, called at all hours of the day to gauge the response of the unit on strip alert. The 1983 invasion of Grenada had done much to add meaning to the endless drills, alerts and training exercises. But that had been a small affair by any standards and, to a unit in the U.S. Army, a long time ago. There were few men in the 2nd of the 517th who wore a division patch on both sleeves.

Captain John Evans, the new commander of A Company, was one of them. At the time of the Grenada invasion he had been a second lieutenant who had just made his cherry jump, a first jump with one's unit. Not having had the experience of numerous alerts and readiness tests that never went anywhere and tended to dull rather than sharpen the reactions of some, Evans had tackled the alert for the Grenada operation with enthusiasm and vigor. His performance at Bragg and on the island had earned him a name as a hard charger and an energetic young officer. As a result, he had found it easy to stay in the 517th, moving from one position to another until he made it to the most coveted position for a company-grade officer in the division, command of an airborne infantry company.

Evans had come down off brigade staff to assume command of Company A less than two months ago. Thus far he had been unimpressed with the company. While there was more than enough effort and enthusiasm on the part of the leadership and the soldiers, the unit lacked a sense of orientation and an ability to really understand what was important.

For example, when the unit assembled at the Green Ramp for precombat inspections, Evans had found that the men were hopelessly overburdened with useless equipment and far too much ammunition. Had they jumped with everything that they had when they initially fell out, the company would never have made it off the drop zone. It reminded Evans of the Grenada operation, when people had taken all of their military equipment with them, only to discard it once they reached the island and found they didn't need it. Today, together with his first sergeant, a veteran of eighteen years in and out of airborne units, he had inspected every man's load and equipment. Anything that was considered to be of no value was discarded into a pile at the end of the company line. When they were finished, the pile was higher than Evans. The inspection had taken the entire morning, but the results were worth the effort. The men in the company looked right to him.

Now all that was left to do was wait. A briefing given by the battalion commander had been the least informative briefing Evans had ever attended. They were told that the current alert was in response to the Soviet invasion of Iran. But that was about all. Several contingencies had been discussed, but none in detail and none that the battalion commander felt confident the unit would execute. Despite this lack of information, the brigade had been alerted for immediate deployment, with a warning order that they might have to make a combat jump somewhere. No doubt, Evans thought, the people in Washington were thrashing about trying to decide what the division was to do. Until a decision was made, the 17th Airborne Division was going to be held in a ready-to-go posture.

As he sat on the concrete, resting against his gear with sweat rolling down his face, Evans looked at his men baking in the hot May sun. You can bet, he told himself, the Soviets aren't sitting around in Iran with nothing to do.

Tabriz, Iran
0410 Hours, 27 May (0040 Hours, 27 May, GMT)

It had been almost an hour since the last Iranian attack. Junior Lieutenant Nikolai Ilvanich carefully raised his head over the edge of the parapet of the shallow trench his unit occupied. He took great care while he did this. Less than two hours before, his company commander had been killed doing the same thing. The deputy company commander had said that it had been a lucky shot. But as far as Ilvanich was concerned, dead was dead, regardless of what luck had to do with it.

In the darkness he could see only shadows and faint images in the no-man's-land between his position and the ditch that the Iranians had come from. The barbed wire that had been strung up by Ilvanich's men in the center of the no-man's-land had been breached in several places during the four Iranian attacks so far. Those attacks had not been easy or cheap. Iranian bodies lay draped across the wire where it was still attached to the posts. In the gaps where the Iranians had succeeded in breaching the wire, a confused pile of corpses and limbs had accumulated. Every now and then a soft moan would rise from the pile, indicating that some of the attackers had only been wounded.

Slowly Ilvanich slipped back down into the trench, coming to rest on the ground and facing toward the rear with his back against the trench wall. He looked at his watch. There were only twenty or so minutes to go before sunrise. He was sure that if they could hang on until the sun came up, they would be able to hold. Ilvanich and his men, what was left of them, were exhausted and drained. The stress and exertion of the last twelve hours had pushed them all to the brink of collapse.

They had parachuted into Tabriz two days before and seized the airport without much effort. The first twenty-four hours had gone well, more like a maneuver than war. Starting just before dawn of the second day, however, Iranian militia forces had begun to make their presence felt. It had begun with sniping that was effective enough to be dangerous.

In the early afternoon of that day Iranians began to arrive in force. The first group drove up in buses and trucks and began to dismount in plain view of Ilvanich's position five kilometers away. Patiently Ilvanich waited for the battalion's mortars or divisional artillery to smash the assembling enemy horde. But nothing happened. He continued to report the location and the growing number of Iranians, but received nothing in return other than an acknowledgment of his report. He was sure the artillery observers could see what he saw. Still, nothing was fired on the enemy as they dismounted from their vehicles. While he watched in frustration, Ilvanich remembered that in his study of Western imperialist armies he had read that even platoon leaders like him could request and direct artillery fire. The book went on to explain how this practice was wasteful and tended to dilute a unit's combat power. As he watched the Iranians go about their preparations for attack unmolested, Ilvanich wished that he could have been a little wasteful.

"Here they come again!" The shout was followed immediately by the crack of small-arms fire and the din of exploding grenades. Ilvanich leaped to his feet and rushed over to the machine gun just to his left.

The crew of that weapon was already hammering away into the darkness. They could not see their targets, but that didn't matter. The crew had the weapon set to fire along a prescribed arc at a set height. Anything standing more than one meter in height entering that zone would be hit. The rest of Ilvanich's platoon was doing likewise. So long as every man covered his zone, in theory no Iranian could reach them alive.

From behind the platoon's positions a flare raced upward, then burst, casting a pale light over no-man's-land. Their attackers were now clearly visible. Numbering in the hundreds, the Iranians piled through the gaps in the wire and rushed toward the platoon's position. With the aid of the flare, the machine gun stopped its sweep and concentrated on the gap immediately to its front, its rounds were clearly hitting in the mass of attackers, knocking the lead rank back. The follow-on rank, however, merely pushed over the bodies of their comrades and surged forward. In their turn they were cut down. And in turn the next rank pressed forward.

This process was maddening to Ilvanich. Each rank of attackers gained a few more meters. The Iranians were closing on the platoon's positions. Ilvanich suddenly realized that the situation he faced was a simple question of mathematics: Did the Iranians have more men than he had bullets to kill them with?

This line of thought was interrupted by a scream to his left. A junior sergeant came running up to Ilvanich and, gasping for breath, reported that the platoon to their left had collapsed and the Iranians were pouring through the gap created. Rushing past the sergeant, Ilvanich began to make his way along the trench to the left flank of his position, stepping over bodies of his men who had fallen during this and previous attacks.

On reaching his last position, he could clearly see Iranians running past his platoon, headed for the airport's runway. The sergeant in command of the squad covering that section of the trench had already reoriented some of his men to face the flank and the rear. His men were firing into the Iranians as they went by, but to no effect. The Iranians were hell-bent to reach the runway.

In the gathering light, Ilvanich saw two BMD infantry-fighting vehicles charge from the direction of the runway toward the head of the Iranian penetration. With guns blazing, the BMDs cut down the lead rank. The Iranians who were on either side of the line of fire moved away from the BMDs and sought cover. Without firing, they allowed the two BMDs to pass.

Suddenly Ilvanich realized what the Iranians were up to. They were going to allow the BMDs to go by, then hit them in the rear. Before he could act, the Iranians began to close on the BMDs from behind. In groups of twos and threes they rushed forward, some with mines, others with explosive charges. Those with the mines were going to shove them under the tracks of the advancing BMDs to immobilize them. Once the vehicles were stopped, the Iranians with the charges would be able to set their charges and blow the BMDs up. With the BMDs destroyed, there would be nothing immediately available to plug the gap. The Iranians with the mines had to be stopped.

Looking back to the front, Ilvanich could see no letup in the Iranians' attacks on his positions. They were still slowly gaining ground. If he switched a machine gun from the front to assist the BMDs, the horde he faced would surge forward and overwhelm his position. By the same token, if the Iranians destroyed the BMDs, eventually they would surround the platoon's position and wipe it out. Without another thought, Ilvanich ordered the machine gun to switch positions to face the rear and engage the Iranians attacking the BMDs. Four riflemen were ordered to cover the machine gun's former zone to the front.

The machine gun was immediately effective. The fire from the rear caused some of the Iranians approaching the BMDs to stop and go to ground. In addition, the crews of the BMDs, alerted by ricocheting rounds from Ilvanich's machine gun that hit their vehicles, realized they were in trouble and began to turn on their Iranian attackers. For the BMD farthest from Ilvanich's position, this realization came too late. With a thunderous explosion, it was flipped up and over onto its top as it ran over a mine. The remaining BMD continued to fight for its life.

A scream from the squad sergeant to Ilvanich was cut short by a gurgling sound. Ilvanich turned back toward his platoon's front to see the squad sergeant sink to the bottom of the trench, clutching his bloody face in his hands. A dozen Iranians stood at the lip of the trench, ready to jump in. Ilvanich ordered the machine gun back to the front. The Iranians were in the trench, however, before it could be brought to bear.

In a blur of actions, the fight degenerated into a hand-to-hand brawl. Ilvanich shoved his pistol into the face of the nearest Iranian and fired twice. Without pausing, he turned on a second Iranian just as the Iranian ran a bayonet into the stomach of one of Ilvanich's men. Two rounds finished the Iranian and emptied Ilvanich's pistol. Not taking the time to reload, Ilvanich threw down the pistol and grabbed an AK assault rifle. In a single upward swing, he fired a burst into a group of three Iranians rushing at him and managed to kill two and wound the third.

Now only he and two other Russians were still standing. All the Iranians who had entered the trench were down, mixed in with his own dead and wounded. Ilvanich looked over the top of the trench, only to see another wave of Iranians approaching. "Get the machine gun!" The three Russians searched but could not find the machine gun, now hidden somewhere on the floor of the trench under bodies.

The Iranians were within twenty meters of the trench. There was no time to find the machine gun. Ilvanich yelled to his remaining men, "Forget the machine gun! Shoot the bastards with your rifles!" He turned to get to the front wall, but discovered that his legs were wedged in the tangle of bodies cluttering the trench floor. Unable to move, Ilvanich realized he was going to die.

At that instant there came the sharp crack of a BMD's cannon and the chatter of a machine gun from the rear. Ilvanich looked in the direction of the noise and saw the surviving BMD moving up to his position, firing as it came. He watched the last of the Iranians stop, waver, then withdraw.

As the sun began to crest the horizon, Ilvanich freed his legs and staggered over to the side of the trench. Panting, he leaned against the dirt wall for support and surveyed the scene before him. There was no distinguishing the body of friend or foe. In the confined trench before him were twenty bodies, twisted and interwoven into a grotesque quiltwork of death. They had held. But it had cost them.

Junior Lieutenant Ilvanich bent over and began to vomit.

Beaumont, Texas
1930 Hours, 28 May (0130 Hours, 29 May, GMT)

The rail loading of the brigade's equipment at Ford Hood and the offloading in Beaumont were going surprisingly well. Annual trips to the National Training Center at Fort Irwin, California, ensured that there were always an adequate number of officers and soldiers in the units who had the skills and experience required for the tasks of planning, organizing and carrying out the movement of the unit by rail.

The 2nd Brigade, 25th Armored Division, had been tagged as the first unit to move by virtue of the fact that it had been in the final stages of preparation for movement to the National Training Center and was to have begun the actual move as soon as the three-day weekend was over. The Soviet invasion of Iran had changed the goal. Rather than going to California to face a U.S. Army unit trained and organized as a Soviet motorized rifle regiment, the 2nd Brigade was en route to meet the real thing.

While the XO of 3rd Battalion, 4th Armor, remained at Fort Hood to handle last-minute details at that end, Major Dixon moved to Beaumont to orchestrate the transfer of the unit's equipment from rail to naval transports and tend to the billeting and messing of the men moving the equipment. The battalion commander had to stay loose, ready to go where he was required the most. Much of his time was consumed by meetings, planning sessions and briefings. At first he would religiously rush back to his staff and provide them with all the information that he had just been given. He stopped this practice, however, when it became apparent that plans and information provided by the division, which changed at every meeting, were only causing confusion within the battalion staff. He therefore decided to wait until a final plan was developed before issuing any type of order. Until then, only that information that was required to prepare and deploy the force was provided.

Upon arrival at Beaumont, it became readily apparent that neither the port nor the Navy was ready to receive the 3rd of the 4th. If there was a plan for loading the lead elements from the 25th Armored Division onto the transports, it wasn't evident on the dock next to the S.S. *Cape Fear*.

The *Cape Fear* was part of the Ready Reserve Fleet. Civilian owned and operated, the *Cape Fear*, like other ships in the RRF, conducted normal commercial operations until activated for use as a military transport during war or emergencies. At the time of activation, ships of the RRF were required to report within a specified number of days, anywhere from five to fifteen, to designated ports, where they fell under the control of the Military Sealift Command. While the Navy routinely conducted readiness tests to determine whether ships could respond. The size and frequencies of the tests had always been limited. The speed with which the current crisis developed, and the size of the force requiring movement and the force designated for deployment, were placing on the transport system a demand that had been discussed but never practiced.

As a result, there was a three-way debate on how to run operations. The Army, which owned the equipment being moved, had its ideas on how, when and what to load. There was the desire to keep unit integrity and place a balanced mix of equipment on all ships in the event that the Soviets intercepted the convoy and attacked it. It would do no good to arrive in the Persian Gulf with all the trucks of the division if the transports with the tanks on it sank.

But loading ships in that manner is wasteful as far as space and time are concerned. As there were few ships in the RRF available to move the corps's equipment and supplies, the Navy wanted to pack each ship as efficiently as possible. The bulk of the Navy's true cargo-handling capability was either scattered around the world or in mothballs. Time would be required to assemble those ships or refit and man those in mothballs. Until then, every ship counted.

The third party was the ships' owners and their agents on the spot, the ships' captains. While the theory of the RRF was fine in peacetime, a severe case of cold feet broke out when the plan began to be implemented for real. Some captains and ships' crews went out of their way to accommodate the Navy and Army personnel. Others were openly hostile, one ship's captain having to be threatened with arrest if he failed to comply with his contract. Most fell between the two extremes, doing what was required of them, but with great reluctance. As one seaman put it, "I ain't in the Navy or the Army. I didn't sign on to get my ass blown off and don't intend to." The number of "unaccounted-for personnel" increased daily. The captain and crew of the *Cape Fear* fell into this middle category.

The *Cape Fear* itself was designed to allow vehicles to simply roll on and roll off without the use of cranes or hoists, hence the name RO-RO ship. She had a crew of thirty-four and a capacity of almost twelve thousand tons, or enough hauling capacity, in theory, to transport two hundred tanks. This was where the problems began.

When Dixon arrived at the dock, he found the unit's equipment being driven off the *Cape Fear* instead of on. Bewildered, he grabbed the first noncommissioned officer he found and asked what was going on. The sergeant said they had been told by a Navy officer with an oak leaf like a major that they were loading the boat wrong and would have to start over again. Infuriated, Dixon stormed off in search of the ship's bridge, with the idea that he might find the naval officer there. Knowing nothing about ships other than what he had seen in the movies, he went up the ramp that the battalion's equipment was coming down on. Once inside the cavernous cargo area, he wandered about until he found a door. His plan of attack was simple: so long as he continued to go up, he was sure that eventually he would find the bridge. Surprisingly, it worked until he was just short of the bridge, when a seaman stopped him and said that the soldiers weren't allowed or welcomed there. They almost came to blows when Dixon tried to bull his way past. Only intervention by a ship's officer stopped the fight.

The officer was the first officer of the *Cape Fear*, and Dixon could tell right off that he was not happy about his ship's current mission. When Dixon asked why equipment was being offloaded instead of loaded, the first officer gave him a quizzical look, then replied that they were doing what they had been told to do by the Navy. He had no idea of the whereabouts of the Navy officer who had told them. That officer, he said, had come aboard after most of the battalion's equipment was loaded, and he had left after seeing the manifest and issuing new orders to the crew. The ship's first officer went on to say that until the military got its act together and decided on what it wanted to do, his crew wasn't going to load another piece of equipment. With that, he turned away from Dixon and went up to the bridge.

Dixon stood there, seething with anger that an entire day had been wasted. He turned toward the dock and viewed the confused tangle of men and equipment there. As far as he could tell, there was no rhyme or reason to the effort below him. In a rage, he stormed back into the passageway he had used to reach the bridge and headed for the dock to search for someone in charge.

Sufian, Iran
0735 Hours, 29 May (0405 Hours, 29 May, GMT)

Major Vorishnov sat in the shade of a fruit tree, listening as the second officer, in charge of intelligence, summarized the regimental intelligence report on Iranian operations to date for him and the company commanders. Across from them the tanks of the 3rd Battalion waited in line, pulled off the road. The crews moved around their vehicles with little enthusiasm, giving the appearance of working on the tanks, but in reality doing nothing. Fuel trucks rolled by, winding down the serpentine road into a narrow defile five hundred meters from where the officers sat. The trucks kicked up dust and almost drowned out the second officer.

The sporadic and disorganized resistance of the first two days had given way to an increase in activities by the Iranians. While the lead division of the 28th CAA had yet to meet any sizable forces, it had been seriously delayed by incessant roadblocks and an increasing number of ambushes. At each of the roadblocks, forces had to stop, deploy, and scatter any enemy forces covering the obstacle. Once that had been done, engineers had to come forward and clear the road. The delays that were thus incurred had shattered the time schedule of the operation and were causing a growing number of casualties. Instead of reaching Tabriz on the third day, the 28th was still short of the objective on the morning of the fifth day. The airborne unit that had been dropped into Tabriz was hanging on to most key installations, but would be hard pressed to last for more than another day or two. Twice, the Iranians had actually gotten onto the airfield, the airborne unit's only link to the outside world, before being thrown back.

Vorishnov turned to watch the fuel trucks while the second officer droned on. As each truck reached the defile, it had to slow, change gears and ease between the sheer sides of the defile. Suddenly Vorishnov saw a flash, a puff of smoke, and a streak of flame that raced toward a truck which had just begun to slow down in the defile. Dumbfounded, he watched the flame hit the truck. In an instant the truck disintegrated into a ball of fire. The force of the explosion caught the second officer off guard and threw him to the ground. Vorishnov could feel the heat of the fireball as it passed over them.

"Ambush!"

The officers scattered. Vorishnov leaped to his feet and grabbed the commander of the lead company. Pointing to where he had seen the initial flash, he ordered the commander to move his three lead vehicles into a position where they could fire on that location. He cautioned him to be careful of other attacks from the flank.

The crews that had been going through the motions of working had disappeared into their tanks. Engines sprang to life as gunners and tank commanders began to traverse the turrets, searching for targets. But there was none to be found. As two tanks from the lead company began to pour machine-gun fire into the area Vorishnov had indicated, another tank, equipped with a plow blade, began to move down the road past the fuel trucks, now pulled off to the side. When it reached the remains of the destroyed fuel truck, it pushed them through the defile and out of the way. Then the plow tank pulled off the road and began to fire toward the area at which the other tanks were shooting. Those two tanks, in turn, ceased fire and moved down the road to join the plow tank.

Vorishnov, by then, had mounted his BTR and followed the two tanks through the defile. Once on the other side, the tanks deployed off the road near the plow tank and began to search the area for signs of the enemy. As Vorishnov also searched the far hill with his binoculars, he realized that their efforts were fruitless. The enemy was gone. Odds were, it had been nothing more than two men with a rocket launcher. Guerrillas, stay-behinds whose sole purpose was to harrass and disrupt the Soviet rear area. Still, Vorishnov thought as he turned to look at the remains of the shattered fuel truck, their choice of targets had been good. In order to reach the Strait of Hormuz, the 28th CAA would depend on a long line of fuel trucks like the one just destroyed. The army couldn't afford to lose too many of them to stray parties of guerrillas wandering about its supply routes. Either the Iranians had been incredibly lucky to hit such an important target or they knew exactly what they were doing and had waited for the fuel trucks. If the latter was the case, the delays the 28th CAA had experienced to date were only a foretaste of hard times to come. Visions of a second Afghanistan began to creep into Vorishnov's troubled mind.

The Pentagon, Washington, D.C.
1635 Hours, 29 May (2135 Hours, 29 May, GMT)

Lieutenant General Weir tried hard to relax on the soft sofa that ran along the wall of the Pentagon office belonging to the Army's Deputy Chief of Staff for Operations. He needed to. Since the beginning of the current crisis he had had little time to do so. The stress, an irregular schedule and poor eating habits were beginning to take their toll on him. He thought back to his days as a younger officer when it had seemed as though he could go for weeks with barely two hours of sleep and one C-ration meal a day. That, however, was a long time ago. Since then he had put a lot of mileage on his body, and it was beginning to tell.

The briefing he had just left had done little to ease his anxiety over the upcoming operation. The initial concept and plan he had been given on the twenty-fourth of May had changed almost daily. Additional intelligence, a better grasp of who all the players were, what the Soviets and the United States were capable of doing and what help the U.S. could expect had resulted in several revisions of the plan. While Weir didn't like the initial plan, he liked the revisions even less. Plans, like most things, do not improve when more people get involved.

The initial plan, called Blue Thunder, had been simple and limited in its objectives. The first phase was to move his 10th Corps, a Marine amphibious expeditionary force and supporting Air Force units to the vicinity of the Persian Gulf and get them assembled. At best, it would require forty to fifty days to move and stage the necessary forces. During that time, the State Department was to work all the friendly governments in the area in an effort to secure bases and overflight rights while the CIA, the NSA and other intelligence agencies built a complete picture of what was happening. The Navy would also have time to establish superiority in the Gulf and assemble the required shipping to support large-scale operations. Given time, there was even the possibility that the Iranian government could be convinced that it would be to its benefit to cooperate with the United States. But regardless of the Iranian response, once the true situation was clear a capable and fully assembled force operating from secure and friendly bases in the area would be able to take effective and meaningful action.

Unfortunately, war is seldom left to professional soldiers to manage. From the very beginning, a hue and cry from the Congress and right-wing political factions called for an immediate response to the Soviet invasion. With the cry of "No more Afghanistans" to rally around, politicians of every persuasion offered their ideas on how to keep the world safe for democracy and punish the Russians. The newly elected President, not wanting to be labeled as indecisive or impotent, was stampeded into selecting a course of action that showed immediate results. The current plan fit the bill, but it was, at best, very risky.

The new plan called for the immediate introduction of the Rapid Deployment Force, or RDF, into Iran. The 17th Airborne Division, working with a Marine amphibious brigade, would seize from the Iranians an airhead centered around the city of Bandar Abbas on the Strait of Hormuz. Reinforced with the 12th Infantry Division (Light) and the 52nd Infantry Division (Mechanized), these units would move inland and west along the coast to establish blocking positions to prevent the Soviets from reaching the Persian Gulf. The 10th Corps, when it arrived, would continue that expansion.

With his head laid back on the sofa, Weir was lost in his thoughts and didn't notice that Lieutenant General Robert Horn, the Deputy Chief of Staff for Operations, had entered the room until Horn reached out and offered him a cup of coffee. Weir and Horn had been classmates at West Point, had served in the same armored cavalry squadron in Vietnam, had commanded armor battalions in the same division at the same time and had attended both the Command and General Staff College and the Army War College together. Throughout the years their careers had paralleled and crossed. They had stayed in close touch, considering themselves the best of friends and confidants on all matters, personal and professional. It was therefore natural that they shared the same misgivings about the upcoming operation in Iran.

Rather than sit at his desk, Horn settled down in a leather chair opposite Weir. After taking a sip of his coffee, he said, "The Chief doesn't buy our argument. The plan goes as briefed."

Weir thought about that for a moment, then laid his head back against the sofa. "Then the Airborne Mafia has won. Next thing you know they'll want to send in another light-infantry division for good measure."

"Don't be so quick. That was seriously considered. I had a hell of a fight cutting that one out."

Weir's head shot up. "You have got to be bullshitting me! It's bad enough that I've lost all priority on shipping. Does that cowboy who commands the 13th Airborne Corps seriously believe he can go toe to toe with Soviet tank units and hold all of southern Iran single-handed using a handful of grunts with oversized rucksacks on the ground? Doesn't anyone do a threat analysis around here anymore?"

"Frank, we have no choice. There's simply too much pressure to do something immediately. The RDF can get there faster than you can."

"And do what, Bob, die? Sacrifice themselves in the name of political expediency? Damn it, Bob, you know that they can't do everything that they've been assigned. At best, they can hang on to Bandar Abbas and a couple of hundred kilometers of the coast. To push them inland along the line of Kazerun–Shiraz–Kerman–Zahedan without the 10th Corps is insane. They have neither the manpower to hold that line nor the transportation to keep it supplied. The Soviets will simply bypass whomever they don't want to mess with and leave them to wither on the vine. Jesus, are we the only ones who see that, Bob?" Weir stopped and sipped on his coffee in an effort to compose himself.

"Frank, between you and me, the Vice agrees. He and I went in to the Chief and presented the same argument, a little less passionately, of course. The Chief, however, felt that the risks were acceptable. As he said, we need to 'get there the fastest with the mostest.' "

Weir pounded his knee with his fist, lowered his head and shook it from side to side. "Damn it. It takes twelve hours to fly from Washington to Tehran. It only takes three hours to fly from Moscow to Tehran. How does the Chief expect us to get around that? And the Iranians? What about the Iranians? Has anyone been watching the news lately? How the hell is the 13th Airborne Corps going to hold the Russians *and* fight the Iranians?"

There were several moments of silence as the two generals sipped their coffee and thought. To date the Iranian government had refused all offers of U.S. assistance. Daily demonstrations in Tehran condemned the United States as fervently as they did the Soviets. Under the original plan, there would have been time to work out some type of arrangement or, at worst, allow the Soviets to get so deep into Iran that the Iranians would have no choice but to accept U.S. help. But the new plan didn't allow any time. The CIA was projecting that U.S. forces would be met with armed resistance by the Iranians. Ground forces would be fighting with hostile forces to their rear as well as their front.

Finally, Weir broke the long silence. "Bob, I know you did your best. Now it's time for me to do mine." With that he stood up and began to gather up his briefcase and hat.

Horn stood up also and walked across the room to bid his friend farewell. With a few pleasantries, the two men parted. After Weir had left, Horn went to the window and stared out at the Potomac. He could not escape the thought that he had not only failed his friend but condemned him to death. How easy, he thought, it had been in Vietnam when they were young lieutenants. At least they knew what they were doing then and didn't have to bother with the politicians, both in and out of uniform.

Chapter 3

*I offer neither pay nor quarters nor provi-
sions; I offer hunger, thirst, forced marches,
battles and death. Let him who loves his
country in his heart, and not his lips only,
follow me.*

—GIUSEPPE GARIBALDI

Birjand, Iran
0135 Hours, 30 May (2205 Hours, 29 May, GMT)

Lieutenant Kurpov's scout-car platoon began to stir. The 89th Reconnaissance Battalion had less than an hour to get ready and move out on its next mission. The promise of resupply by air and a twenty-four-hour rest halt had to wait until the airfield outside Birjand had been secured.

The battalion had closed on Birjand on the afternoon of the twenty-ninth after a trek of over three hundred kilometers through the desert. An attempt of the recon battalion, reinforced only by the advance guard, to rush the town and seize the airfield had been repulsed by Islamic Guards dug in along the approaches. Attempts to find a weak point north of the town had also failed. It was therefore decided to wait until the lead motorized rifle regiment and division artillery closed up before trying again. In the meantime, the recon battalion was to bypass the town to the west and check out an unguarded route that had been found the night before. If the route was clear, the recon battalion was to use it to lead a motorized rifle battalion past the town. Once south of the town, the rifle battalion would support the main attack by hitting the Iranians from the rear.

As the officers of the recon company received last-minute instructions, the crews of the BRDM armored cars and BMP reconnaissance vehicles began to crank up their engines and check their weapons. Sand, heat and lack of water were greater problems than the officers and men in the recon battalion had expected. The division had deployed from a garrison in Poltava in the Ukraine to the desert and then into the attack with little time for acclimation. Neither had they received any special instructions on desert warfare or how to deal with the conditions they would find. It was therefore natural that the men would continue to operate as they had been trained while in the Ukraine. The result was a high number of maintenance failures and weapons stoppages. The light coat of oil that had protected their machine guns from the spring rains in the Ukraine attracted sand that jammed them in the desert. During their first serious run-in with an Iranian roadblock on the second day of the invasion, Lieutenant Kurpov's platoon was embarrassed when only one machine gun in the entire platoon fired. In a panic the platoon pulled back into a wadi, where in record time the crews broke down their weapons and cleaned them. Since that time, the men faithfully checked their weapons and kept them clean and free of oil.

Kurpov watched impassively as the other scout-car platoon moved out of their laager and headed west. Behind them went two BMPs. Kurpov's platoon would follow at a distance, ready to lead the rifle battalion through or swing farther west if the route taken by the lead platoon was blocked. This suited Kurpov fine. He had grown tired of being in the lead, always out front, always the first to find the enemy or be found by him. On two separate occasions his BRDM had barely survived a direct hit by rocket-propelled antitank grenades. It would be a welcome relief to follow someone for a change.

A bright three-quarter moon made it easy to track the progress of the lead scout-car platoon. Kurpov felt as though the whole world were staring down on them as they swung west onto a narrow dirt track. Through his vision blocks he monitored the progress of his other vehicles and the rifle battalion's advance guard behind them. It was following far too close. If the Iranians hit them, the rifle battalion would have little room to maneuver or back out. They were becoming sloppy, too lax.

The BMPs, now about one thousand meters to his front, turned slightly to the left and continued forward into the shadows of the surrounding hills. Ahead of them the BRDMs had already entered the dark void and were out of sight. Despite the cool of the night, Kurpov could feel the sweat roll down his spine. This was no good, far too easy. It was inconceivable that such a route would be left open.

A flash, a streak of flame and the detonation of an antitank missile on a BMP raped the stillness of the night and heralded a rush of pandemonium and violence. Contact. Green and red tracer rounds crisscrossed as Iranians engaged the lead scout-car platoon and were in turn engaged by the BRDMs and the remaining BMP. The reports coming from the platoon leader of the scout-car platoon betrayed his confusion and panic. The recon company commander yelled back, demanding a clear and accurate report, but got no response as artillery began to strike.

Kurpov was at a loss as to what to do. He stared through his vision blocks, trying hard to make sense of what was going on before him. But that was not possible. The flashes of gunfire, the bright streaks of tracers and the impact of artillery merged with blotches and fading images of rounds long since fired, distorting Kurpov's sight. Another bright flash and a streak of flame from the shadows of the hills sought out the second BMP. This time the impact of the missile resulted in a thunderous explosion as the BMP's own ammo and fuel ripped it apart, sending a ball of fire into the sky. Men were dying. His comrades. And still Kurpov was at a loss as to what to do.

The Iranians were no fools. What appeared to Kurpov as random and uncontrolled violence was as methodical as it was deadly. They knew exactly what they were doing. The heavy antitank guided missiles were used to destroy the greatest Soviet threat, the better-armed and -armored BMPs. With the BMPs destroyed, the BRDMs were no match for dug-in troops who could easily dispose of them with heavy machine guns and hand-held rocket launchers. The shower of tracers that mesmerized Kurpov came from dug-in .50-caliber machine guns and from the BRDMs' own machine guns' returning fire.

It was an uneven contest as the Iranian machine gunners raked the thin-skinned BRDMs with telling effect while the BRDMs simply thrashed about, firing wildly and randomly. The platoon leader of the lead scout-car platoon never gained control of his three BRDMs. Each fought its own battle and died a hard, slow death. A burst of machine-gun fire hit the flank of the platoon leader's BRDM, killing the driver. It careened wildly, hit a shallow ditch and rolled over on its side. The panicked crew clawed at the hatches in an effort to escape, oblivious to the fact that all guns that could be brought to bear were now hitting the BRDM. As the first man emerged he was hit by a burst of well-directed machine-gun fire. He simply dropped, half in and half out of the vehicle, dead. His comrade behind him screamed and pushed on the body, not realizing the man was dead. With strength born of desperation and fear, the second crewman pushed the body clear and in his turn was killed as he began to emerge. The platoon leader could not reach the hatch. Machine-gun rounds, ripping through the bottom of the BRDM, had hit him. As he lay there against the side of his vehicle, bleeding to death in the dark, he blocked out the horror and noise of the battle outside and dreamed of his home and his family. Gone from his mind were war and death. Before him were images of white puffy clouds racing across a blue sky above windswept seas of sunflowers rooted in the dark Ukrainian earth. For a moment, the young lieutenant smiled as he slipped into the dark abyss.

Without waiting for orders, Kurpov's platoon and the accompanying BMP had gone to ground, seeking cover in a shallow wadi. Kurpov's own driver, reacting to a strong sense of survival as well as to his training, had brought the BRDM to a halt in the wadi next to the BMP. The destruction of the lead scout-car platoon and the two BMPs had bought time for Kurpov and his platoon to find cover and get a grasp on the situation. That was, after all, part of the recon battalion's job.

Somewhat composed now, Kurpov opened his hatch and stood on his seat in order to peer over the lip of the wadi they were in. The wild firing had died down. In the distance he could see the BMPs and the BRDMs burning. The stillness that had descended was punctured by random pops and detonations as on-board ammunition cooked off in the burning vehicles. Putting his binoculars to his eyes, Kurpov scanned the area. Slowly he was able to construct a clear picture of what had happened and the approximate locations of the Iranian positions. Because only two missiles were fired from the same general area and only after a considerable interval, he was convinced there was only one anti-tank-guided-missile launcher. At least, that was all he could be sure of. All the machine-gun fire had come from the area to either side of where the trail should have been when the lead platoon was hit. As best he could determine, there was no more than a single company dug in across the road and supported by a single antitank-guided-missile launcher. He called to his other scout cars for reports. What their commanders told him corroborated what Kurpov had already determined. Only when he was sure he had as clear a picture as he was going to have did he call his company commander to report.

The company commander received the report in silence. When Kurpov was done, the commander asked a few short questions, which Kurpov answered with a simple yes or no. Satisfied, the company commander instructed him to continue to observe while he in turn reported Kurpov's information to the commander of the rifle battalion that was following. As Kurpov waited for new orders, he took off his helmet and leaned against the open hatch, thinking about the fight. With a dirty rag he wiped the sweat from his face. His hand still quivered from the adrenaline in his system. Five vehicles and their crews had been destroyed finding out information that took less than thirty seconds to report. And were it not for a simple decision by the company commander that the other platoon was to lead, it would have been Kurpov's platoon that paid for that information. A decision that had been so easy for the commander to make had such terrible consequences for the people who had to execute it.

A radio call from the company commander brought Kurpov's thoughts back to the present. He got his helmet on in time to hear that the rifle battalion was deploying and moving forward to assault the Iranian position. From behind, Kurpov could already hear the rumble of the rifle battalion as it began to advance. His job for that night was over. It was now up to others to flush out the enemy. There would be no need for Kurpov to guide the advancing elements of the rifle battalion forward toward the enemy's positions; the burning BRDMs proved to be good markers.

Ras Banas, Egypt
0015 Hours, 30 May (2215 Hours, 29 May, GMT)

The progress of the attacking platoon was painfully slow. From his position with the defending platoon, Captain John Evans could see every move that they made. The three-quarters moon and the exposed route the 2nd Platoon's platoon leader had selected made it almost impossible to miss them. For the last hour Evans had been tracking their progress with nothing more than ordinary daylight binoculars. Impatiently he watched as the platoon first moved out of a wadi and arranged themselves in a tight formation. Next he watched as they marched across the open desert and away from the rocky knoll that was their objective and where the defending platoon waited. It took over forty minutes for them to figure out their error and another ten to sort out their true objective. Evans wanted so badly to fire a mortar or something at them, anything. People that stupid needed a shot in the head. But he had nothing. All he could do was sit and watch them mess all over themselves in the open.

The platoon leader defending the knoll was less patient. After seeing the troubles 2nd Platoon was having, he decided to add to them. He sent one of his squads down and around the rear of the attacking platoon. The idea was to have that squad trail the 2nd Platoon closely. When, and if, the 2nd Platoon finally began its attack, the trailing squad would strike from behind. Stripping away one third of his force was a gamble, but the performance of the attacker up to that point made the risk seem reasonable.

The soldiers on the knoll had a difficult time staying awake as they waited for something to happen. They were beginning their second day in Egypt and had not fully recovered from the effects of jet lag. On top of that, they were having difficulty acclimating to the desert heat. Evans was glad that they had the time in Egypt to do so. Not that it was by choice. The 17th Airborne Division had to deploy to forward staging areas before they jumped into Iran. It was not possible to stage and deploy from the States directly into Iran the size force required for the operation. Because of this, any hope for surprise was lost. No doubt there were scores of Shiite Muslims watching the coming and going of the transport aircraft, counting the units and probably even monitoring their radio nets as the 17th Airborne did some last-minute unit training.

The training exercise had come as a shock to many in the company. They had expected to simply lie around and rest in preparation for the big jump. Instead, less than three hours after landing, Evans had his platoons lined up with full combat gear and moving across the desert on foot. While they were there Evans wanted to take every opportunity available to train and prepare. As he continued to watch the 2nd Platoon, he was glad they were doing so. The platoon leader of that unit was actually far better than his current performance would indicate. Second Lieutenant Hal Cerro had been with the unit for over six months and had participated in several major exercises. None of them, however, had been in the desert.

The desert is a harsh environment that has its own rules. People brought up in a sophisticated society in a temperate climate are unprepared for the sheer nothingness of the desert. Simple survival is a challenge. Maintaining unit cohesion and combat effectiveness and conducting active military operations in the desert border on the impossible.

Logistics, or supply operations, is indicative of the nature of the problem. Each man requires each day slightly over two gallons of water which weighs almost twenty pounds. Add to this six pounds of food, and, because the force is engaged in combat, ammunition to the tune of an average of twenty to forty pounds per man. This total of forty-six to sixty-six pounds does not include the weight of fuel required to haul the supplies to the soldier, the weight of repair parts required to maintain the trucks, planes and ships hauling the supplies or the supplies consumed by the people hauling the supplies while they are doing the hauling. When all of this is tallied up, it is quite possible to reach a requirement demanding the movement and consumption of two hundred pounds of supplies per soldier in the combat area per day. When all is considered, getting the combat soldier to the theater of operations is the easy part; keeping him there and keeping him functional are where the real problem lies.

For Captain Evans, the immediate problem was how to get his people over the severe case of the dumbs that they had suddenly come down with. The 2nd Platoon had finally begun to move onto the rocky knoll it was supposed to have taken two hours ago. But rather than deploying for an attack, they advanced in two loose columns up the face of the knoll. What was even more disturbing was the fact that Evans could see the trailing squad coming up behind the 2nd Platoon. It was apparent that no one in the 2nd Platoon was paying attention to the rear. The defending platoon simply waited. They were going to let the 2nd Platoon get to within two hundred meters before they fired. Even this infuriated Evans. In the desert, you always take advantage of long-range engagements whenever possible. The defending platoon was pissing away a one-hundred- to two-hundred-meter advantage.

With blank ammunition quietly supplied to the 17th Airborne Division from Israel, the defending platoon opened fire on the 2nd Platoon. The initial reaction of the attackers was one of surprise and sudden paralysis. Dumbstruck, the men simply stood where they were or fired from the hip or the shoulder. This was too much for Evans. Jumping up, he yelled for a cease-fire above the din of small-arms fire. The men, sensing their commander's anger, stopped firing almost instantaneously. For a moment there was a hushed stillness as all held their positions and waited for further orders.

"Platoon leaders, form on me, *now!*"

In the darkness, two second lieutenants scrambled to find the source of the enraged voice, daring not to ask where it came from for fear of adding to its anger. They knew that their commander was, to say the least, less than pleased. To Lieutenant Cerro, it was like going to his father after he had been caught doing something wrong. Cerro could feel his stomach muscles tightening up. He knew that Captain Evans couldn't whip him as his dad had done. But that didn't lessen the effect of the brutal tongue-lashing he was about to endure.

His performance and that of his platoon since they had landed in Egypt had been less than satisfactory. It was almost as if during the flight to Egypt the men had forgotten everything they had ever been taught. The men were apprehensive about going into combat. In a platoon of thirty-eight men there was not a single combat veteran. There was no one to whom they could turn for guidance or reassurance. While the first sergeant had been in Vietnam, and both the CO and the first sergeant had been in Grenada, they were aloof from the men in the 2nd Platoon, not by intention but by necessity. The platoon therefore found itself facing the dark mysteries of combat for the first time with no idea of what it was really going to be like.

Rationalizing why the platoon was doing poorly was one thing. Doing something about it was another. One thing was for sure. If they didn't do any better in their first battle than they had just done on the aborted attack on the knoll, there would be no second battle for the 2nd Platoon. Captain Evans belabored that point as he drove home each error they had committed that night. While his men formed up and prepared for the fifteen-kilometer foot march back to their laager area, Lieutenant Cerro racked his tired brain for a method of getting his men over their fear of the unknown and ready for combat. He decided that the solution would come to him as soon as he had mastered his own fears.

Headquarters, 28th Combined Arms Army
Tabriz, Iran
0855 Hours, 2 June (0525 Hours, 2 June, GMT)

Despite the fact that Tabriz had been "officially secured" on 31 May, there was still sporadic gunfire throughout the city as snipers took pot shots at small groups of Soviet soldiers, even in daylight. At night the Soviets didn't move unless they were in an armored vehicle. The curfew, which ran from one hour before sunset to one hour after sunrise, simply stated that anyone seen on the streets at night would be shot. Nervous soldiers enforced this rule with a vengeance, often with deadly results for their comrades, since they fired at anything that moved, including friendly patrols.

As Colonel Pyotr Sulvina entered the headquarters of the 28th Combined Arms Army, he studied the two guards at the entrance. They were young men, neither one older than nineteen. They crouched behind their sandbag emplacement until Sulvina was too close to ignore. Both popped up and saluted, returning to their crouched position behind the sandbags as soon as Sulvina returned their salute. Their uniforms were dirty. Their faces were haggard from a combination of fear, anxiety and lack of sleep. With dark circles around their eyes and two days of stubbly beard on their chins, they looked more like the defeated than the victor.

Inside, posters that called for sacrifices in the name of Allah still hung on the walls. Sulvina couldn't read all the messages, but found it amusing that posters calling for death to the godless Americans were almost as numerous as those aimed against the Iraqis. None mentioned the Soviet Union. Fools, Sulvina thought. They feared the snake that was never there and didn't see the bear.

His thoughts were interrupted by a warm greeting from the army's chief of staff, Colonel Ivan Ovcharov. There were a few moments of small talk, the chief of staff asking how the weather was in Moscow and Baku as he walked Sulvina to his office, where they could get down to business. Once the door was closed, Ovcharov's jovial face turned cold. "Well, what is the verdict?" he asked.

Sulvina removed his hat and placed it and his briefcase on a chair. He then walked over to the window, considering his answer.

"It is not a good idea to stand before an open window like that, Comrade. The army commander has already lost an aide in this building doing the same thing."

Sulvina looked at the chief of staff with raised eyebrows as he slowly backed away. "Are they still that active?"

The chief of staff looked at him quizzically. "Still? After last night, there is every indication that it is getting worse. We have already commenced reprisals. It will be several days, however, before that has any effect."

Reprisals, Sulvina thought. What a useful term for making the practice of shooting civilians in retaliation for the shooting of Soviet soldiers seem justifiable. Perhaps it is necessary. War has its own rules.

"So, are you going to tell me the results of your trip to see our intrepid General Staff officers at STAVKA and Front Headquarters, or must I guess?"

"I am afraid, Colonel, you already know the results. All plans remain the same, and the forces committed will not be reinforced. Our losses do not yet justify that. Nor do we have authorization for the use of chemical weapons yet."

The chief of staff considered for a moment. "Yes, I expected no less. And STAVKA's appraisal is correct, we have not been handled too roughly. We have succeeded everywhere we have gone. But it is taking us too long. Do you realize that it has become a common practice now to stop at every roadblock and conduct a deliberate attack against it with artillery and tanks? Do you know why? It is because we no longer have any recon units able, or willing, to go forward without an artillery preparation being fired on the high ground overlooking the roadblock. It is saving us men but consuming tremendous amounts of ammunition and, more important, time. We no sooner clear one roadblock than a few kilometers down the road there is another. Even when we place airborne or air assault forces behind the Iranians, they still build their roadblocks."

The chief was angry and frustrated. Sulvina was one of the few officers in the army he could trust, which was why he had been selected to go to Front Headquarters to report on the army's situation and why the chief could talk freely to him. One had to be careful what one said. No doubt one or more of the 28th Combined Arms Army's staff officers was KGB, which was probably how STAVKA had found out about the army's slow progress.

"What about ammunition? We are now using three times the amount of ammunition that had been projected. Are we going to get any relief in that area?"

"Colonel, I am afraid that even if Front was willing to increase its allocation of ammunition, which it will not do, it does not have the means to deliver it to us. As it is, attacks against supply columns have taken a terrible toll of the trucks we have for resupply. Air resupply will be increased for some critical commodities, but bulk shipments of fuel and ammunition will still have to come over the roads. To relieve pressure on the supply system, STAVKA intends to delay the movement of the 17th Combined Arms Army south behind us. Even they understand the need to keep our lines of communication clear and supplies flowing."

"Roads," the chief interrupted. "Roads that require continuous guarding and siphon off combat troops from the front. On one hand the 17th CAA would help by guarding those roads, and on the other they would block them with their own units and supply columns. Either way, we suffer."

"When I mentioned that, the Front Commander merely remarked that we have yet to use a fraction of our men at the front, making the argument for commitment of parts of the 17th CAA or an increase in ammunition resupply weak."

"Perhaps the Front Commander would change his tune if he had been here when we stormed this miserable excuse of a city." The chief stopped for a moment. Ignoring his own advice, he went to the window and looked out. Without turning to face Sulvina, he continued. "What news of the other fronts?"

"In the east, Mashhad has fallen, but only after a bloody fight. The 89th Motorized Rifle Division is hung up around Birjand. Because they need the road that runs through it and the airfield for resupply, they have commenced a siege of that city. The bridgeheads along the Caspian continue to build up, but, as with us, forward progress is slow. The Elburz Mountains they face are far more formidable than the ones we have to deal with. And in the west, our good allies the Iraqis attacked, as planned, and lost ground, as expected, without tying down any appreciable Iranian forces, as hoped."

Still looking out the window, the chief asked, "And the Americans? What about them?"

"STAVKA is less sure about the Americans' intentions than it used to be. There is now an airborne brigade in Egypt, with more on the way. A Marine brigade is being flown into Diego Garcia. Air Force units have also been reported in Egypt. Naval activity in the Arabian Sea has increased, and the addition of a carrier group is expected."

In a monotone, the chief asked, "How long before the Americans enter Iran?"

"Two weeks at the earliest, probably four at the outside."

The chief of staff thought about that. He turned to Sulvina. "And when that happens, my friend, we will have a whole new war to fight before we finish the first."

Somewhere in the Arabian Sea
2335 Hours, 2 June (1935 Hours, 2 June, GMT)

The pinging of the sonar on the hull of the submarine was clearly audible to the commander, Captain Vladimir Gudkov, and the crew. They had been found again. For the third time in sixteen hours the Soviet *Oscar*-class submarine had failed to penetrate the escort screen of the carrier battle group. A series of orders resulted in a rapid dive and several sharp turns as the submarine attempted to break contact.

The men in the control room looked to their captain. In the eyes of all of them Gudkov could see the same sense of frustration that was accentuated by fatigue. The cruise from Cam Rahn Bay in Vietnam to their patrol station in the Arabian Sea had been routine. Even their patrol had been routine until the captain opened his special orders on the twenty-fourth of May. After that, they played the same cat-and-mouse game with U.S. Navy ships in the area they had always played, but now they did so in deadly earnest. The threat of war brought new meaning to their games.

Daily the submarine, named the *Iskra*—Russian for "spark"—raised its antenna at a prearranged time to receive the code word that would tell the captain when to initiate hostilities and against whom. When the hard-copy orders had been written, the Red Navy did not know who, for sure, would be involved and when. To cover all contingencies, each potential enemy was given a color code word. "Black," for example, meant the United States Navy. "Blue" was for the Royal Navy. "Green" was for the French, and so on. All Moscow had to do was send a simple message with the appropriate code word or words, and all ships on station would commence attacks against the nation's warships and shipping at 0600 hours the next morning. To ensure that there were no errors and that commanders knew their communication systems were functional, code word "White," which meant "Continue peacetime patrol routines," was transmitted daily when there were to be no hostile acts the next day.

The *Oscar*-class submarine had received its White signal as usual, and continued its peacetime mission, which was to maintain contact with the carrier battle group operating in the Arabian Sea and place itself close enough to the American carrier to be able to strike it. The American escort ships, however, were keeping the *Oscar*-class boat from doing that. In order to strike, the submarine had to get close without being detected. Each time it was found, the submarine had to break contact, back away from the escorts, and try from a different angle. Each attempt was time-consuming and wearing on the nerves. The crew knew that whenever the Americans found them, they could kill them with ease. Therefore every discovery was treated as a defeat.

The submarine continued to swerve and change depth in rapid and random patterns in an effort to break contact. As it was doing so, the captain decided to stop any further attempts until his crew could get some sleep. He didn't want to push them too much before hostilities. In the first place, there was always the chance that someone, on either side, just might get too excited and, in the heat of the moment, make a mistake and push a button too soon. In the second place, he and his crew needed all the rest they could get while they could. When war came, he wanted his men able to push the right buttons at the right time.

While the submarine wiggled and bobbed in an effort to lose itself in the dark, cold depths of the Arabian Sea, the pursuing destroyer escort commander pushed his crew in an equally determined effort to maintain contact.

Thus ended another day of "peace."

Chapter 4

Duty is the sublimest word in our language.
Do your duty in all things. You cannot do
more. You should never wish to do less.

— ROBERT E. LEE

The two target panels rose up and locked into place. The crew of the M-1 tank, however, did not see them until the control-tower personnel set off, by remote control, at the target locations, explosives known as the hostile simulators. The flash and the puff of smoke from the simulators brought an immediate reaction from the crew.

Slewing the turret toward the targets by using his control handle, the tank commander began to issue his fire command. "Gunner, Sabot. Two tanks—left tank."

With his eye to the primary sight, the gunner searched until he saw the targets while his right hand danced across the face of the primary sight's control panel, arming the main gun, switching the ammo-select lever to SABOT and coming to rest on the magnification level. Without bothering to key the intercom, he yelled, "Identified!" as soon as the targets came into his field of vision. He then switched his sight to a higher magnification and began to track his first target.

The commander let go of his control and turned to watch just as the loader finished arming the main gun, moved out of its path of recoil, and in his turn announced, "Up."

The tank commander shouted, "Fire!"

It was now up to the gunner and the driver. As the driver strove to maintain steady speed and course, the gunner laid the gun sight onto the center mass of the target. When he had a good sight picture, he hit the laser range-finder thumb switch. Before he could remove his thumb from the switch, the range readout appeared at the bottom of the sight. A quick mental comparison of the size of the target and the indicated range showed that the range was about right. Satisfied, the gunner relaid onto the center mass of the target, yelled, "On the waaay," and squeezed the trigger on his right control handle.

Nothing. Nothing happened. The gunner announced, "Misfire. On the waaay." With that, he pulled the trigger on his left control handle. Again, nothing. "Shit! Misfire!"

It was now the tank commander's turn to try. Grabbing his control handle and crouching down so that he could view through his sight extension, the tank commander laid the sight onto the target's center of mass, hit the laser range-finder switch and watched for the readout. Satisfied that he had a good range and sight picture, he announced, "From my position—on the waaay," and pulled the trigger.

Nothing. The tank continued to roll down the course road. The tank commander continued to track the targets. And the targets continued to stand, unhit. Totally frustrated, the tank commander ordered the driver to stop, then called the tower to inform them that he had to clear a misfire.

In the control tower Major Scott Dixon pounded his fist on the table and let out a stream of obscenities. This was the third run that day that they had failed to complete. With their own equipment en route to the Persian Gulf, the units of the 25th Armored Division had to train on borrowed stuff while they waited to be flown over. The whole arrangement was less than ideal. What they received from the Armor School was already well used when it arrived at Fort Hood. No doubt the Armor School was careful to keep the better equipment to meet its own surge in training. Continuous use by different units did not permit serious preventive maintenance. The result was a high number of malfunctions and mechanical failures that frustrated the battalion's attempts to prepare for combat.

The officer in charge of the range turned to Dixon. "Do we let him continue or pull him off?"

Without looking at the officer, Dixon thought for a moment before answering. "See if he can clear it through the tube. If not, pull him back and have maintenance find out what the problem with *that* one is. In the meantime, push them through as fast as you can. We only have the rest of today and tomorrow to finish the battalion, and we aren't even halfway through." Then Dixon turned to the young captain and asked, "Paul, do you think you can get 'em all through?"

Captain Paul Tait, the battalion S-3 Air, tried to think of something witty to come back with, but couldn't. He simply replied that he would do his damnedest. With that, Dixon left the tower, signaling his driver to crank up his hummer—the new M-998 high-mobility multipurpose wheeled vehicle, or HMMWV. He didn't know for sure where he was going to go. Wherever he went, it had to be more productive than standing around on the range watching tanks break down and, as the crews said, "go tits up." Hopefully the battalion was getting something from the crash training they were conducting instead of merely marking time while waiting for deployment.

Fort Campbell, Kentucky
1735 Hours, 4 June (2335 Hours, 4 June, GMT)

Like clockwork the two A-10 ground-attack aircraft came rolling in on their run and began to fire on the crest of a hill. From the concealment of a stand of pine trees, four M-113 armored personnel carriers of a mech infantry platoon came rolling out. One thousand meters to their right, the gun tubes from four M-60A3 tanks poked out and began to belch fire as they also engaged targets on the hill that was their final objective. The A-10s had by now turned and were making their second, and last, run in, firing their 30mm. GAU-8 gun along the length of the hill. Satisfied with the results of their effort, they overflew the control vehicles, wiggling their wings as they skimmed along at treetop level.

No sooner had the aircraft cleared the area than 155mm. artillery firing high-explosive and white phosphorus rounds began to hit the hill. The first mech infantry platoon was joined by a second platoon that followed it out from the tree line and came up on its left. Together, the two platoons advanced on their objective as the tanks and the artillery continued to work it over. This continued until the M-113s of the two mech platoons reached a predesignated point less than five hundred meters from the hill. When they did, the artillery-fire-support officer issued a curt order to the firing battery. On cue, the guns lifted and shifted fires to a new target beyond the hill. The tanks continued to fire, but now concentrated on targets on either side of their objective.

With the fire lifted and only two hundred meters to go, the M-113s stopped and dropped their ramps. Infantrymen of the Tennessee National Guard came pouring out, running to either side of the M-113s in staggered lines. On signal, the M-113s and the lines of infantry began to advance. Only when the dismounted troops and the M-113s masked the tanks' fields of fire did they cease fire. The track commanders of the M-113s stood upright, firing their .50-caliber machine guns while the dismounted infantry fired from the hip as they went into the dust and smoke that now shrouded the hill.

From their observation point the battalion commander and the executive officer of the 2nd Battalion, 354th Infantry, watched the end of the last run of the day of the company combined-arms live fire exercise. Turning to his XO, the battalion commander asked why they had never been able to do that in Tennessee. The XO, Major Ed Lewis, simply stated, "When the Army got serious about sending the unit to war, all kinds of wonderful things were possible. The last ten days are ample proof of that."

After being mobilized, the battalion had assembled at Fort Campbell in accordance with its mobilization plans. Surprisingly, its first mission was to prepare its equipment and ship it to New Orleans for embarkation. This was quickly accomplished, but left the unit nothing to complete its postmobilization training with. Initially, the battalion had been slated to move immediately to Fort Hood to join its parent Active Army unit, the 2nd Brigade, 25th Armored Division. This, however, was canceled. Fort Hood was already overcrowded with units trying to train with small amounts of borrowed equipment. Instead, the 2nd Battalion of the 354th Infantry was left at Campbell. Heated discussions between the unit commander, the state, the National Guard Bureau and anyone who would listen did not change the ill-conceived peacetime mobilization plan. Instead of training for war with its parent unit, the battalion was left to its own devices, training in isolation while the rest of the 25th Division rushed to complete its preparation for war.

Training at Fort Campbell, however, did have its advantages. With the 12th Infantry Division in the throes of deploying, there were plenty of maneuver areas and ranges available. The 2nd of the 354th, being a round-out unit and high on the deployment list, had a higher priority over other Guard and Reserve units assembling at Campbell. Equipment, including a fully manned tank company with which to train, was borrowed from the Kentucky National Guard. Although the personnel carriers were the old M-113s instead of the M-2 Bradleys, they were better than nothing.

In addition to equipment, ammunition for live fire training was not a problem. Whatever the 12th Division left at the ammo storage point on Campbell was given to the 2nd of the 354th. It was in live fire training that the battalion spent most of its time. The commander felt that the men needed to get used to handling their weapons and getting the feel for what it would be like when everyone was blasting away. Men who had been assigned to the unit as TOW and Dragon antitank-guided-missile gunners for years finally had an opportunity to fire a live missile. Sometimes the results were quite embarrassing, as when the shock of firing their first live missile caused the gunners to jump and send the missile spiraling into the ground. As Lewis, the battalion XO and full-time training officer, said, "Better to miss at Campbell and be embarrassed than miss in Iran and be dead."

While training was progressing well, Lewis was worried about what was coming next. It was all well and good to get their equipment off to the Persian Gulf as soon as possible; and, likewise, using the time while the equipment was in transit for postmobilization training made sense. It was the act of getting the men and the equipment together again that concerned Lewis. To offload the ships in Iran, the Army needed at least one secure and functional seaport. Likewise, to get the troops in, a secure and functional airfield was needed in close proximity to the seaport. More than that, the air over these facilities had to be relatively free of enemy air activity. It would do no good to have all the equipment arrive in port and have the people who were to man it spattered on a runway in Iran by a hotshot Russian jet-fighter jock as the transport plane came in for a landing. A lot of coordination between the Army, the Navy and the Air Force needed to happen to make this operation work.

There was serious work to do, however, right there at Fort Campbell. What happened in Iran was still in the future. Lewis' main concern at that moment was to prepare the battalion for battle as best he could. Success or failure of the deployment phase of the operation was in the hands of other people, people he would never know. As his jeep, also borrowed from the Kentucky National Guard, bounced along the tank trail back to battalion headquarters, Lewis flipped through the unit training schedules for the next day to ensure that everything had been coordinated and set. There was precious little time for screwups.

Tabriz, Iran
0555 Hours, 5 June (0225 Hours, 5 June, GMT)

In any profession there are requirements and duties that are necessary and important but unpleasant. Often, as an unwritten rule, these jobs are given to the most junior man. This practice is passed off as being part of the new man's development, while in fact it is nothing more than passing off a dirty chore to someone else. An equally common practice is to continue passing off un-pleasant duties until there is no one else to push the duty off onto. The Army is probably the greatest practitioner of this method of dealing with its dirty little jobs. Junior Lieutenant Nikolai Ilvanich knew this from his training as a cadet and a junior officer. It was part of the system. This rationalization, however, did not make his current task any easier.

Since being relieved by the 28th CAA, the 285th Guards Air-borne Regiment had been recovering and reorganizing. Ilvanich's company was typical of the condition of the regiment as a whole. The company had dropped into Tabriz with seven officers and seventy-eight enlisted men. After six days of sustained combat, there were only two officers and thirty-three enlisted men who were not dead or wounded when the ground forces finally arrived. The 285th Regiment's parent division was equally depleted, re-quiring reorganization and amalgamation of units. During this effort, the 285th was assigned garrison and patrol duties in and around Tabriz while the 28th CAA continued to advance south and west.

One of these duties was the apprehension and punishment of

Iranians who violated the curfew. The punishment was death. Ilvanich did not realize what he and his men would be required to do when he reported to the garrison headquarters on the afternoon of the fourth. He was taken to a KGB major who would brief him and supervise him and his platoon during the performance of their duties. The KGB major was relatively young, Ilvanich guessed not more than thirty-two. He stood a bit over six foot and had a medium build. His looks and dress were average. But the fact that he was KGB made him different, a difference that one did not dare forget.

At first Ilvanich thought that his men were to be prison guards. Slowly, as the KGB major talked, it dawned upon him that he was going to lead a firing squad and summarily execute anyone who had been apprehended for violating the curfew. Anyone, that is, who was not shot by the patrols.

When this revelation finally hit him, Ilvanich flushed. For a moment he felt lightheaded, as if he were going to faint. Then he noticed the KGB major staring at him. The major asked whether there was something wrong. Ilvanich, mustering all the strength he could, collected himself and replied that he was simply tired, not fully recovered from his first battle. The KGB major appeared to accept that, heaping praise on the bravery and sacrifice of the airborne soldiers before carrying on with his briefing. When he got to the portion of the briefing where he described the duties of the officer in charge of the firing squad, he spoke slowly and looked into Ilvanich's eyes. The KGB major was searching for weakness or hesitation. Ilvanich returned the stare, turning his thoughts away from the task he was being given.

That night, for the first time in his career, Ilvanich struggled with his duties and his conscience. In the dark room where he was billeted, sleep did not come. He tossed and turned in his sweat-soaked bunk, trying to clear his mind and to reason out his current problem. His whole life revolved around duty to the State and the Army. The two were inseparable. There was, in his mind, no other purpose to his life but to serve the State. He had performed, without question, his duties when he and his men were dropped into Iran. Despite the horrors, he was able to deal with what he was doing because the Iranians were the enemy, enemies of the State, armed and ready to do harm to the State. His role as an executioner, however, was different. He was being directed to shoot civilians whose sole crime was being in the street at night.

Granted, some, if not most, were probably terrorists or guerrillas. But this killing was going to be different. On the front it had been so quick, so necessary. Now the process was going to be slow and the reason not so clear.

In the cool of the early morning Ilvanich paraded his firing squad. Still unsure of himself and how he would react, he did his best to hide any show of emotion and chose his words carefully as he issued his instructions. His men quickly detected his stress and tension. But they, like their platoon leader, understood what was at stake and followed suit, doing exactly as they were told without any sign of feeling or hesitation.

The KGB major watched from a corner of the small prison courtyard as the first group of Iranians were brought out and stood against the clean whitewashed wall. His eyes were riveted on Ilvanich standing on the flank of the firing squad. Ilvanich could feel the major's eyes on him. He also felt himself getting dizzy again as he surveyed the prisoners. Of the ten people, four were women, two were boys who could not have been more than twelve years old, and one was an old man who walked with the aid of a wooden stick. How, Ilvanich thought, could any sane person consider this motley group a threat to the State? It was ludicrous. Carefully, he turned his head to where the KGB major stood leaning against the prison building, staring at him. With a simple nod, the major indicated it was time to proceed. Turning his head back to where he could face his men without seeing the people they were about to execute, Ilvanich began to give the orders.

"Ready."

His men raised their rifles to their shoulders.

"Aim."

They tucked their cheeks against the stocks of their rifles.

Ilvanich steadied himself and closed his eyes.

"Fire."

The noise that reverberated off the courtyard walls was deafening. It caused Ilvanich to jump. Opening his eyes, he looked down the line of men as they fired. Some fired a single burst, with their eyes closed, then stopped. Others fired continuously, dipping their rifles to shoot into the bodies after they had fallen. Some fired until their entire magazines were empty.

Ilvanich did not issue an order to cease fire. He merely waited until the shooting stopped, then ordered his men to attention. While still looking along the line of his men, he reached down, unsnapped his holster and drew his pistol, holding it at shoulder level and pointed in the air. At last he turned toward the wall where the prisoners had been. The white wall was now splattered with blood and pockmarked with bullet holes. Streams of blood ran down the wall onto the ground to where the prisoners lay in a tangled heap. For a moment Ilvanich remembered the trench. His stomach muscles tightened as he felt a tinge of bile rise in his throat. He fought for and gained composure before he proceeded.

Mechanically, he marched to the wall, staring not at the bodies but at one of the bloodstains on the wall until he reached the wall. When he got there, he stopped and looked down. The first person was a young woman, not more than twenty. For a second he wondered what had caused her to become an enemy of the State.

Ilvanich turned and looked in the direction of the KGB major. The major was still in the same position, leaning casually against the building. With the same nonchalant nod, he signaled Ilvanich to continue. Without further thought, the junior lieutenant lowered his pistol and fired one round into the head of each of the bodies before him. When he was finished, he turned and marched back to his post on the flank of his firing squad while other Iranians came out, dragged away the bodies of the first prisoners and prepared to take their place against the wall. Ilvanich did not watch. He merely replaced the magazine in his pistol with a fresh one, returned the pistol to his holster and stood by until the next group was ready.

As he waited, he saw the KGB major give him a faint smile and a nod of approval. Ilvanich and his men had performed their duty to the State well. Socialism in Iran was a little more secure.

Fort Hood, Texas
2205 Hours, 4 June (0405 Hours, 5 June, GMT)

The officers' club hadn't done as well as this in years. It seemed that everyone was stopping by after a tough day in the pits to undergo liquid "stress reduction." In the beginning, First Lieutenant Amanda Matthews couldn't understand why officers would want to spend all day beating themselves to death at the office and then, for relaxation, go over to the club and spend more time with the same people from the office. For the first few days she left post as soon as she could, showered, changed out of uniform and tried hard to blend into the rest of society for a few hours. She wanted to leave the office and the grim business she dealt in on post.

The more she tried, however, the less she succeeded. As she wandered the shopping mall, Soviet orders of battle raced through her mind. She found that it was difficult to talk to her civilian friends. She felt out of place as they talked about their jobs, stereos and cars, things that now meant little to Matthews. Issues such as Soviet offensive chemical and tactical nuclear capabilities in Iran had become her all-consuming concern. Not finding escape in the outside world, she sought at the officers' club the company of others who, like her, pondered the imponderable and needed escape.

From across the crowded lounge, another military-intelligence lieutenant from the division staff beckoned her to join him. Matthews, feeling no pain after her second scotch, figured there was nothing to lose. After all, misery enjoys company.

First Lieutenant Tom Kovack was one of the more junior officers in the division G-2 shop. Although he was one of the most arrogant and conceited people she knew, he had been a very good source of back-door information for Matthews in the last ten days. She suspected his motives, for good reasons, but felt she could handle him. After all, she had three inches over him.

Without rising as she came to the table, Kovack asked, "Do you always drink alone, Amanda?" Some men took seriously the fact that they were no longer commissioned "an officer and a gentleman."

"Only when there is no one worth drinking with."

"That's cold, Amanda. Besides, I'm supposed to be the conceited one."

Taking advantage of the opening, she gibed, "And so you are, I'll drink to that," and drained her glass.

She had hit him off guard and on the mark. His smirk disappeared and his ears turned red as he bit back a nasty remark. He changed subjects quickly. "You know the G-2 is beginning to lose his patience with your estimates of Iranian resistance. Do you really believe they're going to try to fight the Russians *and* us? I mean, it doesn't make sense."

Matthews looked at Kovack for a moment. She found it hard to believe that the two of them, with the same training and background, could look at the same information and come up with two entirely different conclusions. "Kovack, I don't believe that even you can be so stupid. Haven't you been watching the news? Ten days *after* the Soviets invade their country, and with them less than a hundred and fifty miles from Tehran, the Iranians are still demonstrating against the U.S. There are just as many anti-American banners in their demonstrations as there are anti-Soviet. These people don't see any difference between us and them. They don't see any difference now and they won't see one when the first Americans land there."

With composure and confidence born from assurance of his convictions, Kovack countered her, point by point, clearly demonstrating, in his mind, the foolishness of her position. "Surely," he concluded, "once we're on the ground and they see we're there to fight the Russians and help them preserve their country, they'll flock to our side."

Matthews merely shook her head. "Kovack, you're an idiot as well as an asshole. We are dealing with fanatics. Fanatics that are part of a proud race of people. Anyone that is not a Persian or a Shiite is their enemy. No one, regardless of motivation, is going to change their minds. They'll go down to a man before they embrace us as friends."

Leaning forward and placing his hand on her thigh, Kovack whispered, "Talking about going down and embracing friends, let's leave. The night's still young."

Matthews stood up without breaking eye contact. "Like the Iranians, I'm careful whom I pick for friends." With that she turned and walked away, followed by Kovack's taunt "I have not yet begun to fight."

Five Kilometers West of Kaju, Iran
0645 Hours, 5 June (0315 Hours, 5 June, GMT)

With a thunderous roar, the bombardment of the Iranian positions commenced on schedule. The lead elements of the 67th Motorized Rifle Division were already unraveling from their assembly areas and deploying for the attack. To their north, the summit of the Kuh-e Sahand looked down on the mass of Soviet armor as it moved east, converging on a single point.

The Iranians had taken their time preparing their defensive positions before the town of Kaju. The town itself was of little importance. What did matter was the rail line that ran through it. It was the main rail line running south from Tabriz, around Kuh-e Sahand and then to Tehran. The Soviets needed it. To secure it, and the road system running south from Tabriz, the 28th CAA had split at Tabriz, with one motorized rifle division and the tank division attacking straight south along the roads while two motorized rifle divisions swung west around the Sahand to clear the rail line.

The Iranians saw this splitting of forces as an opportunity to defeat the Soviets. Everything that they could muster, including most of their pitifully small tank reserve, was concentrated either at Kaju, to block Soviet efforts to clear the rail line out of Tabriz, or at Bastanabad, to block the Soviet advance along the roads leading south from Tabriz. The Iranians did not want to lose any more of the northwest than they had to. Besides, the farther the Soviets pushed south, the easier the terrain became. The Iranians were gambling on a winner-take-all proposition.

The Soviets, on the other hand, welcomed the stand by the Iranians. Instead of reacting to Iranians in small, isolated ambushes, the 28th Combined Arms Army would be able to fight the kind of war it was trained and equipped for. The commander of the 28th CAA prepared to fight a battle of annihilation. His goal was to pin, trap and destroy every organized Iranian unit deployed against him. The plan was simple and well proven. It was, in fact, nothing more than an updated version of the German blitzkrieg.

Units of the 28th CAA would close up on the Iranians, feeling out their positions for weak points with air, ground and electronic reconnaissance. Once the Iranian units had been located, weaknesses identified and command posts targeted, the point of attack would be determined and a breakthrough assault would be launched.

Soviet doctrine calls for the concentration of numerical superiority at the point of attack in attacker–defender ratios of at least five to one in infantry, four to one in tanks and seven to one in artillery. Superiority is achieved by the use of artillery and rockets; air attacks including attack helicopters, electronic warfare including radio direction-finding and jamming on command and control nets; and masses of men and tanks on the ground. The well-orchestrated assault designed to break through the defender commences with a violent twenty-minute artillery attack at the selected point. Not only does the artillery kill some defenders and destroy equipment, it also covers the advance of the attacking force by pinning the defenders and obscuring their observation.

The main instrument for a Soviet breakthrough assault is the motorized rifle regiment. Its battalions, normally deployed two abreast in a first-attack echelon and one back as a second echelon, start in columns five to ten kilometers from the front. As a motorized rifle battalion approaches, it breaks up into company columns, with four tanks normally leading a company of ten to twelve armored personnel carriers. When the battalion reaches the five-kilometer point, it breaks down into platoon columns, with a tank leading each rifle platoon of three or four personnel carriers. Finally, at the two- to three-kilometer point, the personnel carriers swing into line as the tanks cut on their on-board smoke generators, shrouding the advancing storm in smoke. All this occurs at a steady, unaltering pace of twelve to twenty miles an hour. At this point, the artillery, which has been firing at a rapid rate on the enemy positions, shifts to the next series of targets. Each battalion now has twelve tanks in line, followed by thirty or more personnel carriers fifty to one hundred meters behind the tanks. If antitank fire is heavy, the infantry will dismount a few hundred meters from the enemy and assault on foot, and the tanks and the personnel carriers will follow with support fire. If the defender's fire is of little consequence, the infantry will remain mounted and the battalion will roll through the defensive positions. Once through, the attacking unit will either continue to drive deep into the enemy's rear or turn and envelop him from the rear.

In addition to the tanks and the personnel carriers, the lead motorized rifle battalion will have two to four self-propelled antiaircraft guns, a battery of six self-propelled artillery guns, and antitank-guided-missile carriers immediately behind the first line of personnel carriers. This force attacks with a frontage of fifteen hundred meters, just under a mile. Two battalions abreast would give the regiment a frontage of three thousand meters. The third battalion, or second-echelon battalion, follows at a distance of five hundred to one thousand meters behind the two lead battalions and is ready to move forward to take advantage of a success of either of them. Soviet practice is to reinforce success. A battalion that fails to break through will be left to its own devices while all support goes to one that is having success or has succeeded.

Once a clean breakthrough has been achieved, the tank battalions, regiments and finally divisions are pushed through. It is the tank unit that is viewed by the Soviets as the decisive arm that strikes deep and smashes the enemy. The motorized rifle units that did not attack will continue to hold and pin the enemy down; they are the anvil. The tanks strike deep and swing around, hitting them in the rear; they are the hammer. To the Soviets, defeat of the enemy requires more than merely gaining ground or breaking through. The enemy force in the field must be defeated in detail, or, in simple terms, annihilated, preferably to the last man.

After almost two weeks of a painfully slow advance into Iran punctuated by brief but sharp encounters with an unseen enemy, the deliberate attack was welcomed by Captain Neboatov and the men of his motorized rifle company. Neboatov tried vainly to maintain visual contact with all of his vehicles. The smoke created by the tanks to his front hid many of his BMP infantry-fighting vehicles from his view. From what he could see, however, all appeared to be going well. The BMPs had swung into line and were maintaining proper distance. Through brief breaks in the smoke he could see that the tanks were beginning to fire while on the move. Their fire would be very inaccurate; its primary intent in such an attack was to suppress the enemy rather than annihilate him.

With the exception of a few stray mortar rounds and an occasional wild burst of machine-gun fire, there appeared to be a total lack of return fire from the direction of the Iranian positions. Neboatov listened intently on the battalion command net for the next order. Very soon the battalion commander would need to decide whether the infantry was to remain mounted or to assault on foot. Neboatov hoped the decision would be to remain mounted. There appeared to be no need to dismount. To do so would cost them their momentum.

Suddenly the platoon leader of the tanks leading Neboatov's

company came over the net and reported he was stopped by an antitank ditch. Neboatov swore. Though the ditch would be of little consequence, it would cost them their momentum and require his men to dismount. Neboatov went on the air and ordered the tanks to cover and the BMPs to close up and prepare to breach the obstacle.

As his BMP pulled up next to the leader's tank, Neboatov saw the ditch. It was ten to fifteen meters wide and two meters deep. On the lip of the far side were rolls of barbed wire. No doubt there were mines in the ditch or along the lip of the far side. Without waiting any longer, he ordered his 1st Platoon to dismount, cross the ditch, secure the far side and cut lanes through the wire. The 2nd Platoon would dismount and cover the 1st Platoon from the near side of the ditch. Although he knew that the battalion commander would already be sending an MTU armored bridge layer that could span the ditch, the 3rd Platoon was ordered to dismount with shovels and begin to knock down the side of the ditch and build ramps for crossing. Better to do something with what you had than wait for something you might never get. Neboatov himself dismounted in order to better observe and, if required, direct the efforts of his men.

His supervision, however, was not needed. As he watched, his men went about their tasks quickly and with little wasted motion even though artillery fire was beginning to fall on both sides of the ditch. Fortunately their own artillery, firing high explosive and smoke, continued to strike just two hundred meters beyond the edge of the ditch, suppressing most of the Iranian positions and obscuring the Iranians' ability to direct artillery fire accurately onto Neboatov's company.

The 1st Platoon reached the ditch and went in with little difficulty, while the 2nd Platoon set up to provide cover. But when the 1st Platoon began to emerge on the other side and cut through the wire, effective fire hit them. The first two men of Neboatov's company had just popped their heads up and begun to cut the wire when a well-aimed burst of machine-gun fire hit them and knocked them back into the ditch. The leader of the 2nd Platoon had managed to catch a glimpse of the Iranian machine gun's muzzle flash. He directed his machine guns to fire on it. The tracers from the 2nd Platoon's machine gun served to mark the target for a tank and the crews of two nearby BMPs. All three opened fire, the tank with its main gun and the BMPs with their

30mm. cannon. They were effective. The Iranian machine gun never fired again.

With a little more caution, the men of the 1st Platoon popped up again and began to cut the wire. Once spaces large enough had been cut, the platoon leader led his men through and set up a shallow arc protecting a breach they had made. By this time, the 3rd Platoon was busy knocking down the side of the ditch with their shovels. Their efforts, however, were wasted. No sooner had they succeeded in completing a ramp that would allow a vehicle to descend into the ditch than the MTU arrived.

Neboatov himself leaped up and directed the MTU to where he wanted the bridge laid. The MTU moved to the edge of the ditch and stopped across from where the 1st Platoon had cut the barbed wire. The operator settled the MTU into a good position and began to play out the bridge. Slowly the bridge extended until it reached across the ditch. When its far edge was past the far lip of the ditch, the operator allowed the bridge to drop into place. Then he disconnected the MTU from the bridge and backed away. Now the tanks began to cross, joining the 1st Platoon's perimeter. When all the tanks were on the other side, Neboatov ordered the 2nd and 3rd Platoons to remount and go over the bridge. As each platoon went over, the little bridgehead expanded until the entire company was on line again. The company moved forward slowly; Neboatov needed to give the rest of the battalion time to cross.

With the antitank ditch breached, the Iranian front lines, lacking sufficient antitank weapons, began to crumble. It was not noticeable at first. The tanks and the artillery from both sides were still creating so much dust and smoke that no one could get a good feel for exactly what was happening. Initially the commanders in the lead vehicles could see only a few hundred meters to either side and submitted only the sketchiest reports. Soon, however, there was a noticeable drop in the volume of fire being directed against them. As the first echelon of Soviet tanks and BMPs rolled through the Iranian positions and continued on, the firing stopped altogether with the exception of random artillery and mortar rounds. Even those stopped as the second-echelon battalion of the regiment reached the point of breakthrough.

Within thirty minutes of the commencement of the attack, the issue had been decided. Five days of work and the best forces the Iranians could muster had failed to stop the Soviet advance. The realization of this and the effects of being pounded by artillery took the fight out of many of the Iranians who watched the Russian tanks roll by. Individually, and then in small groups, the Iranians left their positions and walked, crawled or ran to what they thought to be the rear and safety. The safety they sought was illusory, however, as the Soviet division commander committed his tank regiment to strike deep and smash any semblance of organization the Iranians had left.

The 28th Combined Arms Army finally was able to realize the success that had been eluding it and to achieve a victory which proved beyond a shadow of a doubt that the Iranian Army could not and would not be able to stop it. Tehran now seemed to be within easy grasp, and reaching the army's final goal, the Strait of Hormuz, only a matter of time and logistics.

10th Corps Headquarters, Ford Hood, Texas
1700 Hours, 5 June (2300 Hours, 5 June, GMT)

The sharp report of the evening gun just outside his office window broke Lieutenant General Weir's train of thought. He had been studying so intently the material spread across his desk that he had not heard the duty officer play "Call to the Colors" over the outside PA system. Slowly Weir rose and went over to the window. He looked out across the front of Building 1 to where the MPs were taking down the post flag. Another day had ended. Our last day of peace, Weir thought. For a while.

When the flag had been lowered, he glanced at his watch. Some quick calculations gave him the time in Egypt and Iran. He turned his head toward his desk and looked for a moment at the plan for the invasion of Iran, then turned back to stare out the window. As he watched the cars passing below him, carrying their operators home from work, he knew that somewhere over Saudi Arabia transport aircraft were lumbering northeast toward their objective, carrying their human cargo to war. Off the coast, a Navy task force carrying a Marine amphibious brigade would be making its final course change and beginning its run into its line of departure. In less than four hours, all hell would break loose as the United States committed ground forces in Iran.

Weir understood his corps's role and the intent of the Commander in Chief, Central Command. He and his staff had gone over the plan again and again. Each reading, however, did little to improve it as far as Weir was concerned. The 17th Airborne Division had the mission of seizing Bandar Abbas, an important seaport located at the head of the Strait of Hormuz. The 6th Marine Division had the task of seizing the port of Chah Bahar, located on the Gulf of Oman. Both divisions had the task of securing a lodgement on the Iranian mainland and preparing their respective ports to receive reinforcements and supplies. Until those ports could be made ready to receive and offload ships, everything would have to come in by air or over the beach. Weir knew that large-scale operations could not be sustained indefinitely that way.

That, however, was only the beginning. The follow-on forces of the 13th Airborne Corps would take more than three weeks to arrive after the initial assault. Once ashore, the assembled units had to move north, establish a perimeter and hold it against anything the Russians, and the Iranians, cared to throw against it, until the heavy forces arrived. These forces, namely Weir's 10th Corps, depended on the ports and the sea-lanes, sea-lanes patrolled by Soviet warships. Whether or not the Soviets would actively interfere was still unknown. To Weir, the whole plan was shaky. Too much depended on precise timing and optimum conditions. The 10th Corps was already starting at a disadvantage, depending on a line of communications that stretched over twelve thousand miles on exposed sea-lanes while its main adversary was less than a thousand kilometers by land from his homeland. If the 10th Corps was delayed or the Soviets made better time than anticipated, the 13th Airborne Corps would be unable to hold them for long.

A knock at his office door gave Weir an excuse to turn his mind away from his troubled thoughts. His aide opened the door slightly and announced that Major Jones had arrived for his 1700 hour office call. Weir looked at his watch again, then told his aide to send the major in.

Major Percy Jones, British Army, entered the room, walked forward, stopped, and saluted with the palm of his hand facing out in the manner of the British forces. "Major Jones reporting as ordered, sir." Jones was an exchange officer assigned to the 25th Armored Division. An American major was serving in a similar capacity in a British unit in Germany.

Weir motioned to a chair. "Have a seat, Major."

Weir's aide brought two cups of coffee from the outer office and set one of them on a small table next to the chair where Jones was seating himself. The aide handed the other cup to Weir. With a slight nod, Weir dismissed the aide, who left, closing the door on his way out.

Weir sat down in a chair across from Jones, sipped his coffee and began. "I have just been informed that Her Majesty's Government has agreed to join the United States and France in our upcoming operations in Iran. An armored brigade, currently slated to be attached to this corps, has been assigned to the Allied Expeditionary Force, along with units of the Royal Navy and the Royal Air Force. Until further notice, you are being reassigned to my staff as an adviser and liaison officer."

Weir paused for a moment and let that sink in before he continued. "One of the primary reasons I want you on my staff is the fact that one of the regiments in the armored brigade is the 7th Royal Tank Regiment."

Jones, calm and businesslike until then, was startled by that bit of information. He belonged to the 7th RTR. His father had belonged to that regiment and had fought with it during World War II. To him, as to most British officers, the regiment was a home, a family, a tradition. The thought that his regiment was going to go to war without him was staggering.

Weir continued. "Though it will be some time before we, and the 7th RTR, actually make it to Iran, I want you to start working with the rest of my staff and provide them with everything we need to know so that we can integrate the brigade into the corps. I am particularly concerned about logistical support of that unit. Your assistance there will be critical."

For a moment, there was an awkward silence. Although Jones had been looking at the General, it was obvious that he had not been listening to what Weir said. Jones blinked and then spoke, hesitantly at first. "I am terribly sorry, General, I was just absorbing the news you have given me. It's all rather sudden. Expected, yes, but still it's quite a surprise. You do understand, don't you?"

Weir leaned back in his chair and nodded. "Yes, I am still having difficulty believing we are actually going."

Again hesitantly, Jones continued. "With all due respect, General, and fully understanding your needs, I must insist on being relieved from my current posting, to rejoin my regiment. This will be the first action the regiment will see since 1945."

"I appreciate your desire to rejoin your unit. I expected as much. And I know that your father belonged to the regiment and what that means to you. You are, of course, free to request reassignment. But I must warn you, I will recommend against it. You, and your knowledge of how we, the U.S. Army, operate, coupled with your intimate knowledge of the armored brigade being attached, are far too important to me to lose. You will be a valuable member of my staff."

Jones stood up, faced the General and stood at attention. "I do understand your needs, but I shall nevertheless request reassignment. Is there anything else?"

Weir looked at Jones. The major was visibly disturbed by the news he had given him. "No, Major, I have nothing else. You will report to the corps G-3 tomorrow and begin work with the planning staff. Good night."

Jones saluted, turned and left. Weir stood, walked over to his window and resumed watching the traffic below. He thought, How easy it would be if we could all just grab our rifles and run out to war. So simple, so direct. But instead, I and the major have the "paper wars" to fight. As Weir turned and went back to his desk, still cluttered with the plan, an old Japanese saying came to mind: "Duty is heavy, but death is lighter than a feather." He decided that he finally understood what it meant.

Chapter 5

Minds are like parachutes. They only function when they are open.

—SIR JAMES DEWAR

Over the Persian Gulf En Route to Bandar Abbas, Iran
0358 Hours, 6 June (0028 Hours, 6 June, GMT)

The gentle sway of the C-130 transport and the steady drone of its engines had managed to lull many of the sixty-five men of A Company, 2nd Battalion of the 517th Airborne, to sleep. The excitement and fear that had gripped them at Ras Banas as they made final preparations and during the early part of the flight had given way to sleep. Word that they were finally going to leave had been greeted with great excitement by some of the men, who, after eight days in the Egyptian desert, were glad to be going somewhere else and gave little thought to the fact that they were going to another desert. The idea that they were going into combat was treated with a similar cavalier attitude. Most believed the rumors that the Iranians would not resist them once the Americans had landed. After all, the Americans were coming over there to fight the Russians. It would be stupid to try to fight both the U.S. and the USSR. Any American could understand that.

Captain Evans drifted back and forth between consciousness and sleep. Their eight days at Ras Banas had been demanding ones but profitable. The men had learned a great deal while they were there and had had an opportunity to get used to the desert. He shuddered to think what would have happened if they had been dropped straight into Iran. As it was, he was concerned that his men were still not prepared for the task ahead. Too many had the idea that the Iranians would welcome them with open arms, as liberators. The President's message, read before their departure from Egypt, had not helped. Phrases like "going forth in the name of freedom and justice" and "seeking out and punishing aggression wherever it rears its head" obscured the cold hard fact that they were being sent into a country populated by a hostile race in order to fight someone else. Evans leaned over and looked down the line of men as they slumped in the nylon seats, over-burdened with equipment and overwhelmed by exhaustion. For a moment he wondered how many of them would be alive that night.

A buzz drew his attention to the transport's crew chief, who was seated next to him. The crew chief reached up and grabbed a phone handset. Before he put the handset back, Evans knew what the message had been. It was time.

The crew chief leaned over and told Evans they were ten minutes out. Both he and Evans unsnapped their seat belts and stood up. The men also sensed what was going on and began to stir, waking those who were still in a deep sleep. At the top of his lungs, Evans called out, "Ten minutes."

As if on cue, the ramp behind Evans began to open, letting in the cold night air, known to the paratroopers as "the Hawk." The blast of air and the buildup of adrenaline one experiences before a jump washed away the cobwebs in the minds of the men who had just woken. They needed that. It was critical that everyone have a clear mind. They began to psych themselves up for the coming ordeal. For some, the awful reality of what was about to happen hit home. They were going, they were really going. As they looked down the line of men toward the gaping hole at the rear of the aircraft, some wondered whether they could really do it.

On signal from the pilot, Evans, extending his arms in an exaggerated raising motion, yelled, "Outboard personnel, stand up."

The men along the side of the aircraft struggled to stand, fighting the weight and confinement of their equipment and the swaying of the transport. Instinctively, they reached up and grabbed the thin wire cable that ran the length of the transport above the aisle between the seats. Once up, they turned and faced to the rear.

Evans repeated his motions and yelled, "Inboard personnel,

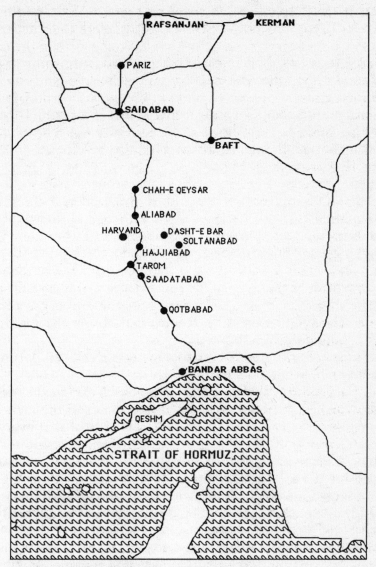

MAP 3: SOUTH CENTRAL IRAN

stand up." The men in the seats arranged down the center of the transport stood up, taking their places between the men already standing. There were now two lines, called "sticks," facing to the rear.

Next Evans raised his hands above his head, formed them into hooks and moved them up and down while he yelled, "Hook up." Each man grabbed the metal static-line hook attached to the reserve parachute hanging on the front of his web gear and fastened it to the cable he was holding on to. Once on the cable, he snapped the small gate shut and gave the static line a tug to ensure that it was hooked up.

When the men were settled, Evans brought one hand up, formed an O with his hand and moved the hand away from him as he ordered, "Check static line." Each man, starting where the static-line hook hung from the cable, ran his free hand down along his gear, touching snaps and links to ensure that all were closed and secured. When he finished his own gear, he checked the parachute of the man to his front that could not be reached by the wearer.

When the men had settled, Evans pointed down the line and yelled, "Sound off for equipment check."

Starting from the front of the transport, or the rear of the stick, the first man slapped the butt of the man to his front and yelled, "OK." Each of the others, in turn, slapped the butt of the man to his front, yelling, "OK." When the last man facing Evans had been slapped, he looked at Evans, pointed to him and yelled, "All OK."

They were ready. The two-minute warning flashed. Evans looked down the line of his men one more time, then turned to face the rear of the aircraft. He was the stick leader and, as such, would be the first to go. As the statue known as "Iron Mike," which stood before Building 4, Infantry Hall, at Fort Benning, implored, he would lead his men into combat.

From his position, he could see the light gray of the Persian Gulf change to blackness as the transports crossed the coast of Iran five hundred feet below them. Behind the C-130 he was in, Evans could see several other transports. They were flying a tight formation, the tightest he had ever seen. At least the battalion would be together when they jumped.

Suddenly, Evans saw flashes on the ground and then several streams of red that streaked up, reaching for the transport. He felt himself go numb with fear. Tracers. They were being fired upon by antiaircraft guns.

Never before had he felt so helpless and exposed. The aluminum skin of the transport would not stop even the smallest round if it was hit. There was nothing he and his men could do but stand there and wait until they were over their objective and it was time to jump. He felt a sudden urge to run out onto the ramp and jump. The sooner he was out of the aircraft, the sooner he would be on the ground, where at least one could hide or, better yet, fight back. Standing there, in a transport, he and his men could do nothing but get hit.

He watched the tracers continue to race up in wild and random patterns. The urge to escape was replaced by a fear that when the time came he would not be able to go out onto the ramp and jump. With a great deal of effort, he turned and looked at his men. Blank expressions and the smell of urine and loose bowels made Evans conscious that the men behind him shared the same thoughts and fears. He wondered whether he was the source of the smell.

A brilliant flash caused him to jerk his head back to the open rear. To his horror, he saw the wing of one of the transports behind them snap off in a great ball of fire. The transport had been hit. It rolled over to the side that the wing had come off and started to go down. Paratroopers began to jump from the rear of the transport, but the sudden explosion, the turning to the side, the low altitude and the steep angle of descent prevented many from escaping. The impact of the stricken transport was spectacular and terrible. Half a hundred paratroopers, America's elite, men who had trained long and hard for battle, had died in a flash without ever having a chance to fight.

The green light, the signal to go, wrenched Evans' thoughts away from the tragedy he had just witnessed. Without thinking, he yelled, *"Go!"* and ran off the ramp. As he felt himself fall away from the transport, he wondered whether anyone had followed him. No time to worry about that now. He was ready. He was confident. In a few minutes he would be doing what he had spent years training and preparing himself for: leading men into combat. Evans tucked his chin into his chest, held his arms tight against his sides, his hands resting on the side of his reserve chute, and waited for his main chute to deploy.

The body of Captain John Evans was traveling close to one

hundred miles an hour when it smashed onto the concrete runway of the Bandar Abbas airfield. In the rush of events, Evans had forgotten to hook up his own static line before jumping.

The jerk of the static line going taut was followed by the shock of the canopy opening. Instinctively, Lieutenant Cerro looked up and at the same time reached to grab the parachute's risers. With a quick circular motion, he checked his canopy and suspension lines. All was in order. Next he reached down and unsnapped his equipment bag and let it fall. When it had reached the end of its suspension line, it gave Cerro a slight tug. He prepared for landing. From an altitude of five hundred feet, a paratrooper has only little more than a minute from exit to impact with the ground when the chute deploys properly.

Only when he had completed his preparations for landing did he notice the tracers rushing up from below him. He looked down into darkness that was punctured by muzzle flashes and explosions. Paratroopers are taught not to look down. As one nears the ground, he experiences ground rush, the sensation of seeing the ground appear to rise; this causes an instinctive tension as the body prepares itself for the shock of impact. Paratroopers are supposed to look out to the horizon and relax, prepared to allow their bodies to collapse in an orderly fashion. Cerro, however, had never been able to do that in training. As a consequence, he always hit hard. His first combat jump was no different.

Cerro landed. Instead of turning and rolling onto the ground on his side and his back, he hit feet, butt and head in rapid succession, which knocked the wind out of him. After coming to rest, he lay for a long time, unable to move, struggling to get himself together as the sound of battle began to grow around him. The tug of his canopy, now reinflated by the wind, motivated him to get moving. Reaching up to the quick-release button located at the center of his chest, he pulled the safety clip, turned the large button and hit it with his fist, so that the harness popped open.

Sitting up, he began to gather his gear from the tangle of webbing, bags and parachute around him. A hand on his shoulder caused him to jump. Whipping around, he found himself face to face with one of his men, who said, "The sarge sent me to get you."

For a moment, Cerro was speechless. Then he yelled at the

soldier, "Jesus! Don't ever do that again, Stevens! You scared the shit out of me."

"I'm sorry, Loot. But Sarge wanted me to see if you was alive."

Cerro continued to police his gear while he hit Stevens with a stream of questions, the first one being how they had found him. Answering without hesitation, Stevens told Cerro that that was easy, since Sarge—Sergeant First Class Arnold, the platoon sergeant—had seen Cerro hit the ground like a sack of potatoes and had known right away who it was.

When Cerro was ready, he got up and told Stevens to lead off to where the platoon was. The two of them, crouching low, ran along the edge of the concrete runway, which Cerro had landed next to. All Cerro could think about was how lucky he had been to hit the dirt instead of the concrete. That would have *really* hurt.

Cerro's thoughts were jarred back to the present when a large-caliber antiaircraft gun four hundred meters to their front cut loose with a burst. As soon as he saw the muzzle flash and the stream of tracers rip through the darkness, he dropped to the ground. Stevens, however, continued on until he noticed that his lieutenant wasn't following. He stopped and called back in a nonchalant manner, "It's OK, Loot. That gun don't know where we are. Come on. Only a few more feet." Cerro looked up. Stevens was really beginning to bug him.

As the two continued running, Cerro became aware of a staggered line of men to his left lying in the prone position and facing out away from the runway. It was his platoon. Stevens hailed for Arnold, who called to them to come over to his location. They veered slightly and ran in that direction.

Arnold was in a shallow ditch beside the runway with four other men. "Damn, Lieutenant, I'm glad to see you made it. Have you seen Captain Evans?"

"Sergeant Arnold, until Stevens came up, I didn't see anyone. How many men have we got and have you seen the XO?"

First Lieutenant Griffit, the XO, answered. He was one of the other men in the ditch. "Hank, as soon as you can, get your platoon moving. We need to get the perimeter out as far as possible before the second drop comes in. The 3rd Platoon is immediately to your right and will begin its move once you go. The 1st Platoon is further down, getting into a position from where they can knock out an SU-23 dug in a couple of hundred meters down the line." The XO indicated the direction from which Cerro had seen the antiaircraft gun fire. The XO continued, "The gun crew doesn't know exactly where we are yet, so keep low. The 1st Platoon should be taking it out soon. Stay on the radio. I'll be with the 3rd Platoon in the center. You got any questions?"

As soon as Cerro shook his head in response, the XO got up and ran along the edge of the runway toward the 3rd Platoon, followed by two radiomen. Cerro watched for a moment, then turned to Arnold. "OK, Sergeant Arnold, we ready to go?"

Arnold answered, "Affirmative," and was beginning to move out of the ditch when Cerro stopped him.

"Before we move out," Cerro asked, "could you tell me exactly where the hell we are and where we're going?"

North of Mianeh
0450 Hours, 6 June (0120 Hours, 6 June, GMT)

The long column of Soviet tanks was easy for the Iranians to track. The dust cloud it produced hung in the still early-morning air like a sail. In a few moments the lead tanks of its advance guard company would be within the kill zone of the Iranian tanks. The tanks of the Soviet combat patrol had been allowed to pass and were already three kilometers farther south. The Soviets suspected nothing. The surprise would be complete.

The Iranian company commander had ordered his tanks not to fire until instructed to do so. The forty-odd M-60A1 and Centurion tanks that made up the composite battalion was the last major force that stood between godless Communists and the holy city of Qom. The Iranian company commander put his binoculars down and looked at the line of tanks tucked into the wadi to his right. Not only were they obsolete in comparison with the Soviet T-80s they were about to face, half of them were missing some part or another of their fire-control system. Years of hard use and lack of repair parts had taken their toll. It would be an uneven contest, despite the element of surprise and the sun to their backs. Defeat of the first Soviet column would only mean that another, larger force would come forward. Once the Iranian tanks of the battalion were gone, there would be no more. Winning or losing, however, did not matter to the company commander. He and his men would die in a just cause in the name of Allah. His only regret was that they were fighting the Lesser Satan. How much better it would have been were it Americans who were about to die.

The company commander turned toward the advancing Soviets. They continued to come on fast, comfortable in the knowledge that their combat patrol was out front and had thus far been unmolested. Now only seconds separated them from death, a just and deserved death.

At a range of five hundred meters, the Iranians opened fire. At such a short distance there is little need for sophisticated fire controls. Nor does special armor protect as well. The Iranians' fire discipline and accuracy were shockingly good. The first volley carried away half of the lead Soviet company. The impact of armor-piercing rounds on the T-80s was followed by catastrophic explosions as on-board ammo detonated and tore the Soviet tanks apart. Those tanks that survived the initial volley shared the others' fate within ten seconds without having been able to take any effective countermeasures.

The commander of the second Soviet company, finding himself in the open, had only a split second to decide whether to attack or to fire smoke and turn away, covering his withdrawal with the tanks' own smoke generators. Instinctively he attacked, ordering an action left. This maneuver, executed with speed and precision, turned the Soviet tanks onto a collision course with the unseen assailant. The gunners and the tank commanders searched for targets but were blinded by the sun now peeking over the horizon. The Iranians brought all their firepower to bear on the desperate charge, with telling effect. Though it cost the Iranians two tanks lost to return fire, the entire second Soviet tank company was smashed. In a space of two minutes, twenty Soviet tanks and the sixty men who manned them were gone.

The 3rd Battalion had been moving all night without letup, resulting in dulled senses and slow reactions. Only the sharp crack of tank cannons in the distance and the near-panicked radio reports of an armored counterattack roused Major Vorishnov from his trancelike state. The battalion commander ordered the battalion to swing left off the road and deploy into columns of companies. Rather than head straight down the road and become involved in the kill zone where the 1st Battalion was, they were going to move east, then turn south, seeking the flank of the

Iranians. The 2nd Battalion, which was following the 3rd, would do likewise, but they would go a little farther east before turning south. In this way, if the 3rd Battalion did not find the flank or the rear of the Iranian position, the 2nd Battalion would.

Vorishnov followed closely behind the battalion commander's tank, all the while listening to reports, orders and calls for artillery fire as the regimental staff strove to organize the 68th Tank Regiment's attack. All was going well until the 2nd Battalion reported that it had run into a mine field and was being hit by tank and artillery fire. Vorishnov stood upright in the BTR-60 with his head protruding out of the hatch. To the east he could see black pillars of smoke rising from tanks that had been hit and destroyed.

In a flash Vorishnov realized that the Iranians had anticipated just such a maneuver and had laid a second trap for the follow-on force. Now the 3rd Battalion was also moving into one. Vorishnov yelled into the radio handset to his commander that they were rolling into a trap. The battalion commander, thinking the same thing, ordered the battalion to move onto line and assume hasty defensive positions. He then switched to the regimental radio and told the regimental commander what was happening and what the 3rd Battalion was doing. The regimental commander, angry at first, ordered the 3rd Battalion to continue the attack, then quickly countermanded that order as the 2nd Battalion's situation became clearer. The wisdom of not pushing his only uncommitted battalion headlong into another fire sack suddenly dawned upon him, to Vorishnov's relief.

This reprieve, however, was only momentary. Seeing the tanks of the 3rd Battalion go to ground, the Iranian tankers facing them began to engage them in a long-range gunnery duel. At ranges of fifteen hundred to two thousand meters, the contest was uneven, with the Soviets having the upper hand. The Iranian tanks had 105mm. main guns, and mechanical range finders, and were not protected by special armor, while the Soviet T-80s had 125mm. smooth-bore guns, laser range finders, and special armor. As an Iranian tank fired, Soviet platoon leaders, under the direction of their company commanders, would direct the fire of all their tanks against that single Iranian tank. The platoon would fire until the targeted Iranian tank began to burn. When finished with one target, the platoon leader would search for the telltale blast and dust produced by the firing of another Iranian tank's main gun and repeat the process.

While this methodical destruction was going on, those Soviet tanks with mine rollers and plows moved forward. When the battalion commander sensed a slackening of Iranian fire, he ordered the lead company to advance behind them while the remaining two companies continued the long-range gunnery battle. Slowly the mine-clearing tanks moved forward, with two other tanks close behind. Every time a mine was run over, the thunderous explosion shook the roller or plow tank and caused it to slow or stop momentarily. Once the crew had sufficiently collected their wits, the tank would move forward again until it hit the next mine.

The Soviets' effort to breach the mine field caused the Iranians to redouble their own efforts against the mine rollers and plows. Hits were scored, but for the most part without effect. The T-80s' special armor easily absorbed the 105mm. rounds and allowed the rollers and the plows to continue their job. The only result of the Iranians' efforts was to give away their positions to the overwatching Soviet tanks. By the time the mine field was breached, the Iranian positions were silent. On order the 3rd Battalion moved through the mine field and formed into battle line as it moved against the Iranian positions. The black pillars of smoke from the burning diesel and rubber of destroyed Iranian tanks served to keep the attackers oriented on their objective.

Vorishnov looked at his watch. In less than thirty minutes the regiment had gone from the brink of defeat to a smashing victory, a victory made possible by the 3rd Battalion. With a little luck, they would go through the Iranian position and be able to continue on to Tehran.

Kuh-e Genu, Iran
0430 Hours, 8 June (0100 Hours, 8 June, GMT)

The flash of impacting artillery followed by the crashing of the explosion reminded Second Lieutenant Cerro of a thunderstorm. In the distance, it had been mildly interesting to watch; as he and his men climbed closer, excitement built up. Cerro wondered how effective the artillery was. Sergeant Arnold didn't think the 105 howitzers would do much good against well-prepared positions that the Iranians, no doubt, had on the mountaintop. Cerro paused for a moment to catch his breath, looking up the steep mountainside. If nothing else, the artillery was at least proving to be a convenient aid to navigation. So long as the artillery went in, Cerro knew where to head.

The first two days in Iran had been hard. The 17th Airborne Division had managed to secure the airfield and the naval base and port facilities there. Organized resistance had collapsed, but there were still a great many groups of anywhere from four to ten Iranians wandering around, setting up ambushes or holding key positions throughout the town and the surrounding countryside. Each group had to be found, pinned and taken out. One of Second Lieutenant Cerro's men had made the casual observation that someone must have issued to every male born in Iran a rifle and forty rounds of ammunition.

The process was simple but nerveracking, especially the first part, finding them. Sometimes the point man was able to detect telltale signs of an ambush or a hidden position. The Iranians, though brave, were not professionals, leaving loose dirt or exposing dirt of a different color near their dug-in positions, using the wrong type of vegetation or simply not covering up their weapons or themselves. Other times, the first hint of trouble was a burst of automatic rifle fire or the explosion of a grenade. When that happened, the men would automatically begin to fire in whichever direction their rifles happened to be pointed. Cerro had the damnedest time getting them to stop and trying to figure out what was really happening.

Once the enemy had been located, part of the platoon would deploy and lay down a base of fire to pin the enemy and cover the movement of the platoon's maneuver element. It was the job of the maneuver element to find an exposed flank or surround the Iranians while the rest of the platoon covered the movement with fire. When the Iranians were trapped, everyone would cut loose until the last Iranian had surrendered or died. Most Iranians preferred the latter. Now that the airfield had been secured, the Sheridan armored assault vehicles arrived and simplified the process with their 152mm. main guns and their machine guns. The paratroopers used the Sheridan like a mobile pillbox to destroy Iranian positions. If a pocket of resistance was hit and there was a Sheridan nearby, someone would summon it. Often all that was needed to break resistance was a burst of machine-gun fire and a menacing maneuver by the ugly tracked vehicle. When true die-hards were encountered, a high-explosive round from the main gun quickly decided the issue.

When word came that the battalion was to move up to seize a place called Kuh-e Genu, the men welcomed the opportunity to end the deadly cat-and-mouse game they had been playing with the small groups of Iranian fanatics. Their enthusiasm evapo-rated, however, when they found out that Kuh-e Genu was the name of the mountain that rose to nearly twenty-four hundred feet above them. Genu dominated the entire area. Until it was secured, it posed a threat to air and port operations in and around Bandar Abbas. The task of seizing the mountain was made even more difficult by the fact that helicopters were not yet available for an air assault operation against the mountaintop. The entire operation would have to be conducted on foot. On the afternoon of 7 June, the battalion moved forward to climb Kuh-e Genu and begin the process of expanding the airhead.

Takestan, Southwest of Qazvin, Iran
0745 Hours, 8 June (0415 Hours, 8 June, GMT)

The halting and frustrating progress that had characterized the first days of the invasion had given way to rapid and unrestricted advances wherever the 28th Combined Arms Army went. After the tank battle north of Mianeh, the greatest delay the army had experienced had been a monumental traffic jam in the town of Mianeh as the two divisions advancing from the west ran into the two advancing from the north. After days of frustrations and delays, no one expected the Iranians to collapse as completely as they did. Plans for organizing the pursuit of shattered Iranian forces were therefore incomplete when the units of the 28th CAA were ordered to execute them.

The 68th Tank Regiment, though badly mauled during the tank battle on 6 June, was the vanguard for the army simply because it was the first unit through the town and didn't stop. The regiment, initially shaken and gun-shy after that battle, over-came their caution and rushed forward with few reservations. All were determined to be the first to reach Tehran and have the honor of parading down the broad avenue to the former Royal Palace of the Shah. Despite the heat, the lack of sleep, the irregular meals and the incessant dust, the men were, for the moment, happy to be moving forward at full speed.

Major Vorishnov, working with the regimental staff, had the task of ensuring that his battalion, the lead battalion, kept moving. Although he was the first officer of the battalion and usually concerned himself with only operational matters, the task of securing fuel, food and other necessary items to keep the drive going was beyond the capability of the battalion's supply officer. In addition, Vorishnov's rank helped, on occasion, to overcome bureaucratic inertia. When his rank failed to impress the rear-echelon supply people, Vorishnov had no qualms about using his vast size and a not-too-subtle hint of violence to get what he wanted. After watching men fight and die to make the break-through possible, he was not about to let a pencil-pushing supply officer stop his battalion. They would reach Tehran ahead of everyone else, procedures be damned.

On his way to the rear in search of fuel trucks that had failed to make it to the battalion the night before, Vorishnov stopped at the division command post. It wasn't much of a command post: several armored cars and personnel carriers, configured as mobile command vehicles, clustered together with canvas spread between them to provide shade for the working officers. The first officer of the division was glad to see Vorishnov. He was having trouble keeping track of the lead unit's progress and could not get accurate reports on the condition of the roads and bridges, what few there were, and other details of what lay ahead. The lead regiment was moving so fast that communications often failed. Therefore anyone coming from the front of the column was pumped for information.

In the course of their conversation, the division first officer made comment about the difficulties the American airborne division was experiencing in securing its airhead around Bandar Abbas. At first, Vorishnov didn't realize what the division officer was saying. Vorishnov had never heard of Bandar Abbas and assumed it was in another Arab country. Only when the division officer mentioned in a disgusted tone that all Soviet naval and air forces were ordered not to engage American forces going into Iran did Vorishnov make the connection.

Vorishnov stopped what he was doing, grabbed the division officer by the arm and asked him to repeat what he had just said.

The division officer, taken aback, looked at him for a moment before he realized that word had never gotten down to him about the American intervention in Iran. Word traveled slowly in both directions.

University of Tehran, in Tehran, Iran
0930 Hours, 8 June (0600 Hours, 8 June, GMT)

The three men seated around the large table were not only from vastly different backgrounds, but figuratively speaking, from different ages. The physicist, noticeably uncomfortable and jumpy, was from the late twentieth century. A man of the future. The Air Force colonel, equally uncomfortable but determined to hide it from the third man in the room, belonged to an age when honor and glory meant something. The man at the head of the table, dressed in the garb of a mullah, was a product of the Middle Ages, in thought and deed.

The mullah leafed through a report on the table before him, then let the pages drop and stared at the physicist. "So, you are not ready, despite your promises."

The physicist jumped. "I . . . I never told you we were ready or gave a date when the device would be ready. I simply said that we had everything we needed and could, given time, put together a couple of devices. This is not easy. If the triggers are not set right, if the material is not of sufficient uniformity—"

The mullah pounded his fist on the table, cutting the physicist off. "*You* have deceived us. A great deal of money and effort has gone into your project. You always reported that things were proceeding well and would be ready soon. For six years, you have said the same thing, over and over. Now is the moment of truth. The Council will not tolerate any more delays. The Lesser Satan is almost at the gates of this city. If he is not stopped here, Qom will fall to him. You will produce or pay with your life."

The physicist was now shaking and stammering. He tried to reply, but could not. The colonel, ever conscious of his delicate position, gambled and intervened on the physicist's behalf. "The doctor is right. While we do have all the parts, putting together a functional device is not easy. None of us has ever done so. If we make an error, just the slightest error, we lose everything. Besides, the time is not right."

The mullah, surprised at the show of support from the colonel, stared at him before asking him to explain why the time was not right.

The colonel explained. "We now have to face both Satans. The Soviets continue to advance and, no doubt, will go as far south as possible. They want the oil and the ports on the Persian Gulf. The Great Satan wants to stop them." The colonel stopped for a moment. He had the mullah's complete attention. "Eventually, they will meet in battle. When they do, there will be much confusion. Then, and only then, will be the right time to set off the device. In the heat of the moment and the confusion of battle, no one will be able to tell who, for sure, fired the device. Both, knowing that we do not have such a thing, will believe the other did it. As is their policy, they will retaliate in kind. In this way, with only a single device, we can serve Allah, His name be praised, and destroy not only the forces of the two Satans in our country but, Allah willing, their homelands too."

The colonel sat back in his chair and watched as the mullah thought over the argument just put forth. The colonel had used all the right words and had given the mullah something more than he could have hoped for—a means to strike at both of the godless infidels. In return, the colonel had, he hoped, bought a little more time for sanity to win out. It was a desperate game the colonel was playing. But the stakes were high. Horribly high.

The mullah looked at him. "Your plan has merit. I will present it to the Council. In the meantime, remove everything you need for the device from Tehran to a safe place where you can continue your work. Destroy all evidence of your work and keep us informed of your progress and when you will be ready."

Without waiting for a response, the mullah stood up and left the room. Both the physicist and the colonel sat there in silence for a moment, staring at each other, wondering what their next move would be and where the unfolding insanity would eventually end.

Chapter 6

Ever forward, but slowly.
— GEBHARD LEBERECHT VON BLÜCHER

Bandar Abbas
0535 Hours, 11 June (0205 Hours, 11 June, GMT)

The crews of the two F-15E Strike Eagles were impatient to go. While the ground crew made last-minute checks around the aircraft, they sat in their cockpits and watched the comings and goings of military transports and of civilian airliners pressed into military service. The sun was hardly up and already the place was a zoo. At one end of the runway, Army equipment taken off C-141 and huge C-5A transports was being marshaled. Next to that area was a supply dump where forklifts shuttled back and forth, moving crates from the runway to a temporary open-air storage site. Along the edge of the runway discarded packing materials and tie-downs were strewn about. For the past five days a steady stream of transports and airliners had been bringing in the rest of the 17th Airborne Division and its support equipment. Despite almost frenzied efforts on the part of the Military Airlift Command, called MAC for short, it would be another five days before the entire division was on the ground and the 12th Infantry Division could begin deployment.

Across from the F-15s a flight of Army UH-60 Blackhawk utility helicopters was winding up, preparing for the day's mission. The F-15s were to provide cover for the flight of Blackhawks, whose mission was to pick up a battalion of the 517th Airborne, one company at a time, and move it to a crossroad town by the

name of Tarom, seventy kilometers north of Bandar Abbas. The
Army was expanding the airhead by leapfrogging units to the
north, east and west along the major avenues of approach leading
to the Strait of Hormuz. The Marines, operating out of the port
of Chah Bahar, were doing likewise. Both forces ran the danger of
overextending and isolating themselves rather than isolating the
people they were bypassing. Risks, however, had to be taken. So
long as the Soviets were still over five hundred miles to the north
and Iranian resistance was disjointed, the risks appeared to be
acceptable.

Finally cleared for takeoff, Major Ed Martain, nicknamed
"Thunderballs," rolled his F-15 out onto the runway and taxied
down to one end. The second aircraft followed Martain's. For a
moment, all traffic was held up for them. As they went past the
huge transports that were scattered about, Martain's weapons-
system operator, or wizzo, commented that it reminded him of
driving on the New Jersey Turnpike. Upon reaching the end of
the runway, the two F-15s turned, got themselves set and began
to increase power. When they were ready, the pilots released the
brakes, allowing the two aircraft to thunder down the runway.
Both Martain and the other pilot, by unspoken agreement, kicked
in their after burners and lifted off faster than necessary. They
wanted to clearly demonstrate to all the trash haulers (their term
for transport pilots) who the kings of the roost were.

Once the planes were off the ground, the wizzos changed over
to the radio frequency of the E-3 Sentry Airborne Warning and
Control System, or AWACS. Martain contacted the AWACS controller, using his call sign for the day, Omaha 01. The controller
gave him an update on the situation in the area of operations.
With everything in order, the F-15s climbed to an altitude of
40,000 feet. Martain's wingman, Omaha 02, took up a position
two miles to Martain's left, a little behind and at 42,000 feet.
When they were set, the two aircraft proceeded north of Tarom,
where they took up station, flying in an oval patrol pattern. In
this way they placed themselves between the most likely threat,
the Soviets, and the air assault operation that was going into
Tarom, while the E-3 Sentry, operating over the Persian Gulf,
scanned the entire area of operations with its powerful radar,
watching for threats from any direction.

.   .   .

Radar, first used in World War II, is a double-edged sword. Radar emits an electronic beam capable of searching and tracking, like a flashlight's beam. And, like a flashlight's beam, it can, itself, be detected by an enemy and used to locate its source. Unfortunately for the transmitter of the beam, it can be detected at a greater distance than it can detect targets. Furthermore, each type of radar has its own peculiar signature, so that a radar beam transmitted by an E-3 Sentry and intercepted by an enemy can be identified as originating from a Sentry. For this reason the F-15s were running with their radars off. Although Soviet radar would be able to see the F-15s, the type of aircraft would not be known until the F-15s turned on their own radars or were within visual range of Soviet fighters.

Before that happened, the Sentry would see the Soviets coming and alert the F-15s. An airborne controller on the Sentry would track the Soviets, estimate their destination and intentions, and relay the information to the F-15s. This information would include a plotted course that would allow the F-15s to intercept the Soviets from a position of advantage. Soviet controllers, working from the other side, would be doing the same for their pilots.

Omaha 01 and 02 had been on station for better than forty minutes when the controller on the Sentry alerted them that two "boggies"—enemy planes—were flying southeast on a course that would take them over Bandar Abbas. As the control relayed information on the targets, the commander on the Sentry decided to commit Omaha 01 and 02 to intercept the boggies. Though Martain's two planes were primarily ground-attack aircraft, there was little use for them in that role and a pressing need for fighters. This suited Martain just fine. He had never liked the idea of becoming a mud mover and relished the idea of playing Steve Canyon, even if it was only for a day. While the pair of aircraft were still over two hundred miles away, the controller began to vector, or direct, Omaha 01 and 02 along an intercept course.

While one controller worked the intercept, others aboard the Sentry were looking for telltale signs of additional Soviet activity. The electronic-warfare operator checked for any signs of interference, jamming or electronic deception, called "spoofing." Other controllers watched their assigned sectors in an effort to find more boggies. The commander of the Sentry contacted headquarters at Bandar Abbas and informed them of the situation. He then instructed the controller working Omaha's intercept to remind Omaha 01 of the rules of engagement: he was not to fire unless fired upon. As yet, there had been no shooting incidents between U.S. and Soviet forces. This was shaping up to be the first confrontation between the two superpowers in Iran.

While the two sets of blips—one representing Omaha Flight and the other the boggies—converged on each other on the controller's radar screen, the commander of the Sentry watched the Soviets intently. He tried to detect any deviation that might indicate that they were being controlled by a Soviet AWACS or ground-control station and were aware of the F-15s' presence. At the one-hundred-mile point, there were no indications of that as the two sets of blips continued to close. The Soviets were coming in fast and dumb. The controller continued to relay information to Omaha 01 and study the two converging plots.

At the fifty-mile mark the F-15s had maneuvered into a position to the left of the Soviets' flight path. This put them out of the area covered by the forward-looking radar of the Soviets, meaning that the boggies could not detect the F-15s on their own. The Soviets continued to fly along their original course without deviating, despite the threat the F-15s now posed, indicating that they were operating without ground or air control. The commander of the Sentry leaned back in his seat, stroked his chin and paused to think about that for a moment. That was dumb, really dumb. The Soviets had AWACS in Iran. They also had forward-deployed ground-control stations. He could not imagine why these two Soviet aircraft were flying blind and without control. The commander knew that the only way to find out what they were about was to challenge them. On board the Sentry, it was decided, therefore, to have the F-15s continue without turning on their radars until they were within missile range.

Two hundred miles away, Martain was becoming anxious. He wanted to gain control of the situation. Although he trusted the controller and agreed that the decision to continue with their radar off until the last minute was probably a good one, he didn't like getting this close to a shooting situation without being in positive control. His wizzo was equally anxious in the backseat, surrounded by millions of dollars of equipment, with nothing to do as they traveled at hundreds of miles an hour toward a potentially hostile contact. Secretly, the wizzo prayed that when the word was given and he hit the switch, all his gizmos would work. Otherwise, they would be very embarrassed.

Finally, at the fifteen-mile point, the controller gave Omaha 01 the word to turn on their radars and intercept, but not engage unless fired upon. At the same instant, both F-15s hit their radars. In a flash the radar screens lit up, showing two bright-green blips at a range of fifteen miles and slightly below. The intercept plot they had received from the Sentry had been so good that the pilots needed only minor corrections before they were able to achieve radar lock on the boggies.

In the Soviet aircraft, radar-warning receivers flashed on, sending a rapid beeping tone through the pilots' headphones. For an instant, the two Soviet pilots were bewildered. Their heads darted about, looking from their radar screens to the outside, unable to detect anything on radar or visually. When the warning changed pitch to a steady tone, indicating that their unseen assailants had achieved radar lock and were about to engage, they both reacted by increasing speed, taking a sharp, turning dive and jiggling their planes in an effort to break radar lock.

Both Omaha 01 and 02 had anticipated the Soviets' reaction. With a "Tally ho!" from Martain, they followed the Soviets' maneuver. Though the Soviets were able to break radar lock momentarily, the F-15s were quickly able to get it back. After several seconds of this, the Soviets realized that if the Americans were going to attack they would have already done so. Having accomplished the mission of their patrol, to test the U.S. reaction and find out how far they could go before being intercepted, the Soviet flight leader ordered his wingman to follow him. Making a sharp turn to the northwest, the two Soviet fighters came about and kicked in their after burners. When the commander aboard the Sentry saw the Soviets break and fly northward, he ordered the controller to instruct the F-15s to break off the pursuit and vector them to a waiting KC-130 for in-flight refueling. From there, they were to return to their patrol pattern.

Martain balked. His heart was racing a mile a minute. His breathing was rapid but controlled. His whole being was riveted on the Soviet aircraft now racing to the north as his thumb stroked the safety cover over the missile-arming switch. He didn't want this to end, at least not like this. For the first time in his life he was doing what he was trained for. He had the drop on the Communist and he wanted to splash him, now. He called for permission to continue pursuit. The controller denied him permission and repeated his orders. Martain came back to argue, but was cut short by the commander, who repeated in a clear and uncompromising voice that Omaha Flight was to break contact and follow previously issued instructions. Martain watched the two Soviets, now mere dots in the bright-blue sky, for a moment before he turned. "Shiiit," uttered in a low and disgusted voice over the open radio net, preceded the turning of Omaha Flight as Martain complied with his orders.

The first serious confrontation between the Great Satan and the Lesser Satan had ended in a moral victory for the United States.

Soviet Embassy, Tehran, Iran
0715 Hours, 11 June (0345 Hours, 11 June, GMT)

Colonel Sulvina stood on the balcony of the Soviet Embassy looking out over the city they had secured almost without a struggle. With his tunic unbuttoned, one hand in his pants pocket and the other holding a half-empty glass of vodka, he listened to the sounds of rifle fire. Mopping up. Here and there small pockets of Revolutionary Guards held out, hell-bent to die for Allah. Intelligence estimates, revised after the 28th Combined Arms Army had entered Tehran, showed that the entire defending force in and around that city had never exceeded four thousand. Why Tehran had been given up so freely baffled Sulvina. It didn't matter, he thought as he scanned the city skyline before him. They would eventually find the bastards somewhere along the line and send them to Allah. If not today, then tomorrow. As far as he was concerned, tomorrow was fine. He was too tired just now, and so was the rest of the army. There was plenty of time tomorrow to make more martyrs.

He took a long drink, then turned his head toward the garden below. Soldiers were still searching for bodies buried there. The staff of the Soviet Embassy had stayed on in Tehran right up to the beginning of the invasion on 25 May. To have evacuated them might have alerted the Iranians that something was about to happen. So for reasons of national security, the staff, including most of the families, had stayed on. The Iranians had spared no one when they entered the emassy on the twenty-fifth. Sulvina watched impassively as two soldiers carefully brushed away dirt from a body in a shallow grave. The body belonged to a girl not more than ten years old. Her pink dress was spattered with dried blood and speckled with dirt. Gently they lifted her from the grave and placed her in a cotton shroud. Sulvina kept telling himself that she had died in the service of the State. He knew that. But to what end her death served the State, he could not say. Such thoughts were disturbing, bordering on treasonous. He turned to walk back into the office.

He stopped, however, in the doorway and stared at the desk before him. Piled to one side were reports from the units on their status, locations and intelligence estimates. On the other side were orders from Front Headquarters and requests for information. He was not concerned about them. They were routine and could be handled by one of his subordinates. It was the single red folder in the center of the desk that he stared at. Sulvina lifted the glass of vodka to his lips and drained it before proceeding any further. Thus fortified, he walked up to the desk, seated himself, opened the folder and began to reread the reports it contained.

Any joy that he had experienced when the 28th Combined Arms Army reached Tehran ahead of the other two armies had been snuffed out when a young KGB major woke him and handed him the red folder two hours ago. As he studied the reports again, he found it hard to believe that the Iranians could do such a thing. If the CAA intelligence officer's estimate was right, this could have terrible consequences for them all.

He carefully read the report of a young captain who had been with the lead elements that entered Tehran; then he reread the intelligence officer's covering report. They supported each other. Sulvina got up, walked over to a map of Iran and began to study it, wondering where he would have taken a half-assembled nuclear device if he were the Iranians. More important, he wondered what they intended to do with it, when and if it became functional.

Tarom, Iran
0845 Hours, 11 June (0515 Hours, 11 June, GMT)

The Blackhawks came in low and fast. Ahead of them two A-10 ground-attack aircraft, affectionately called Warthogs, were working over several positions with their 30mm. guns. From where he sat in one of the Blackhawks, Second Lieutenant Cerro could see two AH-64 Apache attack helicopters coming up. The Apaches would take over covering the air assault when it actually touched down and the A-10s left. Because they were out of range of friendly artillery, the Warthogs and the Apaches were the sole fire support the men of A Company, 2nd of the 517th Airborne, would have as they went in. Although resistance was expected to be very light, the division commander was going to ensure that everything would be done to keep up momentum while minimizing losses. He had the firepower available and would use it whenever possible.

The Iranians on the ground, on the other hand, did not have the firepower they needed to combat the Great Satan on equal terms. All they could do was lie low in their foxholes and bunkers and wait until the enemy had landed. Once the enemy was on the ground, the Iranians could employ their advantages—superiority in numbers and a belief in their cause that bordered on fanaticism. While the balance sheet showed that they were losing everywhere, it also showed that neither the United States nor the Soviets were winning. The leaders of Iran knew that they could not win a war against both, or even one, of their opponents. What they could do, however, was keep both of their enemies from winning. In a no-win situation, Iran would come out ahead.

The commander of the local militia, Major Hasan Rahimi, was a veteran of many desperate fights. He had been a battalion commander, in the war against Iraq before he lost his right eye. No longer fit for front-line duty, he had been assigned to command regional militia forces and a small training center near Tarom. His hopes of serving his country and Allah as a fighter had almost died. Now, with the Great Satan striking north, he again had the chance to lead men in battle.

Rahimi had been ordered to hold the crossroads at Tarom. To do so, he had fewer than three hundred men and only a couple of mortars. More men could have been fielded, but there were no weapons for them. Other militia units would eventually arrive, but until then he and his men would have to hold. The Americans, using helicopters to strike deep and almost without warning, made it difficult for Rahimi to decide where to concentrate his forces. After studying the area, he established dug-in positions at the most likely landing zones, with alternate positions covering the road leading up from Bandar Abbas, in case there was a ground attack.

His plan of battle was simple. Holding half of his force as a mobile reserve, he dispersed the rest to the dug-in positions. The men occupying those positions would hit the transport helicopters as they were about to land. That would be when the Americans were most vulnerable, with the landing transport helicopters blocking the supporting fire of the attack helicopters. Rahimi, leading the mobile reserve, would lead a counterattack as quickly as possible against those Americans who were able to land. He could not allow the Americans to become established. Once they were, they would be able to bring all their awesome firepower to bear, firepower Rahimi could never hope to match.

Even though Lieutenant Cerro preferred air assault operations to jumping, they, like all military operations, were not without their hazards. As with the combat jump, the soldiers are useless as long as they are in the helicopters. Helicopters are able to fly low and maneuver about, using terrain to hide and cover their move. Transport planes, on the other hand, fly high and in relatively straight lines, making their routes predictable. Flying low, however, exposes the helicopters to small-arms fire that transports need not worry about. Anyone on the ground with a rifle can, and usually does, take potshots at low-flying helicopters.

Air assault operations share the same hazards as airdrops during the initial buildup stage. The small force in the airhead is exposed to counterattack and does not have all its support on the ground such as artillery and heavy mortars. These items, which are normally part of the follow-on forces, all must come in by air, just as the initial assault force did. Only, the follow-on forces do not have the element of surprise to protect them. The enemy on the ground knows exactly where the airhead is and, as a result, knows where the follow-on forces will come. This allows the enemy the ability to mass antiaircraft weapons around the landing zones or along the routes leading into the landing zone. Often, it is better to be with the initial force going in than with the follow-on force. Besides the antiaircraft weapons, artillery and mortars massed to fire on the small, well-defined airhead are a great danger to the follow-on forces while the helicopters are on the ground disgorging their cargoes.

The assault force that Cerro was with waited until the last

minute before making its final approach, in order to keep the Iranians guessing as to where the landing zone would be. When the Blackhawks were less than a kilometer away from the landing zone, they made a sharp turn to the left and began their descent. The A-10s were gone by this time, but the Apaches were coming in on either side of the assault force, ready to hit any target that appeared. Cerro, looking out the open cargo door, could clearly see dug-in Iranian positions as the Blackhawks made their approach. There was, however, little ground fire. The A-10s must have done their job well, Cerro thought—they had either killed the defenders or caused them to reconsider the value of martyrdom.

Suddenly all that changed. At one side of the landing zone Iranians popped up out of hidden positions. The door gunner seated in front of Cerro began to fire wildly. An Apache flew by, firing rockets at positions out of Cerro's field of vision. Tracers from the defenders could be seen racing up toward the attackers while tracers from the door gunner's machine gun and the Apaches rained down upon the defenders. The crash of rockets threw up fountains of black smoke and dirt. In just a few seconds, Cerro and his men would be dropped into the middle of that caldron.

First Lieutenant Griffit watched intently the scene unfolding below him. Having assumed command of the company after the death of Captain Evans, Griffit was "the Man." Until the battalion commander arrived, he would be in charge of the operation on the ground. Success or failure of the entire operation depended on his actions during the initial phase, and he was nervous. Griffit had had it easy as the XO. It was the company commander who had to make all the hard decisions. It was the commander who was responsible for everything the unit did or failed to do. Evans, dynamic and a workaholic, had run the company almost single-handedly, leaving Griffit to deal with little details. Now, even with reassurance from the battalion commander, and with several small combat operations under his belt, Griffit was unsure and hesitant. He knew that he would eventually grow used to the awesome responsibility of command and the need to make rapid life-and-death decisions, given time. But there was no time.

He had a few seconds left to memorize the view below him— the lay of the land, enemy dispositions and key terrain features—

which he would not have again once he was on the ground. His initial decisions during the first few minutes on the ground would be based on these quick observations. Griffit, engrossed in watching the battle before him and screwing up the courage he would need to carry him through his next ordeal under fire, did not notice the tracers reaching up at them from the other side of the helicopter. The pilot, however, did, and he knew what they meant. Instinctively he tilted the Blackhawk over to avoid the hail of bullets, watching the tracers rather than where the aircraft was going.

Griffit felt the Blackhawk tilting, but paid no heed until it began to buck violently. Falling debris caused him to look up and straight out the open door. To his horror he saw the blades of his Blackhawk hacking away at the blades of the Blackhawk across from them. In the effort to escape the machine-gun fire from the ground, the pilot of Griffit's helicopter had flown into another.

The pilot and the co-pilot struggled to control their aircraft while the Blackhawk they had hit fell helplessly away. Then, unable to regain full mastery of the helicopter, the two men fought to reduce their rate of descent and at least control their crash. There was, however, too much damage. The blades, no longer balanced, wobbled wildly. In one sweep, a section of torn blade angled down and cut into the crew compartment, decapitating the pilot and showering the co-pilot with deadly splinters of Plexiglas and aluminum. All semblance of control was lost as the Blackhawk rolled over on its side, then nose-dived into the ground.

Cerro watched the two Blackhawks go down. He knew that the XO was in one of them. The first smacked into the ground on its belly. One of the paratroopers on board, wanting to escape, rushed out before the blades stopped spinning, not realizing that they were lower to the ground than normal. A blade seemed to pass through his body, tossing it about like a rag doll. The second Blackhawk, the XO's, went in at a steep angle, nose first. The entire aircraft, the crew and the cargo of paratroopers disappeared in a fireball that rose above Cerro's own helicopter.

He sat there transfixed. In an instant his Blackhawk swept by the scene of the crash and prepared to land. The image of the crash had come and gone, but Cerro did not move, paralyzed. The first clear, conscious thought that came to his head was that he, the senior surviving officer, was now in command of the company.

The thump of the wheels on the ground jerked Cerro back to reality. He unsnapped his seat belt instinctively and jumped down from the Blackhawk into a swirl of dust. Cerro ran forward alongside his men for several meters, then flopped down onto his stomach. Once all the paratroopers were clear, the Blackhawks lifted off, made a hard bank and flew back to Bandar Abbas to pick up their next load.

The paratroopers stayed put for a moment, waiting for the dust to settle so that they could get their bearings. The Iranians didn't wait. With the helicopters gone, they leveled the barrels of their machine guns and began to sweep the landing zone. The paratroop squad leaders and platoon leaders sized up the situation in their immediate areas and began to issue orders. Those who were not pinned by the machine-gun fire maneuvered their units against the nearest Iranian positions. The techniques the paratroopers used were the same they had used against the Iranians while mopping up Bandar Abbas: find them, pin them, get around them, kill them. The Apaches assisted in this effort. They circled overhead, trying to sort out good guy from bad guy. When they had a positive ID on an Iranian position, they went after it with 2.75-inch rockets or 30mm. cannons. Between the Apaches and the ground attack, the Iranian positions in the immediate vicinity of the landing zone were overwhelmed and silenced within ten minutes.

After the firing stopped, Cerro turned command of his platoon over to Sergeant Arnold and made the rounds to determine what the situation was with the rest of the company. He was pleased to find that, despite the loss of two Blackhawks, casualties had been light. The Blackhawk that had crashed on its belly had lost only one man, the paratrooper who had run out into the blades. The crew of that aircraft, dragging their door guns with them, had joined the company. The XO's Blackhawk, on the other hand, had taken everyone with it. The entire company headquarters element, except for the first sergeant, was dead. There were only a few other casualties, however—not enough to keep the company from carrying on with its mission.

Satisfied that all was in hand, Cerro gave one of the company's three remaining radios to the other platoon leader, Second Lieutenant Robert Kinsley, and ordered him to hold the landing zone with his platoon until the follow-on forces arrived. Cerro, with 2nd and 3rd Platoons, would begin to move into Tarom. The faster they got moving, the better chance they had of seizing their objective while the enemy was off balance. Besides, taking the battle to the enemy kept them away from the airhead and increased the odds for the follow-on force. With a three-man point team two hundred meters in front, A Company started for Tarom.

Rahimi watched the Apaches circle overhead, then turn to the south and fly off. Satisfied that they had left the area, he assembled his counterattack force and briefed his subordinates. He divided his men, sending a group of fifty under a young captain directly against the airhead to draw the Americans' attention. With a force of one hundred men and the mortars, he would swing to the north and hit the airhead from the flank or the rear. Ideally, the smaller force would cover the move of the encircling force and suppress the Americans when the encirclers made their attack. However, Rahimi had no radios with which he could coordinate his two forces. They would have to trust in Allah to see them through.

The paratroop company had covered half the distance between the landing zone and Tarom when one of the men from the point team came running back with the report that a force of forty to fifty Iranians was headed straight for them. Cerro halted the company, gathered his platoon leaders and issued orders to prepare an L-shaped ambush. Moving the company back to a curve in the trail that the Iranians would be using, he placed the 2nd Platoon on one shoulder so that they could fire down the trail; they were the base of the L. The 3rd Platoon was deployed twenty meters off the trail along the length of it, forming the stem of the L. If the Iranians continued down the trail, A Company would be able to hit them with a crossfire.

The platoons dispersed and prepared. Cerro sent the point man to find a spot within view where he could both watch the Iranians' advance and warn the company of their approach. The men in the two platoons forming the ambush set up their machine guns, claymore antipersonnel mines and 60mm. mortars and found the best firing positions they could. In less than five minutes, all was set.

Cerro lay among the rocks, watching the lookout man and the

trail. When the lookout gave the signal, Cerro relayed it to the platoon leaders. Everyone hunched down as low as he could and waited. The Iranians came on as a group. There were two men out in front, their point, but they were too close to the main body. Any trap they fell into would also involve the others. The Iranians in the main body, instead of being spread out as was the practice in the U.S. Army, were huddled together, almost shoulder to shoulder. Cerro watched and decided that they had to be militia. The motley assortment of uniforms and weapons and the way they moved showed they had little training. That suits me fine, Cerro thought. I've had enough challenges for the day.

Seemingly by accident, one of the Iranians in the middle of the column noticed something out of the ordinary along the side of the trail. The man stopped and looked toward the unusual object for a moment, then called to one of the officers. The two went over to examine it—a dark-green claymore mine sitting among the sand-colored rocks. Cerro watched the pair while the rest of the column continued into the ambush. Another thirty seconds and the entire column would be in the kill zone and he could spring the ambush. Just thirty seconds.

The paratrooper holding the detonator for the claymore didn't give Cerro the thirty seconds. Feeling that the two curious Iranians were close enough, he hit the detonator when they were less than five feet from the mine. The explosion shredded the curious Iranians and caught both ambushers and ambushed off guard. For a moment everyone hesitated. The paratroopers recovered first, cutting loose with a hail of fire and a volley of claymore mines. Those Iranians who survived the first volley were caught in a withering crossfire punctuated by 60mm. mortar explosions. Panicked, they turned away from their attackers and attempted to escape.

Bullets travel faster than a man can run, however. It took a few seconds for the survivors to realize this. Then, seeing no escape and with their leaders down, they turned either to fight to the death or to surrender. This resulted in confusion as the Iranians desiring to surrender found themselves next to those resisting. The paratroopers didn't take the time to sort them out at first, firing well-aimed bursts at anything that stood or moved. Only when Cerro ordered a cease-fire did the paratroops take better aim, killing only those who chose to become martyrs.

·   ·   ·

The firing coming from his flank caught Rahimi off guard. He halted his column for a moment to check his bearings. Satisfied that he was still headed in the right direction, he came to the conclusion that his other column had been hit before it reached the American perimeter. It was in trouble, but there was nothing he could do to help it. Besides, its mission was to divert the Americans' attention. From the sounds of the fighting, it was doing so. Rahimi continued forward.

The 2nd and 3rd Platoons had just finished rounding up their prisoners and checking the dead when they heard explosions and machine-gun fire from the direction of the landing zone. Even before Lieutenant Kinsley radioed his spot report, Cerro knew what was happening. He looked at his map, then asked Kinsley whether he could hold for ten minutes. Without hesitation, Kinsley gave him an affirmative.

Although he felt uneasy about doing so, Cerro divided his force again. Leaving a small group to cover the prisoners, he took the balance of his men and began to move toward the sound of the firing. It was his intent to circle around the Iranians and hit them from the flank rather than go head to head with the attackers. He ran the risk of running into an ambush like the one he had just sprung on the Iranians, but there seemed to be no alternative that made sense.

Rahimi drew his men back to regroup. Their first attempt to break the American perimeter had failed. The fact of the matter was that he had not been able to organize a proper attack. The lead element had stumbled onto the American positions and become involved in a firefight. Before all surprise was lost, Rahimi had rushed forward with his entire force, attempting to bull through, but failed in the face of superior firepower and organization. Seeing no hope of succeeding on the first try, Rahimi broke it off. They had suffered heavy losses. He now had fewer than sixty men and two dozen mortar rounds. If they didn't succeed on their second attempt, there wouldn't be enough for a third.

While his men gathered, he listened for signs that the fight to his rear was still going on. There were none. Not wanting to be surprised, he sent a small detachment back to provide security.

·　　　　·　　　　·

As the two platoons moved forward, Cerro kept contacting Kinsley for updates. Neither one knew for sure why the Iranians had broken contact or what they were up to. There was the very real possibility that the Iranians were turning against Cerro's column. If that was the case, Kinsley was to remain in place. The second lift was due in momentarily. The landing zone had to be held.

As a precaution against surprise, Cerro had his two platoons disperse. Advancing in a line, they could go over to the attack or assume a hasty defense if attacked. Cerro could feel the tension building as they approached. Every step took them closer to an unseen enemy who might or might not be waiting for them the way Alpha Company had waited for the first Iranian column. Their current situation suddenly reminded him of a great game of hide-and-seek. It was a hell of an analogy. But at that moment it was true.

Wanting to get on with it, Rahimi gave the signal. The two mortars began to choke down their first rounds as two heavy machine guns hammered away at the American positions. With a yell, Rahimi raised his arm and led his men forward. The first burst of American return fire hit him square in the chest, throwing him back against one of his own men. The militiaman eased his leader down and asked what he could do to help. Rahimi, gasping, simply told him to go forward in the defense of Islam. After the militiaman left, Rahimi fought off any fears or doubts about his impending death. He was, after all, dying as Iman Husain had died, in the defense of Persia and Islam. What more could a man ask for?

Rahimi did not hear the sound of Lieutenant Cerro's attack or the approach of attack helicopters that were the vanguard of the American follow-on forces. His death preceded those of his men by mere minutes. They had failed. The American airhead held.

Fort Hood, Texas
1905 Hours, 11 June (0105 Hours, 12 June, GMT)

Major Dixon was clearing away the last of the day's work from his desk. All those items he had worked on but had not completed were returned to their proper folders and filed away in his lower-right desk drawer. Those items that were new but hadn't been acted on went back into his in box. He'd deal with them in the morning. Finally, those items he either didn't want to deal with or didn't know what he would do with were lumped together and thrown into a box labeled TOO HARD.

Content with his shuffling of papers, Dixon was preparing to leave when the phone rang. For a moment he debated whether he should answer it or simply go. His mind had become fried after dealing with a mishmash of deployment issues. It amazed him how ridiculous and misguided some of the division staff could be. On one hand he had to prepare the battalion for war when his equipment was already loaded and en route to Iran, and on the other he was being required to schedule time for inventories of station property the unit would leave behind when it finally did deploy. Fighting the urge to walk away, Dixon answered the phone with a slurred, disheartened "S-three, 3rd of the 4th Armor."

"Scott, Michaelski." It was the brigade S-3. "I thought I'd give you a heads-up. Orders are coming in now at Corps. We roll in fourteen days." Dixon remained silent. "Scott, you still there?"

"Yeah, I'm here. Is this good poop or rumor?"

"It's fact. Word is the Russians are headed south at full speed and the people in Washington are getting a little nervous with nothing on the ground but grunts."

Dixon thought about that for a moment. "Will our equipment be there?"

"The Navy assured the corps commander it will. In order to save time, the convoys haven't been running zigzag in the Atlantic. We also have permission to move them through the Suez. It will be there." The brigade S-3 seemed so sure.

"Is there anything we need to do right away? You planning any briefings or other bull tonight?"

"No, Scott, nothing. We won't have hard copy on this till morning. I'll be ready to talk to the S-threes sometime in the early afternoon. See you then."

"OK. Thanks for the warning, Mike. See you then." Dixon hung up the phone and looked at his watch. Time to go home. The next few days would surely be zoo time. Getting up, he put on his hat, pulled all the papers from the box labeled TOO HARD and dropped them into the trashcan as he walked out of his office.

Chapter 7

Shoot first and inquire afterward and if you make mistakes, I will protect you.
—HERMANN GÖRING

The sleek gray frigate slid through the night with ease. Its decks were deserted and stripped clear of all but its weapons. The gun encased in its automated turret stood motionless but ready. Canisters sat benign, hiding sophisticated missiles the way a cocoon hides a wasp. The breaking of waves and the steady hum of machinery were the only outward signs that the ship was alive. Only in the center of the frigate, where its heart and mind were, was there a semblance of activity. There, in a small room called the combat information center, men sat before electronic devices, watching and listening to sensors that monitored the air and the sea about and below them.

To the casual observer it would have been difficult to tell whether the equipment was an extension of the senses for the men who sat before it or whether the men were simply another piece of the equipment. If the latter was true, then the man was the least reliable and most error-prone portion of the equipment. Somewhere in every system a man, susceptible to all the frailties that humans possess, was a part of it. The most complex computers and processors of combat information that are capable of spewing out data in nanoseconds dump it eventually on a human who has to see, consider and decide what it means and how to use it.

The job of the men in the combat information center was to find an elusive submarine that had been stalking the carrier battle group they had been assigned to protect. This was not a simple task. The sea, far from being uniform and even, complicated the efforts of the frigate's crew with currents and thermal layers that hid and distorted sounds of creatures and things that passed through them. While the use of active sonar would ease the task of searching the sea, it would be akin to a hunter stomping through the woods and announcing his presence. So the frigate moved across the sea quietly, like a cat seeking a prey, its ears perked up and alert for any sign of movement or noise, sliding into the darkness.

Below the frigate a shadow passed undetected. The *Oscar*-class submarine's propeller turned ever so slowly, providing only enough motion to keep the vessel on course and under control. Captain Gudkov found it hard to believe his good fortune. After two weeks of effort he was finally penetrating the escort screen of the American carrier battle group he had been stalking.

The vessel's navigator, with little better to do as the submarine bobbed and weaved to break contact after one of the failed attempts, reviewed their movements over the previous two weeks and those of the carrier battle group. He found what appeared to be a pattern to the wanderings of the carrier battle group. When the navigator showed his findings to Captain Gudkov, the captain began to work on a way of using the discovery to accomplish his mission. Anything was worth a try.

While the crew rested after another failed attempt followed by a ten-hour pursuit, Gudkov and his navigator worked up a plan. The navigator, projecting the probable course of the American carrier battle group based on the pattern he had observed, estimated when the center of the group, where the carrier would be, would pass over a certain point. Assuming that the carrier battle group would follow a set pattern, Gudkov estimated where the *Iskra* could find the carrier at any given time. By being placed along the projected path of the carrier, the *Iskra* could shut down its engines and allow the carrier and its escorts to pass over the silent submarine without detecting it.

Gudkov thought the plan over and discussed it with his officers. Most, already frustrated with their failures, were willing to try anything. The political officer was a little uneasy about trusting so much to luck, guesses and rough calculations. But, though a good submariner in his own right, he did not have the knowledge or the experience to prove Gudkov wrong. In the end, he threw his lot in with the rest. Anything was worth a try. Besides, if it worked once, they would be able to repeat the maneuver if, and when, hostilities were initiated.

The *Iskra's* entire crew had been on edge since they shut down their engines and settled in to wait. It was important to maintain control of the vessel while minimizing their signature. The engines were used sparingly and only when needed. There was a hush throughout the submarine when they detected the passing of the first American escort above them. The noise of the frigate's engines and the turbulence it made passing through the water were easily detected by the *Iskra's* sensors. The crew waited apprehensively as the frigate approached, passed nearby, then left without any sign that it had detected the *Iskra*. The crew was elated, barely suppressing the urge to cheer. They had succeeded. Less than an hour later, another escort passed, causing the crew to tense up as it approached, then relax when it passed without incident.

Shortly after the second escort passed, the noise of a large vessel could be detected. Gudkov listened as the sonar operator relayed information to the *Iskra's* weapons officer concerning the new contacts. It took only a few seconds for him to compare and confirm from computer-stored data that they were in the presence of the carrier that had eluded them so long. Success. But now the hard part began. Finding the carrier was one thing, maintaining contact quite another. The *Iskra* was now in the center of the American carrier battle group. The ships accompanying the carrier would, in all probability, be less vigilant than the escort frigates. Gudkov, however, had to exercise extreme caution when he increased power and began to follow the carrier. Even though hostilities between the U.S. and the USSR had not been declared, a Soviet submarine in their midst might cause the Americans to overreact or make an error. A bad call on one man's part could mean the end of the *Iskra*. Nor did the *Iskra* dare raise its antenna to receive the prearranged code word that would tell Gudkov whether or not they were about to go to war. Their success had brought them new problems.

When the carrier had passed, the *Iskra* slowly came about and left the sanctuary of the current to follow it. The silence that ran throughout the submarine for the first five minutes was deafening. All eyes were on the captain, who watched his instruments and listened for the sonar man to report any sign that they had been discovered. After ten minutes that seemed to last an eternity, Gudkov relaxed, confident that he had been undetected and could remain so as long as he wanted.

Unfortunately, the strain of the effort had worn out the crew. With the immediate danger gone, a wave of exhaustion swept over them, dulling their senses and causing some to drift to sleep. Gudkov endeavored to keep the men alert but could not fight human nature or needs. Even his young weapons officer dozed off for a brief time, during which the calculations needed to engage the carrier were not updated. A sharp rebuke snapped him back. Under the watchful eye of his captain, the weapons officer diligently updated all firing calculations for a while, but began to drift off again.

Seeing that more was needed to maintain vigilance and wanting to ease the tension, Gudkov ordered that hot tea be brought up to the control room. A sailor brought it, exercising extreme care so as not to make any noise or spill the tea. Gudkov was standing behind the weapons officer when the sailor entered the room. He put his left hand on the shoulder of the weapons officer, turned away to the sailor with the tea and said, "Give me one for the weapons officer," as he reached out with his right hand.

The hand on his shoulder startled the weapons officer. He jumped, then realized that he had fallen asleep on duty again. On top of this horrible realization he heard the captain order, "Give me one, Weapons Officer." Without hesitation, the weapons officer leaned forward, flipped a red protective cover up, pressed the red button numbered 1 on the cruise-missile launch-control panel and announced, "One fired."

The release of compressed air and the rushing noise of the cruise missile racing for the surface were heard on a half-dozen ships. Information from sensors fed data into computers that analyzed it, compared it to historical data on different sounds and threats and sent its output to the officers on duty. For a second most of them failed to realize, or refused to believe, what the warning meant. Acceptance was rapidly followed by action as alarms blared, shattering the silence of the night with warnings given too late. The missile broke the water's surface, went into level flight and raced for the carrier.

Gudkov's hand closed like a vise on the weapons officer's shoulder as the *Iskra* stopped shuddering from the release of the missile. Color had run from his face. Transfixed, he watched the information display as the submarine's own sensors and computers tracked the progress of the missile. Thoughts raced through his mind as it scrambled for a solution. It had been a mistake. A horrible mistake. But that didn't matter. He had no way of telling the Americans that. He had no way of proving that. They had no way of knowing that. All the Americans would know was that they had been attacked. They would now strike back, immediately, without hesitation, without mercy.

Gudkov had only two choices that made sense. Break now and run, hoping for the best without any further offensive actions, or finish the carrier while he could, then run. Whether the war started accidentally or not no longer mattered. The *Iskra* was in a position to strike down the carrier that it might never be able to achieve again. Without further thought and to the surprise of all present, Gudkov ordered missiles 2, 3 and 4 fired.

The weapons officer, now fully conscious of what he had done, froze. He was unable to act, move, think, or deal with the calamity he had initiated. He simply stared at the panel before him, dumbfounded, and began to shake uncontrollably. Gudkov realized that the weapons officer had lost control of himself. With all the force he could muster, he shoved the young man out of his seat, reached over and hit the red buttons labeled 2, 3 and 4. When the last missile had been launched, he immediately issued a string of orders to commence evasive maneuvers as the *Iskra* became the hunted.

Aboard the U.S.S. *Franklin* in the Arabian Sea
0413 Hours, 16 June (0043 Hours, 16 June, GMT)

The crew of the aircraft carrier U.S.S. *Franklin* were not ready to greet another day of war. After ten days of it, they were tired. The routine was the same each day. Morning air strikes off the deck before sunrise, a quick turnaround for an early-afternoon

strike, another turnaround for a late-afternoon strike and preparation of a night strike by the specially equipped aircraft.
Throughout the day there was continuous patrolling by fighters
and E-2 Hawkeye AWACS. After each mission, maintenance and
repairs, rearming and refueling and preparation for the next round
were needed. Aircraft thundered across the deck around the
clock, both taking off and recovering, sending vibrations throughout the ship and making sleep difficult for those off duty. Added
to the physical strain of their job was the mental stress produced
by the presence of danger, the close quarters, the irregular hours
and the unending missions. A steady routine of war wears on the
efficiency of men and results in less than optimum performance
and in errors of judgment or downright negligence.

The men of the *Franklin* were preparing the planes for the
early-morning strikes and routine patrols. Topside fuel handlers
dragged their heavy hoses from aircraft to aircraft as they topped
them off. Ordnance crews were below deck, carefully loading
bombs, rockets and missiles from carts scattered about and between the aircraft in the cavernous hangar deck. Plane pushers
were pulling readied aircraft to the elevators that would lift them
to the flight deck with small tugs. On the flight deck, aircraft
maintenance crews were conducting preflight checks on planes
of the first wave. The catapult crews were preparing to receive
their first aircraft of the day. Farther below decks the pilots were
moving from breakfast to the briefing room to receive their mission and conduct their strike planning. Throughout the *Franklin*
the ship's crew went about their tasks of operating, controlling
and maintaining their ship and its planes.

The squawk of the general-quarters alarm caught the crew off
guard. Most couldn't understand why the Skipper had picked that
time for a drill. They were not prepared, physically or mentally,
for the impact of the first missile. Though the vast size of the
carrier absorbed most of the explosion, there was a sudden tilt
and a shudder. Men standing on their toes or performing a delicate operation were thrown off balance. An ordnance crew squatting under the wing of an F-14 Tomcat were about to secure an
air-to-air missile when the impact of the missile knocked them
down. The air-to-air missile dropped to the deck and rolled into
the path of a tug pulling a plane to the elevator. The tug driver,
startled by the alarm and unnerved by the impact of the missile,
saw the missile drop and roll out. Without hesitation, he jerked

the wheel of the tug and rammed into the wing of another aircraft that was heavily laden with bombs, missiles and fuel. The impacts of the next three missiles were masked by the thunderous series of explosions that ripped through the *Franklin.*

A great fireball rolled through the confines of the hangar deck, incinerating crewmen where they stood, detonating munitions lying on the deck and hung from aircraft, and feeding itself on fuel in the aircraft and in ruptured fuel lines. Crews of the *Franklin's* escort watched in awe as the flames vented out from the hangar deck into the predawn darkness. The flight deck itself was ruptured as munitions from below blew great gaps in it. The all-consuming fire turned inward as well as outward, seeking out and passing through passageways that crewmen had neglected to close and through the holes created by the explosions. Men running down narrow corridors to their battle stations were met head on by the tentacles of the fireball. Those in compartments below the hangar deck were crushed by the force of explosions and fragments that ripped through the deck from above. In less than a minute hundreds of men were dead and many horribly burned.

The fireball dissipated. A stunned silence punctured by random exploding munitions was rapidly followed by a flurry of reports and activation of the ship's damage-control system. The captain knew that his ship was hurt badly. The helmsman reported loss of steering, followed rapidly by the report that there was a complete loss of propulsion despite the fact that the engine room had escaped damage. The captain quickly deduced that the missiles which had hit his ship in the stern had damaged the rudders and the screws. Already he could feel the *Franklin* slowing. The captain turned his full attention to saving his ship while escorts around the carrier scurried in a vain effort to track and kill the attacker.

Though the captain and the surviving crew would struggle against the inevitable for hours, the *Franklin* was mortally stricken. Too much damage had been caused to too large an area too fast. Power lines and water mains that were needed to fight the spreading fire were ruptured. Many members of damage-control parties had been swept away in the first minutes of the calamity. By midmorning the fire was out of control. Reluctantly the captain turned his crew's efforts from saving the ship to saving as many of the men as possible. The transfer of the wounded was begun and preparations for abandoning the ship were made. When the *Franklin* finally rolled over and sank in the early evening of 16 June, she took twelve hundred men and a piece of each survivor with her.

The Pentagon, Washington, D.C.
2230 Hours, 15 June (0330 Hours, 16 June, GMT)

Like everyone else on the staff, Lieutenant General Horn was confused as to what the Soviets were up to. On one hand they attacked the U.S.S. *Franklin* and on the other they maintained the same routine patrol patterns and activities throughout Southwest Asia that they had been running since the U.S. had gone into Iran. Even the Soviet carrier group in the Indian Ocean was maintaining its past level of operations without any hint of deviation. Initial reports from Iran showed that ground and air operations were at the same level as they had been for the past four days. The first satellite photos of the day showed that the Soviet 28th Combined Arms Army was where intelligence had projected it would be at first light. Soviet aircraft continued the same level of operations north of their self-imposed limit. Only the submarine attack was out of the norm.

There had been a lively debate between the intelligence officers of each of the services and the Joint Staff as to what was happening. Many felt that the commander of the submarine had jumped the gun and had launched his attack too early (as had happened just prior to the invasion of Finland in 1940, when a Soviet artillery officer had fired a preparatory bombardment twenty-four hours too soon). Another theory was that the Soviets were simply trying to slip in a cheap shot, hitting just one ship in the hope that they could provoke the U.S. into overreacting or could take out a major warship without the U.S. reacting at all. A few believed that the Soviet attack was meant as a warning, an attempt to scare the U.S. off from going deeper into Iran. One young naval commander had even put forth the idea that the sinking of the *Franklin* had been an accident, that someone had gotten excited in the heat of the moment and fired.

Whatever the motivation or reason, the facts were that a Soviet submarine had attacked a U.S. warship in international waters and, according to reports so far received, had caused tremendous damage and hundreds of deaths. The President had asked for recommendations from the Joint Chiefs of Staff by midnight. An initial briefing on the situation, followed by presentation of several recommendations, had taken less than an hour. Horn now had thirty minutes to review the situation and present to his boss, the Chief of Staff of the Army, his recommendation on not only what should be done in response to the attack but also what changes, if any, the Army needed to make in current plans and operations. The Navy was already preparing to initiate operations against Soviet forces in the immediate area. The Chief of Naval Operations had ended his briefing to the Chairman of the Joint Chiefs of Staff by saying laconically, "Just give me the word, and those bastards are history."

Horn believed that the attack was a warning and an intentional act. The 17th Airborne and the 28th Marine Regiment had consolidated their toeholds in Iran and were expanding them. The 12th Infantry Division's lead elements were landing at Bandar Abbas at that very moment. The convoy carrying the 10th Corps's equipment was entering the Indian Ocean. The Air Force was well established and in strength in Iran and Oman. These developments, coupled with intelligence reports that the Soviets were having severe logistical problems complicated by guerrilla activity along their lines of communication, led Horn to the conclusion that the Soviets were desperate. Desperate people do desperate things in an effort to correct the situation.

Horn intended to recommend that the U.S. retaliate in kind immediately. The current situation and Soviet logic and actions reminded him of the story of Brer Rabbit and the Tar Baby. The rabbit, finding himself with one hand stuck on the Tar Baby, hit the Tar Baby with his free hand, only to get it stuck. When that happened, the rabbit kicked the Tar Baby in an effort to teach the Tar Baby a lesson and free himself. That also failed. The rabbit continued to attack the Tar Baby until he was so stuck that he had no hope of freeing himself. The Soviets, with one hand stuck in the fight against the Iranians, would now find their other one stuck dealing with the U.S. Navy. Horn's only concern was what would follow. Would the Soviets continue to fight the Tar Baby until they were totally committed or would they see the light and back off?

In the Indian Ocean
0845 Hours, 16 June (0545 Hours, 16 June, GMT)

The crews of the aircraft carrier *Gorki* and her escorts had been at general quarters for over two hours without a clue as to why. Aboard the *Gorki* all they knew was that something out of the ordinary had happened. The officer on duty had roused the Admiral before dawn. Shortly after that the fleet went to general quarters and began to take evasive maneuvers. At first light half of the Yak-36 fighters had scrambled from the *Gorki*. It wasn't until 0800 that the ship's captain had begun to release the men for breakfast and then only one third at a time. While the men ate, no one dared speculate or inquire as to why the unusual behavior. They would be told in time, one petty officer said, if they needed to know.

Admiral Boleylev and his staff would not have been able to give their men a clear answer if they had wanted to. They were operating in the dark just as the crews of their ships were. The call to general quarters, the evasive maneuvers and the combat air patrol were in reaction to a series of reports that were not clear and could mean anything. The first report, with which the duty officer had woken the Admiral, was that there had been a sudden and unexplained surge of encoded communications traffic from the American carrier battle group operating to the north of them in the Arabian Sea. They had even intercepted several uncoded ship-to-ship communications from the U.S.S. *Franklin* and her escort that talked about transfer of wounded and survivors. This had been rapidly followed by an increase in air patrols by the U.S.S. *Hornet*'s carrier battle group to the south of them and initiation of electronic jamming of the *Gorki*'s long-range radars. The *Gorki* was now running blind.

Boleylev sat in the officers' mess but could not eat. The only reason he was there was that he needed a break. His stomach was upset by acid from too much coffee and from nerves. He was pushing himself too hard. Not that he had much of a choice. The orders given to him before they sailed from Vladivostok were to proceed to the Indian Ocean, where his fleet would put pressure on and harass U.S. naval forces. On order he was to neutralize the base at Diego Garcia and commence operations against U.S. convoys headed into Iran. The *Gorki* and the task force built around her were outnumbered in ships three to one and in carrier aircraft four to one. Rather than Boleylev's putting pressure on the Americans and harassing them, the Americans were doing it to him.

There were two carrier battle groups, one north of him, built around the U.S.S. *Franklin* and the battleship U.S.S. *Utah*, and one south of him with the U.S.S. *Hornet*. The day before, the *Utah* had detached itself from the *Franklin*'s battle group and headed south toward the *Gorki*. Contact had been lost shortly before nightfall yesterday. This worried Boleylev, especially since patrols from the *Gorki* had so far failed to find the *Utah* that morning. In addition, the normal morning recon flight made by U.S. aircraft had not yet been reported. The two U.S. carrier battle groups tracked the *Gorki* constantly and alternated "practice" strikes against Boleylev's task force daily in an attempt to keep him off balance and wear down his men. On one such occasion, all the planes from both carriers popped up over the horizon and came in from all points of the compass toward the *Gorki* at full speed. The speed of the attack and the surprise it had achieved had almost resulted in a shooting incident. As a result, very tight control was maintained on the ship's surface-to-air missiles. Standing orders were that they could be fired only on Boleylev's orders. He did not want to start a war with the U.S. accidentally.

In the *Gorki*'s operations center the air-defense officer stared at his radar screen and his instruments. For the last hour and a half he had seen nothing but static. The Americans were jamming his radar. Though that could be considered a hostile act, the air-defense officer was sure nothing would come of it. The strength of the jamming indicated that the source was relatively near, probably a carrier-launched EA-6B Prowler, an aircraft specially built to conduct electronic-warfare operations. Whatever the source, it rendered the ship's radars ineffectual except for very close in. To overcome this, the escorts had dispersed more widely than normal in order to increase the early-warning distance for the task force and, in particular, the *Gorki*.

It was the electronic-warfare officer who detected the incoming missiles. Faint signals were heard. The electronic-warfare officer leaned forward and listened intently. When he was sure of the signals, he notified the air-defense officer that multiple Harpoon missiles were inbound. A computer plot indicated an intercept course with the *Gorki* and the cruiser *Kynda*, which was providing close-in protection for the *Gorki*. The air-defense officer hesitated. He had not seen anything quite like these plots before. The radar was still unable to provide the computer with the clear data needed to positively identify them. Whatever they were, their number continued to grow: from six to ten, to fifteen, to twenty-one and still more coming. The air-defense officer finally recognized the missile attack for what it was just as a wave of similar plots began to appear from the south.

He hit the ship's alarm and shouted over the intercom that they were under attack from thirty-plus antiship missiles. With the incoming missiles too close for the jamming to have any effect, the *Gorki*'s computer began to relay accurate information to the ship's officers and weapons systems, and antimissile missiles were automatically trained on the incoming missiles. Green lights flashed on the control panel, indicating that the systems were locked on and ready to fire. All that was needed was the initiation of the automated defense sequence.

The air-defense officer, however, did not initiate it. He was, as the standing orders stated, waiting for the order from the ship's captain. The captain, in turn, was waiting for the order from the Admiral, who was, at that moment, scrambling up a ladder to the control room, wondering why the antimissile missiles had not yet been launched. Boleylev stormed into the control room, out of breath and yelling, *"Fire, damn it, fire!"* just as the first U.S.-made Harpoon missile slammed into the *Gorki* just above the waterline.

Bandar Abbas
1107 Hours, 16 June (0737 Hours, 16 June, GMT)

The C-141 was coming into Bandar Abbas low over the Persian Gulf as instructed. Aboard it, Major General Edgar Thorton, commanding general of the 12th Infantry Division (Light), was miffed. The General wanted to make a grand entrance into Iran. Skipping over the water like a stone seemed undignified somehow. At least he had taken the precaution of sending his chief of staff and the division's public-affairs officer, or PAO, with the advance party to ensure that all would be ready when "Condor Six," as Thorton was called, came walking down the ramp into the war.

The greeting Condor Six got was far from the one that he had planned for. As he walked down the ramp of the C-141 onto the runway, what he saw was an MP lieutenant and two hummers with machine guns mounted and manned. The 12th Division's band, the PAO and his photographers and the special honor guard with the division's colors were not there. Thorton stopped midway down the ramp and let out a stream of obscenities. Refusing to continue, he ordered his aide to find out from the MP lieutenant what was going on and why the reception for the division was not ready.

Dutifully, the aide trotted down the ramp, spoke to the MP lieutenant and trotted back up to his general's side to report. The MP lieutenant, according to the aide, knew nothing of the planned reception, had no idea where the 12th Division's chief of staff was and had orders to take the General to meet with the corps commander without delay.

Thorton swore loudly. Totally put out by the failure of his people to do as they had been told, he was in no mood to hop into a hummer with a second-lieutenant messenger boy and miss the chance of a lifetime. The first units of his division were due to arrive momentarily. He intended to greet them with full honors, a speech and a review of troops. He began to issue a string of orders. His aide was sent to find a photographer from somewhere. A major was sent with the MP lieutenant to find out what the corps commander wanted. Another officer was instructed to begin marshaling the soldiers of the division into ranks as they deplaned and to find a suitable place from which the General could address them when they were assembled. The 12th Infantry Division was going to march into Iran and be greeted by the division commander in a manner befitting the occasion.

The preparations for the General's greeting to his troops were interrupted by a pair of hummers that came careening across the airstrip and stopped in front of the adhoc reviewing stand. Thorton was beside himself with rage until he saw the deputy commander of the 13th Airborne Corps get out of the lead hummer. As if he had flipped a switch, Thorton's face changed from anger to a broad grin, and he walked over to greet the deputy commander, extending his hand.

Instead of accepting the hand, the deputy blurted, "Thorton, what in hell do you think you're doing? The corps commander is waiting for you and is fit to be tied."

Thorton stopped. Obviously the people at Corps were in a foul mood. Continuing to grin, he tried to put the best possible light on the subject. "Gee, Tom, I sent one of my people to find out what the corps commander wanted while I stayed to greet my people as they came in."

"Don't give me that crap," the deputy said. "You ignored the commander's instructions so that you could stay here and put on your Hollywood production. Don't you know there's a fucking war going on?"

The deputy had gone too far, had hit too near the mark. Thorton changed expressions and went over to the attack. "Yeah, I know there's a war on. And the division that's going to take care of those camel herders is coming in and is going to receive an appropriate welcome. The Muslim ragheads can wait another hour before we make them martyrs."

The deputy looked at Thorton for a moment before he continued. "Obviously, General, you don't understand what's going on. We're no longer concerned with the Iranians. It's the Russians we're concerned with now. Since this morning we have been at war with the Soviet Union. Now get off your high fucking horse and get in the hummer. The corps commander is waiting."

Thorton was dumbfounded. He had had no idea that the Soviets were now fighting the United States. Without further ado, he followed the deputy and headed off to see his commander.

Memphis, Tennessee
0237 Hours CST, 16 June (0837 Hours, 16 June, GMT)

Like most of the men in the 2nd Battalion of the 354th Infantry, Ed Lewis had taken advantage of the three-day break they had before departing for Iran to visit his family and say goodbye properly. He was almost sorry he had. The situation at home was very strained. Everyone, including Lewis himself, was trying hard to make believe that this was nothing more than another training exercise. No one talked about Iran or Lewis' impending departure. This pretense made everyone even more uncomfortable and on edge.

Each night Lewis' wife would lie next to him awake, unable to settle down. When she thought he was asleep, she would get up and go into their bathroom and cry. Lewis heard her tonight, but said nothing. When she finally calmed herself and returned to bed, he rolled over and put his arm around her. With her emotions vented, and comforted by her husband, she drifted off to sleep. When she had done so, Lewis got up carefully and went downstairs to watch the news on the cable network, something that he didn't do when his wife was awake, for fear of upsetting her.

The news of the U.S.S. *Franklin* and the retaliations by aircraft from the *Hornet* against Soviet warships in the Indian Ocean did not surprise Lewis, disturbing though it was. A confrontation had been inevitable. Everyone had expected it. In fact, now that it had happened, things seemed clearer, easier.

What did disturb Lewis the most was that while he watched satellite films of the *Franklin* burning, while men were dying thousands of miles away, the news program was interrupted by commercials for a product to shrink swollen hemorrhoids and for a new improved panty shield to protect ladies' underwear. The new war, obviously, wasn't interfering with the pressing demands of life in the United States.

Chapter 8

Logistics is the ball and chain of armored warfare.

—HEINZ GUDERIAN

When the farewell ball for the brigade had been proposed by the wife of the brigade commander, it had seemed like a good idea—at least to her and to some of the other older wives. True, no one was sure of what proper etiquette demanded when it came to sending one's spouse to war. The last war that anyone had any experience with had been Vietnam. But that war had been far different for the wives, who had seen their husbands go to war one at a time except in a few rare cases. They remembered it as a very lonely and personal affair. It was because of this that the older wives pushed for the ball. It would give them a last night together before the two groups, the husbands and the wives, parted and dealt with their own little wars.

The commencement of hostilities between the U.S. and the Soviet Union had acted like a wet blanket on the entire affair. While it had been disquieting to imagine one's spouse going to war against the Iranians, it was even more so now that the Russians were actually shooting at Americans. The more realistic wives said that it had been inevitable, some even claiming it had been planned. But even the most cynical had hoped that somehow that conflict could be avoided. There had always been the hope that this crisis would blow over and go away. The latest news reports coming from Southwest Asia crushed those hopes, however, on a daily basis. First there was the commitment of the 17th Airborne Division, followed by strong resistance from the Iranians and by mounting casualties. The sinking of the U.S.S. *Franklin* and the *Gorki* began a cycle of retaliation and escalation. Air battles between American and Soviet planes over the Iranian desert and combat at sea had become daily features of the news. There was no doubt that once U.S. and Soviet forces met on the ground, they would do so with drawn knives and with blood in their eyes.

The ball was already degenerating by ten in the evening. Husbands and wives who desired to spend as much time as possible alone with each other or their families were already bidding good night to their commanders and their commanders' wives. The bachelors had rallied around the bars and were preparing to move down to the pub to continue the party. A few couples danced, while others sat at tables cluttered with glasses and coffee cups and talked about everything but the war.

Scott and Fay Dixon sat with some of the other officers of the 3rd Battalion of the 4th Armor and their wives. The wives talked about the children and other subjects while the men listened to them or conducted encrypted conversations among themselves. Dixon sat to one side watching the whole affair with a cynical eye as he slowly got himself drunk. Fay had been so busy that she had not noticed how much he was putting away. No doubt there would be hell to pay once she found out. She never did approve of drinking to excess, especially since it usually made Dixon sick.

Dixon watched a group of young officers from the battalion at one of the bars. In the middle of them was First Lieutenant Randy Capell, the battalion's scout-platoon leader. Capell was, for the most part, a good officer. Technically proficient, he handled his platoon well. On the debit side, Capell had a tendency to be impetuous to the point of recklessness and self-assured to the point of arrogance. While in moderation those were good qualities for a scout-platoon leader, Dixon would have preferred a slightly more timid man leading the battalion's scouts. He had spent a great deal of time with Capell trying hard to train him in his duties and what was expected of the scouts. Given a little more time, Capell would do well. But time, as Dixon knew, was a commodity he didn't have.

At that moment, Capell appeared to be doing quite well with Lieutenant Amanda Matthews, the assistant brigade S-2. The two were obviously quite tipsy and becoming far more intimate than protocol normally permitted. Dixon thought about that for a moment as he watched Capell run his free hand down Matthews' side, letting it come to rest on her hip. She simply smiled and drew closer. At the rate they were going, it wouldn't surprise Dixon one bit if Capell screwed her right there.

With that thought in mind, Dixon turned and looked at his wife. She was talking to the battalion XO's wife and ignoring him. He turned, placed his hand on her knee and ran it up her thigh. This sudden and unexpected contact startled her, causing her to jump and turn. Then she slapped his hand and scolded him as if he were a little boy, "Scott Dixon, you behave."

Dixon leaned forward, running his hand up higher on her thigh and said, so that all at the table could hear, "I don't want to behave, that's no fun."

Fay blushed and turned to the others at the table to apologize for his behavior. She was cut off, however, by Dixon announcing to them, in slightly slurred voice, "Now, if you ladies and gentlemen will excuse us, my wife and I are going home to reenact the consummation of our marriage."

Without waiting for a response or saying another word, he stood up and dragged his red-faced wife away by the hand as she finished apologizing, halfheartedly now, for her husband's behavior. In truth, she hoped that Scott wasn't so drunk that he couldn't deliver on his promise.

Amanda Matthews was enjoying herself. She had met Randy Capell at the club on night during an evening "stress reduction" session. The two had talked for a while but nothing more. A few nights later they had met again by accident and had dinner together. Matthews found herself drawn to Capell. He was tall and solidly built, with a physique that suggested great power, yet he carried himself with an easy grace. His sandy blond hair and blue eyes were soft and inviting. He was the image of what a soldier should be—a warrior. He was also brash, self-confident, boastful and, on occasion, crude. In short, Capell was all those things that a modern woman was supposed to disdain in a man. Yet Amanda found that those traits were enjoyable and exciting.

When she saw Capell at the ball she decided to find out how

interested in her he was. But rather than charge forth, she decided to charm him. Not sure how an officer went about seducing another officer, Matthews started by making sure she was sufficiently conspicuous at her unit's table that she and Capell could make eye contact. At first, Capell was so engrossed in his conversation with other people at his table that he didn't notice her. In desperation, she excused herself and went to the ladies' room. On her way back to her table she took a roundabout way that let her pass right behind Capell and brush against him. It worked. He turned, his face showing anger at first until he saw who it was. Matthews stopped, put her hand on Capell's shoulder, leaned over and apologized. Capell turned to face her, putting his hand on hers while they talked. His touch sent a warm, tingling surge through her. She felt herself blush as she stood there staring into Capell's soft blue eyes. When she finally told him she needed to get back to her table, her speech was faltering and barely audible.

As she walked back she felt embarrassed and happy. Embarrassed that she was acting like a schoolgirl who had a crush on a boy for the first time, and happy that she had gotten his attention. She wasn't sure, however, whether he was interested or not. Throughout the rest of the meal the two exchanged glances. When the formal part of the evening was over, Matthews forced Capell to make the first move by restraining herself from bounding up and rushing over to him. When he stood and began to approach, she beamed with a childish glee, proud that she had succeeded and excited about the prospects that the night held. She hadn't felt the way she did since her high-school prom. That thought caused her to wish she were wearing something more feminine. The occasion called for a sleek, low-cut black gown, with bare shoulders and slit skirt, not her dress-blue uniform.

That bothered her until they danced for the first time. Capell crossed the room and asked if she would like to dance. Matthews, trying hard to conceal her excitement, simply answered, "Yes, I'd love to." The two started at a respectable and proper distance that didn't last long. Matthews drew closer to Capell, looked into his eyes, then rested her head on his shoulder. As they danced, she felt Capell become aroused, and her own excitement increased. She turned her face toward his and smiled. In response, he leaned over and kissed her.

For a brief moment they stood still, lost in the passion of the moment. Then slowly their lips parted, and they began to sway to the rhythm of the music again. With his arms around her, she put her head back on his shoulder and followed his lead, letting herself relax and enjoy the moment. She had no doubt where the night would lead them and eagerly looked forward to it.

Major Percy Jones watched the couples dance while he sat in his own little corner and quietly got drunk. After two years with the 25th Armored Division, the British officer still had difficulty accepting the large number of women the American Army had in its ranks. It just didn't seem proper. The two young lieutenants, however, seemed perfectly at ease dancing with each other. The blond female intelligence officer, a striking beauty by any measure, was quite competent and professional. Jones had worked with her on several occasions and, despite his prejudices, had come to depend on the intelligence products she developed. Still, it didn't seem quite proper.

As they disappeared into the middle of the group that was dancing, his thoughts returned to his own plight. Despite his best efforts, he had been unable to terminate his assignment to the corps staff and return to the 7th Royal Tank Regiment. This failure had hit home when he and several other officers from the corps staff flew to Britain for a liaison visit with the British 33rd Armored Brigade, to which his regiment belonged. The regimental mess had been alive with young officers eager to have a go at the Iranians. The older officers, while doubting the wisdom of the commitment the British government had made, were, in their own way, just as eager to get on with it. Though everyone was friendly, Jones, for the first time in his life, did not feel at home in the mess where his father's picture hung in a place reserved for the regiment's most honored members. After one visit to the mess, he avoided it for the rest of the trip, spending his time alone in his room instead. And now the American unit he had worked with for so long was also going and he was staying behind with the corps staff. Eventually he would make it over to Iran, but not for some time. This last indignity was almost too much to bear.

As the anger within him began to build, he stood up. This action served only to show how drunk he was as he staggered forward uncontrollably and bumped into a table, sending half-filled glasses and cups flying. A couple passing him stopped, the young captain asking whether he needed any help. Jones waved him on, with muddled thanks. He looked around the room, trying to regain his balance and composure. Well, as usual, Sarah was right, he told himself. It was a bloody stupid idea to come here tonight. Best crawl back to my little hole before I make a complete ass of myself. With that thought, Jones began to carefully pick his way between the tables in search of his wife.

Despite his best efforts, Dixon could not make the room stop spinning. He lay in the dark for another minute, sweating, trying desperately to keep what little he had left in his stomach, but decided that he wouldn't succeed. Without a moment to lose, he threw the sheets off and dashed for the bathroom, arriving at the toilet seconds before the first wave of nausea crested.

He knelt there before the great porcelain bowl for what seemed like an eternity. What a hell of a way to spend my last night at home—that thought and a stream of obscenities passed through Dixon's muddled mind. When he was sure he was finished, he stood up and went to the sink, looking into the mirror as he brushed his teeth and took some aspirin. The face that he saw looked like death warmed over. Well, at least the outside matches the inside, he thought. When he was through, he turned off the bathroom light and returned to the bedroom.

Only the sound of the air-conditioner broke the stillness. He crossed the room, carefully avoiding the clothes and shoes that had been discarded carelessly about the room in a rush of passion. When he reached the bed, he paused for a moment and looked down at his wife. In the faint light he could see her naked body curled up before him. He wanted to reach out and touch her, but didn't for fear of waking her. She looked too peaceful and lovely to disturb. Instead, he pulled the sheet up and covered her before turning away.

Stumbling toward the closet, Dixon groped about until he found some running shorts. He pulled them on and left the bedroom, closing the door carefully so as not to awaken Fay, then plodded down the hall toward the kids' room. Exercising even greater care than before, Dixon picked his way through a maze of toys strewn about the floor until he reached the bunk bed where his two sons slept. As he had with Fay, he covered them and looked at each of the boys for a moment. In turn, he reached out and stroked his fingers through their hair. Tears welled up in his eyes as he thought how much he would miss them, wondering when he would see them again.

Robat-e Abgram, Iran
0830 Hours, 25 June (0500 Hours, 25 June, GMT)

The physicist leaned against the building and looked out across the desert. Even in the shade he was sweating as he smoked his second cigarette in a row. This was the first break that he had allowed himself since late the night before. He needed it. No doubt it would be the last for a while. The Air Force colonel was pushing him to complete the first device as soon as possible. The physicist and his team were working almost around the clock, under primitive conditions and with few capable helpers, in an effort to meet the joint demands of the holy men and the military to deliver functional nuclear devices. Surprisingly, for the first time the physicist finally was able to announce with certainty that he would be able to do so. After having run several tests, he and his small team had a functional triggering system. Early that morning they had completed a test with a full-scale model containing everything but the plutonium. It had worked. All that remained was to assemble the entire device and put it into a deliverable package. That task would be completed within two weeks, three at the outside. After that, it was in the hands of the colonel and Allah.

The motivation of the colonel bothered him. At one moment, the colonel appeared to be against the project, doing everything in his power to delay it. The next moment, he would turn around and breathe fire in an effort to speed it up. Whom, the physicist wondered, was he working for? Was he still loyal to the Shah and part of the resistance? Was he Tudeh, attempting to delay development until the Russians finally caught them? Or was he simply like the rest of them, torn between their loyalties and common sense, and praying that Allah, in his infinite wisdom, would show them the way?

The physicist considered that for a moment as he watched members of the Revolutionary Guard patrol the area. His thoughts then turned to the more practical problems at hand. How would the colonel deliver the device? Because of the bulkiness and the odd shape, a missile or a rocket was out. Hiding it in a truck and driving it to the target was too risky. Only a plane could penetrate enemy lines and get the device to its intended target quickly and in good shape. But the device was not a bomb that could be dropped. There were no provisions for that. No doubt it would be a one-way trip for a group of young religious zealots anxious to achieve martyrdom in a most spectacular manner. A two-megaton explosion would serve their needs well.

The physicist threw down his cigarette, crushed it and rubbed his eyes. There was still much work for him to do before the young lions could do Allah's work. The greater questions of right and wrong would be left to those better able to deal with such things. He was a scientist by training. Science was what he could understand, and he endeavored to confine himself to its narrow spectrum.

Yazd, Iran
0830 Hours, 25 June (0500 Hours, 25 June, GMT)

The elation of their victories at Tabriz, Mianeh, Tehran, Qom and now Yazd was beginning to wear thin. Thirty days of campaigning had taken its toll on the men, the equipment and the leaders of the 28th Combined Arms Army and, in particular, the 68th Tank Regiment. Life in the field is difficult, at best. The men lived on a steady diet of combat rations that provided little more than calories. Dust and dirt penetrated everything, drying out nasal passages and throats, causing everyone to hack. Extremes in temperature and the failure of some of the soldiers to put warm clothing on before late in the evening resulted in congestion and colds that often led to bronchial infections. The water used by the men to quench their thirst was never plentiful enough and carried the seeds of diarrhea and typhoid. Lack of sleep coupled with brief periods of intense combat and stress followed long stretches of boredom and road marches that dulled their senses. Only now was it becoming apparent to the men of the 28th CAA that each new victory brought them only another opportunity to exist in conditions that barely sustained life and to fight another battle that exposed them to fear, sickness, mutilation and death.

The equipment fared badly as well. The same heat, dust and stress that wore on the men attacked their equipment. Dust ingestion in the engines, turning oil and grease into a paste that acted like sandpaper rather than as lubricants, caused a steady steam of maintenance failures. The army's line of march was marked by abandoned equipment that had broken down and had not yet been recovered. Even equipment that managed to stay with the advancing columns suffered from malfunctions to fire-control systems, electrical components and weapons. Heat and the steady vibration of tracks on poor roads was especially hard on sophisticated fire-control computers on tanks.

Major Vorishnov watched the unending columns of combat vehicles, artillery and trucks roll by. Behind him his battalion sat in a loose laager, refueling and resting after another all-night move. Eighteen tanks of the original thirty-one remained with the battalion on this morning. Of the thirteen missing, only two had been combat losses. The rest had broken down and been left behind. Vorishnov would never see them again.

Tanks lost by the battalion due to combat or a maintenance failure were not returned to the same battalion. Instead, those vehicles that had fallen out of the line of march were picked up by maintenance teams following the army. These teams repaired them and formed reserve units with them. The reserve units were manned by using the crews of the tanks that had fallen out due to maintenance failure, survivors of tanks hit in combat and wounded men returning from the hospital. Units in the vanguard of the army would get the replacements needed to bring them back up to full strength by receiving entire companies or, in the case of a regiment, a battalion from the reserve unit. If a unit was too badly depleted, it would be amalgamated with other depleted units to form a complete one. Officers from the staff-officer reserve would be used to provide leadership in the amalgamated units.

In the Soviet Army, units are used until they are no longer capable of performing their mission. In the West, a unit is considered to begin to become combat ineffective when it drops below 70 percent of its authorized strength. The Soviets are more sanguine, using units until they are anywhere from 60 to 40 percent strength. When that happens, the next unit behind is passed forward to continue the mission. The spent unit loses priority on everything and is pulled out of the way and sent to the rear or, in the case of a rapid advance, left in place until the army's combat service support, or logistic, units can move forward. The spent unit is then resupplied with all classes of supply, vehicles are repaired and losses in both equipment and men made good from reserve units. This effort is referred to as reconstitution. If several units are equally depleted, they will be amalgamated. When ready, the reconstituted unit is placed back on the line of advance and awaits its turn to be passed forward into combat.

In theory such a system is easy and manageable. Its practice, however, was proving to be quite difficult, especially in Iran. The major problem facing the 28th CAA was the lack of roads. This limited the amount of traffic that could go forward or to the rear. The army ran the road like a railroad, directing who could be on it and establishing priorities. The highest priority went to combat units in the vanguard and those units required to support them, such as artillery, air-defense and chemical-warfare units. Next came fuel and ammunition resupply convoys tailored to keep the vanguard units moving. Behind them came the army's main body, support units to keep critical equipment in operation and, again, supply convoys. All this was one-way traffic, with only the empty supply trucks being allowed to return.

Vorishnov was not happy with the decision to pull the 68th Tank Regiment out of the lead. He had become used to setting the pace and pushing forward, always up front. He did not relish giving up the position of honor and falling into the line of march behind the motorized rifle division, as they had done during the first days of the war. Vorishnov, however, understood the rationale for the decision. Soon the 28th Combined Arms Army would make contact with the Americans who were preparing to bar the army's route to the Strait of Hormuz. In accordance with Soviet doctrine, it was the role of the motorized infantry to make the breakthrough attack and prepare the way for the tank units. The tank units, suffering heavily due to maintenance failures, needed time to recover and reconstitute themselves. They had to be ready to exploit the success of the motorized rifle units.

Turning his back to the unending traffic on the road, Vorishnov surveyed his battalion. As he did so, he threw his arms above his head and stretched his body. He was sore from traveling many miles in the cramped confines of an armored personnel carrier. The wire seats covered with thin canvas did little to cushion the body from repeated blows and jerks when the vehicle moved down a road that was nothing more than a collection of potholes. As he took stock of his aches and pains, Vorishnov thought that a little rest and a couple of days off the road might not be bad after all.

Rafsanjan, Iran
0845 Hours, 25 June (0515 Hours, 25 June, GMT)

Under the watchful eye of their platoon sergeant, the men of the 1st Platoon, B Company, 3rd Battalion of the 503rd Infantry, went about their task of laying antitank mines in front of their positions. Normally, if the mines were simply laid on the surface and not covered, this wasn't a particularly difficult task. Their platoon sergeant, Sergeant First Class Duncan, insisted, however, that the mines be dug in and buried. The rocky ground made a simple job a real pain.

The platoon worked in teams. Two men, working with one of the squad leaders, went about marking the locations where the mines would be placed. The squad leader, using a compass, would establish a direction for one of the men to move in. Carefully stepping off from where the squad leader was located, the man would count his steps until he had moved a predetermined distance. Once there, he would stand still until the squad leader came up to him. Marking that point, the squad leader would set three stakes two meters out from where the pace man stood. The stakes marked where the mine layers would place mines. The third man was the recorder, carefully making up a sketch map of the mine field so that they could recover the mines at some future date or, if the company was relieved by another, so that the new unit would know where the mines were.

Behind the people marking the locations of the mines came the diggers. At each site where there was a stake they would scrape out a hole just wide and deep enough to accommodate an M-21 antitank mine. An assistant squad leader was in charge of this crew and had the responsibility of ensuring that the holes dug were neither too deep nor too shallow.

While scraping holes in the rocky soil was hard, the task of the mine layers was nothing more than mindless hauling of the heavy mines from where the helicopter had dropped them to where the holes were dug. The mines had to be uncrated and taken out of the protective packaging. Two men did this while the rest carried the mines to where their squad leader directed them. Most men carried only two mines per trip. For this task Duncan used an entire squad. Today he used the squad that was on his shit list.

The final and potentially most dangerous task was performed by an NCO and one other man. They armed the mines and covered them. The M-21 mine can be detonated either by a pressure fuse, which drives a striker into a detonator when the proper amount of pressure is applied, or by a tilt rod, which releases the detonator when tilted at a certain angle. Duncan directed his people to use the tilt rod, which stood higher than the center clearance of most vehicles' hulls and thus could activate a mine when a vehicle passed over it, even if the vehicle's tracks did not run over the mine; upon detonation, a metal penetrator would be driven up into the vehicle or would at least sever the track if the track ran over the mine. As the two men armed the mines, they would randomly booby-trap one by putting a hand grenade under it in such a way that the grenade would be detonated if someone tried to lift out the mine. This was done to discourage the enemy from creeping into a mine field at night and removing the mines in order to clear a lane for attacking forces or use them later against their former owner.

The third squad of the platoon stayed in their positions and overwatched the work party in the mine field. These men provided security. The Russians were still many miles away, but the Iranians were always near at hand, willing to snipe at Americans or seize a lone and unwary soldier and butcher him at their leisure. A man in C Company who had wandered off to relieve himself had been captured by the Iranians and brutally tortured before being killed and dismembered.

As Duncan watched his men, he thought about the situation they were in. They were preparing defensive positions from which they were expected to fight Russian mechanized forces. This in itself was a formidable task for a light-infantry unit deployed in the farthest forward location occupied by U.S. forces; the failure of the Iranians to cease hostilities made the battalion's position even worse. Only one truck convoy had been able to make it forward to them overland. A second had been ambushed by the Iranians and turned back. Their battalion commander claimed that it was the Iranian Communists who had done it. Who had done it, however, made little difference. The fact was that the battalion was isolated, with helicopters being their only secure link to the rest of the U.S. Army. This did little to instill confidence in Duncan or his men. Because of their tenuous position, each man understood how critical it was that they hold. If they were not able to stop the Russians, there would be nowhere safe to hide among a population that was as hostile as the enemy they faced to their front.

The battalion's main defensive positions were several kilometers south of Rafsanjan, on high ground that flanked the main road and offered excellent fields of fire to the Americans. The battalion's scout platoon was located on the forward edge of the town. Duncan did not envy them their position. He and his platoon had made a sweep of the town when the unit first arrived. In all his life Duncan had never imagined such filth or squalor. The houses were mud-brick structures of one or two rooms that held only the barest of primitive furniture. Through the center of the dirt streets ran an open ditch that served as a sewer. The people consisted of women, children, old men and horribly maimed young men, veterans and refuse of the war with Iraq. All were thin as rails and watched the Americans with barely concealed contempt and hate. The platoon had been sent in to find the village mullahs and search for arms. Neither mullahs, weapons nor able-bodied men of military age were found. No doubt they would make their appearance at a time of their choice.

The company was arrayed with two platoons abreast and a third behind them. This gave the company's position depth and, at the same time, all-around security. Four heavy TOW antitank guided missiles reinforced the company in addition to the unit's thirteen Dragon medium antitank guided missiles. Four 66mm. light antitank rockets, called LAWs, per man and extensive antitank mine fields to their front rounded out the company's antiarmor capability. C Company was deployed to B Company's right, A Company was to the left, and D Company deployed to the rear, giving the battalion defense in depth as well as a reserve. A 105mm. howitzer battery was in direct support of the 3rd Battalion. AH-64 attack helicopters operating from an airfield at Kerman provided backup if needed to deal with a serious Soviet threat.

The officers and most of the men of the battalion felt they could hold against anything the Soviets sent against them. Duncan and a few of the more cynical men had their doubts. He had

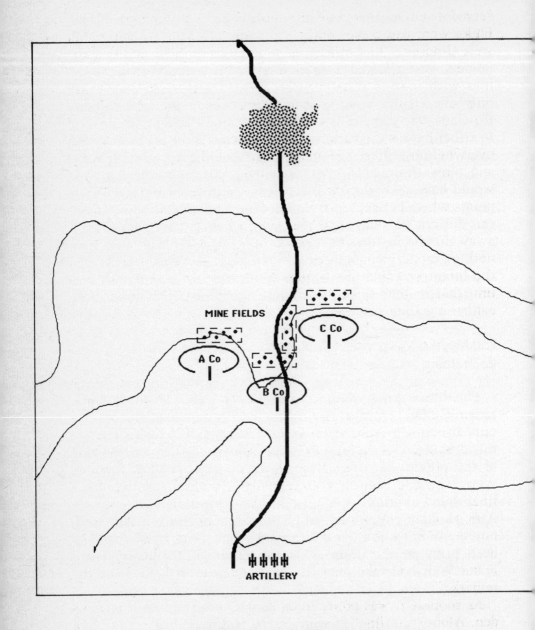

MINE FIELDS

C Co

A Co

B Co

ARTILLERY

DEFENSIVE POSITIONS OF
3RD BATTALION, 503RD INFANTRY

served in a mechanized infantry unit in Germany and knew what tanks were capable of doing, even the old M-60A1 tanks that were dinosaurs in comparison to the Soviet T-80 tanks. If the Soviets were allowed to mass their artillery and hit the companies with masses of armor, the light infantrymen would have only one chance to stop them. And even if the first wave of Russians was stopped, a second wave would be brought forward to either bypass the battalion or conduct a deliberate attack with overwhelming firepower and armor. Should the Soviets succeed and blow through the 3rd Battalion's positions, the battalion would have to withdraw into the desert to predetermined rally points where helicopters from Kerman could pick them up. Duncan did not like having to depend on helicopters that were far away, nor did he like the prospect of facing a horde of tanks with nothing more than a hole in the ground for protection. He cursed the Infantry Branch assignments NCO who had sent him to a unit that marched twenty-five miles for fun and thought a .50-caliber machine gun was big.

Fort Meyers, Maryland
2330 Hours, 24 June (0430 Hours, 25 June, GMT)

The dinner party for Lieutenant General Weir hosted by Lieutenant General Horn and his wife had been a small affair attended only by close friends. Horn's wife, in an effort to lighten the mood, said it was the least they could do for the hero-to-be. None of the officers in attendance, however, even cracked a smile. Weir, who had been in Washington for the past two days for a final round of briefings and updates before leaving for Southwest Asia, thought the remark in bad taste. Betty Horn meant well, but she didn't know what the men in the room knew. Had she been privy to the discussions and briefings her husband and Frank Weir had taken part in, she would never have made the remark.

As soon as it was polite to do so, Horn hustled Weir into his den. Alone, and finally beginning to feel the effects of the fine white Rhine wine served with the meal, Weir turned to his host. "OK, Bob, you've been wanting to get me alone all day. Here's your big chance."

Horn pointed to the bar. "Help yourself and take a seat."

Weir, being in a surprisingly playful mood, furrowed his brow.

"Is that an order directly from the Deputy Chief of Staff for Operations?"

Horn stopped and looked at Weir, then shook his head. "Yeah, that's an order. Fix me one, too, while you're at it."

While Weir poured two tall glasses of bourbon over ice, Horn took off his jacket and sat down. "You know, Frank, you can forget about most of that bullshit you got today at the White House and the Pentagon. You know what your real mission is?"

Weir answered while he handed Horn his drink and sat down. "Let me guess, end this war before it becomes unpopular?"

"Close, but not quite. No, your job is not to lose."

Weir took a sip of his drink before answering. "Now, that's a hell of a note to send a soldier off to war with. Why don't you just do as the Spartan mothers used to do and tell me to return home with my shield or upon it?"

Horn leaned forward and in a soft but serious voice continued. "That, my old friend, is exactly what you are *not* to do. You will be the first American commander faced with the real threat of defeat in the field since the Korean War. Frank, right now there are four U.S. divisions in Iran. When your corps is fully committed, that will make seven. Those units represent thirty-three percent of the active-duty ground-combat strength of the Army and the Marine Corps. We can't afford to lose that, regardless of what happens to Iran, the Persian Gulf and the whole damned region. If the Russians annihilate that force, there's no telling what will happen in Korea, Central America, Africa and especially Europe. Do you realize that the only reason the Brits and the French are committing forces is so that we don't send more units tagged for NATO into Iran? Those people are quite concerned, to say the least, that if we go down the tubes the Russians will say, 'What the hell, let's take out Western Europe too.' Regardless of what happens, you must preserve your force."

Weir leaned back and considered Horn's comments for a moment before he spoke. "Bob, are you telling me to avoid a fight?"

"No. No, that's impossible. You're going to have to duke it out with the Russians. That's the only way we, or, more correctly, you, will be able to stop them. But you're going to have to be damned careful about when and where you pick your battles. We can't afford any long-drawn-out war of attrition or, on the other end of the spectrum, a high-risk operation. Stop them, bloody their nose, but not at the expense of your force."

"That's just great, Bob. 'Go out and kill Commies, but be careful.' Care to tell me how I'm going to do that?"

Horn was becoming agitated. "Damn it, Frank, you know what I mean. And furthermore, you know what's at stake."

Weir held his hand up as a sign of peace. "I know, I know. I've thought about the whole ugly mess, and came to the same conclusion. After years of talking conventional deterrence, we finally are going to find out if it really works. And what if it doesn't? What if the Russians can't be stopped with conventional ground, sea and air power alone?"

Neither man answered that. Both simply sat back and sipped their drinks. They already knew the answer to Weir's question.

The Arabian Sea
0955 Hours, 25 June (0555 Hours, 25 June, GMT)

Patience, planning and a good measure of luck were about to reward Captain Gudkov and the crew of the *Iskra* again. Late the previous evening their sensors had detected the sounds of numerous ships traveling at a little under twenty knots. Gudkov, going on the assumption that these noises were coming from a convoy headed for the Persian Gulf, plotted an intercept course that would place him near the front of the convoy. With no sign of escorting vessels in its immediate area, the *Iskra* sprinted until it was close enough to pick up strong, discrete signals and was within torpedo range. From that point, as the *Iskra* closed the distance between it and its target, Gudkov slowed the boat, reducing the noise and the turbulence it created. There was no need to go charging in, letting the convoy's escorts know that he was there.

Still relying on its passive sensors, the *Iskra* continued to track the convoy and began to ease into attack position. Now the sonar man was able to differentiate the signals and provide Gudkov with a better picture of what the *Iskra* faced. Four escorts and seventeen cargo ships of various sizes were now within range. The weapons officer on duty, who had previously been the engineer officer, was already selecting targets and computing engagement data. The former weapons officer was confined to sick bay. Immediately after the incident with the American carrier, he had become emotionally unbalanced and withdrawn. His being relieved of his assigned duties pushed him over the edge. Depression lapsed into a catatonic state. Only an occasional stream of gibberish, followed by fits of crying, reminded the crew that he was alive. To ensure that he did not create unnecessary noise, he was heavily sedated as the *Iskra* went about pursuing a war he had precipitated.

Gudkov reviewed the flow of information and monitored the actions of the weapons officer. Four cargo ships were targeted for engagement. The *Iskra* could make the shot at any time, but Gudkov waited. He studied the movements of the escorts and watched for a break when they would be the farthest from the *Iskra* or moving away. While sinking cargo ships was important, it was equally important that he save his boat so that it could sink more in the future. Gudkov knew that one serves one's country best by killing the enemy, not dying for it.

As he watched, the sonar man announced that a line of sonar buoys had been activated on the far side of the convoy. An anti-submarine-warfare helicopter was obviously working in that area. After a few minutes, the sonar man announced that two of the escorts appeared to turn away from the *Iskra* and head toward that area, where a second line of sonar buoys had been dropped and activated near the first line. Gudkov guessed that the Americans were pursuing a possible submarine on the far side. Now that the convoy was open to attack from his side, without hesitation he ordered the firing of four torpedoes. When all were away, the *Iskra* made a sharp turn, dove for deeper waters and began to take evasive actions as the escorts realized the danger and turned away from the phantom submarine they had been after.

The torpedoes' sensors began to track their targets. The range and direction in which they had been launched made this easy. One after the other, they located a noise source, automatically activated their active sonar homing device and began to run for their targets at full speed. The convoy's escorts, blaring a warning, turned to find and attack the Soviet submarine and keep the incoming torpedoes from hitting their marks. But the initial surprise, the close range and the confusion handicapped their efforts to stop the torpedoes, and the speed of the attack and the skill of the submarine captain kept them from finding the attacker.

The outcome had already been decided when the *Iskra* fired its torpedoes. Only the results needed to be harvested. Two torpedoes ripped into the hull of a cargo ship built to haul material, not survive torpedoes. The detonations sent geysers of water straight up into the air high above the ship's superstructure. Below decks, the force of the explosion smashed in the side of the ship and buckled bulkheads. Crewmen who had been in compartments where the torpedoes hit were crushed or shredded by the explosion and by chunks of metal. As the explosion dissipated, water that had been pushed away from the hull of the ship when the torpedoes' warheads detonated rushed back toward the ship and into the gaping holes.

On the bridge, the ship's captain felt his vessel heel over away from the explosion, poise precariously on a steep angle, then swing back toward the side that had been hit. Below decks, tons of equipment and numerous armored combat vehicles ripped free of the tie-downs that held them in place. Crewmen who were off duty were tossed about their confined cabins as if thrown by a giant invisible hand. Those who were lucky were knocked unconscious or killed instantly. The others suffered numerous injuries when they were impaled upon pointed objects or slashed by sharp edges or had bones snapped or crushed as they were slammed against bulkheads, cabinets, bunks and tables. Efforts to regain their footing and get out onto the deck were frustrated by injuries, darkness, a clutter of obstacles and the failure of their ship to steady herself.

As the ship tilted again, the cargo, no longer restrained, slid across the deck and crashed against the vessel's damaged side. The sudden shift in cargo, coupled with tons of water rushing into the gaping holes, pulled the ship over onto its side. Within minutes it capsized and began to go down. Of a crew of forty-two, only three men survived the sinking of the *Cape Fear*.

Chapter 9

Go, sir, gallop, and don't forget that the world was made in six days. You can ask me for anything you like, except time.
—NAPOLEON BONAPARTE

Bandar Abbas, Iran
0340 Hours, 28 June (0010 Hours, 28 June, GMT)

In the distance a huge C-5A Galaxy transport could be heard rumbling down the runway. The whine of its engines cut through the clear night air as they strained to lift the cavernous body of the plane aloft. Like an approaching locomotive, the noise grew in intensity, increasing to an ear-splitting sharpness until the aircraft lifted clumsily into the air and turned toward the far horizon. The engines' pitch changed to a low roar that trailed off behind the aircraft like an invisible tail.

Ed Martain sat on a gray metal folding chair outside his tent and peered into the darkness in the direction of the departing C-5A, trying hard to see it. He knew it was impossible to do so; its marker lights were already cut off and would remain off until the aircraft was one hundred miles out over the Gulf. There was no need to make it easy for the Soviets and their friends who tracked the comings and goings from Bandar Abbas. Unable to sleep and restless, Martain listened to the nonstop activity out on the runway. Each time a transport lifted off, he would wonder about its pilots and crew, where they would sleep that night and whether they would see their families. While he had always wanted to be a fighter pilot and derived endless pleasure from pushing himself and his aircraft to the limit, he envied the trash haulers who flew the long-range transports from their home station at Dover Air Force Base in Delaware to Bandar Abbas and back. Despite the monotony and thanklessness of their job, they were lucky. Every thirty-six hours they would be able to walk into their homes and be greeted by wife and kids.

Martain thought about the strange lives the transport pilots led. They would walk out the front door and go in to work just like any other day. Mission briefings, preflight checks and normal prep, just as always. Lift off from a real airbase talking to real air controllers and dodging normal civilian flight patterns. The long, tedious transatlantic flight would be no different from any other flight at any other time. Only when the transport swung lazily toward the northeast over Saudi Arabia did the mission profile change. That was where the insanity began. The turn, no different from any other flight maneuver, was a signal to the transport crews that they were heading into danger. No doubt they felt the same buildup of tension that he felt before going into combat. The mind begins to focus. Images begin to sharpen. Pulse rates slowly climb as the body prepares itself for sudden action and reaction. Though the transport pilots faced only the potential of combat, it made no difference to the mind or the body. Danger is danger, and the potential of mutilation or death elicits the same response from everyone.

The lumbering transports flew along invisible air corridors that changed daily to keep the Soviets from planning raids on them. The pilots strove to maintain their aircraft within these established corridors, which not only acted as a means of controlling traffic going into and out of Bandar Abbas, but also represented the only place in the sky where the transports were safe from friendly antiaircraft fire. As they flew closer to Iran, people on ships prowling the Persian Gulf and combat air patrols flying between the air corridors had greater freedom to engage unidentified aircraft. The sky was divided up into areas other than air corridors. There were missile-free zones where any aircraft that was not positively identified by friendly forces could be engaged by heat-seeking or radar-guided missiles, missiles that could not read nation symbols on aircraft mistaken for enemy and break off the attack at the last minute. There were positive-identification zones where the pilot had to have visual ID of his target before engaging. The United States could not afford to allow its pilots the freedom to go about gunning down anything that flew and that didn't answer special electronic interrogation signals called IFF—identify, friend or foe. The skies over the Persian Gulf were still crowded with civilian air traffic despite a thirty-day-old war and the declaration that the Gulf was a war zone. There were many civilians who insisted on exercising their right to fly over international waters.

Once on the ground at Bandar Abbas, the transport pilots entered an alien world. It was a world of substandard living conditions where Americans had to make extraordinary efforts simply to maintain life. The seemingly utter chaos, destruction and clutter were in sharp contrast to the neat, clean airfields at home, with their grass-bordered runways, well-painted buildings and efficient organization. Here air raids left craters and scars, and hasty offloading operations resulted in mountains of discarded packing and blocking materials along the runways. The shuffling of aircraft, Army and Air Force, combat and transport, added to the confusion. Without exception, the transport pilots dreaded most the wait on the ground. After a long flight, they were thrust into a dangerous and confused environment over which they had no control. They eagerly sought to make their stay in Iran as short as possible. Through careful control, well-planned and -executed defense of the air corridors, and the extreme range that Soviet pilots had to travel to get at them, losses to the transports had been "minimal and acceptable." This, however, was a concept that was incomprehensible to a four-year-old child who was told that her daddy wouldn't be coming home anymore.

For a moment Martain was overcome by a desire to go home. In that instant nothing mattered to him more than to see his wife and daughter. He wished there were some way he could go back with one of the transports for a day, a half day, an hour. All he wanted to do was hold his wife in his arms, feel her arms around his neck, run his hands down her sides and embrace her. Martain dreamed of looking into the round smiling eyes of his young daughter as he lifted her. The smell of baby shampoo in her hair and the ceaseless sweet babble of her stories without beginnings or ends evoked tears as the soft images passed through his mind.

Martain stood and began to walk in an effort to compose himself. He would not be going home today. Nor tomorrow or the next day. Instead he would fly two or three missions, the same as he had done yesterday and the day before. He would continue to fly until the conflict had been resolved or he could no longer fly. Already the squadron had lost three of its aircraft and two crews. One crew had died with its plane as it disintegrated after being hit by a Soviet air-to-air missile. The crew of a second aircraft had ejected safely but had landed in the no-man's-land between the advancing Soviet and U.S. forces four days prior. Attempts to recover the crew had been unsuccessful. If the Iranians didn't take them the desert would.

Omaha Flight had, to date, been successful in surviving and in carrying the war to the Russians. Martain had accounted for three confirmed kills, and his wingman had one to his credit. Martain's first kill had been so simple that he had difficulty accepting the fact that he had actually shot down another fighter. All he had done was listen to the AWACS as it vectored him into a position where his wizzo picked up the target. When the wizzo had a good track on the target and the target did not respond to the IFF interrogation, Martain fired from a range of fifteen miles. The blip that had represented a multimillion-ruble jet fighter simply disappeared from his plane's radarscope and that of the AWACS. His second combat, a real knife fight during which he used his guns, was more like what Martain had expected. High-speed maneuvers with turns that pressed his body into his seat as the invisible vise known as Gs tore at his frame were countered and followed by the Soviet fighter he pursued. One minute Martain was the hunter, the next the hunted as the two opponents hurled themselves at each other. He had enjoyed that victory. He had worked for it and could see the shattered remains of the MIG plummet toward earth in a ball of fire.

His thoughts were interrupted by the sound of a sergeant running from tent to tent waking the squadron's air crews. Martain looked at his watch. It was still too early for normal operations. Something was up. He was about to turn when the sound of a C-5A transport rumbling down the runway caught his attention. Another transport was headed home, without him.

Over the Persian Gulf
0405, 28 June (0035 Hours, 28 June, GMT)

The buildup of Soviet air activity had been slow and near normal that morning. Transports on routine flights deep behind the lead elements of the advancing Soviet forces lumbered to and fro.

Activity over Iraq started to build earlier than normal and began to appear as if it had a purpose for a change. Soviet recon flights, sent aloft to get a picture of the situation at first light, lifted off airfields around Tehran and were detected by the AWACS' radar and tracked by its computers. Operators at their stations watched and reported but were not concerned. Another day of war was beginning.

With a suddenness that bewildered the operations officer aboard the AWACS, the entire situation changed. The clear screens of the operators degenerated into a cluster of static and sparkling clutter. Powerful electronic jamming from what had been thought to be transports en route to forward bases began to blanket the AWACS' radar frequencies. A war waged by computers and electronic devices began as the AWACS' computer flipped its radar frequencies in milliseconds in order to escape jamming, and the Soviet electronic-warfare aircraft beamed barrage after barrage of static toward the AWACS in an effort to degrade or jam its radar. For brief seconds the operators were able to see clearly before the Soviet radar and computers found the AWACS' new radar frequency and jammed it.

From the brief glimpses, the operations officer began to put together a picture of what was happening. The aircraft that had been loitering over Iraq had turned and were now making high-speed runs toward the Gulf. The aircraft that had been mistaken for recon flights were likewise headed for the Gulf. The computer, working with these brief glimpses, began to piece together an attack profile. The straight flight patterns being followed by the Soviet aircraft and their speed left the operations officer no doubt as to what was happening. The Soviets were making for Bandar Abbas, for the air corridors that transited the Gulf and, worse, for the AWACS.

Orders immediately went down to the air wings in Iran, Oman and Saudi Arabia to scramble all fighters and intercept the incoming bandits. The F-15s in Iran were directed to cover their base, those in Saudi Arabia were dispatched to cover the air corridors, and the Oman-based fighters were called to wrap themselves around the AWACS. In addition to the scrambling of the fighters, incoming transports were waved off to alternate landing sites out of range of the Soviet threat. The AWACS began to leave their oval tracks and fly south, attempting to put as much distance as possible between themselves and the incoming attack. Given time, the Soviets would catch up with the AWACS if the American fighters didn't make it. Every second, however, helped in combat.

In the flurry of activity and orders, the controllers, now personally involved in the life-and-death struggle in the sky for the first time, did not see the real threat of the day wind its way slowly and insidiously toward the American front. Like snakes slithering through tall grass, hundreds of transport helicopters from the north began to converge on several points along the perimeter held by the men of the 12th Division and the 17th Airborne.

Aboard an MI-8 Helicopter North of Kerman
0415, 28 June (0045 Hours, 28 June, GMT)

The move from Tabriz to bases south of Tehran had been greeted with mixed feelings by the men of the Soviet 285th Airborne Regiment. Some of the men had become quite comfortable with their garrison duties and were in no hurry to put themselves again in danger of mutilation or death. Others had found their duties either boring or distasteful and sought combat as an acceptable form of escape.

Junior Lieutenant Ilvanich was one of those who sought escape. His duties as an executioner had been a source of pain and conflict to the young lieutenant. Hiding behind the excuse of duty did nothing to wipe away the images of dead civilians falling before the rifles of his men with a regularity that was maddening. Each day he promised himself that he would leave what he did during the day in the confines of the courtyard where the executions took place. Each night, however, he failed as the images of the dead crept into the small room where he struggled to sleep. Only the intervention of the KGB major who had given him the task in the first place saved Ilvanich from total insanity.

The KGB major took a liking to the young lieutenant and his men, and, content that Ilvanich was deserving, he arranged for better billeting and rations for them as a reward. Ilvanich, though at first reluctant, accepted the improved conditions. A few days later, the major began to use Ilvanich for special missions, including courier and liaison duties. For this Ilvanich was given a vehicle that, the major casually mentioned, could be used by Ilvanich when he wasn't needed for official duties. The young lieutenant, taught from an early age to distrust the KGB, made sure to do only what was required and not abuse his freedom or status. This behavior, noted by the major, in turn resulted in greater trust and new duties, including the guarding of the KGB headquarters in Tabriz by Ilvanich's men. Though boring, it was preferable to being executioners.

The greatest surprise came when Ilvanich was made a Hero of the Soviet Union for his role in stopping a breakthrough at the airfield in Tabriz during the opening days of the war. Though he was pleased to receive the honor, realization that the KGB major had probably been instrumental in securing the award for him frightened Ilvanich. Slowly he was being drawn into the KGB major's power. The major had adopted the young lieutenant and seemed to be preparing him for other duties that the State required. It was therefore a blessing when orders came down to report back to the regiment and prepare for future operations.

The regiment had changed. In his old battalion there were new officers and men. Ilvanich was surprised to find that a captain from the division staff, rather than the old deputy company commander, had been put in command. From the beginning Ilvanich and Lvov did not get along. The captain had not made the jump into Tabriz and had no combat experience. He knew how to give a good political indoctrination to the company, but that failed to impress those of the unit who had survived the jump. Ilvanich, on the other hand, was looked up to by all the officers and men. First, he was a veteran, a recognized leader and a decorated hero. Second, he had been able to take care of his men by securing special privileges and rations for them. Finally, the men could trust him and talk to him. They felt comfortable in his presence and he in theirs.

Captain Lvov sought to humble the young junior lieutenant in an effort to solidify his position as the commander, but failed when Ilvanich responded with cold but proper military courtesy. As the unit trained and prepared for the upcoming mission, the junior lieutenant always had his men ready before anyone else and without fail was always one or two steps ahead of the captain in anticipating requirements or reading the tactical situation. Rather than use his lieutenant's ability to his advantage, the captain only redoubled his efforts to break him. Public ridicule and dressing-downs for trivial matters became a routine for Ilvanich. This treatment, however, never seemed to bother him. Lvov's

efforts to evoke a hostile response with abuse were always returned by a cold, hard stare from Ilvanich's steel-blue eyes and
expressionless face. There was nothing the captain could do to
penetrate the hard shell that the junior lieutenant had created
and withdrawn into out of necessity.

The interior of the M-8 helicopter was black as a coal mine.
Yet Ilvanich could feel the captain's eyes on him. The feeling was
more than mere paranoia. When the company began to assemble
and prepare for the mission, the captain always seemed to be
behind Ilvanich, watching him. Ilvanich's men had noticed the
captain's behavior and casually asked whether there was something the young lieutenant needed. Each time one of his squad
leaders asked him that question, the lieutenant merely answered
that he would not require any assistance in doing what was necessary. Ilvanich clutched his assault rifle and pondered what
would really be necessary.

The announcement by the pilot that they were fifteen minutes
out tore Ilvanich's thoughts away from his dilemma and
switched them to the impending operation. Two battalions of the
285th Airborne Regiment were going in to seize the airfield at
Kerman by air assault. Defending the airfield was a battalion of
Americans from the elite 12th Light Infantry Division. This
would be the first confrontation between Soviet and American
ground forces. The men new to the regiment were uneasy, not
knowing what would happen and unsure how they would act.
The veterans, almost to a man, slept. Only Ilvanich, clutching
his rifle, was awake, peering into the darkness in the direction of
his captain.

Over the Persian Gulf
0422 Hours, 28 June (0052 Hours, 28 June, GMT)

Like a thunderclap, the realization of what the Soviets were up
to hit the operations officer of the AWACS. As an Air Force
officer, he had looked at the situation from a purely Air Force
view. The incoming raids, oriented on obvious targets of concern
to the Air Force, had evoked the reaction the operations officer
had been trained to execute and the Soviets had hoped for. At the
time when the massive Soviet air assault forces were still air-

borne and thus the most vulnerable, U.S. aircraft that could have smashed the assault had been placed in a defensive posture well to the south.

With precious little time, the operations officer had to completely reorient his attention. While the situation over the Gulf continued to build and demanded attention, forces had to be shifted to the north against the air assault. A quick analysis of the enemy situation and the location and status of friendly forces resulted in few good choices. The Air Force could defeat the threat to U.S. forces in and along the Gulf or its aircraft could charge north and strike at the Soviet air mobile forces. To attempt both would run the risk of failing in both areas.

As the operations officer discussed the situation with the small staff of the AWACS, he watched the situation screen and half listened to the reports coming in. The wing from Bandar Abbas, the one nearest and best capable of influencing the situation to the north, was beginning to engage the incoming Soviets near its base. In another minute, it would be fully involved in combat and unavailable for commitment to the north. The next group available were the fighters scrambling from Oman, which were tagged to protect the AWACS. Options narrowed rapidly. One, send the F-15s from Bandar Abbas north, leave that base open, and accept, at best, severe damage to the airfield and the port facilities. Two, send the fighters coming from Oman north and jeopardize the AWACS. Third, have the fighters from Oman cover Bandar Abbas and have the F-15s go north. Fourth, do nothing about the north and leave all fighters to perform their assigned missions.

The seconds passed and the window of opportunity to influence the situation slipped as the opposing aircraft joined battle. Already new radar tracks representing air-to-air missiles could be seen on the screen. The Soviets had achieved surprise. Realization of the error in assessing the situation came too late for effective reaction. By saying nothing, the operations officer could let all orders stand. It would be so easy not to make a decision. But no decision was a decision, a decision that would have terrible results for the Army.

Despite the fact that the radar tracks representing the first wave of Soviet helicopters were descending on their targets, the operations officer decided on a compromise. He ordered a squadron from the F-15 wing at Bandar Abbas north to Kerman. There was little probability that they would make it there in time to influence the situation. The effort, however, had to be made.

At 42,000 Feet, North of Bandar Abbas, Iran
0423 Hours, 28 June (0053 Hours, 28 June, GMT)

Martain could not believe that they had just received the order to break contact and head north. Most of the aircraft had already engaged or were about to enter combat. Omaha Flight was on the verge of bouncing a flight of four MIGs when the order to recall came. From the backseat Martain's wizzo exclaimed, "Shit! Another thirty seconds—that's all we need."

Martain looked at his displays. He had complete situation awareness. All was in order. Everything was set for their attacks. He and his wingman could each get a single short-range missile shot, kick in their after burners for a second, clear the remaining MIGs before they could react, and be on their way north. There was no sense in pissing away a perfectly good setup. Without further thought, he hit his radio transmit button. "Omaha Two, this is Omaha One. I got my fangs out. Follow me."

He had no sooner finished his transmission than the squadron commander came back and ordered Martain to break off his attack. Martain's mind, however, blocked him out. All Martain's thoughts were focused on making the kill. He watched his displays and listened for the radar tone. For the next fifteen seconds his eyes were glued to the heads-up display to his front. Ever so carefully he guided his F-15 through an easy turn as he aligned the blip representing the MIG with a small box in the center of his display that represented the proper angle for a missile attack. As soon as the blip and the box were aligned, he got a steady tone. Launching a missile, he yelled to his wizzo to hang on, threw the F-15 into a violent turn and kicked in his after burners.

Only when they had passed the speed of sound did he acknowledge the squadron commander's order. A rebuke from the commander was followed by confirmation from an AWACS controller hundreds of miles away that Omaha 01's missile shot was a kill. Fuck the Old Man—even he can't argue with a kill, Martain said to himself.

Rafsanjan, Iran
0425 Hours, 28 June (0055 Hours, 28 June, GMT)

The men of 1st Platoon, recently stirred from their sleep, slowly made their way into their fighting positions from a wadi to their rear where they had bivouacked. Duncan, watching them, could hear the lieutenant yelling to the men to pick up the pace and get into position. While some of the platoon sergeants didn't mind having a second lieutenant who tried to do everything himself and therefore left little for them to do, it pissed Duncan. He hadn't worked to become a senior NCO and platoon sergeant just to have a lieutenant fresh out of Fort Benning come into his unit and try to run the whole outfit single-handed. Duncan was a proud man. He took pride in his abilities as a soldier and an NCO. He loved his work and the training. It therefore bothered him when his young platoon leader didn't let him do what he was supposed to.

Two quick explosions, a small one followed rapidly by a bigger one, to the front of the platoon's positions, startled Duncan. Instinctively he dropped to the bottom of his position, shifted himself from the rear to the front wall and listened. Immediately a machine gun from the platoon's positions began to fire. Duncan slowly raised his head over the lip of the fighting position and surveyed the scene. In the darkness he could see nothing to his front except the tracers from the machine gun. At the top of his lungs he repeatedly yelled, "Cease fire!" until the machine gun stopped. When silence returned, he listened. Nothing. Nothing could be heard or seen to the front.

Slowly, men who had been in the open when the explosions went off crawled or moved in a crouch to their positions. Duncan didn't bother to turn around when the lieutenant tumbled into his fighting position. The lieutenant sat on the floor of the hole with his back against the wall facing Duncan. Out of breath and excited, he blurted, "What the hell was that? Mortars?"

Duncan continued to peer into the darkness, searching for an answer, while he replied, "A mine. A grenade and a mine. Someone was out there fucking around and tripped a booby-trapped mine."

"Maybe an animal tripped a mine."

Still watching to the front, Duncan calmly replied, "If an animal had tripped a mine, the mine would have gone off first, not the grenade. Someone was out there fucking with our mines and got lucky."

"Iranians?"

"Maybe. Maybe Russians. Didn't the Old Man tell us we could expect their recon elements anytime?"

The lieutenant, now composed, got up and made his way to the front wall, next to Duncan, before replying. "Why would the Soviets bother messing around with our mines?"

"Maybe they wanted to clear a lane. Maybe they wanted to lift the mines and put them to our rear. Shit, Lieutenant, you tell me."

The lieutenant didn't reply. Slowly he lifted his head over the lip of the fighting position and began to search for any telltale sign that would answer his question. As much as he wanted to know why, the young officer was not sure he would like the answer.

North of Rafsanjan, Iran
0425 Hours, 28 June (0055 Hours, 28 June, GMT)

A flash cut through the darkness and caught the attention of the young Soviet recon-platoon leader. Immediately he put his night-vision device up to his eye. He watched as machine-gun tracers stabbed out into the darkness, and made a mental note of where they came from. Twelve seconds later he heard the two explosions, followed by the report from the machine gun. Then nothing. He scanned the area for other signs of activity or firing, but could not detect any. Slowly he lowered the night-vision device, then pounded his fist on the top of his armored car and cursed. His men had failed. Instead of clearing a path through the mine field and marking it for the dawn attack by the 381st Motorized Rifle Regiment, they had killed themselves and alerted the Americans.

The lieutenant considered his options for a moment. There wasn't enough time to send another team forward. Even if there had been, the Americans were alerted. He hoped his other patrols would be able to make it back without incident. He looked at his watch. In another thirty-five minutes he had to make his final report. The thought of reporting that his men had been detected made the lieutenant ill. At least he had been able to locate all of the Americans' forward outposts and their main positions. If the remaining patrols came in with the command-post and artillery locations, perhaps he could be forgiven for not clearing the lane. That thought passed quickly, however. His commander was the type that was never satisfied with partial results. There would be hell to pay for that mistake.

The Airfield at Kerman, Iran
0430 Hours, 28 June (0100 Hours, 28 June, GMT)

The sudden flash of explosions just ahead of the helicopters alerted the paratroopers that they were about to go into battle again. Lieutenant Ilvanich could feel his heart pounding in his chest. The palms of his hands were sweating as he continued to grip his AK assault rifle. One minute to go, two at the most. Flashes of light from the explosions lit the interior of the helicopter for brief seconds. Ilvanich could see others in the cabin shuffle and squirm. The new men leaned forward, glanced to their left and right and tried hard to see what was going on. The veterans merely sat back in their seats, their faces fixed in an expressionless stare to their front. They knew what was going on and what was about to happen.

Ilvanich watched for the landing. Tracers were dashing wildly between the approaching helicopters. The Americans were alert and returning fire. The pilot was bringing the helicopter in fast and would no doubt hit hard. Instinctively, Ilvanich yelled, "Get ready!" When the aircraft was a couple of meters from the ground, he unsnapped his seat belt and swung himself in front of the open door.

A sudden jolt left no doubt that they were on the ground. With the battle cry of "Follow me!" Ilvanich leaped from the helicopter and charged into the darkness without looking back. He dashed for ten meters, then dropped to the ground. To his left and right other men from the helicopter dropped, too. Automatically they began to search the area immediately to their front for threats and targets. While they waited for the helicopters to finish disgorging their passengers, Ilvanich attempted to get his bearings. To his front at a distance of two hundred meters there were several American helicopters burning. The light from those fires was more than enough to allow him to make out the hangars and maintenance shops on the far side of the runway. The mission of his company was to clear those hangars and establish defensive positions three hundred meters beyond, facing away from the airfield.

Just after the last of the empty Soviet helicopters from the first wave had lifted off, several of them exploded, lighting up the sky and showering the paratroopers below with fragments. Ilvanich, who was in the process of getting up, dropped again and covered his head as the fragments pelted him on the back.

Over the Airfield at Kerman, Iran
0436 Hours, 28 June (0106 Hours, 28 June, GMT)

Neither Martain nor his wizzo had ever seen anything like it before. Dozens of targets suddenly popped up on his screen at the same instant. Omaha Flight, flying low and fast, suddenly found itself saturated with them. While most of the squadron had gone in high to deal with Soviet air cover, two flights of two ships each had gone in low, looking for the helicopters. Martin had no doubt they had found them. "Omaha Two, this is One. Check six, then follow me. There's more than enough for both."

"Roger that, Omaha One. Nothing behind or above. I'm coming through."

There was no problem lining up on the slow-moving targets. Once Martain had the first blip aligned in his sight, he let fly a missile and turned to line up the next shot. His wingman did likewise, with terrible and swift results. The wizzo watched his screen in fascination as helicopters scattered in a mad rush to escape them. It was like shooting fish in a barrel.

On the Ground at Kerman, Iran
0438 Hours, 28 June (0108 Hours, 28 June, GMT)

The roar of the jet engines just above their heads was deafening. The thought that American fighters had made it through the protective fighter screen was a shock to Ilvanich. For a moment he watched the burning crumpled wreckage that was the helicopter he had just exited. Without effective air cover, there would be no follow-on waves. The men in the first wave were on their own.

Ilvanich turned his attention back toward his objective. He could hear the volume of American small-arms fire increase. The enemy was now bringing mortars to bear on them. The effect of the assault's initial surprise was being lost. Ilvanich knew they couldn't stay there. Their only chance was to go forward with force and violence. He glanced to his left and right. "Where's Captain Lvov?" No one answered.

Ilvanich raised himself on one elbow and turned to search to his rear. "Captain Lvov?" There was no response.

He had to be dead. Why else had he not answered or taken charge? No loss, Ilvanich thought. His only regret was that he hadn't had the pleasure of doing it himself.

Without further thoughts on the subject, Ilvanich got to his feet and faced the company. "Men of the 3rd Company. Our objective is to clear those hangars over there and set up positions beyond them. Follow me. For the Motherland. Attack!"

As in the helicopter, the young lieutenant turned and went forward without bothering to look behind to see whether his men would follow. He knew they would. Rushing forward in a half-crouch, Junior Lieutenant Nikolai Ilvanich, Hero of the Soviet Union, charged into the inferno of burning helicopters and buildings and exploding mortar shells. Like a great white shark on the prowl, he turned his head from side to side as he went, his eyes going from point to point searching for targets. When something moved, without slowing he fired from the hip until it stopped moving. There was no more thinking required. No need for fancy maneuvers. Just attack, attack, attack.

Chapter 10

War is at best barbarism. . . . Its glory is all moonshine. It is only those who have neither fired a shot nor heard the shrieks and groans of the wounded who cry aloud for blood, more vengeance, more desolation. War is hell.

—WILLIAM TECUMSEH SHERMAN

Ras Banas, Egypt
0510 Hours, 28 June (0310 Hours, 28 June, GMT)

The morning sun greeted the men of the 3–4th Armor and warmed them as they lay in clusters not far from the flight line, the aircraft parking and servicing area. Most slept soundly in spite of the noise of the planes coming and going on the flight line. This was the first time in over thirty-six hours that they had had an opportunity to sleep horizontally. Since Fort Hood, it had been one plane after another. Marshal at the airfield, manifest, board the plane, fly to another airport, get off the plane, marshal somewhere else, manifest for the next flight, board the next plane, on and on. The misery of their odyssey was to have ended that day. They had deplaned at Ras Banas in order to transfer from the commercial 747 to military transports for the last leg of the trip. With the Russians fast approaching Bandar Abbas, it had been judged too risky to send commercial charters straight into Iran. The transfer, however, did not take place immediately, despite the fact that there were a number of Air Force transports sitting on the ground. Rumor had it that there was a big air raid going on.

Whatever the reason, their misery continued. Upon arrival at Ras Banas, the men had been directed to an area just off the airfield tarmac. Their duffle bags, which contained their sleeping bags, were left on the aircraft. The only things the men had were their individual weapons and ALICE packs, rucksacks that held the bare-bones necessities such as a change of underwear, shaving kit, a sweater and clean socks. Rallying by company in small clusters, the men settled down in the sand as best they could, using the ALICE pack as a pillow. They soon found that there were no toilets. Those unlucky enough to be in the center of the mass of soldiers had to wander through the knots of sleeping men out into the desert before relieving themselves. These arrangements, however primitive, were still preferable to staying on the overcrowded transports.

Major Dixon found it hard to sleep once the sun had risen. As he sat up, his body was racked by spasms of pain. He felt as if he had been beaten up. His eyes were puffed out, his mouth and throat dry, his nasal passages clogged with dirt. While he sat sipping water from his canteen, he considered whether he should save his water for drinking or use some of it for cleaning up. His mind, like his body, was in terrible shape. Jumping time zones, being crammed into the confines of an airplane for hours on end with little to do, facing one delay or diversion after another, had reduced Dixon's brain to mush. Slowly he considered the pros and cons of washing up. Since the troops had been issued their kevlar helmets with fixed webbing, he could no longer use his helmet as a washbasin. That meant he had to use his canteen cup, which was, to say the least, a pain in the ass. Making small decisions was hard. "What the hell," he mumbled to himself as he began to dig through his ALICE pack for his shaving kit. "At least I can look decent."

By the time he was finished, Master Sergeant Nesbitt came up to him carrying two cups of coffee. "And a good morning to you, Major. Welcome to Egypt."

Dixon reached out and took the cup Nesbitt offered him. "I trust you came across this legally."

"Sir, would I ever do anything wrong or illegal, like? I mean, what do I look like, a supply sergeant or something?"

As Dixon sipped the coffee, still hot enough to steam his glasses, he thanked the Lord for being blessed with a man of Nesbitt's talents. It seemed the more senior an officer became, the more helpless he was. That was why it was handy to have a talented sergeant around to deal with the mundane tasks such as keeping the unit running and taking care of the officers. "Sergeant Nesbitt, there wouldn't happen to be any food nearby that's worth the walk?"

"The Air Force people I got this from said the mess line will be open over by those hangars in about thirty minutes. They're going to be serving hot A's. Real food, not that T-ration shit."

"What's the matter, Sergeant Nesbitt, creamed beef over chunks of potatoes not to your liking? Why, didn't you know that tests have proven that the T rations have revolutionized tactical feeding?"

Nesbitt got a disgusted look on his face, turned and spat. "Tests my ass, sir. When I was growing up my mom threw away leftovers that looked better than the stuff they expect us to survive on. Let the bastard who invented that shit try living on it for a couple of weeks."

Nesbitt was old Army, a tanker for over twenty years. He missed the old days and many of the old ways. Vietnam, VOLAR and other "reforms" had changed the Army. Each year after his twentieth year he had told his wife that he was fed up with the Army and was turning in his retirement papers. And each time he went to do it, someone always talked him out of it. Dixon had been the last in a long line of officers to do so. The only reason Nesbitt had stayed the last time was because of Dixon. He had served with him in Germany. They got along well and were friends. Besides, Nesbitt liked tanking and the battalion.

"Hey, Major, have you heard about our young scout-platoon leader this morning?"

Dixon stopped what he was doing and looked at Nesbitt. "What's Capell gotten into now?"

With a twinkle in his eye, Sergeant Nesbitt replied, "Lieutenant Matthews."

Amanda Matthews lay next to Randy Capell and watched him sleep. Although it was already becoming hot in the small tent where they had spent the last few hours, she didn't mind. The more she got to know Capell, the more she was overcome by his charm and his strange ideas of romance. Not in her wildest dreams had she imagined that he would be waiting for her when the transport with the brigade staff on board landed in Ras Banas. Even more amazing were the arrangements Capell had made. They included an Air Force hummer, a tent with an ad-hoc double bed in an area that had been abandoned by the 17th Airborne Division, a meal of cold cuts and fresh bread, and even water to wash up in. When she protested that it wouldn't be smart to leave the group, because the unit might depart on a moment's notice, Capell had reassured her that he had it from reliable sources that no one would be leaving before noon that day. Besides, he continued, his platoon sergeant knew where he would be and would get them if either one of their transports was alerted for movement.

Matthews rolled over on her side until the length of her body was against Capell's. Propping her head on one hand, she ran her free hand across his chest. Matthews felt guilty for a moment. Here she was, enjoying herself, sleeping with Randy, while the rest of the brigade staff had only the desert for a bed and the sky for a roof. No doubt she would get an ass-chewing, at the least, for wandering off from the rest of the staff. But it would be worth it. Besides, with the brigade going into Iran, a minor indiscretion such as this might just be overlooked.

Capell began to stir, and Matthews slowly ran her hand across his stomach. As she began to fondle him, she leaned over and softly nibbled on his ear. The reaction was predictable and immediate. Capell smiled as he opened his eyes. He turned and kissed her before he spoke. "Well, trying to sneak up on me when my guard is down, I see."

Matthews smiled back. They kissed again. "From the looks of it, Lieutenant, that's the only thing that you let down."

With speed that startled her, Capell bounded over on top of her, pinned her shoulders down and stared into her eyes, all signs of a smile gone. While she lay there, wide-eyed and unable to move, Capell bellowed in a deep and threatening voice, "It seems I'm going to have to teach you what the price of attacking a defenseless man is." With that as a prelude, they began another long, passionate session of love.

The Airfield at Kerman, Iran
1000 Hours, 28 June (0630 Hours, 28 June, GMT)

The sergeant had a devil of a time rousing Junior Lieutenant Ilvanich, who lay in the shallow foxhole with his back against a side wall, his AK assault rifle cradled in his arms. Ilvanich opened his eyes slightly and looked about him. He was totally disoriented and not quite conscious. When the sergeant was sure the lieutenant's mind was in the receive mode, he told Ilvanich that the captain was looking for him and wanted him to report immediately.

For a moment, Ilvanich was puzzled. Slurring his words, he asked haltingly, "What captain?"

The sergeant, confused for a moment, replied, "Captain Lvov, of course." Then he added, "The company commander."

Ilvanich stared at the sergeant for a second, then sat upright. "Lvov? Where in hell did he come from? Where is he?"

The sergeant pointed to their rear. "Over there, near the hangars. Come, I will take you to him."

Ilvanich slowly stood up. Standing in the shallow hole, he stretched himself, slung his AK over his shoulder and pulled his canteen out. After taking a sip of water, he turned and surveyed the area around him. The desolate landscape he viewed bore no resemblance to the wild and chaotic scenes he had lived through just hours before. To either side there stretched a line of shallow foxholes like the one he was in. They belonged to the remnants of the company. Dotting the landscape all about them were the bodies of his dead and wounded and those of the enemy. Medical teams were going about picking up the wounded and marking the dead. Smoke still lingered at scattered points about the airfield. Helicopters were coming and going at a seemingly lazy pace. In the distance other units could be seen moving about, forming up or going about their assigned tasks.

"What is the final count this morning, Sergeant?"

"One platoon leader, besides you, and thirty-eight men." Then, as an afterthought, the sergeant added, "And Captain Lvov."

Forty-one out of seventy-eight. Not bad. Better than Ilvanich had expected. The battle had been short but extremely violent. Once the Americans had gotten over their initial shock, they had fought like tigers. The final stages of the fight had been hand to hand. In the predawn twilight men grappled with each other using knives and fists as the battle swayed in the balance. Only the sudden appearance of the regiment's follow-on forces finally decided the issue. Even then the American infantry had refused to yield, withdrawing into the desert rather than surrender. Only American ground crews and support personnel had been captured.

The sergeant, watching his lieutenant, tactfully reminded him that Captain Lvov was waiting. Ilvanich thought as he returned his canteen to its case, Fuck Lvov. We fight all morning and lose half the company before he shows up. His story, no doubt, will be fascinating. Then, to his sergeant, "Lead on, Sergeant, I am anxious to report to our commanding officer." The cutting sarcasm was not lost on the sergeant, who smirked and replied, "Yes, Comrade Lieutenant, we must not keep our commanding officer waiting."

Lvov was talking to the battalion's first officer when Ilvanich entered the hangar. The captain acknowledged the lieutenant's presence with a nod, but continued his conversation. Ilvanich stopped several meters away and waited. As he stood there, arms loosely folded across his chest, his AK dangling from his shoulder and his eyes riveted on his captain, Ilvanich fought back his anger. The bastard, he thought. He loses contact with his company all night, he has not been seen by anyone since the battle began, and he has no idea what the company's positions look like. Instead of running out to the line, he stands there like a pompous ass, talking to the battalion staff and summoning me like a schoolboy. As Ilvanich thought about Lvov and what had happened that morning, his hand slowly dropped to his AK. If I were half sane, I would kill the bastard right now, he told himself.

Finished with his chat, Lvov slowly walked over to him. Ilvanich, fighting back his urge to choke the captain, came to attention and rendered a smart, regulation salute.

"Junior Lieutenant Ilvanich reporting as ordered, Comrade Captain."

The captain was pleased. "What is your report, Junior Lieutenant?" Lvov had accentuated the "Junior."

"Third Company has accomplished all assigned tasks. We cleared the hangars, pushed out from the airfield a distance of three hundred meters and established our portion of the defensive perimeter as ordered. Current strength is two officers and thirty-eight men. Ammunition resupply has been effected. Total losses for the action to date are twelve dead and twenty-one wounded. Senior Lieutenant Anatov is among the wounded."

The two men looked at each other while Lvov thought about Ilvanich's report. The captain had clearly winced when Ilvanich stressed the "*we*." After a moment, Lvov replied, "Thank you for your report, Lieutenant. It is unfortunate that Lieutenant Anatov is wounded. Until he recovers, you will assume his duties as the deputy company commander."

Lvov waited for a response from Ilvanich, but did not get one. Awkwardly, he continued. "I became separated from the company last night when the American jets came in. I went forward as soon as the helicopters lifted off. Unfortunately, the men did not follow, because of the jets and the air battle."

Ilvanich thought, You lying bastard. This company always follows. How convenient that the Americans provide a nice cover story.

Lvov, talking more to himself, went on. "When I found there was no one behind me, I went back to the landing site, but the company was gone. Unable to find them, I attached myself to the regimental staff. I am glad to see that things were able to work themselves out."

For the first time Ilvanich thought of his commander as a coward. That anyone would believe his story was incredible. The two men stood and stared at each other for several seconds. Only the intervention of the battalion commander interrupted their private thoughts.

"Comrade Captain, the regimental commander wishes to see Lieutenant Ilvanich at regimental headquarters immediately."

Ilvanich turned to his battalion commander and asked why he had been summoned. His colonel replied that he did not know but that Ilvanich, Lvov and he had best go over and find out.

The three officers were greeted at the entrance of the airfield's administration building by a regimental staff officer, who escorted them to a conference room. Upon entering, Ilvanich froze. The entire regimental staff was assembled in the room, standing against the side walls. At the front of the room were the division commander and the regimental commander. Between them were the regimental colors, guarded by two stern-faced paratroopers.

The regimental commander, standing at attention, called out, "Junior Lieutenant Nikolai Ilvanich, come forward."

As he made his way past the unsmiling faces of the staff officers, he suddenly became painfully aware of his disheveled appearance and of the AK loosely slung over his shoulder and banging against his side. Once he was at the front of the room, the regimental commander guided Ilvanich to a position between him and the division commander. Behind Ilvanich were his regimental colors.

With a nod, the regimental commander signaled the regimental adjutant to begin.

"In recognition of his heroism and leadership during the capture of the airfield at Kerman, Junior Lieutenant Nikolai Ilvanich is being awarded the Order of the Red Star. Through his efforts and example, his men were able to seize the initiative, overcome numerically superior enemy forces and allow the regiment time to reinforce and capitalize on the success achieved by 3rd Company. Lieutenant Ilvanich's leadership and courage are of the highest order and deserving of the appreciation of the Soviet people and the Soviet Union."

Ilvanich was dumbfounded as the division commander pinned the medal on his tunic and congratulated him. Even more surprising was the division commander's announcement that it was high time Ilvanich was given the rank he deserved. On cue, the regimental adjutant handed two lieutenant's epaulets to the division commander, who in turn handed one to the regimental commander. The two commanders removed Ilvanich's junior lieutenant's epaulets and replaced them with the others. In the excitement of the moment, Ilvanich did not notice that there were bloodstains from the former owner on the "new" lieutenant epaulets. He was overwhelmed. Someone shoved a glass of vodka into his hand while the staff officers congratulated him and patted him on the back. The division commander, raising his glass high, offered a toast to the young hero.

For the moment, all was smiles. The 285th Airborne Regiment had again succeeded, by the narrowest of margins. It was time for a brief break from the stress of battle, the arduous task of burying its dead and preparing for the next battle. It was time for the victor to decorate its heroes and count its losses. A new battle streamer would be added to the regimental colors. New names would be inscribed in the regiment's roll of honor. The officers in the room were all smiles and good cheer. All except one man. As they drank up, Ilvanich saw his company commander across the room. He did not drink the toast. Lvov merely stood there, glaring at him. Waiting.

Rafsanjan, Iran
1935 Hours, 28 June (1605 Hours, 28 June, GMT)

The day had been long and difficult for the men of the 1st Platoon. They had been on alert all day, waiting for an attack that never came. Reports of Soviet activity just to the north of them and attacks at other points of the division's perimeter put the men on edge. Rumors that the airfield at Kerman had been overrun added to their nervousness. Sergeant First Class Duncan's platoon leader had moved up and down the platoon line almost constantly all morning, checking the men, their positions and their equipment. It wasn't until noon that Duncan was finally able to convince him that all was in order and that the best thing he could do for the platoon was to settle down and wait, like everyone else.

Duncan was almost sorry that he had succeeded in settling the lieutenant down, because the lieutenant decided to stay with him in his foxhole. Every few minutes the lieutenant would ask a question about a noise or movement to their front, make a line check on the telephone that ran to the squad leaders, or check the action on his M-16 to ensure that it was functioning. That had gone on all afternoon. Duncan could understand the lieutenant's nervousness. He was nervous himself. Still, Duncan wished his platoon leader would go away and bug someone else for a while.

North of Rafsanjan, Iran
1938 Hours, 28 June (1608 Hours, 28 June, GMT)

In little clusters the men of the 381st Motorized Rifle Regiment waited for the attack to commence. All day they had waited, sitting in the open without cover or relief from the sun that beat upon them and their armored vehicles. Their first orders had been to attack immediately once they had made contact with the Americans. That had been changed, however, when a patrol accidentally alerted the Americans to their presence. With the element of surprise gone, the decision was made to conduct a deliberate attack rather than hit the Americans from the march.

Preparation for battle began shortly after dawn. Information concerning the location of American positions gained by the regimental recon unit as well as air recon was received at the regiment's headquarters. There it was carefully reviewed by the first officer, responsible for operations, the second officer, responsible for intelligence, and the artillery officer. Based on that information, the three officers developed a plan of attack, a schedule of artillery fires and orders. The plan of attack incorporated the concepts of maneuver and shock. The motorized rifle battalions, reinforced by companies from the regimental tank battalion, provided the maneuver, while massed artillery would provide the shock.

Orders were issued to the attacking battalions and the follow-on units. Details outlining the routes they would take from their assembly areas to the line of departure, their axis of advance, lines of deployment, intermediate and final objectives for the first attack echelon and follow-on echelons of the regiment were all addressed. They could have attacked sooner in the day, but it had been decided to hit just before dark. In that way, the first-echelon battalions would be able to make the breakthrough during the daylight, while the exploitation force would be able to move forward and drive deep under the cover of darkness.

The artillery battalions supporting the regiment received their orders in the form of a schedule of fires, a detailed listing telling each battery of guns what targets it would fire on and when. Based on this schedule, the regimental and division artillery were brought forward and emplaced, along with ammunition required to fire the preparatory bombardment and other missions listed in the schedule of fires. Carefully worked-out formulas specified how many rounds were required by each caliber of weapon to achieve the target effect desired. For this attack, besides the regiment's own 122mm. self-propelled artillery battalion and the heavy mortars of the battalions, two additional 122mm. artillery battalions, a 152mm. artillery battalion and a battalion of BM-21 multiple-rocket launchers were allocated for support. These units would be grouped together under the command of the regimental artillery officer into a regimental artillery group.

A twenty-minute preparatory bombardment would commence at 1940 hours. American command posts, artillery units and key positions would be hit. The preparatory bombardment would also cover the noise of the maneuver battalions as they deployed. In accordance with the schedule of fires, the artillery would shift their fires to selected targets at 2000 hours. Some of the batteries would concentrate on the Americans' forward positions to pin or destroy the defenders. Some batteries would fire smoke rounds to cover the attacking force. Other batteries would hit targets deep in the Americans' rear. The multiple-rocket launchers were to be held back for the purposes of counterbattery fire and attacking command posts identified through radio direction-finding. As soon as the American artillery began to return fires, Soviet counterbattery radar units would be able to locate where the American rounds originated and feed that data to the multiple-rocket-launcher batteries.

In the shadows of the setting sun, the 2nd Company, 1st Battalion, 381st Motorized Rifle Regiment, waited to move forward. Captain Neboatov had received his orders early in the afternoon. Along with the battalion commander and the other company commanders, they had gone as far forward as was prudent.

For Neboatov, the plan of attack was simple. It was, in fact, nothing more than the battle drill that they had been trained in and had used so effectively to date in Iran. The battalion would leave the assembly area in a column of companies. At a predesignated point, the battalion would split up and move, with each company on its own route. At a second point, the companies in turn would split off into platoon columns. Finally, at the line of deployment, the two lead companies would deploy into a line with the tanks in the lead, followed by BMPs of the rifle companies. Neboatov's company was the second echelon for the battalion, which meant he would follow the battalion command group and be prepared to replace one of the two lead companies or punch through, if one of them succeeded, to the battalion's final objective of the day.

While the battalion was moving forward and the artillery bombardment was going in, Neboatov's company would unfold from the march column into the line of attack. Neboatov had no doubt that his men would be able to execute their maneuvers without a hitch. This would be the third breakthrough attack that the battalion had conducted since the war with Iran had begun. What concerned Neboatov was the unknown quality of the American fighting man.

Since his days as a cadet he had studied American tactics, so-

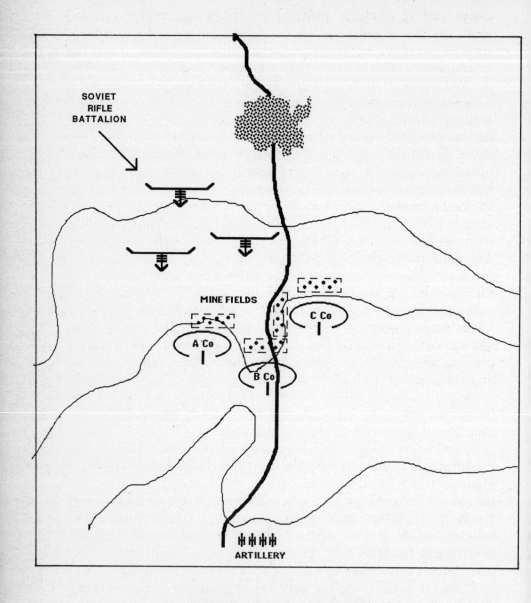

SOVIET RIFLE BATTALION

MINE FIELDS

A Co

B Co

C Co

ARTILLERY

ATTACK, 28 JUNE, ON THE
3RD BATTALION, 503RD INFANTRY

ciety, culture, politics and history. While the books provided clear, concise answers as to American tactics and equipment, some of the more informed instructors always cautioned that the Americans were a strange race of people who did not follow norms. Nor were they a predictable breed. Their history and politics were filled with contradictions and strange actions and reactions to world events. In one instance, they allowed the Iranians to hold their embassy for 444 days without doing anything. Within a few years, they turned around and launched an invasion of a tiny island country simply because the government had changed. One passage that Neboatov had read summed up the problem by stating: "One of the serious problems in planning against American doctrine is that the Americans do not read their manuals nor do they feel any obligation to follow their doctrine." The American fighting man, a product of that unpredictable society and philosophy, was an unknown that Neboatov and his men now had to meet and deal with.

For the fourth time in as many minutes, Neboatov raised his left arm and glanced at his watch: 1939 hours. Sixty seconds. The die was cast. All was set, all planned. Now all they had to do was execute the plan. How simple that seemed. How awfully bloody and simple.

Rafsanjan, Iran
1940 Hours, 28 June (1610 Hours, 28 June, GMT)

The sound of fifty-four howitzers, eighteen heavy mortars and eighteen multiple-rocket launchers firing simultaneously appeared to the 1st Platoon as a distant rumble, like a thunderstorm far away. The lieutenant, nodding off to sleep in Duncan's foxhole, opened his eyes and asked what the rumbling was. Duncan, peering out to the side of the foxhole's parapet, replied casually, "Artillery. I think they're—"

The whine of large-caliber artillery projectiles passing overhead and the impact of 120mm. mortars on the platoon's positions cut Duncan's answer short. The sudden overpressure of near-misses hit all those in his foxhole like a sledgehammer. The clear evening air was corrupted with dust, smoke and fumes. Across the front the men of 1st Platoon cowered in the depth of their foxholes, foxholes that suddenly seemed dangerously shallow. The shock of their initiation to combat was a fearful and lonely experience as each man withdrew into himself in an effort to survive or block out reality. Combat, long prepared for and discussed, was upon them.

Within seconds, the impact of individual mortar and artillery rounds was no longer distinguishable. A steady pounding and an unending chain of detonations dulled the men's senses. Dust and fumes settled down in the bottom of the foxholes where the men sought escape. Those who had presence of mind tied handkerchiefs or bandanas over their noses and mouths. Those lost to panic simply gagged and choked. Eardrums shattered and bled. Men no longer able to control themselves defecated and urinated where they sat, crouched in the corner of their foxholes. Minute after minute the pounding continued. Steady, unending, terrifying. The sobs of men broken by the experience of their initiation to battle could not be heard above the din of explosions by the men next to them.

For the lucky, death came quickly. The probability of a mortar round landing right on top of a foxhole is slim. But even when the odds are a thousand to one, there is always that one. Fire enough rounds in a small area, and probability begins to take its toll. The overhead cover that protected the men of 1st Platoon did well to stop shell fragments but was sadly insufficient when a direct hit was scored. When the shell's fuse setting was on superquick action, the round detonated as soon as it touched ground. In those cases, the force of the explosion rammed the overhead cover that was meant to protect the foxhole's occupants down on top of them, crushing or burying them. When the shell's fuse setting was on delayed action, the shell penetrated the overhead cover and detonated in the foxhole among the occupants. Death was instantaneous. All signs that the foxhole had once been occupied by humans were eradicated in a twinkling of an eye.

In this manner, 1st Platoon, B Company, 3rd of the 503rd Infantry, received its baptism of fire.

The speed of the attacking columns began to pick up as Neboatov's company moved into the open. Neboatov elected to remain standing in the hatch of his BMP, to better control his company and maintain his orientation. It was dangerous but necessary; buttoned up, he was as good as blind. To his front he could see the regiment's preparatory artillery bombardment going in. He was impressed. The entire forward slope of the far ridge was exploding. That anything could live through that seemed unlikely. But there would be survivors, survivors that he would have to deal with.

The battalion was now moving forward at a steady pace of twenty-four kilometers an hour. The lead companies remained in platoon columns, BMPs following the tanks with mine plows and rollers attached to them. Obstacles that had taken hours to emplace would be brushed aside with little effect. Neboatov held the hatch cover firmly as his BMP rolled forward and hit bump after bump. With skill born of practice, his body swayed instinctively to maintain balance while he watched the advance of his company and the progress of those in the lead. The artillery to his front stopped. Neboatov looked at his watch: 2000 hours. The initial barrage was over. Time for the guns to shift to their next targets.

The stunned silence was welcome but frightening. For a moment Duncan sat and listened. Then, with his body pressed against the front wall, he slowly began to rise to peer over the lip of the foxhole. The dust hung in the air like fog. At first he could see nothing. Slowly, in the distance, he could make out the images of the advancing Soviet armored columns, moving forward as if on parade. As he watched, Duncan was conscious of the lieutenant next to him. At first neither said a word, they only watched. Then the lieutenant moved away from the front wall and began to climb out of the foxhole. In confusion, Duncan called out, "Where're you going, Lieutenant?"

Without stopping or turning back, the lieutenant shouted, "I— I gotta get back to my position. Call for artillery."

"Get back here in the hole. You'll never make it. The bastards are only shifting fires." Duncan turned and lunged to grab the lieutenant's leg, but missed. The lieutenant climbed out of the hole and stood upright just as the first round of the next artillery barrage impacted.

The explosions hammered Duncan down to the bottom of his hole. He stayed there for a moment, then rose to see what had become of the lieutenant. The first sight that greeted him was a hand hanging over the lip of the foxhole. The fingers, forming a half-clenched fist, twitched and jerked randomly. Then Duncan saw the lieutenant, lying on his back. His right arm reached out toward Duncan and quivered. His face, turned up to the sky, also quivered in spasms. There seemed to be no wounds. Perhaps he was simply stunned. With a single boost, Duncan pulled himself out of the hole so that he could help his lieutenant.

In an instant, he knew he couldn't. The entire left side of the lieutenant's body was a bloody pulp. From his thigh to his face the lieutenant's body was shattered and covered with bright-red blood that oozed from innumerable wounds. Bone and organs lay exposed in the dirt. The sight of the half man overcame Duncan's last reserves of self-control. Involuntarily he vomited as he leaned over the remains of his lieutenant, adding his own vile fluids to the gore before him. Only the intervention of the radio operator who shared the foxhole with Duncan and who pulled him back down saved him from sharing his lieutenant's fate.

With the smokescreen in place and the battalion clear of the mine field, it was time to deploy into line and commence the final assault. The order had gone out to remain mounted throughout the assault. With few exceptions, there had been no return antitank fire to speak of. Artillery fire had been light and had missed the fast-moving columns. Every time American artillery did fire, a volley of rockets from the multiple-rocket launchers screamed overhead in return. All was in order, all going forward as planned.

It was at this point that Neboatov became nervous. All seemed to be going too well. It was much too easy, like a summer maneuver. The Americans were waiting. They were intentionally holding their fire until the battalion was in a fire sack. Nervously he glanced from side to side for telltale signs of a trap. He saw none. The lead companies continued forward, disappearing into the smoke laid by the artillery and generated by the tanks in the lead. No orders or warning came over the radio. Nothing to indicate a change in the situation or a trap. The battalion rolled forward at twenty-four kilometers per hour on a collision course with the Americans.

The second artillery barrage stopped. The rumble of the advancing Soviet vehicles could be felt before it was heard. Duncan stuck his head up over the lip of the foxhole and peered into the smoke and dust thrown up by impacting artillery. He could see nothing. But he could hear. The squeaking of tank sprockets and the rumble of their engines were joined by the higher-pitched whine of the BMPs, the chatter of machine guns, the pop and whoosh of antitank guided missiles being fired, and close-in detonations. The two companies in the forward positions were in contact with enemy forces.

Duncan reached down for the field phone and tried to ring up the platoon's squad leaders. No one answered. No doubt the wires had been severed by the artillery. He turned to the radiotelephone operator and ordered him to contact the company commander. While the operator tried in vain to raise anyone on the company-command net, Duncan raised his head again to see what was going on.

To his left he saw one of his Dragon gunners prop up his missile launcher in preparation. The sound of advancing tanks and BMPs grew louder. So did the machine-gun fire. The bursts of M-16 and SAW rifle fire were overriden by the sound of unfamiliar small-arms fire. Russian PKs and AKs, probably. Every now and then a tank main gun would fire or the sharp report of a 30mm. cannon would rip through the air. Still Duncan could see nothing.

Suddenly, it was there. Like an apparition, the T-80 tank burst forth, its main gun sweeping from side to side menacingly. It was searching for targets, Duncan's men. The blast of a Dragon firing caught Duncan's attention. He turned and saw that the Dragon gunner who was to his left had let fly his missile at a tank farther to the left. Duncan watched the flight of the missile as it raced for the tank. But it never made it. Instead, the missile looped up, hung in the air for a moment, then grounded itself in a great explosion. Duncan turned back to see what had caused that. The Dragon gunner was no longer visible. The launch tube was lying on its side, its bipod legs turned askew in the air. The gunner had been hit. He was probably at the bottom of his foxhole, wounded or dead.

The image of a great dark form in the corner of his eye caught Duncan's attention. He dropped to the bottom of his foxhole just as the track of a T-80 tank crushed the overhead cover. Broken beams, dirt and sandbags rained down on Duncan and his radio operator. The earth shook and quivered as the BMPs following bypassed Duncan's shattered position. Desperately the two men struggled to free themselves.

Once clear of the rubble, Duncan stood up and looked to his

left and right. The line of tanks and BMPs that had overrun his platoon's positions was clearly visible to their rear as they continued to roll south. To the right, the second-echelon company was passing through where the 2nd Platoon's positions were. Down in the valley before him he could see more Soviet vehicles moving toward them.

In an instant, he knew there was nothing more they could do there. Yelling to his radio operator to follow, Duncan grabbed his rifle and bounded out of the foxhole. The two men ran down the platoon's line of foxholes, stopping at each one while Duncan reached in and shouted to those men who appeared to be alive to get their gear and follow him. Some obeyed. A few didn't. Many couldn't. Those who could leaped out of their holes and followed their platoon sergeant at a dead run as they sought escape to the west, away from Rafsanjan and into the vast wasteland.

Neboatov didn't realize that they had actually overrun the American positions until his company went rumbling past smashed 105mm. artillery pieces. He was shocked. He stood upright and turned to his rear, trying to see where the defensive positions had been. He couldn't. It had all been too easy. Perhaps they hadn't yet hit the main defensive belt. Perhaps the Americans had withdrawn to better defensive positions during the day. Bewildered, Neboatov returned his attention to the front and continued to follow the progress of the lead companies, watch the alignment of his platoons and listen for orders on the battalion radio net.

Chapter 11

Nothing is easy in war. Mistakes are always paid for in casualties and troops are quick to sense any blunder made by their commanders.

—DWIGHT D. EISENHOWER

Bandar Abbas
2055 Hours, 30 June (1725 Hours, 30 June, GMT)

The offloading of the ships was surprisingly easy and fast despite the poor facilities and the damage to the port. Sufficient ramps and piers had been cleared to allow the RO-RO ships to come in and disgorge their contents with the speed and ease for which they were built. Had all the ships arrived, the whole movement from the States, with a few exceptions, would have been a complete success.

Not all the ships had made it. Four had been sunk en route and another badly damaged. Two of the ships lost had been carrying munitions and supplies. Two had equipment belonging to both the active-duty maneuver brigades of the 25th Armored Division and the division's support command. While the loss of any one of the ships was serious, the loss of four and the nature of the loss were crippling. Rather than being able to field two fully equipped combat brigades, the division now had only enough equipment and supplies to field one weak brigade with two maneuver battalions instead of the normal three.

The bulk of the division's personnel had been held at Ras Banas, outside the war zone, until it could be determined which units would provide the people to man the limited amount of equipment that was available. It wasn't until the evening of 28 June that the 3rd of the 4th Armor and the 1st of the 29th Infantry were alerted that they, along with the 5th of the 55th Field Artillery, would deploy the next day to receive what equipment was available and form the 2nd Brigade. These units, once in Iran, would be equipped by pooling together the remaining equipment. Plans to use U.S. Army equipment prepositioned in Europe were being discussed in Washington and at NATO Headquarters in Brussels, but no decision had been made. Every new move to divert units or equipment tagged for NATO was met with alarm by the NATO Allies. Still, in time, some equipment from Europe would be made available. Until then those personnel not required and without equipment stayed in Egypt until the equipment was available or they were required as replacements.

The arrival of the ships in the early-morning hours of the thirtieth was greeted by the personnel of the three battalions, the brigade headquarters and support units. Those selected to drive the vehicles off the ships and out of the port area stood and watched the ships of the convoy enter the port and tie up to the piers. At first an effort was made to offload the ships in an orderly manner, one unit at a time. This, however, quickly broke down due to the manner in which the ships had been loaded and intermittent air raids that sent ships' crews and military personnel alike scrambling for cover. Instead, the first driver who was handy and who thought he could operate the next vehicle in line was grabbed, put into the driver's hatch or behind the wheel and directed to drive to the appropriate equipment holding areas around the port area. MPs at the exit leading from the dock were instructed to direct all tanks to one area, all artillery pieces to another, trucks to a third, Bradley fighting vehicles to a fourth, and anything that didn't look like the others to a fifth area called the Mox Nix area, from the German *macht nichts*, "it makes no difference."

This caused great confusion as unit commanders and supply officers sorted through the holding areas in an effort to put their units together. Beyond the initial marshaling areas, a staging area for each unit had been designated. It was the task of the battalion commanders and their staffs to find the vehicles they needed, gather up drivers needed to move them to staging areas, and assemble their units. There full crews married up the vehicles, and the process of forming platoons, then companies and finally battalions was begun. This assembling of the equipment and personnel and formation of units, however, did not complete the preparations. The combat units still had to draw supplies, fuel and ammunition, commodities that were on other ships and that had to be retrieved and issued by supply units, once they had assembled and formed.

Major Scott Dixon sat in the driver's seat of a hummer that Sergeant Nesbitt had procured earlier for him and watched the comings and goings along the dock areas. It was the scene at Beaumont, Texas, all over again, only in reverse. How much easier it would have been had the battalions been loaded as entire units. So simple. Then it occurred to him that he had not seen the S.S. *Cape Fear*, the ship that the equipment of the 3rd of the 4th had originally been loaded onto. For a second, his curiosity was piqued. He wondered whether the *Cape Fear* and its crew of obnoxious seamen had made it. The thought soon passed. He had a hell of a headache and was not about to wander up and down the docks looking for a ship that might not even be there. Besides, whether it was there or not made no difference. The unit had already secured enough tanks and Bradleys to reach full TOE strength. Perhaps, someday, if he survived this campaign, he would look it up in a history book and see whatever became of the *Cape Fear*.

Headquarters, 13th Airborne Corps, in Bandar Abbas, Iran
2105 Hours, 30 June (1735 Hours, 30 June, GMT)

Since his arrival in the country, Lieutenant General Weir had been greeted with one shock after another. He had come ahead to study the situation and prepare himself and his staff for when the 10th Corps headquarters was activated and assumed operational control of its subordinate units. His arrival, however, could not have come at a worse time. He was able to observe the collapse of the 13th Corps's defensive perimeter firsthand. A current situation update given to him before leaving Washington had not prepared him for what he found and in no way matched reality as viewed from Bandar Abbas.

Tactically, the situation was, at best, desperate. The corps had been deployed almost haphazardly as its subordinate units arrived in the country. The 52nd Infantry Division (Mechanized) had only its two active-duty brigades. That division, last to arrive, was deployed in the west, sent there because the main Soviet threat had appeared to be coming from that direction. It was now obvious that that threat had been a grand deception to draw the 13th Corps's attention away from the true main effort. Unfortunately, the 52nd Division was now too heavily committed and was unable to break contact without endangering the entire defensive perimeter.

The 17th Airborne Division, first in, was deployed in the east. After it had secured the initial airhead and pushed it out as far as Tarom, the follow-on division, the 12th Division, had leapfrogged over it and assumed responsibility for the center. The 17th Airborne had reassembled, rested and then redeployed two brigades with the mission of linking up with the 6th Marine Division operating out of Chah Bahar, but could maintain only very tenuous contact because of the vast distances between the two units. The third brigade of the 17th had been held in reserve by 13th Corps at Saadatabad, ready to respond to a penetration at any point or deal with Iranian guerrillas.

The penetration that came on 28 June had been against the 12th Division. Two Soviet divisions, one motorized rifle and one tank, reinforced with additional assets from the 28th Combined Arms Army, formed the main effort that hit at Rafsanjan. A motorized rifle division moving through the Zagros Mountains had been responsible for conducting deception operations and supporting attacks against the 52nd Infantry Division.

While the 52nd was able to hold its own, trading ground for time, the 12th had, after two days of combat, ceased to exist as a combat-effective division. Of nine infantry battalions assigned to the division, four had been overrun on the first day of the attack and had not been heard of since. Two had been cut off and encircled. Two of the remaining three battalions had been mauled as they attempted to fight a delaying action at Pariz on the road that led from Rafsanjan to Bandar Abbas. An assault at Kerman had crippled the division's combat-aviation brigade, destroying many of its helicopters and most of the maintenance and support units required to maintain them. While the rest of the division base, consisting of the headquarters, supply and maintenance units and engineer and air-defense units, remained relatively intact, the combat elements were gone.

The Air Force was committing everything it had in an effort to sever the Soviet advance from its lines of communication. Strikes against the Soviets' supply lines and identified supply dumps were run round the clock. The Soviets, however, anticipating such an effort, had reduced the number of ground-combat units committed to the bare minimum and used all the air-defense units from uncommitted units to cover their lines of communication. The smaller number of units required fewer supplies, and the roads needed to move those supplies along were better protected. As a result, the efforts of the Air Force had yielded few tangible results in comparison to a high cost in lost aircraft and pilots.

On the ground, the corps reserve had been committed, but in a piecemeal fashion. Since it was clear that the paratroopers would not be able to stop the advancing Soviet columns, company-sized units were being inserted by helicopter along the Soviets' main axis of advance, to conduct antiarmor ambushes, a form of delaying action. The idea was to establish a roadblock with mines and craters under cover of darkness. When the Soviets hit the barrier, they were attacked with antitank guided missiles launched from covered and concealed positions. The company was then evacuated by helicopter before the Soviets were able to turn on the ambushers in force. Done properly, it was an effective method of delaying an enemy. But it only delayed them. To stop and defeat the Soviets, heavy forces—tanks and Bradleys—were needed. That was where the 25th Armored Division, and particularly the 2nd Brigade, came in.

What disturbed Weir more than the tactical situation, grim as it was, was the state of despair that permeated the corps staff. The commander of the 13th Corps, once a boastful and somewhat arrogant man, always in charge, had said barely two words throughout the entire evening update briefing. When Weir asked him directly what his intentions were concerning the employment of the 25th Armored Division, he had looked at Weir rather absentmindedly and said, "I'm not sure. We're going to have to study that some," then turned and walked away to his office. There was the smell of defeat in the air throughout the headquarters of the 13th Corps. Because of this, Weir fought orders that temporarily attached the 25th Armored Division to that corps.

Weir contacted the Commander in Chief of CENTCOM, demanding that the 10th Corps be activated immediately. The CINC listened to Weir's recommendations but decided that it was unwise to change commanders and headquarters in the middle of the battle. The CINC wanted the situation to stabilize before he committed the 10th Corps so that he could use it to conduct a counteroffensive. To commit the entire corps to the defense would mean pissing away his only viable offensive ground-maneuver force. Weir countered that unless the 10th Corps was committed, there would be no ground left to conduct the counteroffensive over. While the CINC was willing to let some of the 10th Corps units join the battle in progress in order to stabilize the situation, he didn't want to lose them all in defensive operations. The bulk of the 10th Corps, in the meantime, would stay out of the battle and assemble in the rear.

For a while, Weir considered going straight to his friend Lieutenant General Horn, then decided against it. Going over the head of his immediate commander could lead to his dismissal. The last thing Weir wanted to do was get thrown out of the war before he got into it.

South of Rafsanjan
2345 Hours, 30 June (2015 Hours, 30 June, GMT)

The grinding of gears and the laboring of truck engines in the distance were the only noises that penetrated the cool night air. A heavily laden supply colum   led by a Soviet BRDM armored car en route to the front was slowly making its way up an incline. In another two minutes the column would come to a bend in the road just before it crested the hill. There it would be met by Sergeant First Class Duncan and the men of the 1st Platoon.

After escaping the Soviet onslaught, Duncan had rallied his men and taken them into hiding a few kilometers away. There he took stock of what he had. That wasn't very much. Seventeen men had followed him out of the foxholes. They brought with them their individual weapons, a couple of dozen hand grenades, some claymore mines, eight LAW antitank-rocket launchers and two Dragon missiles. Food was almost nonexistent, and they had only the water in their canteens. The one thing that the platoon had plenty of was 5.56mm. ammo for their rifles and squad automatic rifles, or SAWs. As Duncan was checking, it became obvious that none of the men, including him, had fired a rifle. There simply had not been any targets that small-arms fire would have had an effect on.

The first major problem Duncan faced was getting his men over the shock of the disaster they had just survived. Once out of danger, they fell into a state of despondency. One man kept asking no one in particular, "What happened? What in the hell happened?" over and over. Duncan himself was bewildered and in a stupor. The image of his lieutenant's body still caused a violent reaction. Never having been confronted with a situation of the magnitude he now faced, Duncan did what came naturally to him, what he had been trained for: being a soldier and a leader.

First he organized his group into two squads and distributed equally all the weapons, ammunition and food. That done, he got the men together and told them what they were going to do. He did not ask for opinions, he did not ask for a vote. As far as he was concerned, there was no alternative for them. They would fight. Duncan was honest with his men. There was no false bravado, there were no promises. The men watched and listened intently as he told them that they would move south, paralleling the road the Soviets were using. When the opportunity presented itself, they would ambush convoys or small patrols. Duncan made it clear that they were going to fight whenever and wherever they could get the drop on the Russians. He held the hope that they would be able to make their way back to their own lines, but stressed that that was only a hope.

The men accepted Duncan's decision in silence. That night there was no further discussion on the matter. They were at war. They were soldiers, American soldiers, renowned for their ability to do things that defied logic. In the tradition of Valley Forge, the Alamo, New Market and the Bulge, the men of 1st Platoon followed their leader and prepared to exact their revenge.

Duncan watched as the BRDM leading the convoy rolled forward. He divided the platoon into teams. The first team consisted of three men armed with LAWs. On Duncan's order they would take out the BRDM leading the convoy. Their firing would be the signal for the main team, deployed just off the road, to fire on the trucks nearest them. These men were further broken down into three-man sections. Each section was to fire on one truck, taking out the drivers and shooting the tires. Once a section managed to stop a truck and the immediate area appeared to be safe, two men were given sixty seconds to raid the truck for food, water and any types of antitank weapons they could find, while the third man covered them. The last team, located at the far end of the ambush, was the security team. Because the platoon was not large enough to deal with an entire column and could take on only a small chunk of it by isolating the lead trucks, the security team's job was to keep the rest of the convoy busy and provide covering fires while the ambush team rummaged through the stopped trucks. Once finished, all teams would withdraw to a predesignated rally point, then move to a hiding place where they would spend the following day.

Like most commanders leading men into battle, Duncan was nervous as he lay there watching the BRDM labor up the incline. His mind was filled with fear and apprehension. Had he thought of everything? Were his men really ready for combat? What happened if the BRDM wasn't knocked out by the team with the LAWs? Were the lead trucks full of supplies or Soviet infantry? Was the security team large enough to deal with the rest of the convoy? What would they do if his men didn't find any food on the trucks? Questions and concerns cascaded through his mind. Despite the cool evening, he was sweating. He wiped his hands and watched the progress of the BRDM.

The image of his lieutenant's body, ripped open and quivering as its life force oozed out, flashed through Duncan's brain. His stomach began to turn and knot up. As he tried hard to compose himself, he wondered what he feared more, death or failure. Death was easier for him. Once he was dead, his problems were over. Failure was the more to be feared of the two. If he failed, his men would pay the price. They would be ripped apart, just like the lieutenant. Other horrible images would crowd his mind. That, to Duncan, was more terrible than death.

The soldier next to Duncan nudged him and pointed. The BRDM was about to reach the point where the team with the LAWs could engage it. Duncan watched, waited and prepared to give the order to fire. In another second, it would be out of his hands.

North of Pariz
0035 Hours, 1 July (2105 Hours, 30 June, GMT)

A convoy of T-80 tanks of the 3rd Battalion, Soviet 68th Tank Regiment, moved through the darkness like a great mechanical snake. Its body turned and slithered along the road relentlessly, always going south. This snake, however, was not alert. Hours of monotonous moving at the same unchanging, slow speed through a countryside that did not vary had drained the last ounce of vigilance from the young tank commanders and their crews. The rhythmic thumping of the tanks' tracks on the road, the steady vibration of the engines, and the silence of the radios and the intercom were more conducive to sleep than to alertness. Instead of standing in their turrets or peering through their sights, watching their assigned sectors, they struggled to stay awake, occupying themselves with thoughts of home. Besides, with security forces out on the flanks and recon elements in front, the danger of an attack on the tanks was minimal.

As the long columns moved, it was not unusual for a tank to slowly drift off toward the shoulder of the road and into a ditch as its crew fell asleep. Sometimes the driver or the tank commander would feel the change in the vibrations of the tank as it moved onto the rough shoulder. When this happened, the driver, startled by the calamity he faced, would jerk the tank back into line, tossing the crew in the turret about. On other occasions, the crew never realized what was happening until the tank literally fell off the road.

Sometimes these incidents resulted in nothing more than a few bumps and bruises and a slight disruption in the column until the tank that had strayed climbed out of the ditch and back into the line of march. On other occasions the consequences were far more serious, particularly when the tank crew fell asleep as the unit was moving along a cliff. Major Vorishnov came across a 2nd Battalion tank in which this had happened. The tank commander, unable to drop down into the safety of the turret, had been crushed when the tank rolled over on top of him as it fell off the cliff.

Vorishnov stopped to see whether there was something he could do. As he watched the recovery operation, he could not help but think what a terrible waste it was to have come so far from home, to have survived several battles, only to be killed in such a manner. Such nonbattle losses were more numerous than his superiors liked to admit. But to stop for rest was to lose their momentum and possibly the opportunity to end the campaign before the arrival of the bulk of the Americans' heavy forces. The decision was made to push on. Better to lose a few now by pushing hard than many because an opportunity was not taken. Such decisions, however logical, did little to lessen the impact on the men who had to lift a forty-ton tank off the body of a twenty-year-old tank commander whose driver had fallen asleep.

Three thousand meters away, fiberglass tubes, protruding from under camouflage nets that fluttered lazily in the cool night air, followed the progress of the T-80 tanks. Under the nets, TOW gunners, their eyes pressed against the rubber eyepieces on the TOWs' thermal night sights, tracked the tank that each had selected for destruction. With ease and steadiness achieved through countless hours of training and practice, the gunners kept the cross hairs fixed on the tank as if they were glued to it. Across the road, in positions similar to those occupied by the TOW gunners but closer, were Dragon gunners. They, like their compatriots, watched through thermal sights as the Soviet column slithered south.

Second Lieutenant Cerro slowly lowered his night-vision goggles. For a moment he was blind, his eyes unable to adapt themselves to the darkness after being exposed to the bright-green light of the goggles. As his night vision returned, Cerro rose slightly from his position and looked to his left. Somewhere, in a rough line on the west side of the road that extended over fifteen hundred meters, there were four TOW-missile launchers under his command. He could not see them, which was the way things were supposed to be, but he knew they were there, tracking the Soviet column as he was. Satisfied that the Soviets were unable to see his TOW positions, Cerro put the night-vision goggles back up to his eyes and looked beyond the column to the east, where six Dragon teams were hidden. They, like the TOW positions, were also invisible.

It had taken the company hours to move up to where they wanted to be and prepare their positions. Every time a column moved down the road, the men would have to stop work and flatten themselves against the ground. When they had scratched out positions that provided some cover, the TOW and Dragon crews draped nets over them. Once finished, they settled into the positions, set up their weapons and waited for the signal to fire. Cerro, the acting company commander, had briefed them all on their roles and how the ambush would go down. When the unit was ready, he would designate the column to be hit. He wanted to go for tanks.

The signal to initiate the ambush would be a green star cluster sent up by Cerro. The TOWs would then fire, hitting the first, fourth, seventh and eleventh tanks in the column, after which the TOW gunners would go to ground and wait. If the Soviets reacted as Cerro expected, the remaining tanks would turn toward the TOWs. When they did, they would expose their rear decks to the Dragon teams. Each Dragon team would then take one shot and run for their designated rally point. Antitank mines lined the road on the Dragon gunners' side in case the Russians decided to turn and pursue them. If Cerro wanted the TOWs to take a second shot, he would fire a second green star cluster. If, however, the Russians appeared to be an immediate threat and the TOWs could not get another clean shot in, he would fire a red star cluster, the signal for the TOWs to withdraw to their rally point.

In support of the ambush a three-gun 81mm. mortar section hidden in a wadi would fire high-explosive and smoke rounds. They would not kill any tanks, but would add to the confusion and cover the withdrawal of the company. Helicopters hidden away in wide wadis not far from the two rally points waited for the ambush to be sprung. Once the firing started, the pilots would crank up their machines, move to the rally points and pick up Cerro's men. With luck, the ambushers would be off the ground ten minutes after the first green star cluster was fired.

Cerro watched and waited. He passed the word to stand by. On the lip of his foxhole sat three star clusters, two green and one red, open and ready for use. The column to their front was theirs.

Unnoticed by the crew, the third tank in line began to weave back and forth across the road. In the driver's compartment, a young man not yet twenty fought to stay awake. His head bobbed up and down as he struggled to open eyes that no longer saw clearly. In desperation he called to his tank commander, to tell him that he was unable to keep his eyes open. The tank commander, however, was already asleep, his head resting against the mount of the 12.7mm. machine gun. The gunner had been out for over an hour. The driver, his head clouded from exhaustion, never noticed the tilting of the tank as it ran off the east side of the road.

Neither was he able to comprehend what was happening to him as the T-80 pushed the tilt rod of an M-21 antitank mine down, setting off its detonator. In an instant, the mine's penetrator was driven up into the belly of the tank, ripping through the ammunition stored below the turret floor. Sparks caused by metal ripping through metal ignited the main-gun propellant charges and gutted the tank with a flash fire in milliseconds. In less time than it took the others in the column to perceive that something was happening, three men were dead and the entire length of the column was lit up by the sheet of flame that leaped from the turret of the disabled T-80 tank.

In an instant Vorishnov knew what was happening. He could see no sign of an antitank guided missile. He had not heard the high-pitched crack of a tank cannon. It had to have been a mine. And if there was a mine, there probably was an ambush.

Cerro was dumbfounded. At first he thought that someone had fired too soon. But he had not heard a missile launch or the popping of guidance rockets. A quick glance gave him the answer. A Soviet tank had wandered off the road and hit a mine. Already other Soviet tanks were maneuvering into firing positions. In the light of the flames coming from the hapless burning tank he could see the other tank commanders closing their hatches, preparing for battle.

With no time to waste, Cerro reached for a green star cluster. He had to start the ambush before the Soviets had completely recovered from their surprise. His men, equally confused by the sudden turn of events, were waiting for the prearranged signal to fire. In the darkness, Cerro removed the star cluster's cover, sliding it over the bottom of the tube. Firmly holding the tube, pointed skyward, in his left hand, he struck the bottom of it with the palm of his right hand, setting off the star cluster. Once the cluster was launched, Cerro dropped the tube, leaned over the front edge of his foxhole and brought his binoculars to his eyes.

He had no sooner done so than the entire area around him was bathed in a bright-red light from the star cluster he had fired.

Cerro froze. He couldn't believe it. He looked down at the edge of his foxhole and saw two unused green star clusters sitting there. In his haste, he had given the signal to withdraw instead of the one to fire. He turned to his right. In the fading red light he could see his TOW crews leaving their positions in accordance with the plan. No doubt the Dragon teams were doing likewise. Cerro pounded his fist against the dirt, shouting a string of obscenities. His plan was going to shit and there wasn't a damned thing he could do about it.

The chatter of machine guns from the tanks on the road brought him back to his immediate problem. The tanks were firing wildly in all directions. The only thing Cerro could do now to influence the situation was order the mortars to fire. Their commander, confused by the single explosion followed by the red star cluster, was calling Cerro over the radio asking for instructions. At least the mortars could cover the withdrawal for a while.

Vorishnov and the battalion commander were at a loss as to what to do. The ditches along the side of the road were obviously mined. It was therefore hazardous for them to maneuver the battalion off the road. The red star cluster, fired from somewhere to the west, had obviously meant something, but Vorishnov had no idea what. Nothing had happened when it fired.

As he tried to sort sense out of chaos, small-caliber mortar rounds, a mix of high-explosive and smoke rounds, began to hit among the roadbound tanks. That explained the star cluster: it was a signal for the mortars to fire. But that didn't make sense, either. What use were small-caliber mortar rounds, particularly smoke, against tanks? Though their aim was quite accurate and they did much to add to the confusion and the general pandemonium, the mortars were really doing nothing of any value. You fired smoke only when you wanted to screen something. What were they screening? Suicide squads? It had to be Iranian fanatics. In the past two months they had done some very strange things that defied all logic and explanation. Whatever they were up to, it was having no real effect on the battalion, except to cause panic and a rash of gibberish over the command radio net. In a booming voice, the battalion commander ordered silence on that net. In an instant, order was restored, at least on the radio.

·   ·   ·

It was easy for the men of the company-command group to follow their commander in the darkness to the rally point. All they had to do was follow the sound of Cerro's cursing. He had screwed up. The men in the command group knew it, and soon the entire company would know it.

At the rally point all the TOW-section leaders counted their men, then reported to Cerro when he arrived. All were present. Second Lieutenant Kinsley, in charge of the Dragon teams to the east, called in that all teams and personnel had reported in and they were in the process of loading up in the helicopters and preparing to lift off. Cerro gave him a roger-out. The mortar-section leader called in and reported that his section had broken down and was also moving to load onto its helicopters. Cerro's acknowledgment to the mortar-section leader was drowned out by the noise of the helicopters coming in to evacuate Cerro and the TOW crews.

As he watched the Blackhawks land, Cerro thanked God that at least the evacuation had come off without a hitch and the entire fiasco had been bloodless. He had read once that any battle you walked away from was a good one. That, unfortunately, was about the only positive thing he could say for this one.

Flames from the burning tank silhouetted Vorishnov and his commander as they walked back to their vehicles. Neither one was able to explain the strange battle that had taken place there. The best that they could figure was that the tank that had exploded had prematurely started the action before the attackers were ready. Rather than stay and fight at a disadvantage, the ambushers had withdrawn. Vorishnov commented that that had been a wise move. It was, in his view, best to walk away from a bad fight and wait until you had the advantage. While the battalion commander agreed, he was quick to point out that even if the incident had been a botched ambush, it had succeeded in stopping them and delaying their advance for thirty minutes while the column got sorted out, the area cleared and the road swept for mines. They could not suffer too many such delays and reach the Gulf before the Americans had built up the strength needed to stop them.

The two men also agreed that they had been incredibly lucky. They knew that they were pushing their luck. The men were tired and the equipment needed maintenance. Resupply was becoming an iffy proposition as the divisions moved farther south. Bypassed pockets both of Americans, now recovering from their initiation to battle, and of Iranian fanatics were beginning to hit the lightly defended supply columns with disturbing frequency. Fuel, critical to maintaining the advance, was becoming a scarce commodity. Even if the Americans were unable to mass enough of their tank forces to stop them, lack of supplies would keep the 28th Combined Arms Army from reaching the Strait of Hormuz. In a briefing to his commanders, the regimental commander had likened their situation to the stretching of a great rubber band. It was their task to stretch that rubber band all the way to the Gulf of Oman without its breaking. In the fading light of the burning tank, Vorishnov wondered if that could be done. And if it couldn't, then what?

South of Hajjiabad, Iran
0645 Hours, 2 July (0315 Hours, 2 July, GMT)

The personnel of the 2nd Brigade headquarters were in good spirits despite a long night. They had traveled over roads that had ceased to be roads years before, suffered delays while moving broken-down vehicles from their path and survived the ever present threat of ambushes by Iranian guerrillas. They had done so with all of their equipment and vehicles and had managed to set up and camouflage before first light. While the value of camouflaging the command post and the vehicles with nets colored to blend into wooded areas instead of the bleak, rock-strewn hills of southern Iran was questionable, anything was better than being in the open. According to Lieutenant Matthews, the Soviets had a satellite passing over southern Iran every two hours. The command post of the only armored brigade standing between the Russians and the Persian Gulf was no doubt high on the Soviets' list of targets to find and eradicate.

The three M-577 command-post vehicles that made up the tactical-operations center, or TOC, of the 2nd Brigade were set side by side. The canvas extensions from all three vehicles were up and connected. This provided a work area for the staff officers on duty. Maps depicting the brigade's situation, the enemy situation, artillery targets and contingency plans were hanging from poles that supported the extensions. Between the maps were status boards showing critical information such as the current organization of the brigade, the status and number of weapons systems available by unit, and radio call signs and frequencies. Radio speakers and hand mikes as well as tactical telephones were placed on tables throughout the TOC so that the appropriate staff officer could look at his map or update a board while talking on the phone or listening to the radio. To a casual observer, the TOC was sheer bedlam. The confined area was filled with people coming and going, three different briefings were going on at the same time, phones were ringing. To the operations and intelligence personnel of 2nd Brigade, it was home.

Matthews sat before the intelligence map and posted information that had been received during the night but had not been posted during the move north. Though the situation was threatening, it was looking better than it had looked two days earlier. The two divisions moving toward them had been slowed down considerably. A combination of ground attacks by forces cut off but still fighting, raids carried out by the 17th Airborne along the Soviets' line of march and attacks by the Air Force had had the effect of slowing the Soviets and buying time for the 2nd Brigade to deploy. Matthews' current projections showed that it would be four to five days before the Soviets could mount a deliberate breakthrough attack against the brigade. By then, they would be as ready as they ever would.

The deployment of the 2nd Brigade bothered Matthews. The tank and mechanized battalions, reorganized into combined-arms task forces, had been placed across the main avenues of approach to the south. The 3rd Battalion of the 4th Armor sat on the road and blocked it. The 1st of the 29th Infantry was covering a secondary avenue to its east. These units, placed in close proximity, could support each other in a pinch depending on where the Soviets made their main effort. But the use of a light-infantry battalion attached to the brigade gave her concern. A valley west of the brigade's main sector ran south from Harvand, past Hajjiabad to Tarom. The infantry battalion was assigned the responsibility of covering this approach. Because the road network was so bad there, the 12th Division G-2 felt that the Soviets would not risk sending heavy forces south through Harvand. If that did happen, the infantry battalion was, in their opinion, capable of stopping the enemy in the restricted terrain there. Failing that, the battalion could delay the enemy long enough for the armored or mech task forces to shift over and reinforce the air assault battalion.

When Matthews volunteered that no infantry unit had yet been able to delay, let alone stop, a Soviet mounted attack, she was politely told to confine her attention to Soviet operations.

While she had some support for her position, no one changed the plan as it stood. For better or worse, the die for the 2nd Brigade's first battle was cast. After thirty-eight days of waiting and twelve thousand miles of travel, they were at the front.

Chapter 12

Russians, in the knowledge of inexhaustible supplies of manpower, are accustomed to accepting gigantic fatalities with comparative calm.

—BARBARA W. TUCHMAN

East of Aliabad
1345 Hours, 7 July (1015 Hours, 7 July, GMT)

The town suddenly became clearly visible in the distance as the two F-15s flew over a low ridge. Martain tilted the plane slightly to the right and began to accelerate. "Aliabad dead ahead. Air defense status?"

The wizzo scanned his instruments. There was no indication of Soviet target-acquisition radar signals. "All clear. Go for it."

"It" in this case was a fuel dump that had been located in the vicinity of Aliabad by an early-morning air reconnaissance. The Soviets were still setting it up and had not had enough time to complete its camouflage before the sun was up. One fuel bladder, completely full, and a partial view of a second fuel bladder being camouflaged, plus a five-thousand-gallon fuel tanker, caught the eye of a photo-image interpreter aboard the carrier U.S.S. *Hornet.* Knowing that fuel dumps were high-priority targets, he passed the photos and his analysis immediately to his supervisor, a staff intelligence officer. The officer confirmed the analysis and forwarded the information and the photos via facsimile to the intelligence section of CENTCOM aboard the U.S.S. *Berkshire.* There the information was again reviewed, this time against photos of the same area the day before. Once it was verified that the target was new and was in fact a fuel dump, the information was passed on to a targeting officer.

The targeting officer reviewed the target profile and analysis along with those of other targets, assigned a priority to the fuel dump and placed it on the consolidated target list. Its place came immediately after nuclear-capable Soviet units and headquarters of divisions or higher units.

Once the target list was completed, assets available to hit those targets were assigned. The targeting process is difficult in that not all targets are marked for destruction and there are never enough assets available to hit all targets. Some, such as "command-and-control nodes," or headquarters, can have high-tech intelligence assets focused on them in order to gain more information. The same command-and-control node could also be neutralized with electronic jammers that would impair its ability to command subordinate elements. If the target is sufficiently stationary, special operations forces could be deployed to strike it. In the case of the fuel dump at Aliabad, a squadron of F-15Es was assigned the task of taking it out immediately.

Once the target list was approved, orders were cut and sent out to the appropriate headquarters. All information concerning the targets went along. The operations officer of the unit assigned to each target developed the unit's plan of attack, or, if time permitted and it was necessary, additional recon of the target was requested before the final plan was developed. The wing operations officer reviewing the intelligence data on the fuel dump decided against additional recon. He had sufficient data to work with.

An air attack involved several different players and was planned in phases. These phases normally included the flight to the target by the attack aircraft, suppression of enemy air-defense elements, called SEADE (pronounced "seed"), by special aircraft, the actual attack on the target, and the return. If the primary target could not be hit or did not require all the ordnance being carried, a strike against a secondary target was also planned.

Travel to and from the target had to be carefully planned by the operations officer of the assigned unit, since the attacking planes would be flying not only over enemy air-defense units but also over friendly forces armed with air-defense weapons. To ensure against errors by nervous soldiers believing in the philosophy of "Shoot them down and sort them out on the ground," temporary air corridors to be used by the attackers would be set up. Army air-defense elements would receive the word about where these air corridors were and when they would be open. The rules are quite simple when it comes to air corridors: Any plane in an air corridor when it is open cannot be engaged by friendly forces unless the aircraft is definitely identified as hostile. If friendly aircraft stray from established air corridors or miss the established times, they are fair game to ground antiaircraft fire.

Dealing with enemy air defenses can be done by hitting the air-defense units or their radars, by jamming the air-defense radars or by simply avoiding them. Specialized aircraft and units, called "Wild Wessels," do nothing but suppress enemy air defense in support of attack missions. They precede the attackers and clear a corridor through enemy air defenses so that the attackers can reach the target and get back. Air-superiority fighters are also assigned to provide high cover against enemy fighters on patrol or intentionally dispatched to bounce the attackers.

An attack such as the one on the fuel dump requires split-second timing and a great deal of coordination. All services practice such operations in peace and rapidly get very good at it once war commences.

Martain was not pleased when he drew the mission to hit the fuel dump. As the squadron's premier fighter pilot, with eight kills to his credit, he felt he belonged with the aircraft providing cover, not playing mud mover. The squadron commander, however, was adamant that everyone do his time in the ground-attack role. "After all," the squadron commander said, "if the government wanted you to be a fighter pilot they would have given you a big watch and a cheap airplane."

Martain and his wingman would be the first of four aircraft that would hit the fuel dump. If Omaha Flight succeeded in taking out the fuel dump on its pass, the remaining two planes would hit an unidentified headquarters located a little farther north. The rest of the squadron was assigned the task of providing high cover to the attacking aircraft. For the mission, both Omaha 01 and 02 were carrying over sixteen thousand pounds of bombs, mostly Rockeye cluster bombs, with four 750-pound general-purpose bombs each for good measure. This was in addition to their Sidewinder and Sparrow air-to-air missiles for self-defense.

As Omaha Flight came screaming up over the ridge and veered to the northwest at a speed in excess of 550 miles an hour, Martain was reminded of how nervous he got when he was moving that fast one hundred feet off the ground. Their attack profile would be a low approach, followed by a quick pop up to identify the target, and a diving attack. Once all bombs were released, which would take only a second, he would go low again, kick in his after burner and get the hell out of Dodge before the people on the ground knew what had happened and got pissed. Omaha 02 would be right beside him, with Vegas Flight thirty seconds behind.

As they approached the pop-up point, Martain again asked his wizzo whether they had been tagged by radar. A short "Negative" was all he had time for before Martain began to climb and search for landmarks. He had only a second to do so. Starting from the town, he looked to the west until he found a small kidney-shaped hill and then a road. Keeping his eyes glued on a point between the hill and the road, he turned his aircraft toward it. The fuel dump was tucked into that area.

All his energies and attention were now totally oriented to that spot. His thumb flipped up the red cover that protected the bomb-release button. With ease born of hours of training, he turned the F-15 over onto its side, then down into a dive, all the time watching the hill as it grew larger and closer. Martain could now see people scurrying from under camouflage nets, running for shelter or weapons. Tracers were racing up at him. The people on the ground knew he was coming and what he was after. A flash and a streak of white smoke to one side of the F-15, seen in the corner of his eye, told Martain he was being engaged by an SA-7 surface-to-air missile. But it was too late. The F-15 was on the mark. The target was in the box in his sight. All was set. Martain hit the button and felt the aircraft suddenly spring up as it became sixteen thousand pounds lighter. In an instant he hit his after burners, flattened out his dive and charged south as fast as his engines could carry them.

Neither he nor his wizzo could see the effects of their work. They didn't need to. The leader of Vegas Flight coming up behind reported that the target appeared to be destroyed and that he was going after the secondary target.

Five Kilometers North of Hajjiabad
1935 Hours, 7 July (1605 Hours, 7 July, GMT)

The sun was casting long shadows on the ground by the time Major Dixon returned to the command post of the 3rd of the 4th Armor. As he approached, the glint of the late-afternoon sun reflecting off uncovered glass caught his eye. As his Bradley grew nearer, he was disturbed to see several vehicles scattered throughout the area without camouflage nets up or cloth covering their windows or mirrors. He could not get over how totally stupid some people were. What use was it to put nets up over the TOC if everyone and his brother who owned a vehicle parked it outside? From the air the CP must look like a used-military-vehicle parking lot.

Even before he was within range, Dixon began to call out for the headquarters commandant. A young captain, too young to command the monster that the battalion's headquarters company was, came out from under a net not far from the TOC. Without shutting down the engine or getting down from atop his Bradley, Dixon bellowed out, "Ellis, get these gawddamned vehicles outa here or I'll run 'em over!" Ellis looked up at the red-faced major and attempted to explain, but was cut off as Dixon yelled, "Now, Captain—today!"

It was only after Ellis had rushed off to find the drivers that Dixon noticed the bumper numbers on two of the uncovered hummers. One of them belonged to the brigade commander and the other to the brigade S-3. Not expecting an answer, he asked himself out loud, "What in the hell is the brigade commander and his three doing running around in hummers?" No doubt they had their reasons, but none that he could think of at that moment. Both had more sense than that, or so Dixon assumed.

Once inside the TOC, Dixon saw his battalion commander talking to both the brigade commander and the S-3. First Lieutenant Matthews was over in one corner talking to the battalion S-2.

Dixon's commander looked up and smiled. "Scott, I thought I heard you bellow. I was going over our dispositions with Colonel Hardin. He seems concerned that we haven't occupied all of our forward positions yet."

Dixon walked up to the situation map. "As we explained during the brief of our OPLAN, back on the fifth, we will not move into our actual fighting positions until either the enemy has committed himself into the attack or we lose our ability to detect him before he enters our sector here along Phase Line Thomas." On the situation map Dixon ran his finger along a black line located in the battalion's forwardmost area. "By keeping away from our actual fighting positions we make it difficult for the enemy to accurately predict where our kill zones and battle positions are. Hopefully, this will dilute his preparatory bombardment and keep him guessing as to where we are until it's too late for him to react."

The brigade commander, with arms folded, leaned back in his chair and studied the map for a moment before speaking. "You two may be right. No doubt the Russians have been studying us under a microscope, using everything from satellites to goatherders. I would, however, feel a hell of a lot more comfortable if you had more firepower forward. Besides, as it stands right now, there's no one that can cover your mine fields and barriers. Intell tells us the other side have been good at picking their way through barriers before the battle starts."

Without waiting for his commander to respond, Dixon said, "The scout platoon, reinforced with a tank platoon, is more than sufficient to cover the entire battalion's frontage, day or night. Vehicles rotate their positions nightly so that the Soviets can't plot them and plan infiltration routes around them. At night, all barriers are covered by dismounted elements from the mech platoons, as well as one tank or Bradley deployed forward to scan the area with its thermal sight. The techniques we are using worked well for the battalion at the National Training Center and should do well here."

The brigade commander leaned forward, putting his hands on his knees. "This isn't the NTC, Major Dixon. Those people closing on us are the real thing."

Dixon could feel himself getting excited. The thoughts that ran through his mind didn't help: Here we are, with the same plan we briefed two days ago. The enemy is expected to make contact anytime, and the brigade commander wants us to change now, in the middle of the night, before our first battle. He's got to be bullshitting us.

He allowed himself to calm down before answering. "You are right, sir, this is not the NTC. I therefore expect the plan to work better, since this will be the first time the Soviets have come across a heavy U.S. unit." Switching to the attack, he continued. "Our concern at battalion is the air assault unit to the west. The large wadi that leads from Harvand to Tarom provides the Soviets with an excellent avenue of approach into our rear and across the brigade's main supply route. If we are hit with a supporting attack and the main attack here," Dixon pointed to Harvand on the map, "we would be unable to displace sufficient combat power to stop a major breakthrough."

The battalion commander shot a dirty look to Dixon. They had been over the subject before, and it was becoming a sore point for the brigade commander.

"Dixon, the 1st of the 503rd Infantry will hold. I've been over their plan with their battalion commander and have walked the ground. They know what they are doing." The brigade commander was clearly agitated.

Dixon was about to state that none of the units in the 12th Division had yet stopped a Soviet attack, but he was cut short by the brigade S-3, who reminded the brigade commander they had to get back for a meeting with the 13 Corps commander.

As the meeting broke up, First Lieutenant Matthews, who apparently was traveling with the brigade S-3, came over to Dixon. "Have you seen Randy, I mean Lieutenant Capell, lately, sir?"

Dixon's anger left him as he looked into Matthews' eyes. "Yes, I just came from there. Randy is doing fine. He's happier than a pig in slop. Do you have a message you want me to give him?"

A smile lit Matthews' face. She reached down into a pocket of her BDUs, pulled out a crumpled letter and offered it to Dixon. "Would you give this to him, sir?"

With a grin, Dixon took the letter. "Sure, and I'll tell him you send all your love."

That made Matthews blush. She saluted, turned and hurried out to where the brigade S-3 was waiting.

When everyone but the people on shift had cleared out of the TOC, Master Sergeant Nesbitt came out of the S-3 M577 command track, carrying two steaming cups. "Looks like you could use some coffee."

Dixon took the cup offered by Nesbitt and began to shake his head in disbelief. "What I need is a good drink, Sergeant Nesbitt. Can you imagine that? The bloody Communists are close enough to spit on us, and the brigade commander wants to change things." He stopped, took a drink of coffee and thought for a moment before continuing. "Well, twenty-four hours from now we'll know who was right."

"You staying here tonight or going back forward?"

"I really should go back out, but I won't. I need to clean up some and get some sleep. You got anything worth a damn to eat around here, Sergeant Nesbitt?"

Nesbitt went back into the command track and returned with two brown plastic pouches., "You have a choice tonight, sir. Pork patties or chicken à la king."

A disgusted look crept across Dixon's face. "Then the answer is no, you don't have anything worth a damn to eat."

"Well, sir, it's your choice, malnutrition or indigestion. I have them both."

"A comedian. I'm starving to death and I get a comedy act. Give me the chicken à la king. At least I know what that used to be." Dixon took the brown pouch offered by Nesbitt, tucked it under his arm and left after reminding the duty officer where he would be and when to wake him.

With everyone else gone, the people on duty in the TOC settled down for what promised to be a long and busy night.

Fifteen Kilometers North of Hajjiabad
1940 Hours, 7 July (1610 Hours, 7 July, GMT)

In the gathering darkness the shadowy area between the opposing forces began to come to life. The Soviet juggernaut, long awaited by the 2nd Brigade, had finally come within striking distance. Rather than crashing into the forward elements of the brigade, the lead Soviet forces slowed, then stopped for reconnaissance. The Soviets knew the approximate front-line trace of the American forces but not exact unit and vehicle locations. Recon elements and patrols would now creep forward under the veil of darkness to verify what information they had and pin exact locations of vehicles and weapons.

Plans at the operational level had been made by the 28th Combined Arms Army and issued the day before. Its subordinate divisions had, in turn, deployed in accordance with the army's orders and issued their own to their regiments. Regimental commanders and staffs decided on the tactical deployment their units would use and issued orders for the execution of those tactics. The exact axis of attack and timing of deployments as well as targeting would be based on intelligence gathered by patrols working their way into the midst of the Americans' positions. At an early-morning briefing just before the attack, the regimental intelligence officers would present a complete picture of U.S. forces to their front. With that information, the regimental commander would issue his final orders for the attack.

Forward of their main defensive positions, both American battalions deployed their scout platoons as a counter-reconnaissance screen. The mission of the scouts was to keep the Soviet recon elements from infiltrating into the battalions' area of operations and deceive them as to where the main defensive positions really were. The success or failure of the attack hinged on the skills of a handful of men sneaking about in the dark.

With darkness upon them, Capell signaled his scout platoon to move into their night positions, which stretched across the small valley that was the battalion's front. His squad leaders knew where to go and what to do. The tank platoon attached to him as part of the screen moved into shallow holes scooped out of the dirt in the center of the battalion's sector; though spread out with a distance of four hundred meters between tanks, the platoon was able to cover the entire center with surveillance and direct fire. Two ground-surveillance radar teams, called GSRs, each equipped with a radar capable of detecting moving personnel at four thousand meters and moving vehicles at ten thousand, also were operating with Capell's scouts. Only a few wadis and cuts along the flanks could not be covered by the M-1 tanks or the GSRs. That was where the scout platoon set up.

Capell and his men had no sooner moved into positions than a GSR team reported two wheeled vehicles eight thousand meters to their front. Several minutes of tracking them left no doubt in Capell's mind that they were BRDMs of the Soviet regiment's recon company. Though he had sufficient information to call artillery on them, Capell held back. He wanted to see where they were going without the Soviets knowing they were being tracked. At a range of five thousand meters, the two vehicles split up. One disappeared into a wadi that ran down the American battalion's western flank. The other moved forward slowly along the eastern flank, still being tracked by the GSR. The scout section on the western flank was notified of the approaching BRDM and was ordered to take it out. The tanks were able to track the other

BRDM on the eastern flank with their thermal sights. They had the task of taking it out when the scouts hit the first BRDM.

Now began a deadly game of cat and mouse as the scouts waited for the BRDM to pop into view. There was always the possibility that the BRDM in the wadi would find cover and slip past Capell's waiting scouts. If that happened, the Soviets would be able to get into the battalion's main defensive areas. Capell worried about this but trusted his initial dispositions. Besides, it was too late to change them.

Across the valley from where Capell was, the low hills were suddenly lit up by the flash of a small cannon firing somewhere down in the wadi. As he slewed the turret of his Bradley in that direction, the *pop-pop-pop* report of a Bradley's 25mm. gun reached his location. Watching, Capell saw a series of tiny flashes, then the eruption of a fireball. The first BRDM had been hit and killed.

The crack of a tank cannon and the streak of a 105mm. HEAT antitank round tore Capell's attention away from the burning BRDM in the far wadi. The tank crews had not waited for the order to fire. Instead, they had seized the opportunity to kill the second BRDM. A flash and a brilliant shower of sparks signaled to Capell that they had succeeded. When silence returned to the valley, Capell called for all sections to report. This they did promptly. Capell in turn consolidated the information into one short, concise spot report and submitted the first of many sightings and contacts that night to battalion.

Headquarters, 28th CAA, North of Aliabad
2245 Hours, 7 July (1915 Hours, 7 July, GMT)

The staff of the 28th CAA's main command post had spent a good part of the day recovering from an early-afternoon air attack. A group of F-15s had hit both the headquarters and a fuel dump four kilometers south of it. Losses in men and equipment had been heavy. Fortunately the commander and the first officer, Colonel Sulvina, had been absent at the time. Upon their return, they found their once efficient and orderly command post the scene of pandemonium and despair. The chief of staff, though alive, had been stunned by the concussion of a general-purpose bomb and was temporarily out of action. Until he recovered, Sulvina assumed the role of chief of staff.

Once order had been restored and the staff was sufficiently recovered from their shock, Sulvina had each primary and special staff officer prepare an update for the commander. He wanted to review the army's plan and capability once more before the battle was joined.

The second officer outlined all current intelligence on the enemy. Reports from the division's recon that night had not yet had time to reach army headquarters. A more complete picture would be ready just before the attack at dawn. The logistics officer, always harried, presented a picture of gloom. Based on statistics on hand and projected, the army did not have sufficient ammunition to conduct more than one major breakthrough attack. He stressed that raids and attacks all along their supply routes were not only keeping ammunition from reaching the army in the quantities needed but were degrading the army's ability to supply itself at all. Each time an ambush hit a supply column, trucks that were needed to haul future supplies were also lost. Even more critical than the ammunition shortage was the fuel situation. The logistics officer stated that the Americans were hitting anything that looked like a fuel dump, and he warned that unless the situation improved dramatically the army would run out of fuel within ninety-six hours.

Sulvina waited to discuss the next day's assault until he was alone with the commander. The 127th Motorized Rifle Division would conduct the main attack through Harvand against light-infantry units. Once the breakthrough was achieved, the 33rd Tank Division would be passed through the 127th MRD, probably in the vicinity of Tarom by midmorning. A supporting attack by the 67th Motorized Rifle Division would hold the American armored brigade in place around Hajjiabad until the 33rd Tank Division was able to cut them off and isolate them.

If all went according to plan, Sulvina said, the American brigade facing them would be crushed in the next twenty-four hours. If the flow of fuel was not diminished any further, they would be able to reach the Strait of Hormuz, seize Bandar Abbas and complete their mission. If, however, anything went wrong, there was little hope for success. All the divisions in the 28th Combined Arms Army were wearing thin. Not only were supplies a problem, but equipment and personnel were also at a critical level.

The 17th Combined Arms Army and the 9th Tank Army,

whose assigned mission was to push through the 28th when the 28th could no longer advance, were no longer following. Instead, their divisions were diverted to other tasks. The puppet government that had been set up to run the Soviet Republic of Azerbaijan was unable to control the Turkic tribes and required two full divisions to maintain order in Tabriz and other towns. Another division was tied down in Tehran chasing the shadows of Iranian rebels. The majority of the 17th CAA was stretched between Tehran and Kerman, fighting remnants of the Iranian Islamic Revolutionary Guard and pro-U.S. Iranian groups being supplied by air. In short, there was no one except the well-worn 28th CAA left to finish the mission.

For better than an hour Sulvina and his commander discussed the situation and their options. In the end, at Sulvina's urging, the commander gave him permission to draft and transmit a message to the Front Commander recommending that the 28th CAA be authorized to employ chemical weapons. Sulvina, upon leaving his commander, returned to his small work area, where he pulled a prepared message from his field desk. He called the duty officer over, handed him the original copy of the message and instructed him to have it transmitted to Front Headquarters immediately. He then called in the assistant operations officer, the intelligence officer, the chemical officer and the artillery officer. He told them to prepare a list of targets that were vulnerable to chemical attack and present it to him for his review and approval by 0600 hours that morning.

After checking the situation reports and the most current intelligence one more time, Sulvina was satisifed that all was in order. With nothing more to do, he left word to wake him in four hours and then went to get some sleep. The next forty-eight hours were going to be critical and hard. The first thing in the morning he would begin to plan the next battle, the one that would take the 28th CAA to the Persian Gulf.

Fifteen Kilometers North of Hajjiabad
0425 Hours, 8 July (0055 Hours, 8 July, GMT)

The reduction in the level of activity hadn't been noticeable at first. In fact, it wasn't until shortly before 0400 hours that Capell realized that the Soviets were withdrawing and that the number of reports had been declining for the past hour. Even then he didn't attach any special meaning to that fact. His mind, like everyone else's, was running at half speed from stress, fatigue and lack of sleep. The reduction in action was greeted with relief and not questioned or considered suspect. Only the assistant intelligence officer at brigade, Lieutenant Matthews, saw the pattern. Together with the report from airborne surveillance radars, she made the correct assessment. The patrols and the probing were over. The Soviets were about to attack.

The warning to prepare for a major Soviet attack going down to the battalions coincided with reports coming up from the scouts of the 2nd Brigade that the movement of large numbers of tracked vehicles could be heard. In the sector of the 3rd of the 4th Armor, tank crewmen and infantry squads scrambled onto their vehicles. Without waiting for or needing permission to move, company commanders rolled their platoons from their hiding positions into fighting positions. Members of the command group, woken with great difficulty, listened intently while they dressed to an update of the current situation given by the intelligence and operations officers who had been on duty during the night. Outside, their armored vehicles were being cranked up. Within minutes the entire battalion was in motion, winding itself up for the impending battle.

The Soviet artillery bombardment came just before the first rays of light began to herald the new dawn. For most men in the armored battalion the artillery barrage was nothing more than a curiosity. Soviet intelligence and artillery officers, confused by the battalion's dispersed nature, and the seemingly random digging by engineers, erred in their targeting. Few units were hit as the Soviet artillery fell on positions where vehicles used to be. While not all companies and platoons were equally lucky, the effect of the bombardment was, on the whole, negligible. Even the Soviet smoke rounds were of little use, as the gunners in Capell's Bradleys and M-1s switched their thermal sights on and continued to scan for signs of the enemy's advance.

In the gray morning twilight, the scout section of the battalion's western flank caught the first glimpse of the advancing Soviet columns at a range of eight kilometers. A quick spot report was followed by a call for artillery fire. Within minutes, U.S. artillery rounds were thundering north. The grim task of killing was well under way.

Dixon's Bradley pulled up into its position as the scouts completed sending in their first series of corrections to the artillery. By that time the Soviet columns were within five kilometers and beginning to deploy into platoon columns. Initial reports showed that they were headed for the western flank of the battalion's sector, where Dixon was situated.

That suited him fine. The battalion, with two tank and two mechanized companies, had deployed in positions that looked like a huge horseshoe on the map. One tank-pure company, Alpha Company, was deployed across the valley floor behind an antitank ditch and a mine field. A pure-mech company, Charlie Company, was deployed on the high ground to one flank, with a tank-heavy company team, Team Bravo, on the other. The fourth company team, Team Delta, had given one tank platoon to the scouts. The other two platoons, both mech, were in positions behind the tank company in the center, which allowed them to fire their TOW missiles over the tanks. If the Soviets continued to drive up along the western flank through the wadis there, they would have to contend with Charlie Company's dismounted infantry and face close-in combat with the Bradleys' 25mm chain gun. If they went in the center, everyone would be able to fire on them. If the Soviets skirted the east, the tanks of both Team Bravo and Alpha Company would be able to deal with them, while Charlie Company's Bradleys on the west flank would have good TOW shots from across the valley.

Once the Soviets were committed, the battalion commander would have the artillery fire two scatterable mine fields, one in front of and one on top of the Soviets' column. While there was no doubt that the Soviets knew where the antitank ditch and mine field were, there was no way they could predict where and when the scatterable mines would go. If they were fired in conjunction with normal indirect artillery and mortar fire, direct fire from the tanks and the Bradleys and, if available, close air support from A-10s, the cumulative effect would be devastating.

Relentlessly the Soviets came on. Capell's scouts maintained a steady flow of reports on the Soviets' progress and actions. By the time the Soviet lead battalion deployed into lines with one company forward and others following the first, it had lost over ten vehicles to artillery and was having difficulty maintaining alignment. Capell's scout platoon and the tank platoon with them

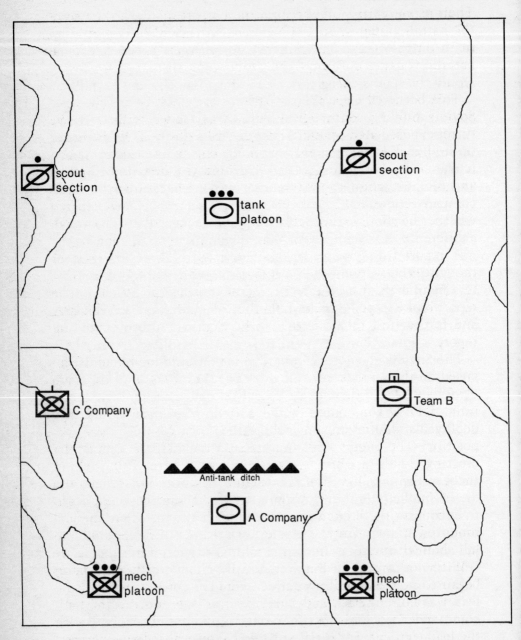

DEFENSIVE POSITIONS
OF 3RD BATTALION, 4TH ARMOR

withdrew to either side of the advancing battalion without firing. Their primary mission, screening and reporting while the rest of the battalion deployed, had been accomplished. They would remain on the flanks and continue to report as Soviet follow-on battalions came into the fight. Only when absolutely necessary would the scouts engage.

This bothered Capell. From the eastern flank he watched the Soviets moving south. His Bradley was hidden with only the turret exposed aboveground. His gunner, with the TOW launcher up and locked, was slowly tracking one of the Soviet tanks. It was a T-80 traveling by itself behind the first line of tanks and BRT-60 armored personnel carriers. It had to be the tank-company commander. For the next few seconds Capell debated whether he should ignore the order not to engage. It won't make a difference, he told himself. Who the hell's going to know?

A report from one of his section leaders broke his train of thought. The second-echelon battalion was in sight, five kilometers behind the trail element of the first Soviet battalion. The report broke Capell's fixation on the T-80 they had been tracking and forced him to go back to his assigned tasks: observe and report.

The Soviets continued forward. Their orientation remained focused on the far-western side of the battalion sector. They were obviously headed there in an effort to skirt the antitank ditch and mine field. Dixon could now see the Soviet companies, all fully deployed and following one behind the other, rushing toward his position. The Soviet tanks had cut on their smoke generators, creating clouds of white smoke that obscured everything behind them to the naked eye. Thermal sights, however, cut through the diesel smoke. In another minute the lead elements would begin to encounter the broken-ground and wadi system where the dismounted infantry and the Bradleys waited. Artillery continued to fall about the Bradleys in spurts, taking its toll.

With nothing to do but wait until contact was made, Dixon began to notice small, obscure details. One of the T-80s in the lead was holding back and swerving from side to side. The tank commander, no doubt, was nervous and did not relish being with the lead element. For the first time, Dixon realized how nervous *he* was. He could sympathize with that tank commander. How much easier it was to be sitting in the defense than running out across the open, knowing that everyone with an antitank missile

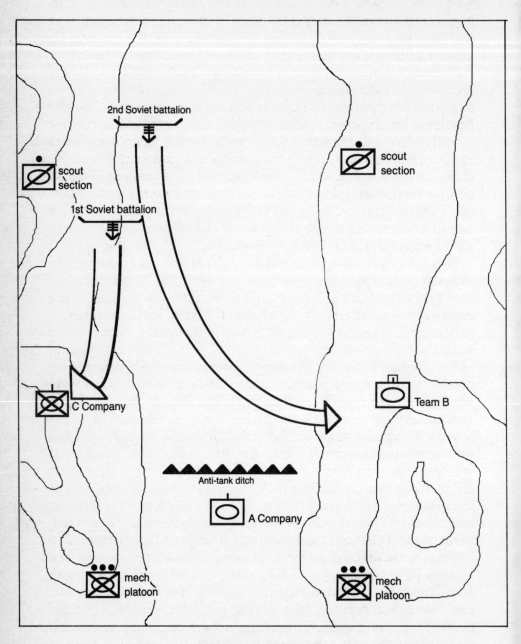

2nd Soviet battalion

scout section

1st Soviet battalion

scout section

C Company

Team B

Anti-tank ditch

A Company

mech platoon

mech platoon

SOVIET ATTACK ON
3RD BATTALION, 4TH ARMOR

was tracking you. Dixon looked down into his own turret. His gunner was calmly tracking a Soviet tank. Their TOW launcher was up and the ready-to-fire indicator was illuminated. All the gunner needed was one word.

The commander of Charlie Company gave that word as the lead Soviet tanks tripped across an imaginary line on the ground and entered Charlie Company's kill zone. Dixon watched as four Bradleys let fly their TOW missiles. The nervous T-80 was quickly alerted to the oncoming danger. He fired smoke grenades and stopped moving, in an effort to screen himself. The TOW that was targeted for him found its mark, however. The TOW gunner merely kept his thermal sight on the center mass where the T-80 had been and let the missile fly into the screen of smoke. A ball of flame followed by a rush of black smoke pushed the white smoke aside. The T-80 was dead.

Not all the T-80s died from their first hits. Reactive armor, explosives in small metal boxes arrayed in front of the turrets of the T-80s, detonated with thunderous explosions and in some cases prevented the TOWs' warheads from penetrating the tanks' main armor. Dixon was amazed that crews were able to survive such a cataclysmic explosion. Some did, rolling on, trailing a thin veil of smoke from smoldering scraps and hot steel. These successes were normally short-lived, however, as other TOWs marked the same tank and bored through. In less than a minute, all four lead tanks were burning or stopped.

With the tanks gone, the Soviet BTRs came rolling out from under the smokescreen generated by the tanks. Their alignment was gone as they drove past burning tanks or zigzagged in an effort to confuse the Bradleys' TOW antitank guided missiles. But the Bradley gunners were not confused by the evasive maneuvers, and the BTRs, not protected by reactive armor, were easy prey: most of the TOW missiles found their mark and took their toll.

Despite the demise of the lead company, the next Soviet motorized rifle company rolled forward, past the foundering lead company. The second company had only two tanks in the lead and five BTRs. Artillery had already made its inroads. The folly of the Soviet deployment in column manifested itself as the second and third companies were, in their turn, smashed by Charlie Company. Rather than hit in mass, the Soviets had presented themselves a little at a time. It reminded Dixon of watching a butcher feed meat into a grinder. Though each motorized rifle company drew closer to Charlie Company in its turn and was finally able to return fire, this gained it nothing but a quicker death as the 25mm chain guns came into play.

For a moment, there was a pause. The firing died down but did not completely stop. A few of the BTRs had made it into the wadis and their infantry had dismounted. A fight, pitting Soviet infantrymen supported by their BTR armored personnel carriers against Charlie Company's infantrymen and their Bradleys, now developed in the broken ground and wadis along the western flank of the American battalion's sector. Charlie Company had more than enough people and firepower to decide the issue if the Soviets were not reinforced. Dixon listened to the reports from the scouts as the second Soviet motorized rifle battalion entered the sector of the 3rd of the 4th Armor.

The Soviet second-echelon battalion apparently did not know that the first battalion had gained a foothold in the wadis. Instead of rushing forward and adding its weight to that fight, it rolled down along the eastern flank. The only reasonable explanation was that the regimental commander, surprised at the strength encountered in the west, had decided to try the left, hoping to find it lightly defended. Since the eastern side of the 3rd of the 4th Armor's sector was more open, the Soviets were able to deploy two companies forward, with the second company close enough to the first to support it by fire.

The same openness also allowed the 3rd of the 4th to mass the firepower of the remaining company and two teams, with telling effect. Once the Soviets were committed, Dixon called for the artillery to fire scatterable mines. These mines, in conjunction with the antitank ditch and the mines already in place, slowed and disrupted the well-orchestrated Soviet battle drill. Despite large volumes of artillery- and tank-generated smoke, efforts to breach the obstacles were frustrated by accurate M-1 tank fire. Soviet mine rollers and plows, along with MTU bridge layers, were destroyed as soon as they ventured forward. T-80 tanks standing off and attempting to provide cover fire for the mine rollers and plows were, in their turn, destroyed. Seeing no way around the obstacle and little chance of bulling through, the Soviets began to withdraw.

As the battle began to ebb, Dixon's assistant called him on the radio and asked if he had been monitoring the brigade-command frequency. Dixon, caught up in the battalion's fight, had not. The assistant S-3 reported that the brigade was having difficulty contacting the 1st of the 503rd Infantry. That battalion had reported earlier that it was being hit by tanks and BMPs, and after several sketchy reports it had stopped answering the brigade's calls.

Dixon was concerned. If the infantry battalion had been hit by a regiment equipped with BMPs, odds were that the main effort was going in against the 503rd and not the 3rd of the 4th Armor. The fight that was dying out to his front was probably nothing more than a supporting attack whose purpose was to divert attention while the Soviets broke through the infantry battalion. Dixon contacted his commander and relayed his conclusions. The battalion commander concurred and, in turn, contacted the brigade commander, with the result that the armored battalion was instructed to make physical contact with the 1st of the 503rd Infantry and clarify the situation over there.

With the scouts forward, Charlie Company still flushing out the Soviet survivors, and the battalion commander needed in the battalion sector, it was up to Dixon to make that contact. Besides, Dixon knew where the two battalions' designated contact points were. Without giving it further thought, he ordered his driver to back the Bradley out of its position.

Even after the Bradley had moved into the infantry sector—having avoided enemy fire by traveling along covered and concealed routes—it inched along with caution. Since they were approaching the other battalion's positions from the rear and were five kilometers from where the front line should be, they had more to fear from a nervous U.S. infantryman armed with an antitank-rocket launcher than from the Soviets.

As they moved forward through a narrow, twisting wadi, Dixon had a crewman in the rear compartment switch the radio to the battalion-command frequency of the 1st of the 503rd Infantry and attempted to raise someone on that net. There was no response. After three unsuccessful attempts, he decided to try a company-command net in that battalion. Just as Dixon lowered himself onto his seat inside the turret and pulled out his codebook to look up the company frequencies, his gunner screamed, *"Jesus Christ!* Back up—no, driver, stop! *On the waaay!"* This was immediately followed by a long burst of 25mm cannon fire as the gunner held his trigger down, pumping out rounds.

Dixon was startled. He looked at his gunner, who had now

stopped firing, and shouted at him without keying the intercom, "What the fuck are you doing?"

The gunner didn't answer, but kept his eye glued to his sight. Then it dawned upon Dixon what had happened. Letting the codebook fall to the floor, he popped his head up out of the turret and looked in the direction the 25mm gun was pointed. To their front, at a range of less than twenty meters, was a burning Soviet BMP, its 30mm gun aimed at Dixon.

Chapter 13

*My center gives way, my right is pushed
back, situation excellent, I am attacking.*
                    —FERDINAND FOCH

Twenty Kilometers South of Harvand
0810 Hours, 8 July (0440 Hours, 8 July, GMT)

Instead of diminishing, the volume of small-arms fire directed
against the advancing Soviet formations was increasing. Isolated
pockets of enemy infantry were coming out of hiding and engaging the men of the 1st Battalion, 381st Motorized Rifle Regiment.
The Americans had not crumpled as before and had, instead, recovered from their initial attack and in some cases seemed to be
counterattacking.

Neboatov's company had again been the second attack echelon
of the battalion. As before, the preparatory artillery bombardment had silenced all resistance as the attacking force approached. Again the battalion had rolled over the American
forward positions and driven for the regiment's objective. This
time, however, the battalion had been hit by a combination of
close-in antitank rockets and long-range antitank guided missiles. The antitank guided missiles, or ATGMs, had been set up
behind hills and in wadis in the Americans' rear areas. From these
well-covered and well-concealed positions, the ATGM teams
were impossible to detect before they fired. Even when the positions were detected, by the time effective fire could be massed
against them the ATGM teams were gone, moved to another
hidden position farther up the valley.

While the American level of fire was insufficient to stop the attacking columns, it slowed the advance, delayed the commitment of follow-on forces and forced the lead regiment to turn against the resisting Americans. This task fell to the 381st Motorized Rifle Regiment. It was forced to dismount its riflemen, in order to clear the shoulders of the penetration in preparation for the commitment of the 127th Motorized Rifle Division's own tank regiment and the 33rd Tank Division.

The resulting fight pitted the regiment's riflemen, backed by their tanks and BMP-2 infantry-fighting vehicles, against an elusive foe that moved from one hidden position in the high ground to the next. American infantrymen, deployed on the lower heights, defended the antitank-guided-missile teams located farther up the hillside. When Soviet riflemen began to close on a position and threaten to overwhelm it, the ATGM teams would move while the infantry covered them. They, in their turn, would move to the next prepared position that covered the ATGM teams already in place.

The problem for Neboatov's battalion was to get past and around the Americans, isolate them, bring superior firepower and numbers to bear and then crush them. While they had the advantage of having BMPs to carry them, the vehicles were easily tracked and often frustrated by obstacles, mines or antitank guided missiles. A hit on a BMP by an antitank guided missile resulted in the dual loss of a fighting vehicle and a squad of riflemen. Cutting off the Americans did not seem to bother them; they remained just as dangerous, moving about along concealed routes in small groups, infiltrating past the surrounding Soviet riflemen. On occasion, they would fall on the rear of Soviet riflemen who were maneuvering against another position. The result was a confusing swirl of battle that knew no front or rear, no friendly lines or hostile positions. Just chaos and sudden death.

After a failed attempt to destroy a pocket of resistance, Neboatov was trying to rally his men and plan their next move. After three hours of playing cat and mouse among the rocks and the wadis, he was running out of ideas and was frustrated. He ordered his driver to tuck their BMP into a small draw near one of his platoons so that they would be out of harm's way while he collected his command and his thoughts. No sooner had they pulled in than his battalion commander's BMP rolled up. Both officers dismounted from their vehicles and walked over to a spot near some large rocks to discuss the situation out of earshot of their men. The crews of the two BMPs, exhausted and hot from driving about buttoned up, dismounted and took the opportunity to relax and eat something. Sitting on top of their vehicles, they picked at their combat rations, drank from their canteens and speculated among themselves what would happen next.

The battalion commander, like Neboatov, was frustrated. The regimental commander wanted the Americans cleared before the division's tank regiment was committed. He, in turn, was being pressured by Division to give the all clear. The two officers knelt to study a map the battalion commander laid out on the ground. As he pointed with a grease pencil to key areas that he wanted Neboatov to clear, sweat from his brow dripped onto the map. Neboatov wiped his own face with a dirty rag as he listened to his commander explain how the battalion would systematically clear the valley. The task would be long and tedious, not to mention dangerous.

A sudden warning shout from one of the BMP crewmen was cut short by a burst of automatic fire. Neboatov and his commander, looking up to see what was happening, watched in horror as the crews of the two BMPs were cut down by accurate small-arms fire. The two officers turned in the direction the fire was coming from in time to see four American infantrymen jump out from behind one of the rocks. The two in the lead were firing their rifles from the hip as they rushed forward. The other two were lobbing grenades in the direction of the BMPs.

The battalion commander was the first to react and the first to fall. The sudden motion as he stood up and reached for his pistol caught the attention of the Americans. One of them stopped in place, turned toward the two officers and, firing from the hip, let go two quick bursts. Both bursts hit the battalion commander square in the chest, ripping it open and throwing him backward on top of Neboatov, who was still kneeling. The impact of his colonel's body sent him sprawling, and he hit his head against a rock.

Though not unconscious, Neboatov had the wind knocked out of him and was unable to clearly focus or react. Pinned beneath the body of his dead commander, his head reeling, he watched the Americans rush forward and drop grenades into the open hatches of the two BMPs. One of the American infantrymen noticed the map on the ground and walked over to recover it. As he was bending over, Neboatov tried to reach for his pistol. His spastic fumbling served only to catch the American's attention. Dropping the map, the American swung around and raised his rifle, its muzzle stopping inches from Neboatov's face.

Neboatov knew he was going to die. He closed his eyes. After what seemed to be an eternity, the familar burst of several AKs caused him to open them. The threatening rifle muzzle and the American were gone. From where he lay, Neboatov could see several of his men from the nearby platoon running forward. While some of them pursued the surviving Americans, a lieutenant and two men came over to give their company commander a hand. Gently, they moved the battalion commander's body off Neboatov and helped him up.

Neboatov scanned the area as he collected his thoughts and caught his breath. He was shaking like a leaf. Two Americans, one of them the soldier who moments before had held Neboatov's life in his hand, were down. The other two were gone. Small-arms fire from beyond the rocks told that they were fighting as they withdrew. The battalion commander's BMP was burning, and ammunition on board popped as it cooked in the fire. Neboatov's BMP was smoking. The bodies, wounded and dead, of both BMPs' crews were scattered about the ground or hanging limp off the BMPs. Half-eaten rations and spilled canteens were scattered among the bodies or held in lifeless hands.

Neboatov walked over to his BMP on shaky legs, stopping where the body of his driver lay. He knelt and pulled the leather helmet from the soldier's head, freeing a crop of dirty blond hair matted down by sweat and oil. The soldier was more boy than man, not more than nineteen years old. He had been born and raised on a small collective farm in the eastern Ukraine, a true son of Mother Russia. Though Neboatov seldom bothered with the enlisted men in his command, he had taken special interest in this youth because of his loyalty to family and country, his skills as a tracked-vehicle driver, and a shy, easygoing manner that Neboatov found refreshing. Now he was gone, killed in a barren land miles from his beloved family and country. The young girl he spoke of often would probably never know how he had died. His mother would never be able to tend to his needs again. He was dead, killed in action in the service of the Party and his country.

Neboatov stood up and turned his face to the rising sun. He felt its heat. How brutal, he thought, this day is going to be.

North of Harvand
0845 Hours, 8 July (0515 Hours, 8 July, GMT)

The two attacking A-10 aircraft were a long time gone before all firing ceased. Once the tank crews did cease fire, they automatically turned 180 degrees, preparing for an attack by a second pair of American planes. Vorishnov knew that the Americans would not come from the same direction again. As he picked himself up off the ground, he looked about in an effort to guess which way they would come if they did return. Deciding that this was an exercise in futility, he turned his attention to more immediate problems.

The 3rd Battalion was scattered about in an open field, dispersed as a precaution against air attack. That, however, had not saved them this time. Two A-10s had come swooping down out of the sun as the tanks sat waiting for the order to move forward, an order that had not yet been given. From where he stood, Vorishnov counted three of his battalion's tanks burning. He was about to heave a sigh of relief when his eyes fell upon his BTR-60. Smoke was pouring from its open hatches. It had been hit.

As he rushed over, the chatter of machine-gun fire announced the approach of the attacking aircraft. The low-pitch ripping sound of the A-10s' miniguns sent Vorishnov diving. As he flattened himself against the ground he imagined he could feel the planes' 30mm. projectiles passing right over him. The *pock-pock-pock* of the rounds hitting metal, followed by a low, rumbling explosion, told him that another tank had died. When the screech of the jets' engines had again passed, Vorishnov picked himself up and ran toward the BTR.

The BTR was a total loss. Flames were now shooting from the open hatches. A man trying to pull out the body of one of the crewmen was beaten back by the heat of the flames. Looking around, Vorishnov saw the battalion's second officer sitting on the ground next to a sprawled-out body. Vorishnov went over to him.

He could see that the second officer, a young intelligence captain, was hit in the shoulder and bleeding. His helmet was off and his face was quite pale. Speckles of blood seemed to cover his tunic. No doubt he was going into shock. As Vorishnov knelt down next to the young captain, he noticed that the body on the ground was that of the political officer. He knew this only from the insignia—the body was without a head.

"Alexis," Vorishnov asked, "are you hit anywhere else?"

The second officer only shook his head in response. He was obviously losing blood.

"Come, we must get that arm tended to."

As Vorishnov helped him up the captain spoke hesitantly, his voice barely audible. "We . . . we were walking away from the BTR, talking about the delay. We heard the planes begin to fire. We both turned to see what the noise was. Then I looked toward Lieutenant Teplov, just as he was hit. A round hit him in the head and exploded. It . . . " The second officer stared into Vorishnov's eyes before he continued. "His head just exploded. It blew apart, all over me. It just . . . it blew apart." As he talked, the captain ran his hands down his tunic, which, Vorishnov realized, was spattered not only with blood but also with scraps of human brain tissue. The young man's eyes were wide and showed his bewilderment and shock. "We must help him. How are we going to fix him, Comrade Major? His head is gone. What are we going to do, Comrade?"

Vorishnov cradled the captain's face gently in his hands and spoke softly, the way his father had spoken to him when he was a boy and was hurt or confused. "Lieutenant Teplov is dead. He has done his duty. We must now take care of you. There is nothing we can do for him. Do you understand?"

Tears welled up in the captain's eyes as reality began to take hold. He looked into the major's eyes for a moment, then nodded that he understood.

"Good," Vorishnov said. "Let us tend to your arm." With that, he led the second officer away from the smashed BTR and the shattered remains of the political officer.

South of Hajjiabad, Iran
0915 Hours, 8 July (0545 Hours, 8 July, GMT)

Throughout the initial phase of the engagement that morning it had been difficult to believe there was a real-life battle going on, a battle that involved killing and dying. Everything had been working so well, too well. The American maneuver battalions submitted their reports on enemy activities and their own status as if this were nothing more than a training exercise. Military-intelligence units operating well forward were picking up all the information they needed to show that the main attack was coming into the 3rd of the 4th Armor's sector. That battalion's reports confirmed that and the battalion's success in defeating the attack.

Everything suddenly changed when the truth was finally known. The discovery of Soviet forces in the rear of the sector of the 1st of the 503rd Infantry, coupled with Brigade's inability to raise that battalion, caused concerns at Brigade and near-panic in 3rd of the 4th Armor. The commander of that armored battalion wanted to withdraw immediately toward Tarom. With the infantry battalion penetrated, he saw no way he could hold where he was. The brigade commander, unsure of how bad things really were, wanted the situation clarified before he began giving ground. Besides, even if the 1st of the 503rd Infantry had been penetrated, Brigade could still shift the 1st of the 29th Mech from the east into the infantry battalion's sector and counterattack. At least that was what the brigade commander wanted. Initial orders to execute that contingency plan were issued. Units began to shift in compliance.

Well to the north, Soviet electronic-warfare units waged a different, silent and unseen war. With electronic equipment that rivaled the best that the West had to offer, Soviet intelligence officers and technicians listened to the airwaves, scanning the full spectrum of FM, HF and AM radio waves. When they caught a transmission in progress, they locked onto it and studied it. Although they could not understand what was being said over the various American command radio nets because of speech-secure equipment, they could determine which nets were brigade command, which were battalion command and so on. When the traffic on the command nets suddenly increased, followed shortly by an apparent shifting of forces from the mech infantry battalion's sector in the east, Soviet electronic-warfare units went into action.

Some of the American locations that FM radio emissions were coming from had already been pinpointed through radio direction-finding and targeted for attack by artillery. But the Soviets held back, waiting for the right moment when disruption or loss of the American command-and-control elements would have maximum effect. With the situation now changing rapidly, the decision was made to take out selected targets.

Orders went out to the Soviet artillery battalions to fire on some of those locations. Other radio nets were simply jammed with high volumes of interference. Some of the jamming was silent jamming, a technique whereby the subscribers to the radio net do not hear any unusual noise or see any effect until they try to transmit over their radio; when they do try but cannot make contact, they often assume their radio is not operating or that terrain is blocking the transmission. Other radio nets were jammed with loud noises and unusual sounds designed to annoy the listener. Regardless of the means used to jam or interfere, the results were the same: commanders could no longer control their subordinate commands or pass information.

The artillery attack (called a fire strike by the Soviets) that had been directed against 2nd Brigade's headquarters was a rude awakening for the brigade staff. The calm, businesslike atmosphere was suddenly smashed as heavy artillery projectiles screamed in and burst nearby. Because the FM radio antennas were located away from the actual command post, the incoming rounds did not hit squarely on the tactical operations center. The effects, however, were devastating just the same. Chunks of shrapnel, some no larger than a pin, others the size of a fist, carried by overpowering bursts, ripped through the canvas sides of the TOC extensions. Maps, paper, books, phones and people were brushed aside. The staff, once they were down on the ground, remained there, covering their ears or their heads as round after round detonated and sent its own wave of heat, dirt and shrapnel into the TOC.

Though the attack lasted less than two minutes, it transformed the TOC from a neat, orderly command-and-control node to a tangled heap of paper, tables, wire and assorted equipment. Moans from the wounded broke the stillness as the staff began to untangle themselves from the debris. Lieutenant Matthews pulled herself up and looked around. The canvas sides of the extensions were shredded and hanging limply from the support poles. The situation map was hanging at an angle from one of its supports. Field desks were overturned, their contents scattered about and mixed with the contents of tables and other desks. Other staff officers and NCOs were also picking themselves up. Some, however, were not.

Matthews began to help those around her by clearing off debris and giving them a hand. When she went to help her boss, Major Price, get up, she noticed the bright-red spot on his back. Bending down, she turned his face toward her. His eyes were shut tightly; his face was frozen in pain. He let out a scream, then yelled not to move him. Matthews stopped, unsure what to do. She called for the S-2 NCO.

Master Sergeant Trent came over and, kneeling next to the major, asked how badly he was hit. Without opening his eyes, Price replied that he couldn't move his legs or feel them. Trent looked at Price's back. Carefully he ripped the BDU shirt. A deep gash ran across the major's lower back. Trent thought the spine might have been severed and said so.

Matthews, fighting back nausea, told them she would get some help. She stood and looked around. Others were beginning to move about and help one another. When she saw the brigade XO, she went over to where he stood. He seemed unaffected by the calamity that had befallen the TOC. Standing in the middle of the remains of it, he was directing the brigade signal officer to sort out their communications status. Matthews waited till he was done before she told him about Major Price. The XO sent her out to find a medic while he walked over to where Price was.

Outside the TOC not much had changed. In the distance Matthews could see numerous shell holes where the antennas had been. Men from the signal platoon were already scurrying about, putting up spare antennas and checking cable connections. Matthews headed for the medical team assigned to the command post. As she approached its area, located on the far side of a small rise that separated the TOC from where the CP's admin-support vehicles were, she heard the sound of tracked vehicles. The ambulance, which was a tracked vehicle, she thought, was cranking up and coming to the TOC. She had almost reached there when the scream "BMPs!" from that direction told her she was wrong.

Matthews froze for a moment and listened. A burst of machine-gun fire, joined by the sound of small-caliber cannon, confirmed her fears. The Soviets had somehow managed to penetrate into the brigade's rear and were attacking the CP. Her immediate instinct, to turn and run, was overridden by the urge to see exactly what was going on so that she could render an accurate report. Dropping down, she rapidly crawled up to the top of the rise and looked over.

To her front she saw six BMPs moving forward in a loose formation. Trucks and personnel from the headquarters company
were scattering about in an effort to escape them. The BMPs,
given so many easy targets, slowed or stopped and fired wildly at
whatever happened to be in their sights. They obviously did not
know that there was a CP on the other side of the hill.

Having seen all she needed, Matthews ran back to the TOC.
The XO had heard the firing and was already directing the remaining staff to throw what was really critical into the M-577
tracked command-post carriers and get ready to move. Matthews
reported to him what she had seen. He thought about it for a
moment, then told her to get the S-2's M-577 track ready and
moving. She asked about Major Price, reminding the XO that
they couldn't move him. He barked at her, telling her to get the
M-577 out of there.

At the back of the S-2 track she saw Sergeant Trent and another
NCO, who had managed to get Major Price strapped onto a long
wooden table and were in the process of carrying him into the
track. Matthews gave a hand as best she could as they eased the
major down onto the floor. Despite the fact that he was in a great
deal of pain, he did not scream. He clawed at the edges of the
table while the lieutenant and two sergeants bounced and
bumped it against the side of the track. His face was contorted in
pain. His knuckles were white. But he did not scream.

Once they were in, Trent yelled to the driver to crank the track
up and raise the back ramp. Matthews looked about and saw that
the intelligence situation map was already loaded. She turned to
Trent, told him to wait a moment and ran out of the track. The
S-3 track was already pulling away, leaving the shredded extensions and support poles as well as field desks and unnecessary
paper and books. Matthews looked around what had been the S-2
area and grabbed a couple of books and binders. The sound of
machine-gun fire grew closer. Sergeant Trent's yells hastened her
search. She looked down at the mass of papers scattered about
the ground and decided that efforts to recover more would be
useless.

She turned and ran up to the crew door located on the rear
ramp, which was now up and locked. With a heave she dumped
the books she held in her arms into the open door and then
hopped in after them. Sergeant Trent grabbed her arm and pulled
her in as he yelled to the driver to move out and follow the S-3

track. Matthews, lying on the floor of the track as it began to move and bounce away, saw through the open crew door a BMP come over the rise. It began to fire at them. With effort, Trent was finally able to close that door just before a burst of machine-gun rounds tapped on the outside of the ramp.

For a moment, all was silent except for the sound of the M-577's engine, the grinding of its tracks and the heavy breathing of its occupants. The four people in the rear sat or lay where they were in the dark interior of the command-post carrier, drained by the close escape. None of them knew what was going on outside, let alone with the battle, a battle now obviously out of control and being lost.

Headquarters, 13th Corps, Bandar Abbas, Iran
1345 Hours, 8 July (1015 Hours, 8 July, GMT)

Despite his better judgment, Lieutenant General Weir had gone into the corps operations center when he got word that the Soviet attack had begun. Anxiously he watched the situation turn sour. Successive cups of coffee did nothing to calm him as the corps staff, already used to a string of disasters, thrashed about in a futile attempt to gain an understanding of what was happening. Weir, pacing and fuming, saw Air Force and Army air units thrown into the fray without coordination at widely scattered targets and enemy concentrations, most of which were not an immediate threat to the 2nd Brigade. Orders to withdraw the entire brigade to Tarom were canceled and then put back into effect twice in the space of one hour.

The deputy corps commander, a major general, went from staff section to staff section in an effort to influence the situation. He alternated between yelling at the corps signal officer and the operations officer, whom he threatened to relieve of his duties unless he got a handle on the situation. Sometime during midmorning the deputy commander received word that the corps commander, who was at the forward corps command post at Saadatabad, had collapsed. Seizing the opportunity to escape the chaos and ignorance of the main command post, the deputy decided to go forward and "get control of the situation." Weir watched and listened as the deputy ordered the corps chief of staff to reorganize the staff as he saw fit, reestablish communications and begin to focus combat power at the point of penetration, wherever that was. The deputy then left by helicopter for Saadat-abad.

Weir stayed for another half hour without seeing any change. Unable to bear sitting there doing nothing while he watched the 13th Corps, and one of his brigades, go down the tubes, he stormed out and headed for his own advance command post. En route, he scribbled notes, his mind racing through options open to his corps. As he did so, he wondered whether any of the naval officers in the area had ever studied the British evacuation at Dunkirk. As distasteful as that thought was, he could not discount the possibility that the U.S. forces could be forced to withdraw. The warning his friend had given him the night before he left Washington, that the United States could not afford to lose all the ground forces in Iran, kept popping up in his mind. He included "Evacuation of forces" on his list of options right after "Request for release and use of tactical nuclear weapons."

At his headquarters Weir was greeted by his own chief of staff with word from the chief of staff of the 13th Corps that the helicopter carrying the 13th Corps's deputy commander had been shot down. Initial reports were that there were no survivors. Given the current situation and the rapid loss of both senior officers, the 13th Corps's chief of staff had requested that General Weir assume command.

For a moment, Weir considered telling him no, or at least consulting with the CINC. That, however, would take time, a commodity quickly running out. Weir asked his chief how long it would be before the 10th Corps headquarters could assume control of the battle. The chief, having anticipated the question, told him that while not all the staff principals were in place, the operations staff, the fire-support element, the plans section and the airspace-management element were preparing to do so and could be ready for a battle takeover from 13th Corps in three or four hours, but that the 13th would need to continue to control all personnel and logistic operations for at least another twenty-four hours. The 10th Corps G-1 and G-4 as well as the corps support command were still heavily involved in assembling the 10th Corps. Satisfied that his chief had the situation well in hand, Weir told him to inform the 13th Corps chief of staff that he was en route back and wanted to see all 13th Corps staff principals and special staff officers upon his arrival. He handed his chief his scribbled notes, told him to have his staff start working on those options, and left.

The greeting he got at 13th Corps headquarters was cold and strained. He was no longer a visitor or an observer. He was their commander, come to replace two who had failed or died. The officers and the men watched him the way the condemned watches the executioner. The staff was assembled in a small dirty conference room, seated around a long table cluttered with scraps of paper. When Weir walked in, they slowly stood to attention. Their faces betrayed a mixture of fear, exhaustion and stress. They're beat, Weir thought to himself as he stood there and looked at them. They've lost the battle and have given up. For an awkward moment, they looked at each other, not knowing quite how to proceed.

In his desperate search for some way to get the 13th Corps staff going again, the Battle of Marengo suddenly came to his mind. During that battle, a French general, Louis Desaix, who commanded a detachment of the main French army, was recalled by Napoleon to save a losing battle. When the two met, a discouraged Napoleon asked what he thought of the situation. Desaix, according to the story, casually pulled out his watch and replied, "This battle is completely lost, but it is only two o'clock. There is time to win another."

The slight smile that flitted across Weir's face confused the staff officers. Without further ado, Weir announced, "Gentlemen, we have much to do. There is a battle that needs winning, and you're going to do it."

Robat-e Abgram, Iran
0215 Hours, 9 July (2245 Hours, 8 July, GMT)

The Iranian major dressed himself slowly. The dim light from an oil lamp gave a soft yellow cast to everything in the small room that was nothing more than a hovel. A mattress on the floor and a chair comprised all the room's furniture. The major's worn flight suit was carefully draped across the back of the chair. How fortunate he was, the major thought, to be selected for this mission. Since the Soviets came he had resigned himself to dying. Doing so was easy. What concerned him was dying in a manner befitting his heritage as a Persian and in the service of Islam.

His selection to fly an F-4, hidden for months, and strike at both Satans was truly a gift from Allah. The Air Force colonel in charge of the operation had personally selected him and asked him to fly the mission. The major had accepted willingly despite the colonel's warning that it would be a one-way trip. He had replied, with a smile, that it would be a trip to glory and martyrdom.

The mission was simple. The major would fly the F-4 along a roundabout route to a point just north of Saadatabad. The Americans and the Russians were locked in combat there, busily hacking away at one another, according to the colonel. The F-4 would carry just one bomb, an atomic one. Once he reached the designated point, the major would hit a switch that would begin the chain reaction. It was not possible to drop the bomb. The device was too crude and the trigger mechanism needed for such a drop was beyond their capability. Even if the aircraft crashed, the device would not go off. Only a precise sequence of firing would cause it to detonate. The F-4 would, in effect, be a manned guided missile. Since little on the aircraft worked, that was about all it was good for.

He did not ponder what would become of his family or the nation. When compared to what he was about to do in the name of the Islamic Revolution, those matters were unimportant. What was important was the punishing of the nonbelievers and those who had defiled his country. He knew that what he was about to do was right. He placed his trust in his skills as a pilot to get him there. Everything else after that was in the hands of Allah.

Aliabad, Iran
0230 Hours, 9 July (2300 Hours 8 July, GMT)

The day that had begun so well and had held so much promise for the 28th Combined Arms Army had turned bad before noon. The breakthrough and encirclement that should have taken place before in a matter of hours never happened. Instead of blowing through the American infantry deployed south of Harvand, the attacking regiment became involved in a slugfest. By the time the last of the die-hard enemy infantry had been dug out or had withdrawn, it was late afternoon and the 381st Motorized Rifle Regiment was combat ineffective.

Even that had not spelled the end of problems for the 28th

CAA. When the 127th Motorized Rifle Division finally committed its tank regiment to pass through the infantry melee and seize Tarom, it was greeted by an American battalion equipped with AH-64 attack helicopters. Constricted by the terrain and the narrow opening held by the 381st MRR, the tank regiment was an easy target. Volleys of Hellfire missiles rained on the tight tank formations and wreaked havoc without the tanks being able to strike back. Only through extraordinary effort and great sacrifices by the Red Air Force was the attack-helicopter threat finally checked. That success came too late for the 127th MRD's tank regiment.

It wasn't until midafternoon that there appeared to be a slackening of the Americans' resistance. Air activity ceased. Troops broke contact and withdrew. For a while, Colonel Sulvina suspected that the Americans were preparing to employ tactical nuclear weapons. To prevent that, subordinate commanders were ordered to reestablish contact and stay close to the enemy. (You don't set off atomic weapons on your enemy when he is so close to your own forces that you will also be affected by your own weapons.) The army's intelligence officer reported, however, that there were few indicators other than the reduction of activity that pointed to imminent use of nuclear weapons. Instead, the withdrawals were felt to be part of a general retreat south to positions below Saadatabad. Still unconvinced, Sulvina ordered the army's nuclear-capable weapons to stand by for immediate use, just in case.

In the meantime, Sulvina decided to commit the 33rd Tank Division. If the intelligence officer was right about the Americans retreating, that was the time to hit and hit hard. Shortly after dark, the 33rd Tank Division rolled forward and began its advance on Saadatabad. As he waited for word from the lead elements, Sulvina considered all the options open to him and the Americans. If the Americans succeeded in making it to Saadatabad intact and establishing themselves in strong defensive positions south of that town, the 28th CAA would not have the combat power or the ammunition to dig them out or conduct a deliberate breakthrough attack. With no fuel reserves, major flanking maneuvers were out of the question. All depended on the 33rd Tank Division catching the retreating Americans while they were still in the open and smashing them. To keep the pressure on, the 67th Motorized Rifle Division was ordered to move south along the main road from Hajjiabad to Tarom. The 33rd Tank, advancing farther to the west, was to race past the retreating Americans and hit them in the flank or, if possible, get around into their rear. All depended on speed.

For the fourth time in ten minutes, Sulvina looked at his watch, then at the situation board. It had not been updated in four hours. He got up and walked over to the operations duty officer. "What word do we have from the 33rd Tank Division?"

The major looked at his reports and began to read off the last status report received from that unit. Sulvina cut him short. "What time, Comrade Major, was that report received?"

The major looked at the time entry and replied, "Twenty-two forty-five hours, Comrade Colonel."

"Don't you think we should find out where they are now and what they have been up to for the last four hours?" Sulvina returned.

"Of course, Comrade Colonel. We have been trying. However, most of the networks are being jammed. The Americans are concentrating most of their electronic jamming from both ground and airborne platforms, against the 33rd Tank Division. The rest are being turned on the 67th MRD. We are having great difficulty—"

Sulvina's face went red as he pounded his fist on the table. He was so angry, spit flew as he yelled, "Damn you, Major! If I wanted an excuse, I would have asked for it. I want to know where in hell they are and what they are doing. Find out, *now!*"

The major, taken aback by the sudden outburst, looked at the colonel, then simply replied, "Yes, Comrade Colonel, at once."

Sulvina walked away and out into the cool night air. He was tired. As he stood in the darkness, smoking a cigarette, he looked at the stars and wondered what they saw to the south. How frustrating it was for him to be there, unable to influence the fight. He wished he were forward, with the lead column. At least there he could so something.

Five Kilometers Northwest of Tarom, Iran
0305 Hours, 9 July (2335 Hours, 8 July, GMT)

In the darkness Major Vorishnov walked along the line of silent tanks. Hours of waiting and dodging air attacks had been replaced by a mad dash south through the dark along goat trails and wadis.

When they had finally been given the word to advance, it was greeted with a collective sigh of relief. At last they were going to have an opportunity to end the fight, once and for all. The speed of the move south strengthened that hope.

Shortly after 0200 hours, however, that hope died. One at a time, tanks began to drop out of the column. Vorishnov, bringing up the rear, stopped at each. At first, he thought the crews were falling asleep. As he approached the first tank, however, he found the crew awake but dismounted. He immediately assumed that the tank had had a mechanical failure. The tank commander greeted him with news that was far more serious. They had run out of fuel. Vorishnov criticized the commander for not refueling and left without waiting for an excuse.

Before Vorishnov's own tank had traveled a kilometer farther he came across a second stopped tank. Its crew was also dismounted, and for the same reason: they were out of fuel. This time Vorishnov did not say anything. He returned to his tank and asked his driver how much fuel they had. The response sent a chill down his back. His own tank's fuel gage was reading empty. He immediately radioed the battalion commander and informed him of the problem. The battalion commander ordered the battalion to pull off the road and halt for ten minutes. That done, he radioed Vorishnov and ordered him to dismount and personally check each tank's fuel status and then report to him.

By the time Vorishnov finished and approached the battalion commander's tank at the front of the column, the regimental commander was there. Vorishnov saluted the two colonels and reported, "As we suspected, the battalion is out of fuel. Half of the tanks' fuel gages, including mine, show they are empty. A commander on one of those tanks said he had no idea what his tank was running on anymore. We also have three tanks that have completely run dry. The rest of the tanks are approaching empty." He was about to add that the battalion could no longer advance, but decided not to. That conclusion was obvious, but the decision had to be made by a commander, not by a battalion staff officer.

The regimental commander spoke first. "We must continue. Continue until we can go no further. Fuel, I am sure, will make its way forward."

The battalion commander did not hesitate to disagree. "Comrade Colonel, we cannot do that. If we run ourselves completely out of fuel, the battalion will be totally strung out and unable to maneuver. We will be nothing more than steel pillboxes dotting the road and easy prey for attack aircraft or a counterattack. We must stop now and laager here into a defensive position until fuel arrives. We should go forward only when we can do so with all the tanks and with some measure of assurance that we will not run out of fuel in the middle of a battle."

"I cannot halt the attack. I do not have the authority to do that," the regimental commander said.

The battalion commander shot back, slightly agitated now, "Comrade, either we stop the attack now, while we are still together and have some fuel to maneuver with, or we wait until the lack of fuel stops us when we are not. Your only choice, Comrade Colonel, is whether you want the regiment to be together and have some fighting capability or whether you want it to be scattered to the four winds. The lack of fuel has already stopped us."

With a sigh, the regimental commander acknowledged that the other was right. Before he returned to his command vehicle, he ordered the battalion commander to assume a defensive posture to the west. The battalion immediately behind would swing to the east and do likewise.

With the regimental commander gone, Vorishnov turned to his battalion commander and asked the question that neither of them had the answer for: "Now what?"

Northeast of Saadatabad, Iran
0355 Hours, 9 July (0025 Hours, 9 July, GMT)

The AWACS controller had been tracking a single-aircraft plot for over fifteen minutes, coming from the northeast. At first he thought very little of it. The plane was flying relatively slowly and very low. Then it dawned upon him that it was a recon flight. He informed the commander and immediately began to search the area for fighters providing high cover. There was none. Both he and the commander thought that odd. Sending in recon without cover was not a normal practice. A single one without air cover was as good as dead. Satisfied that all was as it appeared, the commander ordered the alert fighters from Bandar Abbas to scramble and intercept. The order of the day was to keep the Soviets from getting any air recon through. The Army was maneuvering about, doing something really weird, and didn't want the Russians to catch on before they were ready.

The order to scramble caught Martain dozing. The entire squadron was dead on its ass after yesterday. Omaha Flight alone had gone up eight times, four of them in the ground-attack role, three times to provide cover for their own air-recon flights and once to squash a Russian recon flight. The men and the machines of the squadron were reaching their limits. Martain had once thought he would never reach the point where he would hate flying. He had been wrong. After yesterday, he was sick of it.

Mechanically, he and his wingman did their preflight. Though the ground crew tried, they too dragged as they did their thing to get the two F-15s airborne. Because of exhaustion, the whole procedure took far longer than normal. When the F-15s were finally up and Martain checked in with the AWACS controller, the controller sneered, "Good morning. Hated to wake you guys up so early."

Martain was livid. "Cut the crap, clown, and give me a vector."

The commander on the AWACS, monitoring the transmission, got on both of them and ordered them to restrict transmissions to proper radio procedures. Martain was about to tell him to fuck off, too, but decided against that. No need to piss off a full-bird colonel that early in the morning.

Following the instructions from the controller, Omaha Flight closed on the boggy. Once they were in the area, Martain's wizzo switched on the radar and began to search for their target. They had no trouble finding it, for the boggy continued on a straight-line course, flying low and slow. While his wingman covered him, Martain went down after the boggy. As he tracked it, the wizzo called out, "Hey, Ed, this guy's a real zombie. He just keeps flying low and dumb. Let's play with him for a while."

Martain thought about it but decided against it. "Screw that, Frank. This is too easy. Let's just bounce this clown and get back. No doubt today is going to be a real zoo, just like yesterday."

The wizzo agreed and gave Martain the final information he needed for the setup. Martain took over, aligned his sights. When he heard the tone telling him he had missile lock, he held his fire for a moment. The boggy continued to fly straight and low, making no attempt to evade. "Jesus, Frank. That guy must be asleep. Or he's in a real hurry to meet his maker."

"Well, Ed, if that's so, go ahead, make his day."

Without further hesitation, Martain launched a short-range Sidewinder air-to-air missile. Both he and the wizzo tracked it until it hit. In the predawn darkness, there was a slight explosion ahead and below them. Immediately after that, the plot disappeared, indicating that Martain had made his tenth confirmed kill.

Chapter 14

Men willingly believe what they want to.
                                    —JULIUS CAESAR

Saadatabad, Iran
0440 Hours, 9 July (0110 Hours, 9 July, GMT)

When the orders to attack were received by the 2nd Brigade, the brigade staff had no doubt that the staff of the 13th Corps was hallucinating. The orders came by courier shortly before 1900 hours at a brigade CP that was a shadow of its former self. Most of the wheeled vehicles were still unaccounted for or lost. The signal platoon, unable to break down its multichannel equipment in time, lost much of it. The TOC itself, while it had not lost any of its M-577 command-post tracks, had little of its equipment left. Personnel losses were equally staggering. Many of the brigade staff who had not been on duty at the time of the attack were either dead, wounded or missing.

Worse than the physical losses, bad as they were, was the psychological damage. The survivors suddenly found themselves face to face with the reality of war. "Battle" was no longer a paper drill of moving little markers about on a map or writing orders. The idea that their primary task was the cool analytical process of thinking about and debating tactics had been smashed. They had seen the face of war. It was the shattered remains of a body left in the dirt. It was Major Price, a first-class runner and all-round jock, reduced to a helpless cripple with a severed spine. It was the smell of fear and the look of panic in the eyes of people with whom they had worked for so long. And, worse, it was the realization that only the dead had seen an end to the suffering and horror.

This was the brigade staff—stunned by their introduction to combat, left with three M-577 command-post tracks, operating with an ad hoc communications lash-up which was less than adequate—that received the order to attack. Their reactions, though slow at first, were surprisingly positive. The senior officers and NCOs led by example and deed. "You're a soldier, start acting like one" was heard time and again. Old habits and training prevailed as the staff began to function. The brigade commander, along with the brigade S-3 and the assistant S-2, Amanda Matthews, analyzed the mission and developed several courses of action based on the enemy situation as they knew it. The status of subordinate·units, their locations and their needs were reported and fed to the command group as the plan evolved. Orders went out to the units, instructing them to break contact with the enemy and move to tactical assembly areas. Combat-support elements were drawn into the plan and began to position themselves. Coordination to refuel and rearm the combat elements was effected.

The corps commander arrived shortly before midnight for the express purpose of ensuring that the brigade fully understood his intent and their role in the counteroffensive. With the brigade commander and his staff, Lieutenant General Weir reviewed the entire operation. The main Soviet offensive continued south toward Saadatabad with two divisions abreast, one division moving along the road and a second division to the west. The third Soviet division, heavily attrited by its attack and the combined efforts of the Air Force and attack helicopters, was now following the two lead divisions. Despite the fact that all the Soviet divisions were less than full strength and were experiencing difficulties with resupply, they were still more than capable of overpowering any defense the corps could create. There simply was not enough ground-combat power available to stop the Soviets. Therefore, Weir stated with a gleam in his eye, "Since we cannot hold 'em, we *must* attack."

The reserve brigade from the 17th Airborne Division had the task of delaying the Soviet forces moving south against Saadatabad. With priority on all close air support from the Air Force until the 2nd Brigade actually made contact, they would act as a matador's cape being waved in front of a bull. Their job was to hold the bull's attention and keep it in check, or at least controlled. In addition to providing close air support to the reserve airborne brigade's delay-and-deception role, the Air Force had the task of gaining air superiority and keeping Soviet tactical air recon in check. Nothing could be done to counter the Soviet surveillance satellites. The best anyone could do was hope that the operation would develop too rapidly for the strategic-intelligence people in the Soviet Union to figure out what they were seeing and provide that information down through the chain to the 28th Combined Arms Army.

In this operation the 2nd Brigade would be the matador's sword. While the Soviets pushed south, the 2nd Brigade, reinforced and supported by all Army aviation as well as Navy and Marine air, would make an end run and attack the Soviets in the rear. Like a rapier, they would drive for the heart. Moving east from Saadatabad along an axis running through Soltanabad to Dasht-e Bar to Aliabad, the 2nd Brigade would cut the Soviets' main supply route and tear up its rear areas. With air superiority all but guaranteed—thanks to the high cost in aircraft that resulted from the Soviets' late-afternoon all-out effort to save the 127th Tank Regiment—most of the operation could be conducted under clear skies and against a half-blind enemy.

Weir continuously stressed how critical the situation was. If they failed, there would be no fall-back positions, no second chance. If they succeeded, maybe they could hold on till the rest of 10th Corps arrived. Everything was being risked on a winner-take-all proposition. "To succeed," he said, "this operation calls for a little deception, some fast maneuvering and ruthless execution." He told the brigade commander that once the 2nd Brigade was in the Soviets' rear, they were to avoid enemy strongpoints but rip up support facilities and units with "the finesse of a chainsaw murderer."

Not all was gloom and doom. Both of the maneuver battalions had suffered little in the fighting on the eighth. Both would begin the operation with over 90 percent of their assigned personnel and equipment available. The brigade's third tank battalion, the 4th Battalion of the 4th Armor, was assembling just north of Bandar Abbas. Sufficient pressure had finally been brought to bear on those reluctant to draw from the NATO war stocks. Tanks drawn from storage sites in Germany and Holland were being flown in by C-5 transports, one at a time. That operation, Weir explained, was costly in human terms as well as in resources. Two of the overworked C-5s, long overdue for routine maintenance, had already gone down with a loss of crew and cargo. The losses, however, were considered acceptable. Although the 4th of the 4th would be unable to participate in the initial part of the operation that was about to commence, it would be ready for any follow-on missions.

By the time Weir left, initial reports from the maneuver battalions were coming in. No resistance had been encountered as units hit their checkpoints on time and intact. The brigade staff, put back on track by the brigade XO, was functioning. Though communications were still shaky and stretched to the limit, they worked. The battle, planned and coordinated by Corps, orchestrated and controlled by Brigade, was now in the hands of the warriors.

Five Kilometers North of Dasht-e Bar, Iran
0500 Hours, 9 July (0130 Hours, 9 July, GMT)

The scout platoon, well forward and spread out like a great net, crossed the line of departure. They were the forward screen, sent in advance to find and fix the enemy. Behind them, at a distance of two kilometers, the battalion's lead companies, Alpha and Bravo, were in the process of deploying; they would be followed by Charlie and Delta. The 3rd of the 4th Armor would be in a box formation when all companies had completed their deployment. In this formation the battalion presented a formidable front as well as good all-round protection.

In the early-morning light Major Dixon watched the companies as they began to spread out. From his vantage point on an M-1 tank behind Alpha Company, he could see three of the four units. Only Delta was hidden from his view by dust and terrain. The battalion commander, now riding in the Bradley that had belonged to Dixon, was between Bravo and Delta Companies. In a surprising move, the battalion commander had asked Dixon whether he would mind giving up his Bradley. An old cavalryman, he did not like operating from the tank. Dixon, with the

BMP incident still fresh in his mind, gladly consented to the swap.

When the main body came up to and crossed the line of departure, Dixon was at ease. With sixty-one tons of tank wrapped around him, and a 105mm gun, he felt invincible. He stood on the commander's platform, his upper torso out of the tank, hands grasping the cupola, body swaying with the motion of the tank. The M-2 .50-caliber machine gun was turned out to the right in order to give him an unobstructed view. He was standing far too high in the hatch, but didn't care. He needed to see what was going on. As he explained to his assistant on many occasions, "Ya gotta see what's happening in order to exercise command and control."

The regular crew of the tank was good but a real diverse lot. From where he stood, Dixon could see the back of the gunner, a Sergeant Maxfield. Maxfield had his eye glued to the gunner's primary sight, scanning his assigned sector. With six years on active duty, he was due for promotion to staff sergeant and a tank of his own. The loader, a Specialist Four Wilard, was up in his hatch and facing to the rear, covering his assigned sector. A farm boy from Idaho, Wilard was far too tall for tanks. When he stood erect on the turret floor, his whole head stuck out of the loader's hatch. During the road march he had a hell of a time staying alert. Only when Dixon told him that they were approaching the line of departure did Wilard's vigilance increase. The driver was a Private First Class Casper, a young black kid from New York City. Dixon, born and raised in Virginia, had a hell of a time understanding him when he talked. But the man could drive, and that, Dixon decided, was all that mattered.

As they moved forward, Dixon listened to the radio and watched the high ground to the north and the south. So far, they had hit nothing, not even a screen line. That the Soviets' flank was so open seemed incredible. The battalion commander and Dixon had cautioned the company commanders to watch out for Soviet fire sacks. Whole battalions, blundering forward blind and unwary, could be swallowed up in a matter of minutes by a well-planned and -executed Soviet defense. The terrain that 3rd of the 4th Armor was now moving into was made for such a defense. Dixon prayed that the deception being run by the 17th Airborne was working. If not, this would be the shortest counteroffensive in history.

Ten Kilometers South of Saadatabad, Iran
0700 Hours, 9 July (0330 Hours, 9 July, GMT)

The young engineer captain from Virginia stood on the edge of
the antitank ditch and watched his last operational D-7 bulldozer
as it scraped another two inches of dirt from the bottom. Two
other dozers, broken down and idle due to a lack of spare parts,
were being loaded onto flatbed trucks. Behind him a crew of engineers were placing round wooden blocks on the north lip of the
antitank ditch, in the same pattern used in laying a surface mine
field. The engineers, along with hundreds of other engineers, had
been busy all night creating defensive positions and obstacles
that would never be used.

The men, used to hard work and doing things that ranged from
not so smart to downright dumb, could not understand what in
hell they were doing. First the captain told them that the Russians were charging down the road at full speed and the world
was coming to an end; every man, he said, needed to do his job or
the foothold held by the 13th Corps would fail. Then he turned
around and ordered them to plant a dummy mine field and dig
ditches where there were no units. As hard as he tried, the captain
could not make his men understand the importance of what they
were doing.

Watching his men, he decided that it didn't really matter what
they thought. They had done the best they could, given the time
and resources available. The Russians would either believe them
or not. It was no longer in their hands.

Headquarters, 28th CAA, Aliabad, Iran
0730 Hours, 9 July (0400 Hours, 9 July, GMT)

The situation that the 28th Combined Arms Army faced was
deplorable and at the same time pregnant with possibilities. The
lack of fuel had brought the attack by both divisions to a screeching halt. Only enough fuel for the recon elements had been
scraped up. Most of that had been obtained by siphoning fuel
from vehicles belonging to the army's second-echelon division.
On orders from Colonel Sulvina, in the name of the army commander, the recon continued to push forward, maintaining contact, gathering information and searching out American weak

points. In all three tasks, they were successful. The information they provided confirmed the intelligence officer's projection. Light-infantry forces, in conjunction with massive close air support, were conducting a delaying action south toward Saadatabad. Agents and an occasional recon flight indicated a great deal of activity south of Saadatabad by engineer units.

Fuel, so simple a commodity, normally so plentiful, had become the key to success or failure. How ironic, Sulvina had thought. Here we are in the middle of a region that contains most of the world's oil reserves, and we run out of fuel. History, no doubt, will laugh if we fail here. No one, however, was laughing that morning in the 28th CAA. Everyone's full attention and energies were geared to obtaining the fuel and pushing it forward. The Red Air Force, depleted by the previous day's efforts, was being pressed by Front Headquarters to clear the skies and provide cover to transport aircraft flying fuel to makeshift airstrips or dropping it by parachute. Helicopters, loaded to maximum capacity, carried fuel drums right up to the front-line units. Despite continuous interference by and heavy losses to American fighters, fuel was being delivered. Anything that could carry fuel was being used.

Not all units were being resupplied. Priority went to the lead divisions. On the basis of the intelligence picture being painted for him by the army's second officer, the army commander was gambling that two divisions would be sufficient to blow through the Americans' final positions and reach the Strait of Hormuz. All other units had to manage with what they had. As a result of such draconian measures, fuel was beginning to reach the forward combat elements in sufficient quantities. By 0900 the lead regiments would be refueled and ready to move. The logistics officer promised that both first-echelon divisions would be refueled and on the move by noon, provided no calamity befell the army. To ensure synchronization of effort and to leave some time for errors, orders had gone out to the lead divisions to reinitiate the attack commencing at 1000 hours with those units that were then refueled. Saadatabad was designated as the army's intermediate objective, with the final objective of the day being Qotbabad. Plans for a joint airborne and ground attack against Bandar Abbas on the eleventh of July were being worked out.

Both the commander of the 28th CAA and Sulvina were exhausted. Neither had slept for more than an hour since the begin-

ning of the attack, on the eighth. Satisfied that all was being done
and that the situation would soon be in hand, they walked out of
the command post for a break. Endless hours in an operations
center with staff officers rushing about, radios blaring, phones
ringing, and half a dozen conversations being conducted at the
same time can best be likened to living in a pressure cooker.
Stress and lack of sleep destroy a person's ability to think clearly
or work effectively. An occasional break, just a simple walk outside, is required every so often in order to maintain sanity and
effectiveness. Outside, the two officers stood fifty meters from
the command post, not far from an SA-8 surface-to-air antiair-
craft-missile battery. Neither said anything. They smoked their
cigarettes and let their minds go blank as they watched a convoy
of fuel trucks move south along the highway. Both knew that
was a good sign.

Five Kilometers East of Aliabad, Iran
0730 Hours, 9 July (0400 Hours, 9 July, GMT)

From his perch, Capell watched a convoy moving south along
the main road. With his binoculars he could see that many were
fuel trucks and that the escort was light, very light. Before leaving
his observation point and returning to his Bradley, he made one
more sweep of the area. Though he didn't expect to see any, he
searched for telltale signs of combat units or defenses. The only
thing that came close was what appeared to be an air-defense unit
equipped with missiles. They could do nothing to his scouts.

Satisfied, he slithered down off the rock pile he was on and
trotted back to his Bradley, where he switched his radio to the
battalion-command frequency and called the S-3. "Bravo Four-
five, this is Mike Eight-eight. Spot report. Over."

"Mike Eight-eight, this is Bravo Four-five. Send it. Over."

With the aid of a preprinted form in which he had filled in the
blanks, Capell began to send his report. "This is Mike Eight-
eight. Two zero trucks with three BRDMs escorting moving
south along the highway at grid four six five, nine eight five, and
one air-defense unit located at three nine six, nine eight zero,
time now. Request permission to engage. Over."

After acknowledging, Dixon plotted the location on his map
and considered Capell's request. "Mike Eight-eight, this is Bravo
Four-five. Do you see any other enemy units or activity? Over."

Capell replied in the negative. Dixon called the battalion commander, who had been monitoring the transmissions. Dixon recommended that the scouts lead off the attack by hitting the convoy. The battalion commander concurred. They had gone as far as they could expect to go without being detected. It was time to go in and begin hacking away at the Russians. Capell, tired of sneaking about and reporting, was looking forward to doing some serious fighting. He did not need to be told twice.

With the six Bradleys of his scout platoon on line, concealed behind a small hill crest, Capell prepared to attack. He stood high in the turret of his vehicle, waved his arm over his head and then dropped it, pointing in the direction of the convoy of fuel trucks. Yelling over his intercom, he ordered his driver, "Kick it in the ass!" The other track commanders in the platoon did likewise. Together, the six Bradleys lurched forward and began their attack.

The platoon crested the rise that had concealed them. Dead ahead, at a range of three kilometers, was the convoy. As the Bradleys began to accelerate, track commanders marked their targets and issued fire commands. "Gunner—HEAT. Moving truck."

With eyes glued to their sights and hands on their controls, the platoon's gunners searched for their targets and yelled out, "Identified!" when the first truck they saw was in their sight. Automatically the track commanders let go of their controls and let the gunners prepare to do their thing.

Rapidly the platoon closed. Two kilometers. Drivers in the convoy and men at the SA-8 battery, their attention drawn by the huge clouds of dust to the east, watched the six tracked vehicles racing at them and wondered what they were doing. Sulvina and his commander also watched. Sulvina was angry that a BMP company commander would allow such a flagrant waste of fuel. He was determined to find out who their commander was and personally rip his rank off him.

Fifteen hundred meters. Two Bradleys strained to keep up, while another slowed to maintain alignment. Capell stood upright in his turret. With goggles down and olive-drab bandana covering his mouth and nose, he held on and swayed with the rocking of the Bradley as it rolled forward. He could almost feel adrenaline pumping into his system. With the sun to his back and their field of fire clear, he keyed the platoon radio net and yelled, *"Fire!"*

The tracked vehicles charging from the east began to fire. In bewilderment and horror the Soviets at the SA-8 battery and Sulvina saw half a dozen fuel trucks explode. The crews of the BMPs must be insane—they were actually firing on their own trucks. Even when one of the officers from the SA-8 battery, using his sight, yelled that they were Bradleys, Sulvina still could not move. His commander shared his disbelief, turning to Sulvina and yelling, "How can this be? Where did they come from?"

The truck drivers either panicked, stopping their trucks and bailing out, or turned away from the attacking Bradleys in an effort to escape. There was no escape, however, as the Bradleys raced forward and began to fire up the fuel trucks with their machine guns as well as the 25mm. cannon. Capell turned the killing over to his gunner. Still standing upright in his open hatch, he scanned the area, keeping track of his platoon and searching for targets. Once the fuel trucks were disposed of, he intended to turn on the antiaircraft battery. Until then, he called for the battalion mortar platoon to fire on them.

The reality of the situation finally hit home when large-caliber mortar rounds began to impact on the SA-8 battery. Crewmen, scurrying about in an effort to prepare their vehicles for movement, were cut down or ripped apart by the mortar shells. Sulvina turned away and raced for the command post. As he drew near, he yelled to several drivers to crank up the commander's and his armored vehicles. He ran into the command center, pushing back young staff officers who were trying to go out to see what was happening.

Once inside, he yelled, "Ground attack. Grab critical items only and get to your vehicles. Rally at the 127th division's command post. Move."

Not waiting for a response, he grabbed his map, a briefcase with orders and papers, and ran out to his waiting vehicle. The commander's BTR was already moving off to the west. Sulvina waited only a few seconds in his own BTR for several staff officers to pile in before he ordered his driver to follow the commander's carrier.

.   .   .

The movement of two BTRs and several trucks heading west caught Capell's attention. He watched for a moment, then realized that he was probably looking at a command post of some sort. What a chance. What a fabulous chance. But there was nothing he could do. His platoon had driven among the burning trucks in pursuit of the survivors, and the smoke and confusion now frustrated his efforts to regain control. He called desperately over the radio for all tracks to rally on him and ordered his driver to stop.

Once stationary, he told his gunner to fire TOWs at the escaping BTRs before they disappeared. Capell watched as the TOW launcher slowly rose into the firing position, then locked. He looked back, to see that the first BTR had already disappeared. He ordered the gunner to aim at the second BTR. The gunner did so, but called out that he did not have a ready-to-fire light. Capell dropped down and looked. The safety was still on. He yelled to the gunner to switch his safety off. When the gunner complied, the ready-to-fire light came on. Capell yelled "Fire!" and stuck his head up to watch the flight of the missile. The missile launched. It popped out of the tube and went several meters before its rocket motor kicked in and it began to pursue the second BTR, now cresting the rise. Seconds, mere seconds, meant success or failure, life or death.

For Colonel Sulvina, acting chief of staff of the 28th Combined Arms Army, the issue was decided in his favor, this time.

Harvand, Iran
0900 Hours, 9 July (0530 Hours, 9 July, GMT)

An enemy that had come out of nowhere was suddenly everywhere. Wild reports from combat support and service unit personnel flooded a communications net that was rapidly collapsing as relay sites were overrun or moved. Rear-area personnel, unused to the proper reporting procedures and to being exposed to danger, added to the confusion rather than clarifying the situation. Some support-unit commanders requested permission to move. Others simply moved without informing anyone and clogged the limited road network. Panic became the order of the day.

Once at the headquarters of the 127th Motorized Rifle Division, the commander of the 28th Combined Arms Army ordered the commander of that division to move his entire unit north.

They were to find, pin and encircle the enemy forces now rampaging throughout the army's rear. The division commander said nothing at first. In his bewilderment, he turned to his staff, but got only looks of amazement or blank stares in return. The army commander, still hyper from his brush with death and faced with the prospect of losing his army to an unknown enemy, became enraged when his order was not immediately acted on. He jumped in front of the division commander and yelled, "Did you not hear me? I ordered you to attack. I expect you to attack—now!"

The division commander began to sweat. The condition of his commander and the serious situation overwhelmed him. He fumbled for words. "Comrade General, we, we . . ." The word "cannot" came hard to him. One did not tell one's commander that one could not do something. There must be reasons for not doing things—unfavorable conditions, enemy activity, failure of a support element to be in place, and so on. Reasons.

For an awkward moment there was silence as the division commander faced his superior. Sulvina stepped in and broke the silence. "Comrade General, the 127th Division cannot attack. They have no fuel." The army commander turned to him. Sulvina continued, "We diverted all they had to the 33rd Tank Division." The army commander's expression turned from anger to shock as it began to dawn upon him that all was lost. Seeing that his commander's mind was foundering under the weight of the disaster and grasping for a solution, Sulvina offered him the only practical one. "We must order the 33rd Tank Division to disengage and move north against the enemy in our rear. The 67th Motorized Rifle Division must also withdraw and assume a defensive posture facing south."

Automatically the army commander refused to break off the attack or withdraw the 67th MRD. He insisted that they must continue the atttack or at least hold what they had. Patiently, Sulvina explained that even if the Americans were cleared from the rear areas in the next twenty-four hours, the army would expend in that effort whatever supplies it had left. A continuation of the offensive was out of the question. "As we speak, Comrade General, the Americans are destroying our support elements and supply dumps. We cannot, I repeat, cannot hope to reach the Strait of Hormuz and be able to stay there in our present state. It is time to save the army."

For a moment, there was silence. Then the army commander, a tired and defeated man, gave in. He ordered Sulvina to issue the necessary orders and seek permission from Front Headquarters to withdraw. As the army commander sat down, Sulvina looked about him at the spartan headquarters of the 127th MRD. To himself he mumbled, That, Comrade General, will be a feat.

Northwest of Saadatabad, Iran
1145 Hours, 9 July (0815 Hours, 9 July, GMT)

The Soviet 68th Tank Regiment rumbled north at breakneck speed. The poor condition of the trail that the tanks followed battered their already exhausted crews about. One of the gunners once compared the sensation of being inside a T-80 tank to that of being in a tin can being rolled down a rocky hillside. The driver, down low and covered with dust and dirt thrown up by the tank less than fifty meters to his front, drove mostly by instinct. The same dust that covered him hid the tank in front of him from view. The tank commander, perched higher above the ground, could see more, but also ate dust and dirt. In addition, while the driver sat and had the controls to hang on to, the tank commander had to grab whatever he could and do his best to sway the right way as the tank bucked and bumped down the road. When he erred in his judgment, his kidneys were bashed against the steel lip of the hatch opening. Inside, the gunner was protected from dust being thrown in his face but from little else. The air he breathed hung heavy with dust that came down through the open hatch. It mingled with the smell of hot oil and grease. There was no air circulation. The sun, pounding down on the steel, pushed temperatures well beyond 110 degrees Fahrenheit. Every stitch of the gunner's black uniform was soaked with sweat. With nothing else to do, the gunner hung on to anything that was fixed to the turret wall and, like the commander, swayed with the motion of the tank.

Major Vorishnov missed his BTR. The T-80 tank was small, cramped and impossible to work from. When the order came down that the regiment was going to move north and execute a movement to contact, to find and destroy the American forces, confusion reigned. A short preparatory bombardment to kick off the attack south had already begun. Requests to confirm the orders or repeat them were met with shrill blasts from harried commanders or staff officers. Apparently something had gone terribly wrong. Neither Vorishnov's battalion commander nor he knew for sure, but their guess was that a large enemy force was in the army's rear. Vorishnov's effort to gain additional information or formulate any type of plan was frustrated by the speed of the move and the necessity of riding a tank. The T-80 he had did not have the proper radio nets, nor could he work effectively or think. As they raced north, all Vorishnov could do was hang on and hope to save his kidneys.

Turning a unit around and attacking in the opposite direction is a feat few commanders master. A combat unit is followed by a tail that drags behind it like a ball and chain. Immediately behind and mixed in with the combat units are combat-support units. These include the engineers and the air defenders. They maneuver at a set distance behind the lead combat elements, ready to rush forward, in the case of engineers, or to support by fire, in the case of the air defenders. Behind them are the artillery units. Battalions and batteries of artillery leapfrog forward at a set distance in order to provide continuous fire support to the ground-maneuver units. In the case of a regiment making the main attack, the number of artillery battalions following and supporting is often greater than the number of maneuver battalions being supported. Behind them are the combat service support elements: medical teams and aid stations, supply units, maintenance units, transportation units, signal units, military-police units and so on. On top of all these units are the headquarters of the regiment, the division, the division artillery, the combat service support units. Finally, there are Army assets such as FROG rocket units, attack-helicopter units, Army-level air-defense units and such.

All those units are stacked up behind the maneuver battalions in a set order. All compete for use of the same roads, require enough space to operate properly in and must be supplied from the same supply route. Simply giving the order "Turn around, attack to the other way" does not work. While a company can do so with relative ease and a battalion with minimal coordination, turning a regiment or a division requires monumental efforts and coordination. As the Soviet 33rd Tank Division rushed north, staff officers at every level and in every unit scrambled to make sense out of the chaos. Planning and coordination that required a day, at best, had to be accomplished in hours. With little direction or information from the army staff, subordinate staffs made do with what little information they had. The situation would no doubt clarify itself once contact was established with the enemy.

Chah-e Qeysar, Iran
1525 Hours, 9 July (1155 Hours, 9 July, GMT)

Outside a tumbledown building that had once served as a garage, the brigade command group caught up with the command group of the 3rd of the 4th Armor. The impromptu meeting, called by the brigade commander, was for the purpose of getting an update on the unit and issuing new orders. While the tanks and the M-113 armored personnel carriers sat outside forming a small protective perimeter, the commanders and their key staff officers met in an open garage bay. Even in the shade of the building, the heat was oppressive. Men long overdue for sleep and given a break from the threat of sudden death or mutilation said little as they gathered. Some fell asleep waiting for the meeting to start.

While the battalion commander and the staff officers spoke, the brigade commander studied them and listened. He could see that they were tired or, more correctly, exhausted. The success of the day, however, added positive notes to their briefing. Overall, their units were in far better shape than could be expected. The day before, the brigade had fought a battle in the morning and conducted a withdrawal under pressure in the afternoon; that night they had planned an operation, conducted a fifty-kilometer movement and rolled in the attack at 0500 hours. Since then the entire brigade had been on a rampage, spreading out and smashing anything and everything it ran across. While their losses had been minimal to date, they could not count on their good fortune lasting much longer. The Soviet divisions that had been poised to strike south for the Gulf had turned around and were beating feet north in a mad dash to clear their rear area and crush the 2nd Brigade. The brigade had accomplished its mission. It was time, the brigade S-3 said, "to take the money and run."

The brigade commander himself stood and began the orders briefing. "Gentlemen, a situation that was hopeless less than twenty-four hours ago is now simply critical." He paused for a moment while those present chuckled. "Good, I'm glad to see some of you are still alive." More chuckles. Turning serious, he began to outline the next operation with the aid of a map board propped against the wall. "Radio intercepts and what little information Corps has been able to get to us show that the tank division that was headed south has been turned around and is charging back north. No doubt he is going to be looking for us. I do not intend to be here when he gets here. We've had our fun and have done what we were sent to do. Commencing immediately, the 2nd Brigade will withdraw to the southeast along the same general route we used this morning. Upon reaching a point northeast of Tarom, we will link up with the 4th of the 4th Armor, now there, and turn either north toward Hajjiabad or south toward Tarom. That decision will be based on the enemy situation at the time. From that point on, our orders are to conduct a movement to contact. Once we have made contact, we will develop the situation. If we encounter only a light screen, we will push on until we find his main defensive belt. When we do find it, we stop, deploy and hang on. The one thing we cannot do is become involved in a slugfest. There are simply too few forces in the country yet to afford that. While we have crippled the enemy and stopped him for now, he ain't dead yet. Be aggressive, but don't piss your units away. There's plenty of fighting left to do." He stopped and let that sink in before he continued. "Now that I have totally confused you, the S-3 will explain what I just said."

With that, the brigade commander sat on a wobbly chair while his staff went over the details.

North of Aliabad, Iran
2015 Hours, 9 July (1645 Hours, 9 July, GMT)

In the gathering darkness the 3rd Battalion of the Soviet 68th Tank Regiment completed its pivot, deployed and began to sweep to the east. The 2nd Battalion was to the south of Aliabad, and the 1st was following the 2nd. Security patrols had been flung out on both flanks to protect against a surprise attack. Patrols from the regimental recon were deployed well forward, seeking any sign of enemy activity or presence.

While they did not find the Americans, they found ample signs that they had been there. Smashed vehicles and equipment dotted the desolate countryside. Scattered around the wreckage were the bodies of Red Army soldiers. Here and there groups of survivors came out of hiding upon seeing the advancing T-80 tanks. This, however, was dangerous. The tank crews, exhausted from two continuous days of movement, physically beaten by extremes of heat and bad roads, were on edge. They were moving into an area overrun by the enemy, an enemy they now sought; everything was suspect and assumed hostile. More than a few Red Army soldiers, relieved to see friendly forces and anxious to make contact, died that night at the hands of their saviors.

To Vorishnov's horror, the opposite was also true. On three separate occasions the battalion had been fired on by soldiers whom it had bypassed and who were expecting the Americans. Such encounters were generally harmless to the tanks of the battalion, thanks to their reactive armor and the inept handling of antitank-rocket launchers on the part of the combat service support troops. Some of the men firing the antitank rockets, however, paid for their error with their lives.

Vorishnov looked forward to the end of the current operation. He began to pray that they would not be the ones who found the Americans, if they were still in the area. He longed for a break from the stress of endless operations, the threat of imminent combat and the pressure of having to produce plans and orders with little or no guidance. How good it would feel to be able to lie down and sleep. That, above all else, was what he wanted, needed. He looked at his watch, then glanced at his map. He couldn't let his mind wander too far. They were out there somewhere. Still, if all went well, the battalion would reach its objective just east of Dasht-e Bar in another two to three hours. There the regiment would assume a hasty defense and await further orders. With luck, orders would not arrive until dawn, maybe later. He could sleep. He would be able to lie down on the ground and wrap a blanket about himself and sleep. How wonderful that idea seemed to Vorishnov. One could always hope.

East of Hajjiabad, Iran
2230 Hours, 9 July (1900 Hours, 9 July, GMT)

The two Bradleys slowly inched their way up the small hill. Their engines were barely running above idle, almost inaudible in the still night air. The sound of track grinding on the sprockets was, on the other hand, piercing. Capell stood in his open hatch, stretching in an effort to see over the top of the hill. He should have dismounted the scouts, now sleeping in the rear of the track, but had decided against it. They were exhausted. The whole platoon was. Since midnight the night before, the battalion had been on the move. An attack in the north, a withdrawal, now a movement to contact the enemy. At least when the enemy was finally found this time, the battalion was to go to ground and hold for a while. Perhaps they would finally have an opportunity to rest. Until then, the battalion, with the scouts out front, continued forward.

The tank commander of the T-80 heard the squeaking but could not pinpoint it. He whispered to his gunner to search the area, but got no response. Looking down, the tank commander saw the gunner hunched over, asleep. With his left boot the commander kicked the gunner in the back. The gunner began to curse, but was cut short when the tank commander curtly reminded him that the penalty for sleeping while on outpost duty was death. When he had the gunner's attention, the commander ordered him to search the area. There was something moving out there.

The gunner switched on his night-vision sight and put his eye up to it. The darkness turned to day. On his first sweep he scanned his sector without noticing anything. But as he traversed the turret back, he saw an antenna, not more than four hundred meters away. He yelled to his commander that he had them. The commander, watching through his sight, also did not see the antenna at first. Only when the turret of the Bradley slowly began to rise above the crest of the hill did he see the source of the noise. Pleased and excited, the tank commander reported the sighting and ordered the gunner to prepare to engage.

As they pulled into a turret defilade, Capell ordered the driver to stop. He keyed the intercom and ordered the gunner to search the area. Using his night-vision goggles, Capell leaned forward and also began to search for signs of the enemy. He never saw the T-80's muzzle flash or heard the crack of the 125mm. gun. A brilliant flash and a shower of sparks that lit the night and washed over Capell were the first indication that they were in the presence of the enemy. The noise of ripping metal was accompanied by the scream of the driver. Capell felt a wave of searing heat rush up between his legs. The gunner, his hatch closed, was engulfed in flames, screeching at the top of his lungs, like a wild animal in agony. The smell of burning flesh and the intensity of his own pain destroyed Capell's ability to reason. With fire racing up his back, he began screaming louder than his gunner.

The detonation of stored TOW missiles stopped Capell's screams, throwing him clear of the turret into the dirt, where he writhed and squirmed, his mind overwhelmed with pain and more pain.

The movement to contact was successful. The enemy had been located.

Chapter 15

Leadership is intangible, and therefore no weapon ever designed can replace it.
— GENERAL OMAR BRADLEY

Moscow, Headquarters, STAVKA
0845 Hours, 13 July (0545 Hours, 13 July, GMT)

Deep in the bowels of the building that served as the Red Army's nerve center, a captain by the name of Dubask sat at a small desk overcrowded with papers and photos. He was hunched over, studying the latest glut of satellite photos. On one corner of the desk was a pile of photos awaiting his review. They had long since swamped the in box, flopping over onto his desk. He had little time to examine each in detail. For his task, however, he did not need much time. Unlike most of the other photo analysts in his section, Dubask was looking for a specific target. He could therefore ignore anything that did not fit his target criteria. He noted in very general terms items of interest he stumbled across, but left the detail analysis to someone else.

The target he was interested in seemed at first as though it would be simple to locate. He had to find a base camp with manufacturing facilities. The KGB major who had briefed Dubask stressed continuously the importance of pinpointing this facility, though no reason was given. Nor was one expected. You did not ask questions unless you really had to. The simple task, however, became frustrating. Dubask was amazed at the number of villages there were in the areas that were officially labeled uninhabited. It took him several days to confirm that most were in fact permanent settlements. His next problem was sorting out the roving bands of Iranian partisans. Once the permanent settlements had been tagged, he concentrated on these groups. Clearing them from the clutter took over a week as Dubask tagged each group and checked for them over the next several days. If they moved, he stopped worrying about that area and reduced his list of likely targets. He didn't even bother with the numerous photos showing small groups, some as small as ten people, wandering about the great expanses of Iran. In Dubask's section, any group that numbered fewer than twenty-five people was considered tactically insignificant and was not reported. There was too much that needed to be reported to waste time on such a small number of people.

On this particular day Dubask came across two photos that caught his attention. The first was of an area in the Dasht-e Lut near a place called Robat-e Abgram. Several days before, when an early-morning photo dated 9 July showed a number of trucks gathered there in a compound of several buildings, he had marked that area as one that needed to be watched. The photos of 8 and 10 July had shown no vehicles present. Digging back, he found that in earlier analyses of the area he had discounted the compound as being a permanent settlement and had scratched it from his list. The unaccounted-for appearance of trucks, however, was out of the norm. He had not seen trucks at any of the other settlements, the Iranians having been reduced to animals and foot for transportation. Dubask began to watch that area with greater interest, alerting his superior that Robat-e Abgram was a possible target.

The second item of interest, though not falling within his target criteria, was also sufficiently significant to warrant alerting his superior. In the southeast corner of the Dasht-e Lut he came across a large number of armored vehicles. A quick check showed that they did not belong to the 89th Motorized Rifle Division, the unit responsible for that area of the front. The American unit opposing the 89th MRD was the 6th U.S. Marine Division, a unit that did not possess large armored formations. The sudden appearance of these vehicles was out of the norm.

Dubask's first reaction was to pass the photo off to someone else, with a simple note on it, as he had done with another such photo on 9 July, the day he found the trucks at Robat-e Abgram. On that day he had come across a photo that showed large numbers of armored vehicles moving north around the eastern flank of the 28th Combined Arms Army. Dubask had thought this odd and important, but it was not his concern. He had already noted the trucks at Robat-e Abgram and wanted to go back and study that photo more closely. Dubask therefore placed a note on the photo and dropped it into an out box behind him. There it sat for an hour, until a runner making his rounds came by, emptied the out box and dumped the photo and the note into another over-filled in box on another analyst's desk. Somewhere in the process, the note and the photo became separated.

It was not until the tenth that Dubask made the connection between the disaster that befell the 28th CAA and the photo of the armor column he had looked at but passed on. All day on the tenth and the eleventh he sat at his desk, fearing that someone would find out that he had seen the photo but had taken no action. He feared what might happen to him and his family when it was found that he could have alerted STAVKA to the threat to the 28th CAA's flank. But no one said anything or even broached the subject. From his desk he watched the routine continue una-bated. Every hour a new glut of photos was distributed on the stack of unviewed photos already in the in boxes of the analysts in the section. Dubask's error went undetected.

Dubask finally satisfied himself that nothing would ever hap-pen. Everyone was too overwhelmed worrying about what was about to happen and did not have time to go back and try to figure out what had happened. Free of his unfounded fears, he began to concentrate on his immediate task, sorting through the stack before him, looking for the latest photos of Robat-e Abgram. He had already made two serious errors, discounting Robat-e Abgram the first time and the 9 July photo showing the U.S. armored column. They had been costly. Dubask doubted he would be as lucky a third time.

Northwest of Chah-e Qeyser
1915 Hours, 13 July (1545 Hours, 13 July, GMT)

The sun had already dipped below the western horizon when Staff Sergeant Hernandez woke his platoon leader, Sergeant First Class Duncan. Hernandez and three other men of the 1st Platoon were completing their four-hour tour of guard duty. This did not mean, however, that they were finished for the day. On the contrary. Since they had escaped being annihilated with the rest of the battalion at Rafsanjan, Duncan and his men had been operating exclusively at night.

By day the platoon went to ground, concealed in the nooks and crannies of the wadis and draws that cut through the Iranian wilderness like unhealed scars. It was only at night, hiding under the cloak of darkness, that they came out like the other desert predators. Their sole purpose in life since the twenty-eighth of June had been survival. They moved south in the forlorn hope of eventually finding friendly forces. Making it back was only a hope—a dim, flickering light at the end of a long, dark and dangerous tunnel. The more immediate tasks of escaping detection and finding sufficient food were the reality of the day, two problems that constantly loomed before each of the men with Duncan.

Simply put, these two tasks were in direct conflict with each other. On one hand, in order to live the men had to avoid being detected by the Soviet patrols searching for such ragtag collections of men. Besides the Russians, Iranian bands also roamed the desert looking for unwary infidels, Americans and Russians alike. On the other hand, Duncan and his men had to hit either the Soviets or the Iranians to secure food, water, weapons and medicine. The trick was to find isolated groups or small convoys moving around at night, sneak up on them and hit them hard, fast and without mercy. They could not afford to take prisoners, who would only compound Duncan's problems. By being selective about whom they hit and backing off from questionable confrontations, Duncan and his men had managed to survive two weeks and put many miles between themselves and their start point.

As Duncan passed from sleep to consciousness, his first reaction was to tighten his grip on the Kalashnikov assault rifle that lay at his side. He had picked the Russian rifle up one night to replace his own M-16 when the platoon became short of 5.56mm. ammo. Hernandez watched this and calmed his platoon leader's fears. "Nothin' happening, Sarge. Just sunset."

Duncan raised his head and turned slowly. Around him he could see the rest of the platoon being rousted out of their cubbyholes by Specialist Four Thorton, one of Hernandez's men. Duncan turned back to Hernandez. "What's for supper?"

Faking an Oriental accent, Hernandez said, smiling, "Oh, no problem, GI. I fix you right up, chop chop." He reached into a wide fatigue-pants pocket, pulled out a clump of foil and offered it to Duncan. "I got just the ticket for you, GI. Number one. Fresh five months ago."

Duncan sat up and accepted the clump of foil. He looked it over before unwrapping it. When he began to peel away the foil, he did so with great care, not wanting to lose a single crumb. The prize in the center was a chunk of black bread. Under ordinary circumstances, he would have tossed it away. These, however, were not ordinary circumstances. Duncan knew that the chunk of bread, captured four days ago in the ambush of a lone Soviet truck broken down on the side of the road, represented his entire evening meal. As he inspected it, he decided that the fuzzy green mold growing on it had to go, starvation or not. He reached into one of his ammo pouches and pulled out a Swiss Army knife. As he carefully cut away the offending mold, he talked to Hernandez, the second man in the platoon's chain of command. "Everyone else get something to eat?"

Using his normal conversational voice, Hernandez replied, "Roger that, Boss. Thorton's passing out the last of the rations as he goes along."

Finishing his carving, Duncan held the bread up before his face at arm's length and inspected his dinner one more time. "I hope they fared better than I did." With that he stuck it into his mouth, tore a chunk off with effort and began to chew, talking as he ate. "Well, looks like it's time to go grocery shopping. What do you feel like tonight? More Russian, or should we try the local cuisine again?"

Hernandez made a face. "Fuck that Iranian shit. I've seen maggots turn down better food than what the Iranians eat. It's no wonder these people are so pissed at the whole world. If I had to eat their food all the time, I'd have a grudge, too."

"Beggars can't be choosers. If we can't find a good target on the road by midnight, we go into the nearest village and grab what we can. We don't have the time to sit around and wait for the Soviets to send us a mess truck."

Hernandez shook his head from side to side. "I don't like going into those villages, Sarge. The last time we did that it took two days to shake those ragheads. We're asking for trouble screwing with 'em, if you ask me."

Duncan turned serious. "I didn't ask you. And in case you

haven't caught on, every time we hit a Russian convoy, we get visits from a pair of attack helicopters for the next twenty-four hours. Either way you split it, we're up shit's creek. We go for what we can deal with and run like hell. One way or the other I'm going to get this platoon back." The two men looked at each other for a few moments before Duncan continued. "You know the drill. Lineup and inspection in ten minutes. Get on it, Sergeant."

Hernandez left without saying a word. What could he say? Duncan was right. Duncan was always right.

As Duncan finished his bread, he dug a plastic bag from one of his pockets with his free hand. He took off the elastic band wrapped around it and pulled out a small dog-eared green army note pad and a pencil. Setting the pad on his leg, he began to write. Since their escape into the desert, he had been keeping a log of the platoon's activities. Each evening Duncan recorded the situation, his plans for the night and his observations on the morale and conduct of the men under his command. Every morning he would summarize the activities of the platoon and describe the land they had traversed, what they had seen and the status of men, weapons, ammunition and food. His comments were terse, often incomplete and at times nothing more than random thoughts scribbled by a hand being driven by a tired and frustrated mind.

What the log did provide was a history of the platoon and its wanderings. Duncan held few illusions about their ultimate fate. They had started with eighteen men on 28 June. On this day there were only thirteen men left with him. Two were dead—one killed outright in an ambush by Iranians and the second during a strafing run by a Soviet attack helicopter. Two men had been severely wounded. Though Duncan had tried to bring them along, the effort slowed the platoon and exposed the wounded men to death from infection and lack of medical care. Both had been left near the road in the hope that they would be found by the Russians and treated humanely as prisoners of war. The fifth man Duncan had lost was missing, unaccounted for. One morning the platoon had settled into hiding with all men present, but that evening Hernandez woke Duncan to report that Private Slatter was missing. Sometime during the day Slatter had up and wandered off on his own. The platoon stayed in place that night in the hope that he would return. He didn't. Nor did he return the next day. With great reluctance, Duncan left the area where they had lost Slatter, never knowing what had happened or why.

This disturbed Duncan—not knowing. This concern for knowing and giving others the chance to know was what motivated him to record what they did. If fate dealt them a bad hand and the platoon was wiped out, the story of their wanderings would be preserved. Duncan hoped that someone would find the log and see it for what it was. Perhaps the Russians would even turn the green notebook over to someone in the International Red Cross. For all the propaganda, Duncan knew that the Russians were, in reality, people. The Iranians, on the other hand, were fanatics. Religious fanatics, yes. But a fanatic is still a fanatic and as such is totally insensible to anything or anyone not conforming to his narrow way of thinking. If the green book fell into the hands of the Iranians and was destroyed, it would mean that the platoon lost more than their lives—they would lose their souls. This Duncan feared more than death.

Watching his men, Duncan gathered his thoughts before he started to write. When he was ready, he jotted down the night's entry.

> *13 July. Nothing to report. Day was quiet. No Soviet patrols or Iranians spotted. Last of the food gone. Tonight we move down to the road and hit the Russians. Need to pick up more Russian weapons and ammo. Only three men have M-16s left and each of them are down to 60 rounds of 5.56. Targets have to be soft tonight, only have one LAW and 2 RPG rounds. If we do not find a good target by midnight, we will go into town and take whatever we need from the locals. Don't want to do this. The bastards chased us the last time we hit them and damned near caught us. Only going to do so if needed.*
>
> Duncan

Hernandez waited until Duncan had finished writing before announcing that the platoon was ready for inspection. Of all the men in the platoon, only Hernandez and Sergeant Younger knew of the green book and its purpose. Both NCOs were under orders from Duncan to recover the book and keep the record going as long as they could if he went down.

Each night before the last ray of light faded and they moved out, Duncan inspected his platoon, checking the men, their weapons and the pitiful remains of their equipment. In spite of the desperateness of their plight, the grim reality of their chances of survival and their deterioration due to fatigue and approaching malnutrition, Duncan demanded discipline. His nightly inspections were a method of reminding the men that they were soldiers. As he stepped in front of each man, Duncan looked him in the eye, searching for his deepest thoughts, gauging his will and ability to go on. He looked for doubts and fear. Usually he spoke to each one softly as he snapped the man's weapon from his hands and inspected it for cleanliness and proper function. After handing the weapon back, he gave the man a once-over, adjusting gear and equipment, judging each man's load as he did so to ensure that everyone carried a fair share. Though some of the men griped to Hernandez about the daily inspection, they stood and were inspected. They were, after all, soldiers, regardless of their plight and situation. Duncan used every opportunity to remind them of that fact.

As the last hint of daylight left the sky, Hernandez and another man took point duty and moved out. Duncan waited a few moments, then led the rest of the men out. Younger took up the rear. As always, they moved south, five meters between men, weapons at the ready. In an hour Hernandez would angle over to the southeast toward the road in search of an ambush site. With a little luck, the platoon would find an easy mark, be able to hit it and be alive in the morning to enjoy a full meal of Russian rations. Regardless of luck, they would be a little closer to friendly lines, wherever they were, in the morning. The pursuit of survival, like their trek, dragged on.

On the Southern Edge of the Dasht-e Lut
1945 Hours, 13 July (1615 Hours, 13 July, GMT)

The lead BRDM recon vehicle and the BMP moved off into the distance. Kurpov watched them with detached interest. His three-vehicle platoon was in pursuit of another phantom. An image on a photo had no doubt caught someone's attention and he had decided it was a danger. An intelligence estimate had been

sent down to Front Headquarters, where it was decided that action was needed. From there, orders had been passed to Army,
Army had issued their own orders, and Division had done the
same. Kurpov leaned down and told his driver to move out, the
final order in the long chain.

Kurpov's mission was to locate an enemy armored column that
had been reported moving north. Despite the dearth of fuel, a
reinforced battalion was being dispatched to deal with the threat.
The commander of the 89th Motorized Rifle Division did not
want to let the enemy get deep into his rear areas, as had happened to the 28th Combined Arms Army. Had aircraft been available, the threat would have been dealt with from the sky.
Everything that could fly, however, had been diverted to the west
to keep a bad situation from getting worse. The 89th MRD, long
since relegated to last priority in everything, had even less.

Kurpov followed the progress of his lead element and checked
off their location on his map as they moved south. He had not
been surprised by the order to move out. For over three weeks
they had done nothing but spar with the American Marines
across a front stretching from the Pakistan border to the Dasht-e
Lut. The battles had been small, violent affairs fought by units
numbering fewer than five hundred in most cases. Both they and
the Americans in the eastern sector were spread thin, responsible
for far more ground than could be properly patrolled, let alone
defended. The result was a strange frontier war in which the
opponents made sudden thrusts to seize key terrain features or
destroy isolated outposts. The thrusts were normally met with a
counterattack from either air or ground forces. The fighting never
lasted for more than a day and resulted in few changes other than
in the number of soldiers left on each side. It did not take Kurpov
long to figure out that the 89th MRD and the American Marines
were engaged in a sideshow, a battle that wouldn't influence the
final outcome of the war. This, however, didn't change the fact
that men fought just as hard and the losers were just as dead.

As his platoon moved into the area known to both sides as no-
man's-land, Kurpov began to grow more apprehensive. There had
been no friendly air recon by either helicopters or the Air Force.
The last report of the Americans was over twelve hours old. The
American Marines had picked up the habit of faking a thrust in
order to make the 89th MRD react. Sitting well to the rear, airborne intelligence-gathering platforms watched and tracked the

movement of the Soviet force reacting to the Marine fake. When enough information had been gathered to make a good estimate of where the Soviet force would be at a given time, attack helicopters were dispatched to ambush sites along the route. More than once the counterattack force rolled into such an ambush. The Americans, however, didn't always have it their way. One Soviet regimental commander, anticipating such a trick, had sent every antiaircraft weapon in the regiment with the counterattack force. In that instance, it was the Americans who had been surprised and had come off the worse.

In the gathering darkness Kurpov ordered his vehicles to close up. To the west he could not see the other recon platoon. Nor could he see the lead elements of the rifle battalion that was following them at a distance of fifteen kilometers. It had been reasoned that that distance was necessary in order to give the rifle battalion time to deploy against an enemy found by the recon patrols. Kurpov scanned the area to his front in frustration. His three little vehicles were totally inadequate for their task. They were moving far too fast to properly check out the entire area. They could drive past whole companies of American Marines hidden in the wadis. It is hard to find someone who does not want to be found, especially when you are not given the time to search. Kurpov likened his predicament to that of a bear crashing through a thicket. If there was an elephant hiding in there, they might find it. But they would never see a snake until it was too late.

Private First Class Chester Hewett, U.S.M.C., was glad to see the sun disappear over the western horizon. A native of Vermont, Hewett had never been in a desert before 6 June. The oppressive heat, the barren terrain, the extreme dryness were foreign to a man raised among pine trees and snow-covered mountains. Parris Island and Camp Lejeune in the Carolinas had been a shock to him. There the men had likened riding about in the monstrous LTVP-7 amphibious assault vehicles to living in an oven. Since their arrival in Iran, they had upgraded the status of the LTVPs to microwave oven. Fortunately their CO had them moving only at night. During the day the battalion hunkered down, with a third of the men on alert and the rest asleep.

In a short speech before moving out on their current mission, the Old Man had told them that they were going out hunting for bear, a term the battalion commander liked to use when they made raids deep into no-man's-land for the express purpose of picking a fight with the Russians. This raid was an all-armored affair. LAV-25 light armored recon vehicles thrown out in the lead had the mission of finding and tracking the Soviets. Once they had done so, the main body, consisting of a battalion of Marine infantry mounted in LTVPs and accompanied by an M-1A1 tank company, would close with the Russians and strike. Hewett's platoon was the rear guard. Their mission was to keep an eye on the back door, just in case it was the Russians who got the upper hand.

With the booming voice that many had likened to that of a beached whale, Hewett's platoon sergeant called in the men on outpost duty. There was no need for whispers here. If there had been Russians around, they would have announced their presence a long time before. Rising from his shallow pit, Hewett picked up his Dragon missile launcher. It was still warm from the sun. A cool breeze hit Hewett as he stood and stretched. It felt good until he remembered that the temperature that night would never get as low as the highest temperature he had ever experienced back home in Vermont. He had joined the Marines to see the world. Looking around at the barren wasteland, he decided that if the rest of the world looked half as bad as Iran, Vermont was all he would ever need for the rest of his life.

In the darkness the recon elements of the two antagonists passed by each other unseen. Had they found each other, the fight would have been a reasonably even match. Instead, the recon vehicles continued to grope about in the night, each rolling forward into a head-on collision with their enemy's main body.

A flash and the explosion of a vehicle hit in the distance signaled the first contact. Kurpov turned in the open hatch and faced west. He could see a red glow in the sky, a beacon marking the spot where an armored vehicle had died. But whose? Kurpov stretched himself until he was standing on his toes in an effort to see what was happening to the west. The crack of the radio and the frantic report by the other recon-platoon leader provided the answers he sought. Tanks! The other platoon had run into a pair of American tanks moving north. Two more flashes lit up the west. Each was followed by an explosion. The sudden termination of the other platoon leader's radio transmission in midsentence told Kurpov that his friend Sasha was dead.

While the rifle-battalion commander, leading the main body still fifteen kilometers behind, attempted to raise Sasha on the radio, Kurpov ordered his platoon to seek covered positions from which they could observe their assigned sectors. When the vehicle commanders had acknowledged his order, he directed his own driver into a position between two rocks from where he could see out to his front as well as the general location of his other two vehicles. The battalion commander, having failed to raise the platoon that had made contact with the enemy, called Kurpov for a report. Kurpov's platoon was not actually in contact. What he told the battalion commander was exactly what he had seen, his current location and his intent.

The commander of the Soviet motorized rifle battalion thought about the situation for a moment. He estimated that he had at least five minutes to digest the scant information he had, devise a plan and issue necessary orders. He assumed that the recon platoons had stumbled upon the enemy recon forces. He did not know that the enemy recon, two U.S. Marine LAV-25s, had passed by his own recon and were now sitting undetected in a wadi at a range of twelve hundred meters, watching his column move south and reporting to their commander. A series of muzzle flashes and the exploding of a BMP in the middle of the main body quickly destroyed the Soviet commander's initial estimate of the situation. In an instant the sky was lit up with tracers as the other Soviet vehicles in the company that had lost the BMP returned fire in the direction from which the attacker had struck. The battalion commander directed his BMP into a shallow defilade and watched for a moment. The hail of Soviet fire continued without any indication that it was hitting anything. Nor could he see any further firing directed toward the column. The enemy had taken a potshot at his battalion in order to make them react. No doubt the enemy was part of a recon force that was probably reporting what it saw even as it was withdrawing.

The battalion commander ordered all units to cease fire and report. Though the firing stopped, the images of tracers and muzzle flashes were burned into the battalion commander's eyes. As he waited for his company commanders to respond, he rubbed his eyes in an effort to eradicate the spots. The pressing seemed only to make the images more intense. Slowly the reports came in. He listened impassively as his commanders gave their inflated reports of kills. Each report fueled the battalion commander's anger. When all units had reported in, he yelled into his handset, demanding that they give him accurate reports, challenging anyone to bring him the head of a dead marine. He didn't really expect his commanders to do so, and they knew it. They also knew what he meant.

As his commanders sorted out their situation, he reevaluated his. The enemy now knew where his main body was. Through deductive reasoning based on the scant information he had, the battalion commander was able to put together a mental image of the battlefield and the relative locations of his forces and the enemy. The enemy had hit the recon platoon deployed in the west. Immediately after that, his main body had been hit by a recon element firing on his battalion from the west. That meant that the enemy force was to his west. Dropping down into the BMP and turning on a small red-filtered light, he looked at his map, quickly drew two simple symbols to show where the enemy was, then looked at the terrain for a moment. He realized what had happened. By sheer chance the two antagonists had brushed shoulders as they moved about in the dark.

Satisfied that his grasp of the tactical situation was correct, the battalion commander began to issue his orders. Like clockwork, the battalion began to reconfigure itself from a column to an attack formation.

Kurpov sat and listened to the reports and the battalion commander's tongue-lashing. The BRDM driver chuckled. "We would not be as lucky if we gave such bad reports."

The comment broke the tension. Kurpov smiled. "Ivan, I consider us lucky any time we stumble into a fight and are able to report."

The crew of the BRDM laughed. For the moment, the nervous stress, the fear and the dread of what would happen next were forgotten. But the war was still out there. The sound of ammunition cooking off in the burning vehicles was muffled by distance, the armor of the BRDM and the crewmen's helmets. Kurpov stood up in his hatch. Slowly he turned, studying the terrain and the immediate area. Nothing; there was nothing to be seen other than his other BRDM and the BMP. To the west and the north the sky glowed faintly red, marking where men had died. They were of no concern to Kurpov. It was the ones who were alive that he was interested in. He knew that at that very moment hundreds of men, manning the most sophisticated combat vehicles in the world, were out there, creeping about, intent on finding one another and killing.

The LTVP-7 came to a jolting halt. The ramp hadn't even hit the ground when the squad leader was up and yelling, "Let's go, Marines. Deploy and hit it!" The LTVP-7 was empty in seconds. Each man rushed out and ran to either the left of the track or the right. As they ran forward the Marines spread out until the squad was in a rough line deployed to either side of the track. As soon as Hewett came around the side of the vehicle and began to run to the front, he searched the darkness for a position. The LTVP was in some kind of shallow ditch. Its prow was up against the side of the ditch, splitting the squad up. Hewett saw a good position that appeared to offer the best protection and headed for it. His assistant gunner followed, carrying a spare Dragon missile. The bulky tub, and the personnel weapons and other assorted equipment hanging on each of them, made running awkward but not impossible. With enough adrenaline, just about anything was possible.

Once in position, Hewett slowly popped his head up and surveyed the lay of the land, checking to see whether he had a good field of fire. The ditch they were in ran along the crest of a small rise. It was almost like a custom-made trench. The ground to his front had a gentle downward slope. From where he was, he had a clear field of fire for better than one thousand meters, more than enough for his Dragon. Satisfied, Hewett turned to survey the back blast area. Firing a Dragon could be just as deadly to friendlies as to the enemy. As he was checking that area, the squad leader came up.

"This looks like a good place, Sarge," Hewett said. "What do you think?"

The squad leader examined the position, then slapped Hewett on the back. "Good to go. Set up here." Without waiting for a response, the leader was gone, moving down to check the next position.

Hewett pulled the boxlike thermal sight from the pouch at his side and attached it to the Dragon missile he had been carrying.

He could not see what he was doing, but that was not necessary. Hours of redundant drilling had made the handling of the missile launcher second nature. Once the sight was in place, Hewett hoisted the Dragon onto his right shoulder, put his eye up to the rubber eyepiece, then flicked the switch with his finger. The darkness disappeared. Through the thermal sight, he viewed the landscape in more detail, looking for any sign of life or movement. Everything to his front was now black and red. He could clearly see everything worth seeing, which wasn't much.

Nor did he expect to see anything. As part of the rear guard, they were looking in the wrong direction. The enemy was to the north. They were facing south, just in case the enemy tried to sneak through the back door. As Hewett scanned the area, he thought about their mission and weighed the mixed feelings that cluttered his head. On one hand, he did not like the idea that they probably would not get a chance to shoot at anyone all night. They had pulled rear guard before on smaller raids. It was frustrating to get all psyched up preparing for combat, then spend several days rolling around the godforsaken country and doing nothing. On the other hand, combat meant danger, the chance to get torn apart, maimed or killed. Every mission completed alive meant that he was that much closer to home.

The thought of home pushed aside Hewett's debate on whether it was better to be in the rear or the front. Instead, images of the lush green pine forest that covered the mountains came to mind. His mountains were alive, vibrant, inviting. The stark black and red images he was viewing were so foreign, so different, so hostile.

The order to find the enemy's flank or rear came as no surprise. Kurpov made one more sweep of the area before he ordered his platoon to move out. This time, the platoon proceeded with great caution. The BMP overwatched as the two BRDMs crept forward. They advanced for a while under the watchful eye of the BMP until the BMP could no longer cover their movement. Then Kurpov held the BRDMs in place until the BMP could advance, find a new position to cover the next move and settle in. As the BMP moved forward, Kurpov and the other BRDM commander scanned their areas looking for signs of the enemy. When the

BMP commander was ready, he signed Kurpov, who then moved out again. Though the process was slow, it was the safest and most thorough.

Because he wanted to find the enemy rear, Kurpov initially moved south. He knew that the enemy was immediately to the west. That piece of information had cost the recon company one of its last two platoons. Only Kurpov's platoon was left of the original company. Kurpov intended to be a live veteran after the war. He reasoned that the Soviet Union already had more than enough heroes. Besides, a dead recon leader provides his unit with no information, other than where not to go.

Only when he was satisfied that they had gone south far enough did Kurpov turn west. He would proceed west for about two kilometers and then turn north. When he did that, he intended to go even slower. Following Kurpov's platoon was a motorized rifle company. They would strike once the rear had been found and plotted by the recon element. Success or failure now hinged on which commander had made the best guess and who found whom first.

Hewett's mind was still wandering about the slopes of Vermont when the faint image of two dust clouds first appeared in his sight. By the time he jerked his mind back to the present, the two BRDMs had stopped in concealed defilade positions. The dust kicked up and heated by the engines' exhaust was dissipated when Hewett made his next sweep of his assigned area.

Kurpov studied the far slope as he waited for the BMP to move into its next position. He wanted to cut north, but did not like the idea of running across the open area that stretched from his position to the next covered position. The BMP would have difficulty covering them all the way. Kurpov was still mulling over the alternatives when the BMP signaled that he was set and ready to cover.

Kurpov was about to move out and continue to the west when the battalion radio net came alive with contact reports. The two main bodies had collided. The battle was on. Kurpov no longer had all the time in the world to sneak about and find the safest, most secured route. He had to find the enemy rear quickly and guide the rifle company following him to a position from which it could launch a surprise attack. The red flashes to the north and the faint boom of tank cannons in the distance galvanized Kurpov into action. He ordered his driver to move out and to the right. They would try to bound across the open as rapidly as possible. Luck favors the bold, Kurpov told himself.

The sound of tanks firing and explosions broke into Hewett's dreams of home. He turned around and looked to the north for a moment. He could see the sky suddenly glow as a weapon fired. Here and there a fireball leaped up, announcing the death of an armored vehicle and its crew. That thought convinced Hewett that rear guard wasn't so bad after all. He turned around, hoisted the Dragon back onto his shoulder and put his eye to the sight. In an instant, the image of two armored vehicles burned itself into his eye. Hewett felt himself go cold. His heart began to beat faster. He could almost feel the adrenaline course through his veins. The enemy.

In a voice that was neither a whisper nor a shout, he alerted his squad leader. In an instant he, followed by the platoon leader, came stumbling up to where Hewett sat transfixed, tracking the progress of the enemy vehicles.

The platoon leader spoke first. "What do you have, Marine?"

"Two vehicles. Looks like BRDMs, Skipper, headed straight for us at about twelve hundred meters."

Reaching for the Dragon, the lieutenant whispered, "Let me see." Hewett relinquished control of the Dragon to him. The lieutenant needed only a second. When he had convinced himself, he turned it back over to Hewett, issuing orders to the squad leader as he did so. "Kendle, find Gunney. Have him report to the CO that we have two BRDMs moving on our position from the south. We are engaging and will hold here until we receive further orders." Turning to Hewett, "Marine, you take out the one on the right. Fire when he gets to five hundred meters. I'll get Thompson to take out the other. Be prepared to get the second one if Thompson misses."

The lieutenant was gone before Hewett could say, "Aye aye, sir." Turning to his assistant, Hewett told him, "No doubt the skipper's telling Thompson to be ready to take out the other BRDM in case we miss. Well, we ain't gonna miss."

His assistant slapped Hewett on the shoulder and acknowledged with "Fuckin' a-men."

Hoisting the Dragon back into position, Hewett set the sight's cross hair on the center of mass of the BRDM on the right and began to track it. His fingers lightly tapped the trigger as he waited for the enemy vehicle to reach the designated range.

They were at the halfway point. Kurpov stood upright in his hatch and looked to his right. The other BRDM was having difficulty keeping up with him. Turning to the front, he could see no sign of activity on the slope that they were fast approaching. There were only six hundred meters to go. Three minutes. Time seemed to stand still. It was taking so long to get there. These things always seemed to take forever.

The image of the BRDM, growing by the second, seemed to fill Hewett's sight. He no longer concerned himself with the one to the left. It was falling behind and not his concern. At that moment, his entire life, his whole being, centered around the image of the enemy vehicle bearing down on him. Time swept by. Any second now. Hewett began to control his breathing, taking in a full breath, letting it out, taking another. He watched the BRDM, he timed his breath, he waited until he felt he could wait no more. At that instant he drew in one final breath, held it, then squeezed the trigger.

Although he was looking right at it when it fired, Kurpov did not immediately recognize the antitank guided missile for what it was. For the briefest of moments, he stared at the bright-orange orb closing on him. *"Missile, missile, missile! Driver, hard right!"* The order surprised the driver, but he responded with a violent jerk to the left. The maneuver threw Kurpov off balance and sent him sprawling onto the floor of the BRDM.

Hewett held his breath and kept the sight glued to the BRDM. Five seconds, that was all it would take the missile to fly five hundred meters. Three seconds were gone, two to go. Hewett had almost anticipated the sharp turn. With ease he followed the BRDM as it now exposed its flank to him. Hewett gripped the launcher tightly, his eye pressed to the sight, and held his breath until the bright glow of the high-explosive warhead on the side of the BRDM lit up his sight.

·   ·   ·

Kurpov was lying on the floor, looking up and struggling to grab on to something when the missile slammed into the side of the BRDM. The dark interior was suddenly lit up by a blinding flash of light. The shaped-charge warhead had detonated on the side of the BRDM and formed a jet stream of molten metal that bored its way through the vehicle's thin armor. As the jet stream pushed through, it added the BRDM's armor that lay in its path, now liquefied and white hot, to the stream. In horror Kurpov saw the stream cut through the gunner. The man's shrieks were cut short by the explosion of on-board ammunition. Blinded by the light, unable to move or avoid the jet stream, Kurpov felt himself being ripped by fragments and peppered by molten clumps of metal tossed aside as the jet stream dissipated. He screamed as his brain was overwhelmed with pain. He was unconscious when the final cataclysmic explosion tore the BRDM apart.

Hewett didn't need to watch the death of the BRDM. The initial impact told him he had scored a square hit. The BRDM wasn't going anywhere anymore. Instead of watching, he turned to the task of taking his sight from the expended Dragon tube and fitting it to the new round held by the assistant gunner. They had just about completed their drill when the sky was lit up by the explosion of the second BRDM. Thompson had also scored.

Hewett finished what he was doing and looked back at the BRDM he had hit. It was now totally involved in flames. Fuel dripped from a ruptured tank, forming a flaming little pond that spread as he watched. For a moment, he considered the crew. That thought, however, was interrupted by the sharp report of a 30mm. gun. In the distance, at a point from which the two BRDMs had come, an automatic cannon was firing. Hewett, seeing that the firing was wild, put his sight up to his eye and began to search for the new enemy. The battle had just been joined. It would be a long and bloody night as two antagonists, each many miles from home, tore at each other in a battle that would, at best, someday be referred to as a sideshow.

Chapter 16

The unleashed power of the atom has changed everything save our modes of thinking, and we thus drift toward unparalleled catastrophes.

— ALBERT EINSTEIN

Kerman, Iran
0730 Hours, 15 July (0400 Hours, 15 July, GMT)

The airfield was visible from a distance as the patrol crossed the open fields. The sight gave the footsore paratroopers heart. After four days of ceaseless patrolling during the day that found nothing and ambushes at night that yielded nothing, the men were tired. The airfield promised them a meal of hot tea and kasha. While they were on patrol campfires had not been allowed, preventing the men from preparing tea to accompany their dry rations of canned meat and black bread. Though they knew they would have only two days, three at the most, before they went out again, any break was welcome.

Before entering the airfield's perimeter, the patrol was stopped by their commanding officer and ordered to straighten out their uniforms and equipment. They would still be dirty, but at least they would give the impression that they were a disciplined military unit. The paratroopers, despite being tired and anxious to get back into the safety of the perimeter, did not complain. No one, not even new men assigned to the unit, complained or hesitated when Lieutenant Ilvanich gave an order. As if on parade, Ilvanich, followed by Junior Lieutenant Malovidov, walked down the line of paratroopers, stopping in front of each. Ilvanich addressed each paratrooper by his full name and chatted or joked with him while he inspected or made an adjustment.

Malovidov watched intently everything Ilvanich did. New to the unit, he had been sent on the patrol to learn from Ilvanich. Intimidated at first due to his teacher's reputation and manner, Malovidov was confused by the time they finished. Most of what the lieutenant did and the way in which he conducted himself had never been taught in the military academy or the officers' training courses Malovidov had attended. Ilvanich often did not follow doctrine or proper procedures. Despite his cold and aloof manner, the men under his command worshiped him, following his every order and direction without hesitation, question or complaint. When combat appeared imminent, the lieutenant became a cold, unfeeling machine, seeing all and spewing out orders rapidly, efficiently. The men responded to him as if they had anticipated his orders. When Malovidov asked Ilvanich why he had done something, the lieutenant often snapped, "Because that is the way to do it." The junior lieutenant, having much to learn, was not sure he could from such an enigma.

Nor could Malovidov penetrate Ilvanich's personal world. Efforts at striking up conversation about home and family were met with silence or curt remarks such as "That is not important right now" or "You should be concerning yourself with military matters, not idle gossip." As far as Malovidov could determine, Ilvanich had no real friends. What free time he had he spent alone, often out of sight of the rest of the unit. This worried Malovidov. He wondered whether he himself would become as sullen and unfriendly once he had been in combat as much as Ilvanich had been. He hoped he would not, but he did not discount the possibility. The young lieutenant had heard that combat did strange things to a man's mind.

As the patrol entered the perimeter, Ilvanich was shocked to see the KGB major for whom he had worked in Tabriz. The major was waiting for him. After the two officers saluted, the KGB major offered a friendly smile, while the lieutenant carefully guarded his surprise and suspicions.

"Lieutenant Ilvanich, congratulations on your well-deserved promotion."

Ilvanich, straight-faced, thanked the major. Then, anxious to find out the purpose of the visit, he asked, "What brings you, Comrade Major, to the garden spot of Iran?"

The major laughed and threw his arm around Ilvanich. "We have a mission for you. Turn your patrol over to the junior lieutenant and walk with me."

A sinking feeling began to grow in Ilvanich's stomach while they walked. The image of the dead prisoners stacked against the wall in Tabriz came to mind. Hesitantly he asked, "What, Comrade Major, is the nature of the mission?"

The major, serious now, spoke slowly, guardedly. "It is a matter of great importance to the State. Much depends on its success."

Everything, Ilvanich thought, is a matter of great importance to the KGB. I wonder how many children we must kill this time.

Headquarters, 10th Corps, Bandar Abbas, Iran
0900 Hours, 15 July (0530 Hours, 15 July, GMT)

The briefing, the atmosphere and the collection of rank overwhelmed Second Lieutenant Cerro. As he sat there, he wished he could slither under the table he was seated at and low-crawl out the door. That option, however, was definitely out. There were too few people in the room. His absence would be noticed. Besides, the corps commander kept watching him, almost as if he knew of Cerro's plans to escape. At the table, along with the corps commander, there were several full colonels, a Special Forces major, a naval officer whose rank Cerro didn't know, and two other airborne-company commanders from Cerro's battalion. Cerro had never seen this side of the Army before. Earlier, as he walked through the corps headquarters with the other company commanders and waited for the meeting to start, he had watched majors and lieutenant colonels scurrying about like office boys, scribbling on paper, posting maps, answering phones. Cerro wondered whether there were any second lieutenants in the corps headquarters and, if there were, what their jobs were.

Once the meeting began, behind closed doors with MPs posted at them, Cerro became more bewildered and, because of the subject, frightened. As the briefers went through their presentations, a story that sounded more like a poor made-for-TV movie plot began to unfold: In a sweep of the battlefield on 13 July, the wreck of an Iranian F-4 fighter-bomber had been found just north of Saadatabad. Shot down on the ninth, the plane was carrying a crude atomic bomb.

Despite the fact that everyone except Cerro seemed to know about the "Device," as they called it, all present still were visibly uneasy every time it was mentioned. When the corps intelligence officer presented his suppositions on what the plane with the Device was up to, several of the colonels questioned him. A lively debate was cut short by the corps commander, who stated, "Gentlemen, I really don't give a damn what they were going to do with it. What I want to know is what we are going to do to find out if they have more and how we are going to keep those fanatics from using them."

The intelligence officer, using a map, explained that by reviewing Air Force records of all air battles fought on the ninth, they had been able to locate where the F-4 had originated. When information obtained from other sources, including a Special Forces team dropped into the area, was added to this, it had been determined that a secret, well-secured base was being operated by the Iranians near Robat-e Abgram in the Dasht-e Lut. Since the F-4 had first been detected by AWACS in that area, the connection was made that the Devices were being either stored or manufactured there. Other than that, intelligence had nothing to offer.

The corps operations officer followed with his report. He stated that CENTCOM, apprised of the matter, had given the corps the mission of following up on the theory that the Device had probably come from either Robat-e Abgram or one of two other sites. It was the task of the 10th Corps to find the real site and take it out. The operations officer presented to the corps commander all possible options available to accomplish the mission, recounted all pros and cons for each option and presented a coordinated staff recommendation. It had been decided that ground attacks, led by Special Forces A teams and supported by an airborne company hitting each site, were best. By going in on the ground, they could confirm whether or not the secret site was in fact the storage place or the plant where the Device was manufactured. In addition, a ground attack would ensure complete destruction of all critical elements, personnel and Devices.

It suddenly dawned on Cerro why he was there. His company would be one of the airborne companies. When the Special Forces major spoke, Cerro listened intently. His suspicions were confirmed when the major casually mentioned that A Company, 2nd of the 517th Parachute Infantry, commanded by Lieutenant Cerro, would provide fire support and security for the Special Forces assault team in the raid against Robat-e Abgram. At that instant, all faces in the room turned to Cerro. He could feel their eyes drilling through him, wondering if he could pull it off.

For the balance of the meeting, Cerro was lost in his own thoughts. How in hell did I get into this one? he pondered. Don't they know about the antiarmor ambush I blew? Isn't there a unit with a more senior commander? These and similar questions swam through his mind until the meeting broke up. As the people in the room began to rise, the corps commander's aide called to Cerro. The corps commander wanted to see Cerro in his office.

When the door was closed and they were alone, Lieutenant General Weir told Cerro to be seated and relax. "I suppose you're wondering why your company is going in."

Cerro responded, "Yes, sir."

"Well, Lieutenant, you're doing it because your unit is ready, it's proven in battle and, most importantly, you've been ordered to. What do you think about that?"

Cerro looked up at the General for a moment. He thought about giving him a "Can do, airborne, sir" yell but decided against that. The General asked what he thought. Fuck it, Cerro thought. He asked, I'll tell him. "Sir, I think you have the wrong unit. You obviously weren't told about the ambush I blew on one July."

A smile flitted across the General's face. "On the contrary, Lieutenant Cerro, I know everything about that action. I also know about your conduct on eight June at Kuhha A Ye Genu, the air assault on Tarom on eleven June and the three successful ambushes your company did pull off. In fact, it was because of your actions when the ambush on one July was blown that I decided your unit should go on the mission."

Cerro stared at the General with a puzzled look.

"Another man in your spot would have tried to pull the ambush off despite the error in firing the wrong star cluster. You made the right choice. In an instant you saw that the ambush could not be salvaged and pulled out, saving your men and equipment for another day. Most second lieutenants would not have done that. Believe me, I know. I used to be one."

Cerro thought about that for a moment. In his wildest imaginings, he could not picture the General as a second lieutenant. Yet, once he had been one, just like Cerro. "Sir, if you're sure, I know we can do it."

"Lieutenant, if I had any doubts, you wouldn't be here."

With that, Cerro jumped to his feet, snapped to attention and shouted, "Airborne!" as he saluted.

West of Kul-e Nay Band, Iran
0254 Hours, 18 July (2324 Hours, 17 July, GMT)

A sandstorm from out of nowhere had sprung up and turned the clear night into a swirling nightmare. The M-8 helicopter carrying Lieutenant Ilvanich and most of Junior Lieutenant Malovidov's platoon, Ilvanich's old platoon, was bucking and being tossed about. Visual contact with Captain Lvov's and the other helicopter had been lost shortly after the storm began. The pilot, worried about midair collisions or crashing or losing his way, wanted to abort the mission. Ilvanich, cradling his AK assault rifle, "encouraged" him to continue. Ilvanich was not overly concerned. Even if the helicopters dropped everyone off at the wrong landing zone, they still had twenty-four hours to rally everyone at an obscure and well-hidden oasis in the hills southwest of their objective in Robat-e Abgram.

As in the Kerman operation, Ilvanich's greatest concern was not with the enemy or how his soldiers would perform. They would do their duty, as always. His concerns were with his company commander. Captain Lvov had become more overbearing since Ilvanich was promoted. Ilvanich, experiencing great difficulty in controlling himself in the presence of his commander, had volunteered for every patrol that took him away from Lvov. The other officers in the battalion and the regiment saw his actions as a dedication to duty and a love of battle. Both he and Lvov knew better.

The current operation had done little to overcome the hatred shared by the two. The KGB major who had brought the mission to the regiment had selected Ilvanich's company for it. The major insisted on speaking to Ilvanich, ignoring Lvov, during all the briefings and meetings. The senior officers of the regiment, seeing this, began to do the same. There was, after all, an obvious connection between the young lieutenant and the KGB, and such connections were not taken lightly. Despite his best efforts, Lvov was unable to change this. As bad as that had been for Lvov, the situation became worse when the company was being briefed and prepared. Whenever one of the officers or noncommissioned officers in the company had a question or a problem, he instinctively turned to Ilvanich. Lvov was careful not to say anything in the presence of the KGB major. In one stormy session when the major was absent, Lvov raged and cursed at Ilvanich, threatening that he had best find himself a new unit after the current mission was over. When Lvov was finished, Ilvanich, face frozen in an expressionless stare, responded as his right hand toyed with the safety of his AK, "If the company is too small for both of us, Comrade Captain, other arrangements can be made."

Above the din of the helicopter's engines and the roar of the storm, the pilot yelled to Ilvanich, "Comrade Lieutenant, we are going down!"

The sudden announcement galvanized Ilvanich. He undid his seat belt and moved up behind the pilot. "What do you mean, we are going down? Are we crashing?"

The pilot was fighting with the controls and peering into the impenetrable sandstorm and darkness. Sweat from exertion and fear covered his face. He answered in a harried manner, "The dust is clogging the engines and the entire system. There are warning lights coming on all over." With a sweep of his hand, he showed Ilvanich a half-dozen flashing red lights on the instrument panel. "Either we land now, while we still have control, or we crash in five minutes."

Ilvanich looked at his watch. "How far to the landing zone?"

Without hesitation, the pilot responded, "Fifteen minutes."

"No, kilometers. How many kilometers?"

"Oh, sorry." The pilot looked at his instruments and thought for a moment. "Fifty kilometers."

"That's too far. You must get us closer. Keep going as long as you can before you put it down."

The pilot protested, "If I wait too long, the engine will seize up and the helicopter will never fly again. We must land now."

Angry, Ilvanich leaned closer to the pilot's ear. "The hell with your helicopter. What happens to it is unimportant. You must get us closer. Do you understand?"

The pilot, his face grim with fear and concentration, nodded in the affirmative. "Yes, Comrade Lieutenant, we will do the best we can. Now go back and strap in, just in case."

Fifteen Kilometers Southwest of Robat-e Abgram, Iran
0610 Hours, 18 July (0240 Hours, 18 July, GMT)

The smell of burnt flesh and rubber permeated the area. The wreckage of a Soviet M-8 transport helicopter sat just inside the patch of green vegetation that surrounded the well. The bodies of its crew and passengers were sprawled about the wreckage. Only one survivor, a major, apparently overlooked by the attackers in the darkness and confusion, had been found. Unfortunately, he was severely wounded and could not, or would not, speak English. While the company medics tended to him, Second Lieutenants Cerro and Kinsley, followed by Lieutenant Commander Hensly, U.S.N., checked out the area. They decided that most of the Russians had been out of the helicopter when it was hit. The discovery of an expended LAW antitank-rocket-launcher tube and small piles of 5.56mm. rounds left no doubt who had hit the Russians as they were disembarking.

Cerro walked up to the helicopter, looked around, then kicked it and let out a string of curses. To date, the whole operation had been plagued with problems. One of the C-130 transports they had been loaded on for the jump blew an engine, requiring some of Cerro's company, overburdened with parachutes, weapons and ammunition, to offload and move to a backup plane while the rest waited. When they were all set, they were put on a weather hold—a sandstorm had suddenly cropped up in the area of the drop zone. After they finally did take off and then made their jump, they found themselves five kilometers from the intended drop zone. As a fitting conclusion to the string of mishaps, the Special Forces team and the pro-U.S. Iranians were not at the well when Cerro's company arrived. Instead of finding them, the company found a smoldering Soviet helicopter and dead bodies, left by the Special Forces team.

Hensly waited for a minute before he asked the question that was on everyone's mind. When Cerro had gotten over his fit, Hensly said as nonchalantly as he could, "Well, I suppose this puts an end to this operation."

Cerro replied, "No bullshit, sir. Unless you happen to know

where the place is, how many troops are there, how they're deployed, how many buildings there are and a few other minor details, this operation is officially over."

Hensly was more surprised than upset. "Didn't they tell you anything?"

With a sneer, Cerro shot back, "Yeah, bring lots of ammo and be on time. The green beanies were going to brief us on all the details once we got here." Looking up at the twisted tail boom of the M-8, he mused, "Guess they had everything figured out except for these yahoos. Wonder what they were after."

"Could be a routine patrol or a strike force looking for our friends the snake eaters and their friendly ragheads. Maybe they were after the same thing we're here for."

Cerro looked at his platoon leader and laughed. "Now, wouldn't that be a trip. Both we and the Reds chasing a bunch of Irans with the Device." Both Cerro and Kinsley laughed.

Hensly, picking through the wreckage, called out, "That, gentlemen, may be right on the money."

"Come on, Commander. Do you know what the odds of that happening are?"

"Before you put your money where your big mouth is, Lieutenant, come over here and look at this."

Their curiosity aroused, Cerro and Kinsley walked over to where the lieutenant commander was picking through what appeared to be a tool bag. Without looking up, he asked, "You know that bag of special instruments I carry around?" He picked up a spanner and several other tools. "Look familiar, don't they?"

Cerro stared at the tools, then at the helicopter. "I'll be damned."

Hensly stood up and looked Cerro in the eye. "We'll all be damned if the Iranians pull off what I think they're after. Lieutenant Cerro, you're in command of the ground operation. I'm here only as a technician to identify anything we find and tell the Army what to blow up. I cannot order you to continue the mission. God knows, we've had enough bad luck as it is. But if we fail, and the Iranians do have another Device that they manage to set off, a lot of people are going to die. And that dying may not be confined to this country."

The two lieutenants thought about that. "You mean that the Russians might think we set the bomb off and retaliate?" Kinsley asked.

"Or, Lieutenant," Hensly replied, "it could be the other way around. Both the U.S. and the Soviet Union have a policy of retaliation in kind. Once we start popping nukes, who knows where it will end."

For a long time the three officers stood there, looking at the burned tool bag and one another. Cerro finally broke the silence. "Well, I guess it's decided. We go for it. Now, anyone got any bright ideas on how we're going to do it?"

Kinsley asked, "What about the Commie major? Maybe he can help us?"

Cerro looked at Hensly, then at Kinsley. "Right. You've been reading too many spy novels." He scanned the wreckage and the bodies one more time, then turned back to Hensly. "Well, standing here isn't getting us anywhere. How about some lunch, Commander?"

Fifteen Kilometers Southwest of Robat-e Abgram, Iran
1425 Hours, 18 July (1055 Hours, 18 July, GMT)

Through binoculars the wreckage of a helicopter could be seen among the trees. Occasional movement could also be seen. What could not be discerned was who the moving people were.

Ilvanich put his binoculars down and considered the possibilities. They could be the rest of the company. Perhaps one of the other helicopters had crashed, like theirs, because of engine failure. That could still leave the other platoon, if they had made it, to join the one with him to accomplish the mission. If that was so, Ilvanich hoped the helicopter that survived was the one with the KGB major.

That thought surprised him. For the first time, he realized that he actually liked the man. In Tabriz he had hated the KGB major at first for having made him play executioner. When the major pulled the platoon off that duty, he had been grateful, but that was all. At Kerman, Ilvanich had actually been able to hold a decent conversation with the man and had found he was human. What really won Ilvanich over, however, was that the KGB major volunteered to go on the mission. In a guarded conversation, he told Ilvanich that he did not trust Lvov, but could not relieve him —Lvov's father was too well connected in the Party. Instead, the major said, he would go as the senior officer. That way he could ensure the success of the mission and protect Ilvanich from Lvov.

When Ilvanich indicated to the major that he could deal with Lvov himself, the major told him to go easy. Lvov was not worth a trip to a gulag. Given time, they could take care of Lvov properly. The fact that the major was truly interested in him and was willing to risk his life in battle impressed Ilvanich.

Putting all thoughts of Lvov and the major aside, Ilvanich considered the matter at hand. If the people moving about were not his, they were Iranians. Hostile ones, no doubt. Sliding back down behind the rise he was on, he turned to Malovidov and his senior sergeant. "Lieutenant Malovidov, you will stay here and cover me. I will go forward with one man and find out who is there. If I do not return in an hour, you will continue with the mission as best you can. Is that clear?"

The junior lieutenant looked confused, but accepted the order. Several men volunteered to go with Ilvanich, forcing him to pick one. Without further ado, the two set out to crawl up to the well and find out who owned it.

Cerro crawled into the rifle pit between its two occupants. In a whisper, he asked, "What's up?"

The sergeant slowly pointed to a spot fifty meters to their front. "Movement. We've been watching them for about five minutes. Looks like one or two guys tryin' to sneak up on us."

Cerro lifted his binoculars to where the sergeant pointed, but saw nothing. "Iranians?"

The private in the rifle pit replied, "Don't think so, sir. Looks like they got some kind of uniform on, camouflaged."

More Russians, Cerro thought. Had to be. Turning to the sergeant, he said, "They're probably Russian. Chances are they're coming in here to find out what we're doing and what happened to their buddies. Take some men and capture them. I want you to do it quietly and without anyone out there seeing. No shooting, no screams. If you have to kill 'em, use the knife."

After the sergeant left, Cerro sat in the pit and watched for a while longer, pondering his next move.

Everything was spinning, and the back of his head hurt. Ilvanich had not felt that bad since his first true drinking bout as a cadet. The glare of the sun did not help his blurred vision. As he sat up, he saw others standing around him. "What happened?"

The answer, given in English, was a shock. "You are a prisoner. Who are you and what are you doing here?"

Ilvanich turned to see who was speaking. The images were still blurry. The one image that was not blurry was the muzzle of a rifle less than an inch from his nose.

The speaker asked again, "Who are you and what are you doing here?"

Still befuddled, Ilvanich anwered without thinking, "Nikolai Ilvanich, junior lieutenant, no, lieutenant, Red Army. Who are you?"

A new voice from behind him spoke. "Sonofabitch, he does speak English. See, I told ya, Hal. Most of 'em do."

Ilvanich's vision cleared. A group of Americans stood near him, a guard in front of him, a second guard farther back with his rifle at the ready, and two men who were apparently officers squatting down beside him. Ilvanich turned to see a third guard and another officer behind him. *Americans.*

The younger officer in front smiled and said, "Give that man a cigar. OK, Ivan, what are you doing here?"

Defiantly Ilvanich asked, "Where is the man who was with me?"

Again it was the younger officer who spoke. "He's with your major. Took a bayonet in the side. He'll be all right, if you coop- erate."

Letting his astonishment show, Ilvanich shot back, "Major? Is he alive? Where is he?"

"Not so fast, Ivan."

Regaining his composure and going back to the attack, Ilvanich replied, "Ilvanich, Lieutenant Ilvanich. What is *your* name and rank?"

Cerro considered the Russian before him. He was a hard cookie. The direct approach didn't seem to work. Maybe he could soften him up some. Perhaps a little give-and-take. "Lieutenant Harold Cerro, U.S. Army. Now, what are you doing here?"

"Before we talk anymore, I must see my major." I must main- tain the upper hand, Ilvanich thought.

The younger officer, the lieutenant named Cerro, seemed to be in charge. Ilvanich kept looking at the other officer, the one with the insignia of an American major, who said nothing. Nor could

Ilvanich detect any signals between the lieutenant named Cerro and that major. Perhaps he wasn't in command.

The one named Cerro turned to the major. "I suppose it won't do any harm. What do you think, Commander?"

He is in command, Ilvanich thought. How strange, though—the lieutenant did all the talking. He must be intelligence or CIA.

Ilvanich was led to the KGB major. A medic and a guard were attending him and the man who had accompanied Ilvanich. The KGB major looked bad, very pale and in pain. When he saw Ilvanich he tried to speak, but could not. Ilvanich knelt down next to him and looked at the wounds. The dressing was clean and neatly tied off. Ilvanich turned to the medic, a young black soldier. "Will he live?"

The medic looked at Ilvanich, surprised that he spoke English. Without a second thought, he began to talk. "He was hit twice by small-arms fire, in the side and the right arm, and he took a fragment, probably a grenade, in the left leg. He's lost a lot of blood, but no major arteries were severed. He was already in shock when we found him, but he seems to be responding well. If we can keep the infections down, he'll do OK."

The American in attendance had to be a doctor. How strange that such a small unit should have a doctor. "The other man, how is he?"

The American doctor looked at the private who had come with Ilvanich. His arm was in a sling. "He's in good shape. His backhand ain't gonna be what it used to be, but he'll get used to it."

The American guard laughed at that.

American humor, no doubt, Ilvanich thought.

The doctor said to Ilvanich, "Let me see your head." He looked at where Ilvanich had been hit. "Hell of a bump. Cut too. I'll clean it." He opened his medical bag and worked on Ilvanich for several minutes. When he was done, he handed Ilvanich two white pills. "You're gonna have a helluva headache. Take these."

Ilvanich looked at the pills suspiciously. A drug to make him talk? He took them in his hand and thanked the doctor before he was led away. While he walked, he let the pills drop to the ground when he was sure no one was looking.

Ilvanich was taken to where Cerro sat alone. Cerro dismissed the guard and asked Ilvanich to sit across from him. Deciding that there was no time to play games and that the Russian was better trained to play them, anyhow, Cerro went straight to the point. "Lieutenant Ilvanich, I know why you're here. You're after the Iranians making the atomic bombs, just like us."

Ilvanich was taken aback by Cerro's statement. He shot back, "I do not know what you are talking about. We were on patrol."

"Bullshit, Lieutenant. My explosive-ordnance expert found your explosive-ordnance expert's tools on the helicopter your major was on," Cerro countered.

The American is after something, Ilvanich thought. But what? If he knows what we were up to, what more does he need? To Cerro, "And if we are, what does that mean to me? I am your prisoner."

Cerro thought for a minute. Years of training had taught him not to trust Russians. If he told the Russian everything, he would be giving classified information to the enemy. But there was little choice. His men could not pull off the raid on their own with the little information he had. It was a gamble, but perhaps the Russian had information, and maybe, just maybe, he would cooperate. Kinsley's far-out idea didn't seem so far out anymore. "We need each other. The people I was supposed to meet ran into your major and his helicopter. Apparently they left after they fired up the helicopter. I have the men to pull off the operation, but I don't know anything about the Iranian installation, troop strength or layout. If you have this information, we can work together."

"What makes you think I might have any such information? I am, after all, only a lieutenant, like you. Besides, we are at war with each other. To tell you anything would be treason. Surely you know that. You are a soldier."

Cerro became angry. "Yeah, I know that, Ilvanich. But I also know that we, both you and I, are at war with Iran. I also know those crazy ragheads have an atomic bomb. They tried to use one on us already. Your people may be next. Do you know what that means?"

Ilvanich thought before he answered. What a strange situation. Three countries at war with one another. Two men, each trained from childhood to hate and distrust the other. Now one was asking the other to trust him. Ilvanich said to himself, I wonder what Lenin would have done. Then to Cerro, "And if we do cooperate, what will happen after the raid? Do we start killing each other again?"

"Good question," Cerro said. "No, at least not right away. I propose we simply withdraw from each other. I let you and your people, along with your wounded, be extracted, and you let me and my men go."

"How do I know you will do this when we are of no further use to you?"

"You don't—at least, not for sure. Just like I don't know for sure if you'll let me go. You'll have to accept my word."

"And if you are killed, what good is your word?"

"Lieutenant Kinsley will honor our agreement."

Ilvanich was confused. Why was the lieutenant doing this? "What about your major? What does he have to say?"

Cerro looked at him, bewildered for a moment, then smiled. "Oh, you mean Lieutenant Commander Hensly. He's Navy. He's my bomb expert. He has nothing to do with running the operation, just checking out the bomb and showing us what to blow."

"Like my bomb expert," Ilvanich enjoined.

"Yeah, like yours. Is it a deal?"

How strange war is, Ilvanich mused. "You realize we may be killing each other in another week."

Cerro looked him in the eye and returned, "If we don't pull this off, none of us may be around in a week."

Chapter 17

Time is everything: Five minutes makes the
difference between victory and defeat.
    —ADMIRAL HORATIO NELSON

Robat-e Abgram, Iran
0150 Hours, 19 July (2220 Hours, 18 July, GMT)

The two lieutenants crept along the ditch to get a closer look
at the buildings in the center. The darkness made their advance
easier. Five hundred meters away six men, three American, three
Soviet, waited for the return of their lieutenants. After agreeing
to work together, the two commanders had decided that a recon
of the site was needed. That would mean delaying the attack
until the next night. They had, however, decided that the intelligence gained was worth the risk. As Ilvanich pointed out, time
spent in reconnaissance was time well spent.

The men of both units were uneasy about the coalition formed
by their commanders. It was, as one American had said, "unnat-
ural." The two lieutenants, however, endeavored to impress upon
their men the nature of the mission and what it meant if they
failed. With great reluctance, the two units had merged, in a way.
Each group had gravitated to one side of the oasis and posted
guards, half of whom watched outward to protect against the
Iranians and the other half inward, to protect against their new
"ally." Even as they approached the Iranian compound, the close
proximity of their new comrades caused more concern than did
the threat of an Iranian ambush.

The two officers came to the end of the ditch. Slowly, they peered over its lip and looked around. Twenty meters to their front was a large building. Light came from several cracks in the boards and from a window. Iranian guards, weapons slung and appearing quite inattentive, paced around it.

Cerro whispered, "That's got to be it. Wish we could get closer, but it's too risky. Let's go back."

Ilvanich turned. "I'll go in. Stay here and cover me."

Cerro grabbed his arm. "No, too risky."

"We must know for sure. It will do us no good if we all run in here and hit the wrong building. I will go, you stay here, Cerro."

"OK, but watch your ass."

Confused, Ilvanich stopped and looked at Cerro. In a serious tone: "I cannot do that. You must."

Cerro chuckled. "OK, I'll watch it. Now go."

Ilvanich watched until the guards were walking away from the near side of the building. Crouching low, he left the ditch and ran up to the building. Once there, he flattened himself against the wall and froze, listening for any sign that someone had seen him. Satisfied he was undetected, he took his knife, turned around and stuck it into a crack between two boards, twisting it slowly to make a small peephole. When he thought it was large enough, he pulled the knife out and peered in. He saw a room filled with metal casings, machine tools and electronic equipment. Men in white coats walked about or worked on various electronic components. This was it. The assembly building had been found.

Satisfied, Ilvanich turned to go back to the ditch. As he did so, a guard came around the corner. They looked at each other for a moment. The guard started to unsling his rifle. Instinctively, Ilvanich rushed him with his knife. The guard, however, hit him in the stomach with the rifle butt, sending Ilvanich sprawling on the ground. Ilvanich, his knife lost, looked up as the guard began to raise his rifle at him.

Suddenly, the rifle dropped to the ground and Ilvanich heard a gurgling noise. The guard slid to his knees, then fell over onto his face. Behind where the guard had been was the figure of Lieutenant Cerro with a knife in his hand. He had cut the guard's throat.

"Grab the rifle and cover the bloodstains." Cerro pulled the guard's body up and slung it over his shoulder, then headed for the ditch.

Ilvanich, now recovered, grabbed the rifle and spread sand over the pool of blood and a thin trail of blood as he followed Cerro. Once in the ditch, he asked Cerro what they were going to do with the body.

"We'll take it with us. Hopefully his buddies will think he went AWOL."

Ilvanich asked, "A-wol, what does that mean?"

"Deserted, over the wall, gone home to Mama. Now let's get the hell outa Dodge."

Although Ilvanich had no idea where Dodge was, he got the idea and followed, covering up all traces of blood as Cerro dragged the body along the ditch.

Fifteen Kilometers Southwest of Robat-e Abgram, Iran
1805 Hours, 19 July (1435 Hours, 19 July, GMT)

Word of the run-in with the guard spread fast and did much to relieve the tension in both camps. Though the men still were cautious, they believed that what their officers told them about the operation was true.

During the morning the two commanders discussed what they had seen and what they knew from before, and formulated a plan. At noon, all the officers and the senior NCOs were briefed. Because the Americans had more men and firepower, they would provide the security and deal with the guards, just as in the original plan. There were four barracks buildings as well as an administration building that needed to be neutralized. Trenches and machine-gun pits ran at regular intervals between the barracks buildings. Two work and storage buildings were in the center. Ilvanich and his men, along with Lieutenant Commander Hensly, would go after those buildings.

While one platoon took on the barracks and trenches on the north side, and another did the same on the south, Cerro would lead a platoon to seize the barracks on the west and overrun the trenches there. Ilvanich and his men would move along the ditch the two lieutenants had been in the night before. When the attack began, they would move in and seize the work and storage buildings. Once they had done so, they would kill everyone there. A special demolition squad of Americans and Soviets who knew how to handle demo would work for Hensly, destroying everything that needed to be destroyed. When they were finished, Ilvanich and his men would withdraw through Cerro. The platoon in the west would cover the withdrawal of the platoons in the north and the south. Cerro wanted to be in and out in less than fifteen minutes. Hensly, however, would make the final decision based on how much needed to be destroyed.

Word that the Soviet major was conscious temporarily broke up the planning session. Ilvanich suddenly became uneasy. What would he do if the KGB major objected? How would he be able to explain the situation? His convictions wavered as he walked over to where the wounded were. What the hell, he thought. What is done is done. The major is in no position to influence the situation.

The major was propped up against a rucksack, and the American doctor was helping him drink from a canteen cup. When the major saw Ilvanich, he waved the American away. For a moment he watched the young lieutenant without expression. Suddenly his face contorted with a surprised look as he focused on Ilvanich's AK dangling from his shoulder. His head snapped to the right in the direction of a group of Americans sitting under a tree cleaning their weapons and joking. By the time he turned back to Ilvanich, the lieutenant was standing before him at attention.

Ilvanich saluted. "I am most happy to see you are responding to treatment, Comrade Major."

The major did not return the salute or say anything as Ilvanich squatted down at his side. The look on the major's face bespoke his confusion.

"No doubt you are wondering what is happening, Comrade Major."

The major regained his composure, his face going blank as his eyes locked on Ilvanich's. Though his voice was weak and raspy, his question was direct and measured. "You have, I trust, an explanation for all this, Lieutenant Ilvanich?"

Ilvanich explained the situation, including what he and Cerro assumed had happened before the Americans arrived at the oasis and found the major and the burned-out helicopter. The KGB major listened without interruption as Ilvanich described in detail the events that had led up to his capture, the bargain the two lieutenants had struck and the results of the previous night's patrol. When Ilvanich finished, the major simply stared at him for a moment. Ilvanich was uneasy but did not allow him to see that.

Finally the major spoke. "What about Lvov, and the other helicopter?"

"We have seen nothing of the captain or the men with him, Comrade Major. Either they went down like me or turned back because of the storm."

"Do you really believe the American, Comrade Lieutenant? Do you really think that once the mission is complete he is simply going to let us walk away?"

"Yes, Comrade. He will."

The major's eyes narrowed. "You are more naive than I thought. I had hoped to make something of you. You had a great future. Do you know what will become of you now if the Americans do let you live?"

Ilvanich felt his anger rising. He fought the urge to lash out at the KGB major. Only when he had regained his composure did he answer. "Have you realized, Comrade Major, what will happen if the Iranians are not stopped? I may not have a future in the Party. And I may be sent to a gulag for cooperating with the Americans. But at least there will be a Party left to send me to a gulag if we succeed. What, Comrade Major, do you suppose will happen if the Iranians do drop a bomb on either the Americans or us? Do you suppose anyone in Moscow or Washington will worry much about who started it? And where will it stop? Here? No, Comrade Major. I will not gamble on the chance that sane heads will prevail. Not when the stakes are Mother Russia herself. I am a soldier. I have a mission to accomplish, an important one. If it means cooperating with the enemy for a moment, then I will do so. After all, did not Stalin sign a pact with the fascists in order to serve the needs of the Soviet Union and the Party?"

The last comment made the major visibly angry. Party members did not like having certain historical events "discussed." Ilvanich knew he had hit the mark as he watched the major consider his comments. After a couple of minutes of silence, the harshness in the major's face softened, then changed to a look of concern. "Do they," pointing to the Americans, "know that I am KGB?"

Ilvanich fought the urge to smile. So, it has finally dawned upon you, he thought. You are slow, Comrade Major. For a moment he thought of toying with the major, to make *him* squirm for once. He decided not to, however. Ilvanich knew that he would be in serious trouble when he and his men eventually returned to their own lines. He would need the support and good-will of the KGB major. If he played it right, he might even escape a tour in the gulag. "No, Comrade Major. They assumed you were my commander, and I have allowed them to continue to think that. Right now they think I am briefing you on the situation in order to gain your approval of our joint enterprise. What should I tell them? Do we continue as planned?"

The major looked in Ilvanich's eyes. He knew that Ilvanich was going to continue, regardless of what he said. He also knew that if Ilvanich told the Americans that he was KGB, he was a dead man. Reluctantly, he nodded and said yes, continue.

As Ilvanich walked away, he smiled to himself. Even the major, like Lenin, he thought, is wise enough to realize there comes a time when reality outweighs ideology and principles.

As the two lieutenants in command ate their evening meal, they talked of many things. Mostly they discussed their homes and families. Cerro told of how he feared heights and hated to jump. He recounted the jump into Bandar Abbas and how his commander had died. Ilvanich did not say much about his conversation with the KGB major, stating only that his "commander" approved of the cooperation. Instead he told the American of the problems he was having with his company commander, wherever he was. He added that he should be so lucky as to lose Lvov as Cerro had lost his commander.

While they avoided any discussion of their units in general or of politics, their talk turned to things they could not tell anyone else. They talked about war, leadership and killing. Both were young men, neither one more than twenty-three years old. Both had led and were about to lead men younger than they into battle where they would kill or be killed by other young men. When it was time to leave for the march to Robat-e Abgram, they both felt unburdened of problems and weighty matters that they had carried about for so long. Each also felt an affinity to the man he had called enemy. They were part of a brotherhood, a brotherhood understood only by those who had seen the face of battle and led men into it. For two days, they would be allies. After that, enemies again, until death. That they did not discuss. They didn't need to. It had always been understood.

Robat-e Abgram, Iran
0059 Hours, 20 July (2129 Hours, 19 July, GMT)

The assault group in the ditch was not visible. Cerro had no way of knowing whether Ilvanich and his men were in place. Nervously he tapped the metal tube of the green star cluster. This time he had brought only one color. One green star cluster was the signal to attack. Two star clusters were the signal for the withdrawal. Cerro would signal the withdrawal only after the assault party had passed through the platoon on the western side of the compound. Once contact was broken, the platoons would move back to the well on their own. Cerro again looked at his watch. Thirty seconds. He prepared the star cluster for firing. Ten seconds. He watched the sweep hand move until it was about to hit the twelve. Holding the star cluster's tube firmly in his left hand, he hit it on the bottom with his right hand.

Most of the Americans did not wait for the star cluster to burst before they fired. When the sound of the rocket was heard whooshing skyward, they cut loose. Two 60mm. mortars located behind Cerro choked out rounds as fast the gunners could drop them in. Grenadiers fired their 40mm. grenades into the open windows of the barracks. Machine gunners raked the area with long bursts, cutting down guards as they looked up at the bursting star cluster.

Ilvanich held his men in the ditch until the first mortar rounds impacted and the firing had begun. He wanted to ensure that they were not running into someone's field of fire. On order, the Russians were up out of the ditch and running for the buildings they were to hit. Hensly did not understand what Ilvanich said, but got the idea when everyone left the ditch. He and his small squad raced behind Ilvanich.

There were several trucks in front of the buildings they were assaulting. Four Iranians standing by the trucks had grabbed their rifles and held them at the ready, but did not know which way to turn or run. There appeared to be firing going on in all directions. Only at the last possible moment did they see the advancing line of Soviet paratroopers and then it was too late. In a single volley of automatic-rifle fire, all four Iranians were cut down. The presence of the trucks puzzled Ilvanich as he rushed past them toward the buildings. He and Cerro had not seen them the night before.

He wondered where they had come from and why they were there.

Once in the buildings, the Soviet paratroopers ceased spraying automatic fire at random. For fear of hitting one another or, even worse, stored explosives, they carefully marked their targets. When Hensly entered the building that Ilvanich had said was the main assembly area, he was blinded by the lights. In the confusion, the Iranians had not killed the generator or the lights in the building. This, along with the fact that there were no fighters in the building, made the task of clearing it quite easy. From behind a large crate, Hensly watched the systematic elimination of Iran's best engineers and physicists. Seeing the Russian paratroopers go about their duty was frightening. He had no doubt American paratroopers doing the same thing would not have looked much different. The mere thought of being in a room full of armed Russians during a killing frenzy, however, was very nerve-racking indeed.

Within two minutes the Russians were done. Ilvanich walked out to the middle of the floor and looked around, his AK held at the ready. A yell from him in Russian brought responses from his people. Satisfied, he let his AK drop to his side and called out to Hensly, "We are finished, Commander. Time for you."

From behind his crate, Hensly came to where Ilvanich stood and began to survey the area. All eyes were on him now, waiting for his orders and directions. He walked a few feet, then stopped and looked some more. Ilvanich, his AK dangling, its barrel still hot from use, followed him. Outside, the sounds of fighting continued unabated. Still Hensly took his time, taking it all in before starting.

When he found what he was searching for he stopped and smiled. Turning to Ilvanich, he asked, "Have you ever seen an atomic device before?" Ilvanich shook his head, annoyed at the time being wasted but not wanting to rush the expert. Hensly, with a sweep of his arm, pointed out six large cylinders on tables. Wires and electronic equipment surrounded four of them. Two that were apparently completed were on small carts with wheels, as if they were about to be moved. "You have before you, Lieutenant, six bombs. We have found what we were after."

Ilvanich, anxious to leave, snapped, "Good, let us get on with destroying them. We must leave, quickly."

When he was ready, Hensly turned to the men in the demolition team and directed them to their tasks. Some were sent to destroy machine tools and equipment used for fabrication of the devices. Two men, one Russian, the other American, followed Hensly from one device to the other, handing him blocks of C-4 detonators and timers. While Hensly set the explosives where he wanted them, the two men set the detonators and timers. At Hensly's direction, Ilvanich sent two other men to find the storage containers for the plutonium. When they returned, Hensly, accompanied by Ilvanich, followed them to the other building in the center of the compound.

As they entered the building, Hensly stopped and gasped. "Jesus Christ! It's a wonder these clowns didn't blow themselves up." Throughout the room large, heavy containers were stacked haphazardly. Each contained the symbol that cautioned against radiation. Hensly walked up to one of the containers and knelt to read the markings on a metal data plate. "Shit. I should've figured."

Ilvanich came up beside him and also knelt. "What is it, Commander?"

"Read the markings from shipping, Lieutenant. Nice friends, eh?"

"Perhaps they had them from before the fall of the Shah?"

Hensly shook his head. "Not likely. Not with the shipping date of January 1985."

Ilvanich was amazed. "That government would allow such a thing to be sold to people like the Iranians? Is that country not your ally?"

Hensly smiled. "Lieutenant, in the West we have an old saying, 'Money talks and bullshit walks.' You are looking at the ultimate in a world that believes in supply and demand. Someone no doubt showed a tremendous annual profit for his company over this deal."

The rattle of machine-gun fire reminded Ilvanich that they needed to hurry. "We must destroy this and be gone. Come, let us hurry."

"That, my young friend, is easier said than done." Hensly looked at the containers for a moment and tried hard to imagine what would happen if they tried to destroy them all. His training and what little he knew of physics had not prepared him for this. A bad call on his part, breaking too many containers and allowing, or forcing, too much plutonium to mass, could set off a chain reaction. At least, that was what he thought. He wasn't sure. Mumbling to himself, he mused, "Well, this is a fine mess you've got yourself into."

After considering the problem for a few more moments, he began showing the men where to place the demo charges and then directed them as they finished the task. He would destroy some of the containers, hoping that he didn't err in judgment and break too many. He wanted to cause just enough damage and dump enough radiation in the area to make everything in the compound too hot to handle. That, however, was a hope, as he had no way to gauge the amount of radiation that would be generated or the degree of damage his demo would cause. There were too many variables that he could not measure. At least the Air Force would be able to come back and level the place if his efforts didn't do the job.

Satisfied that he had done his best, Hensly paused for a moment before leaving. He took out his pocketknife and pried the metal data plate off one of the containers. No doubt the CIA would be interested.

Seeing this, Ilvanich did likewise when Hensly was not looking. The KGB major would be proud of him.

When the two green star clusters streaked skyward, the platoons on the north and the south increased their rates of fire, then began to back off. The platoon with Cerro withdrew outside the compound and took up positions two hundred meters from the outer perimeter. There they stayed in place, waiting for the demolitions to go off. Cerro, Hensly and Ilvanich watched and waited. Two machine guns and the mortars continued to sweep the compound in order to keep the Iranians pinned and away from the demolitions.

As they lay there and waited, Hensly asked, "By the way, has anyone considered which way the wind is blowing?"

Ilvanich asked why.

Hensly turned to the two lieutenants. "I hope you gentlemen realize that when that demolition goes off and starts cracking the protective shields of the plutonium containers, we could have a radioactive accident that will make Three Mile Island seem like Disneyland."

Ilvanich turned to Cerro. "What is a three-mile island?"

Glumly, Cerro replied, "America's Chernobyl."

Any further discussion was cut off by the first blasts of the demolitions. Hensly was on his feet first. "Let's get the fuck out of Dodge!"

As they ran, Ilvanich called to Cerro, "Where is Dodge?"

Fifteen Kilometers Southwest of Robat-e Abgram, Iran
2035 Hours, 20 July (1705 Hours, 20 July, GMT)

The winds that day had been from the west. While the raiders were quite relieved, the Marines and the Soviet 89th Motorized Rifle Division in eastern Iran would experience a period of alarm and near-panic as radiac meters and Geiger counters registered the passing of the radiation cloud and the fallout.

The two lieutenants had agreed not to tell each other of their plans for extraction. With the mission over and the common goal met, there would always be the temptation to turn on the temporary ally. Once all were assembled at the well, Cerro and Ilvanich reorganized their companies. As Ilvanich had wounded and the American pickup zone was several kilometers away, Cerro let the Russians have the well. When the Americans prepared to depart at twilight on the twentieth, neither lieutenant knew how to bid the other farewell. As they stood facing each other, many thoughts raced through their minds. They were so much alike, had so much in common. Men who should have been friends under any other circumstances were returning to serve in the defense of people who would never know the horrors of battle or the trial of leadership in combat as they knew it. In the end, they simply said goodbye and saluted each other, before Cerro turned and walked away.

Chapter 18

A single death is a tragedy, a million deaths are a statistic.

—JOSEPH STALIN

Frankfurt-am-Main, Federal Republic of Germany
2130 Hours, 23 July (2030 Hours, 23 July, GMT)

The crowd at the Club was unusually heavy despite the fact that payday was still a week away. The lure of live showgirls and a discount on all drinks until nine o'clock that evening did wonders to bring the GIs out on a night cooled by a late-afternoon shower and a lingering drizzle. The Germans who owned the shops along the cobblestone street were long gone, tucked into their homes or visiting their own local *Gasthaus*. Only the American soldiers and "the ladies" populated the street in front of the Club, a local establishment that, if called a dive, would be giving it more class than it deserved.

To its patrons, however, it was where it was happening, at least for the moment. Inside, the smell of stale beer and cheap perfume, mixed with cigarette smoke and an occasional whiff of a controlled substance, permeated every nook and cranny. Dim lights hid the faces of most of the patrons from anyone more than a few feet away. The blare of music and the continuous chatter of numerous conversations were as numbing to the body as the beer the Club's patrons drank and spilled. Except for small knots of friends here and there, most of the people there that night were strangers, people with nothing in common except the desire to escape the boredom of the barracks, training that of late seemed endless, and homesickness that no amount of beer could wash away.

A block down the street from the entrance to the Club, a non-descript Volkswagen van sat parked. Four men dressed as painters, with their black hair covered by hoods or hats, sat in the van. They said nothing. They only watched the Club in the van's rearview mirrors and occasionally looked at their wristwatches. The man in the driver's seat leaned back and tried to relax, but the drumming of his fingers on the steering wheel told that he could not. They were tired, having spent the entire day working in the basement under the Club. To the casual observer, their presence should have been suspicious. But the Germans who lived on the street and the police who patrolled it were used to strange comings and goings because of the Club and the foreigners it attracted. It was obvious that the four men, probably Turkish workers earning money for families they had left behind, had nothing better to do.

As nine-thirty approached, the man seated next to the driver raised his arm for the last time and looked at his watch. When the sweep hand reached that time, he said in Farsi, "Now."

The stillness of the night was shattered by a series of explosions that ripped through the Club. Balls of fire, followed by great sheets of flame, erupted from every window and door of the building. Fragments of glass and splinters from window and door frames flew in all directions, showering the street. Two American soldiers and a young "lady" who had been talking in front of the Club were cut to ribbons. In a second, all was silence again. Only the hiss of the flames billowing out from every opening interrupted the stunned quiet that momentarily returned to the street.

The man next to the van driver turned away from the scene and muttered, "Allah be praised." Then the van drove away.

Five Kilometers West of Harvand, Iran
0005 Hours, 24 July (2035 Hours, 23 July, GMT)

Like shadows, the ten figures moved slowly and silently among the rocks. The path they weaved doubled the distance they traveled but avoided positions defended by the enemy or areas under observation. They were not interested in killing the enemy and didn't bother to find out what was in each position. The leader of the small platoon had but one goal in mind, to get past the enemy without detection and back to friendly lines. Since 28 June, that goal had become an obsession with Sergeant First Class Duncan.

The closer to no-man's-land they advanced, the more difficult it became to avoid the enemy. In the rear areas units are more spread out and less vigilant but this did not mean that Duncan and the survivors of the battle at Rafsanjan had it easy. Soviet patrols, on foot, mounted and heliborne, were constantly searching for guerrillas throughout their rear areas. By day they would sweep through suspected hideouts and at night set up ambushes along trails. The Iranians, both civilians and guerrillas, were also a constant threat. The civilians hid the guerrillas, fed them and supplied information. A sighting by civilians was almost as dangerous as one by the Soviets. Duncan had found this out the hard way after going through a small village one night. The next day their hideout was hit by a group of Iranian guerrillas.

Contact with Soviets and Iranians was not completely avoided by the platoon. When commodities such as food, water and weapons were running short, Duncan would move closer to supply routes or track down Soviet installations. From carefully reconnoitered ambush sites, his men would wait for a small convoy or, even better, lone vehicles. Once the ambush was sprung, selected men would rush in, grab whatever they could that looked useful, and run like hell for the rally point. When Soviet convoys appeared to be out of the question, Iranian villages were hit. They were, after all, the enemy too. Besides, fresh fruit from the Iranians was a welcome change from canned Russian meat and bread.

These raids were not without cost. Eighteen men, including Duncan, had started out on 28 June. By 24 July there were only ten left. Some had been killed. As regrettable as that was, those killed outright presented no problems to the platoon. Duncan would simply take one of the dog tags, write in his little green notebook the time and circumstances of the death, and, if possible, bury the man. Duncan had no idea where they were and could not record the grave's location. Nor could he mark it, for fear of leaving a trail that Soviets or Iranians could follow. Once they interred a friend in his lonely grave in a hostile land far from home, it was forever.

But wounded had always been a problem. As the platoon neared their goal, Duncan reconsidered his decision to leave the seriously wounded behind. Simple wounds that did not debilitate the man were patched up using a Russian medical kit. In those cases, infection, pain and loss of blood were the greatest concern. Duncan himself carried a grenade fragment in his left arm. It was the men who could not go on and would die without medical attention who had presented Duncan with his greatest leadership challenge. The first time a man was seriously wounded, they tried to carry him with them. The wounded man did the best he could to keep quiet but soon became delirious from fever caused by unchecked infection. Without drugs or hope of saving him, Duncan had been forced to decide whether to abandon him and hope the Russians would find and care for him or to relieve the man's misery himself.

For two days Duncan had put off that decision, until the platoon suffered another severe casualty. The agony he had experienced when he finally made the choice still haunted him. He recalled every detail, every footfall as they moved down close to the road, carrying their wounded. Mercifully, both men had been unconscious as a result of pain and infection. When the road was clear of traffic, the two wounded men were set on the shoulder. Duncan himself placed a stick with a white rag, held up by a pile of rocks, in the middle of the road and watched from a hidden position until the first Soviet column came along. He had to satisfy himself that all would be well, that the wounded men would be recovered and cared for. It was not long before a column did show up. The lead vehicle stopped and dismounted troops to check out the flag and the area. They found the wounded. After checking to ensure that the wounded men were not bait for an ambush, the Russians loaded them on their vehicle. After that incident, two more men from the platoon had been left to the clemency of the enemy. Duncan was relieved, but not satisfied. He had abandoned his wounded, he could never forget that.

As hard as it was, he had to turn his mind to the immediate problem at hand. That their odyssey was near an end was hard to believe. After the battle at Rafsanjan, their life had been reduced to seemingly aimless wandering, constant hunger and the ever present threat of sudden death, or worse. To actually be in a position to end their ordeal, one way or the other, was welcomed.

The platoon faced two problems. First, they had to get past the Russians' positions and through their kill zones without detection. As they were approaching the Russians from the rear and the Russians' attention was focused mainly on the front, this would be, relatively speaking, the easy part. The hard part was getting through the American mine fields, kill zones and positions without being killed. Duncan had no idea what unit's sector they were going to enter, what the password was or even what the land looked like. They were going in blind. And if, while they were between the lines, someone accidentally started a firefight, both the Russians and the Americans in position, knowing they did not have anyone out there, would fire up Duncan's platoon.

In single file they followed Duncan. He would creep along for several meters and stop, look and listen. When he was sure they had not been detected, he would decide which way to move and creep along another forty to fifty meters before stopping again. Progress was slow, but that was the safest, and only, way to do it.

The first serious obstacle they came across was a barrier of barbed wire. Leaving the platoon behind, Duncan crawled up to it and checked it and the area around it. The wire was not the type used by the Army. It was Russian. Worse, on the other side Duncan could see small dents in the ground. A mine field. That meant that they were at or near the very forward edge of the front lines. He had the choice of either low-crawling through the mine field or following the barbed wire until it ended. No doubt the Russians had the mine field covered by fire. By the same token, if the platoon tried to go around, they could just as easily run into a Russian fighting position covering the mine field.

Duncan rolled over on his back and stared at the sky. He was tired of making decisions. For the last twenty-seven days he had had to not only live by his wits but lead others in and out of danger. His decisions had cost the lives of four men, maybe more if the Russians had killed the wounded. Days of wandering and physical exertion, malnutrition, the stress of combat, the pressure of leadership, the agony of making life-or-death decisions, little rest and less hope had all worked to reduce Duncan's effectiveness and ability to function. As he weighed the two alternatives, he wondered whether their efforts had been worth it and what value, if any, their wandering had had.

He rolled back onto his elbows and looked at the mine field again. There was less than a quarter moon. He decided to go through the wire and the mine field. As it would be dawn soon, there was little time to find another way around. Besides, he was anxious to end it that night, one way or the other.

Before returning to the platoon, Duncan moved along the wire to find the nearest Russian position. Thirty meters from where he had been, he came across a machine-gun pit with three men in it. They were covering the mine field in that area. Only one man appeared to be awake. It would be so much easier if that position was silenced before they started. Besides, it would create a blind spot. Returning to his platoon, Duncan briefed the plan and selected two men to go with him to take out the machine-gun pit.

The three men crept forward, their bayonet-knives at the ready. The one Russian on guard was leaning against the forward edge of the pit, wrapped in a blanket and watching to the front. Duncan would go for him. The other two Russians were sitting with their backs against the rear wall, asleep. The three Americans inched forward with Duncan in the middle. When they were at the rear edge of the pit, Duncan raised his left hand with three fingers up. The men with him watched the hand. He dropped one finger, then a second. When the third came down, the man on either side reached down, put his free hand over the mouth of a Russian leaning against the back wall and, with a long arching swing, drove his knife into the Russian's chest. Duncan jumped up and bounded across the open pit, diving for the Russian on guard. The Russian rolled over and opened his mouth to scream. The thrust of Duncan's bayonet into his throat stifled the scream before it could come out.

Finished, Duncan called the other men in the platoon forward and prepared to cross the mine field. They would move forward in single file behind Duncan. He had considered asking for a volunteer to lead the final leg, but decided against that. He would go all the way. Using the dead Russians' rifles, they propped up the barbed wire and crawled under it into the mine field. Duncan, leaving his helmet behind, rolled up his sleeves and took off his watch. That way he would be able to feel on his bare arms any trip wires that might be strung between the mines. With his bayonet he began to probe for mines across his front. Slowly he slid it into the ground at a forty-five-degree angle. As the mine field was old and the people putting it in had been sloppy, loose dirt placed over the buried mines to cover them had sunk down. This left an easily detected depression wherever there was a mine. Duncan still probed, however, just on the off chance that there were new mines or that someone had buried some properly.

As he moved forward, the sweat rolled down his brow and into his eyes. It would have been so much easier to let someone else lead. Inch by inch he moved forward, probing for mines. He wondered how deep the mine field was. The rumble of artillery in the distance reminded him that other people were awake and alert, ready to kill. Slowly he crept on, fighting the urge to make larger sweeps as he probed for mines. He wondered how often the Russians checked their outposts. Duncan cursed himself for not checking to see if there had been a phone or a radio in the pit. How stupid. He was getting tired. Inch by inch he moved forward. The mine field seemed to be never ending. How many mines could the Russians have used? Inch by bloody inch he crawled, probing, sweating, praying.

Suddenly Duncan realized they were no longer surrounded by the shallow depressions that marked where the mines were. Slowly, he raised himself and looked around. The barbed-wire fence to their rear was no longer visible in the darkness. To his front were dark hills and a wadi. Turning to the man immediately behind him, he told him to hold there while he checked out the area in front. Unslinging his rifle and cradling it in his arms, Duncan crawled forward. He watched for telltale signs of mines, but found none. Satisfied that he and his men were clear of the mine field, he signaled the platoon to follow.

It took them an hour to cover the two or more kilometers between the mine field they had left and an antitank ditch that blocked their way. As before, Duncan crawled forward and checked it out. It could be Russian or the beginning of the Americans' barriers. With the platoon following, Duncan moved slowly along the edge. When they found the end of the ditch and began to go around, Duncan probed for mines. Finding none, he led the men on until he saw what appeared to be the outline of a fighting position. Slowly he crept forward. There was no sign of movement. When he reached the edge of the hole, he carefully peered over. There were two men in the hole. Both were asleep. In the faint light, he could make out an M-16 rifle.

They had made it. The long nightmare was over.

Former Iranian Naval Hospital, Bandar Abbas, Iran
1540 Hours, 26 July (1210 Hours, 26 July, GMT)

Her excuse that she needed to ask more questions of the sergeant from the 12th Infantry Division who had infiltrated from Rafsanjan was very transparent. Everyone in the 2nd Brigade headquarters knew that Lieutenant Matthews' real objective was her wounded scout-platoon leader. The brigade XO let her go, however. He reasoned that she needed the break. Since the loss of the brigade S-2, she had been working harder than any two people in the TOC. The results of her efforts showed. Matthews and her section produced intelligence that kept the units in the brigade one step ahead of the Soviets and allowed the commander to make effective plans and decisions. It would do little harm to let her go while there was a break in the action.

As anxious as she was to see him, Matthews became apprehensive as she approached the ward where Capell was. She had been told by Major Dixon that he had been severely burned over much of his body when his Bradley was hit. The burns, along with wounds from on-board ammo going off and several broken bones, had nearly killed him. That he lived, according to Dixon, was only due to the fact that Capell was either too stubborn or too dumb to die. Meant to cheer her up, this only increased her fears. She knew Capell would still be the same person inside. She knew it wasn't his fault that he had been wounded. What she didn't know was how she would react when she saw him. Nor did she know whether she could look at him and love him as she did before. She told herself that it didn't matter what he looked like so long as he was alive, but she knew that that was a lie.

Prepared for facing Capell, regardless of what he looked like, she entered the ward. Instead of being full of patients, the room was full of empty bunks with their mattresses turned up. The only person in the room was a soldier mopping the floor with soapy water that smelled of disinfectant. She called to him, "Excuse me, but is this Ward Four B?"

The soldier turned around and saw her for the first time. "Sorry, ma'am, didn't see ya. Yes, this is Four B, but ain't no one here anymore. They all got shipped out this mornin'."

"Damn!" she mumbled. "Do you know when they took them to the airfield?"

"Didn't go to the airfield. There's a hospital ship in the harbor. Started takin' 'em out after breakfast this mornin'. Could be they're still there."

Seizing any chance to see Randy, she thanked the soldier for his help and ran down to the hummer she had come down to Bandar Abbas in. She directed the driver to head for the docks and see if he could find out where they were loading the hospital ship. The sergeant who was riding shotgun warned her they needed to be heading back. He didn't want to be on the road alone after dark. Looking at her watch, she told him they had plenty of time. Without further discussion on the matter, she ordered the driver to move out.

Their entrance into the dock area took far longer than expected. Equipment from a newly arrived unit was being moved from there to its marshaling area outside Bandar Abbas. As she waited impatiently in the hummer watching a column of National Guard Bradleys go by, she was struck by the apparent difference in age between the men in the Guard unit and those in Capell's battalion. No doubt they knew what they were doing. Perhaps, she thought, older men would be less impetuous and more cautious, unlike Randy.

Once the hummer had been admitted, it raced down the line of piers, weaving between crates and vehicles just offloaded. It was stopped once by a Navy shore patrolman who cautioned the driver to slow down and provided directions to the pier where the hospital ship had been tied up. That pier, however, was empty when they arrived. In the distance, the white hospital ship could be seen moving out to the open sea.

Disappointed and struggling to hold back her tears, Matthews ordered the driver to turn around and head back. The sergeant suggested that they stay in Bandar Abbas for the night, but she did not hear him. Her mind was on other things. At least, she thought, Randy was safe. When the current mess in Iran was over, they would have plenty of time together.

Movement from the docks into the unit's staging area went without a hitch. Some of the officers had been worried that the men would have problems moving the equipment after being away from it for several weeks. The battalion XO, Major Ed Lewis, laughed. "What are you talking about? Back home we meet once a month and get to use our equipment once every two months, maybe three. Then we march off to summer camp and expect our people to hop in and drive away. Why should this be any different?"

It *was* different, however, and Lewis knew it. Summer camp, as annual training was still called by many, lasted only two weeks, then they all went home to their families and their civilian jobs. No one had any idea how long the war in Iran would last. Some thought they would be there only a few months. Others brought up the fact that they were committed for the duration —however long that was—and a year. Regardless of how long the war and their commitment to the federal government lasted, even the most optimistic among them knew that some would not return home. The loading of a hospital ship that morning served as a reminder to them that they were actually entering an active war zone.

Upon arriving in the marshaling area, Lewis met up with his battalion commander and the S-3, both of whom had gone up to the headquarters of the 25th Armored Division the previous day to receive an operations order, while Lewis had been left with the job of supervising the offloading and marshaling of men and equipment. The three officers now met at the dock and watched before they went to the battalion TOC, then in the final stages of being set up, and sat before the S-3 situation map. As the S-3 read the order out loud, Master Sergeant Kenneth Mayfree, the operations sergeant, posted the operational graphics on the map. Once the battalion had assembled and completed arming and refueling, it was to move from its current location to a tactical assembly area south of Saadatabad. There it would become part of the 25th Armored Division's 3rd Brigade. The three officers had expected to join the 2nd Brigade, the active-component brigade they had normally trained with. The nature of the operation, however, required a large counterattack force, of which the 2nd Battalion of the 354th Mech Tennessee National Guard was now part.

All three men accepted their mission with a feeling of relief. By being in reserve, they and their company commanders would have more time to prepare their men and units for battle. Training in the marshaling area and the tactical assembly area, while limited, was better than none. The prospect of rolling off the ship right into combat had haunted them for the past three weeks. While they did not underestimate the difficulties they would face, at least they would not have to face a battle-hardened Soviet army their first day in the country. Every day they had in which to prepare and train increased their odds of success.

Headquarter, 10th Corps, Qotbabad, Iran
1650 Hours, 26 July (1320 Hours, 26 July, GMT)

Lieutenant General Weir reviewed the information papers and reports before going into the 1700 hours briefing. Shortly after he assumed control of the 13th Corps, he had been appointed overall commander of all ground forces in Iran by the Commander in Chief of CENTCOM. While this meant more work for Weir and his staff, it simplified the coordination of operations between the 1st Marine Corps in the east and the two Army corps in Kerman Province to the south.

The briefing that evening was an important one. Decisions made during it would shape the next round of operations. The corps G-3 was going to present the revised operations plan for the upcoming campaign. While the U.S. situation had improved tremendously in the past two weeks, they were still far from ready to assume offensive operations. All the reports pointed to the fact that the Soviets, despite the best efforts of the Air Force and Special Forces to interdict the flow of supplies, would be ready to commence their offensive before the 10th Corps was completely assembled. It was simply a matter of time, space and numbers. The Soviets, at the end of a shorter supply line, were able to make good their losses and deficiencies faster than the U.S. forces in Iran could. In addition, the number of heavy ground-combat units available to the 10th Corps was limited, while the Soviets had many. In fact, the Soviets had more heavy divisions in Iran at that moment than the U.S. Army had throughout the world.

With the writing on the wall, the 10th Corps had no choice but to accept the Soviet offensive before commencing their own. This, however, was not all bad. Properly done, the 10th Corps could channel the Soviets into those areas where Weir wanted the Soviets to go, bleeding them all the way and setting them up for a counterblow. Once the Soviets' main effort was identified and contained, the 10th Corps could pile on and destroy it. With the Soviets broken and weak points uncovered, the 10th Corps could then launch its own offensive in conjunction with the 13th Corps, now recovering, and the newly formed 1st Marine Corps operating to the east.

Not all was bleak. Weir had a few aces up his sleeve. One of them was the British 33rd Armored Brigade. That brigade was ready for commitment. Through a great deal of effort and deception, the brigade had been "smuggled" into Iran. Though the world knew that the British were committed to send troops, a sham movement of forces and troops kept the media occupied while the 33rd Armored Brigade was brought into Iran on U.S. ships, then moved in small groups at night and assembled in the forward areas. Weir was betting that the psychological impact of the sudden and unexpected appearance in Iran of ground forces from a NATO ally would give the Soviets great concern and cause them to question their intelligence analysis. The French Airborne Division, operating with the 6th Marine Division, had, by accident, had that effect. Weir intended to hold the 33rd Armored Brigade back, using it at the right moment to kick off his counterblow, the first step to the counteroffensive that would, with luck, smash the Soviet forces then facing them in the central area.

Weir's aide came in and told him the staff was ready. As Weir was leaving his office, he looked at the map on the wall. "Well, Ted," he said to the aide, "what it all boils down to is that we've got to keep the enemy from breaking through and wear him out without him doing the same to the 10th Corps. Pretty neat trick if we can do it. I sure hope the 25th Armored can pull it off."

Moscow, USSR
1620 Hours, 26 July (1320 Hours, 26 July, GMT)

The shock of returning from the front to Moscow was overpowering. Colonel Sulvina had expected things to be different. He wasn't quite sure what should have changed, but surely something had to be different. After all, the Soviet Union was locked in battle with the United States. Yet as the Army sedan moved through the streets of the city, he saw no change. People still came and went to work. Women queued up to buy everyday necessities. Grandmothers walked babies and watched as children played in the parks. Even the radio news, what little Sulvina heard, treated the war as just another news story.

Less than twenty-four hours before, Sulvina had been ordered to appear at the Moscow headquarters of STAVKA, the General Staff of the Red Army, concerning his written report on the operations of the 28th Combined Arms Army. That report, forwarded to Front Headquarters and STAVKA before the army's new commander had arrived, had been disturbing to both. It was to have been sent back to Sulvina to be rewritten. Instead, someone had forwarded a copy to a member of the Politburo. Rumors were that it was a STAVKA officer working for the KGB who had done that in an effort to discredit the Red Army and its conduct of operations in Iran. Now Sulvina, after a grueling session at STAVKA, was on his way to answer to the Politburo.

Colonel Sulvina was not politically naive. He understood the State and the system. He was, after all, part of it. He was, however, a soldier, first and foremost. Schooled in all aspects of military science, with years of command and general-staff experience, Sulvina believed that it was his duty to keep his commander and higher headquarters informed of the situation as it really existed, not as they wished it to be. He had been taught from his first year as a cadet that commanders can make the proper decisions only if they have good, accurate information. It was in that vein that he had written his report. Not to blame or condemn, or to record excuses. Sulvina wanted to record what had happened so that corrections could be made before the next offensive.

His debriefing at STAVKA that morning had been a rude shock. Only slowly had he realized that some saw his report as a threat to them and their position, while others saw it as "the whimperings of a man unfit for a position of great responsibility." When he was told personally by a Marshal of the Soviet Union to answer only yes or no to all questions of the Politburo, Sulvina knew he was on trial for telling the "wrong" truth.

For two hours Sulvina sat in a chair in the center of a room. Before him sat the eleven Politburo members who ran the Soviet Union. They alone determined national policy. They alone decided how the Soviet Union would achieve its national goals, goals which they established. Each member had before him a copy of the report. Each member, with the exception of the Foreign Minister, asked Sulvina questions, most of which skirted the real issues at hand. Diligently, Sulvina answered their questions with either a yes or a no. The questioning was punctuated by discussions, sometimes heated, between the members as some of the senior members became annoyed at the cat-and-mouse game.

Finally, the Foreign Minister dropped the report, folded his hands before him and said, "We have all read the report, Comrade Colonel. We have all asked you many questions. I want you now, Comrade Colonel, to tell me in your own words what happened."

The General Secretary, visibly upset, leaned forward and glared at the Foreign Minister, but could not get his attention. Failing that, the General Secretary turned to face Sulvina.

Sweat ran down Sulvina's face. His eyes turned to the Minister of Defense. The Minister of Defense returned the stare. Looking back to the Foreign Minister, Sulvina replied, "Comrade, the report before you is my own words. It is what I believe to be the truth." Sulvina did not look again at the Minister of Defense.

The Foreign Minister said after a moment, "Yes, of course. Now, Comrade Colonel, what must we, the Politburo, do to prevent another disaster such as this from happening?"

Sulvina was taken aback by the term "disaster." Without realizing it, he went into the attack. "Comrade, there was no disaster. The actions of the commander of the 28th Combined Arms Army prevented a disaster. We merely withdrew so that we could regroup, resupply and reestablish conditions that favored the resumption of the offensive and the seizure of the Strait of Hormuz. A setback, yes. A disaster, no."

For a long time, there was silence in the room. Then the Foreign Minister asked the question again, in a harsher tone this time. "What must we do to prevent another disaster, Comrade Colonel?"

Sulvina considered the question before continuing. For a moment he wavered in his convictions. Then he decided that if there was nothing he could do to save himself, perhaps he could do something to help those who would soon have to face the same situation he had faced. "First, Comrade, we must employ chemical weapons. The Americans have little in the way of retaliatory capability. Even if they assume a fully protective posture, which they will, the heat casualties from wearing the protective clothing will be just as devastating to their efficiency as would losses to the chemical agents employed. Our troops, better trained, equipped and used to working in a chemical environment, will have a great advantage. Next, we must mass all combat power in Iran. If insufficient forces are available in the country, they must come from the reserves if necessary. Finally, we must strike at the source of American supplies. The war zone at sea must include the entire Indian Ocean, the Mediterranean, the Red Sea and the Atlantic. It does us no good to wait until they reach Iran to kill them."

Again there was a long silence. This time the Foreign Minister smiled when he broke it. "You must understand, Comrade Colonel, there are certain political realities that come into play at the strategic level. We cannot use chemical weapons. We know the Americans' limitations in that area, but if we did use such weapons the entire world would condemn us. Even those who support us now in the United Nations would be reluctant to continue that support. Nor can we afford to spread the conflict without endangering our interests in other areas. To do so could push America's reluctant allies into the conflict. And you know as well as I that the economy cannot sustain a large-scale mobilization. So, given those realities, what can we do?"

The General Secretary, agitated by the discussion, nonetheless allowed the Foreign Minister to continue his game. The colonel, after all, was expendable. Perhaps, if the Foreign Minister played out his fool's hand, he would discredit himself and give the General Secretary sufficient cause to replace him.

Sulvina knew he was a lost man. Nothing he said mattered anymore. There was no going back. He had, by doing what he believed correct, dug his own grave. He straightened up in his chair, looked each member in the eye and spoke, "Then we must stop the war. If, Comrades, we are going to fight this war, we must fight it with every means available. If we want to win, the nation must be mobilized behind the effort. Otherwise, Comrades, we are asking our men to die for nothing. I cannot go back and order our soldiers to go forward and die in the name of the State if the State is unwilling to provide the means for victory."

Colonel Sulvina jumped into his grave with both feet and a clear conscience.

Aboard the Hospital Ship U.S.S. *Tranquility* in the Gulf of Oman
2205 Hours, 26 July (1805 Hours, 26 July, GMT)

Between bouts of pain and short periods of restless sleep, Randy Capell pondered his current state and his future. Lying on his stomach with most of his body encased in bandages, Capell could do nothing on his own. That he had lived, he had been told, was nothing short of a miracle. The battalion aid station, overwhelmed by incoming casualties, had classified him as being beyond help. He had second- and third-degree burns over half of his body, multiple fragment wounds, several broken bones and a severe loss of blood. A medic gave him morphine and set him aside while those who could be saved were worked on. Eventually the physician's assistant did work on him, stabilized his condition and had him evacuated.

In the two weeks he spent at Bandar Abbas, Capell began the slow and painful process of recovery. While there he sent several notes to Amanda Matthews. A medic had to write them for him. In return, he received two letters. The medic had to read them for him. As Amanda was quite graphic in describing her love for him, this proved embarrassing to Capell. His only regret was that he had not seen her before he was shipped out. Capell kept consoling himself with the thought that they would have plenty of time together after the war was over.

Besides, he was not sure he wanted her to see him as he was. That might have been hard for Amanda to accept and could have put an end to their relationship. By leaving, he would have time to recover and get back into shape. There were only two things that mattered to him now: Amanda Matthews and getting back into shape so that he could pursue his career. Capell pondered which was the more important of the two.

The launching of several cruise missiles from a submarine set off alarms on escort ships throughout the area. By the time the missiles broke surface, fire-control computers were already feeding data to the Seasparrow point-defense-missile launchers. On cue from the computer, air-defense officers began to launch the Seasparrows. While Soviet missiles flew toward their marks in the darkness, American missiles raced toward the Soviet missiles in an effort to head them off. Great balls of fire blossomed in the distance every time one of the defensive missiles found its target and destroyed it.

Not all Soviet missiles were felled by the Seasparrows. American radar continued tracking the surviving cruise missiles and preparing the close-in defense systems. The phalanx gun systems, set to automatic mode, picked up their targets and tracked them. The 20mm. minigun, controlled by a computer, fired a stream of projectiles into the night in a last-ditch effort to bring down the remaining cruise missiles. As with the Seasparrows, each success was marked with the violent explosion of a Soviet missile.

When all active measures had been expended, the computers on the escorts began to fire chaff. Millions of tiny strips of aluminum were blown out of launchers, creating instant clouds to confuse the cruise missiles' targeting radar. Those ships that had chaff escaped as the missiles broke radar lock and flew about, searching for a new target, until they ran out of fuel. Those ships that didn't and were marked, died.

As in a nightmare, Capell heard the ripping of metal and the detonation of the cruise missile's warhead. Unused fuel from the missile was ignited by the explosion and propelled forward by the momentum of the missile. The burning fuel was sprayed across the ward, covering everything in a sheet of fire. The bandages wrapped about Capell's body to protect his burns now provided fuel to the fire that engulfed him and his ward mates. Only the crushing rush of seawater and the mercy of drowning saved Capell from burning to death.

Five Kilometers South of Saadatabad, Iran
0545 Hours, 27 July (0215 Hours, 27 July, GMT)

The mounted patrol, making its morning sweep of the division's main supply route, came across an overturned hummer and the dismembered remains of three people. In a single glance they could tell it had been done by Iranians. Russians weren't in the habit of mutilating the dead.

As the platoon leader watched his patrol check the vehicle and the bodies for booby traps, his platoon sergeant came up to him. "No signs leading away from the ambush site. All we found were a few shell casings. What do you suppose they were doing out here alone last night?"

The platoon leader leaned against his vehicle and pulled out his canteen. "Doesn't really matter what they were doing, does it? They're dead now." The lieutenant took a drink from his canteen. "Hell of a way to start the day."

The platoon sergeant watched as two men checked a body. "You don't suppose that the Iranians . . . well, do you think they . . . ?"

Finishing a second drink, the lieutenant looked at the body. "You mean raped her? I really don't want to know, Sergeant. And you have no need to know. If some shit in grave registrations wants to find out, that's his business. We just find 'em, mark 'em and report 'em."

A soldier picked up something from the body and brought it over to his platoon leader. A pair of dog tags. The lieutenant poured water from his canteen over one of the tags and wiped away the blood. "Well, Sergeant Mullen, at least we'll be able to notify the next of kin of one Matthews, Amanda, that their daughter died in the service of her country."

Chapter 19

God is always with the strongest battalion.
—FREDERICK THE GREAT

Fifteen Kilometers North of Hajjiabad, Iran
0500 Hours, 1 August (0130 Hours, 1 August, GMT)

For weeks forces had been moving forward on both sides of no-man's-land, assembling within striking distance of each other. Savage little skirmishes between Soviet recon units and American armored cavalry units, sent forth to screen friendly preparations and uncover those of the enemy, punctured the lull. Units jockeying for positions from which to defend or attack clashed in the night, holding when possible, drawing back when faced by superior force. Therefore, the simultaneous eruption of over eight hundred howitzers, guns and mortars that heralded the commencement of the "final" offensive came as no surprise.

The Soviet 17th Combined Arms Army, the main instrument to be used in destroying U.S. forces in Iran and seizing the Strait of Hormuz, was well rested and prepared. For this purpose it had absorbed the remnants of the 28th Combined Arms Army, so that it now had four motorized rifle divisions, two tank divisions and several independent regiments, one of which was the 285th Guards Airborne Regiment. Front artillery and air units made the 17th CAA a formidable force with over 1600 tanks, 2500 armored personnel carriers and other armored vehicles, 900 pieces of artillery and heavy mortars, and close to 100,000 men.

To oppose the 17th CAA, Allied ground forces in the central area, the area of operations, consisted of the bulk of the 10th

Corps and the 13th Corps. The 10th would be responsible for taking on the main Soviet force. For this it had three divisions—two armored divisions and one mechanized infantry—an armored cavalry regiment and a British armored brigade. Units from the 13th Airborne Corps were available if needed. The 17th Airborne Division was being held ready for use in either the air assault mode or a combat drop deep in the Soviet rear once the counteroffensive began. A French airborne armored-car regiment had been transferred from the eastern sector, where the 6th Marine Division was operating, to reinforce the 17th Airborne in preparation for those operations. The 12th Division, though a shadow of its former self, had the role of securing the rear of the central area. The primary force to be used for this mission was a brigade comprised of four reconstructed and reorganized infantry battalions that had survived the fighting in late June. It was called the Phoenix Brigade, and each and every man in it was ready and anxious to avenge the earlier defeats.

Though the Allied ground forces in the central area were outnumbered and, initially, on the defense, the goals of the ground-force commander, Lieutenant General Weir, were far more ambitious than merely stopping the Soviets from reaching their goal. Weir intended to allow the Soviets to attack first and smash themselves upon the 10th Corps. When they were broken, he planned to seize the initiative and attack north, destroying them through the use of slashing ground attacks in conjunction with bold airborne and air assault operations against critical Soviet command, control and support facilities. Over his desk hung a hand-painted sign reminding his commanders and staff to THINK NORTH. Not to be outdone, his operations officer had a sign that told his people, TEHRAN OR BUST. With more flair than his superiors, the corps G-3 plans officer created his own sign that advertised SKI TABRIZ.

The lofty plans of the corps commander and his staff depended, however, upon the performance of men living at the far end of the spectrum. Cavalrymen watching from their Bradleys, armored crewmen manning M-1s and infantrymen huddled in their rifle pits girded themselves for the coming of the Soviets. Few knew of the plans the corps commander and his staff had. Most did not fully understand the part they were supposed to play in the final defeat of the Soviet forces in Iran. What they did know was that their survival depended on how well they and the other men in the crew or squad performed their duties.

The crew of the M-1A1 tank watched the T-80 tanks roll forward. Their tank commander, Staff Sergeant Steven Pulaski, stood high in the turret as he tracked the Soviet tanks with his binoculars. He listened to the platoon sergeant report his sightings to the platoon leader. Since he had nothing to add, Pulaski did not report. He watched, fascinated, as the Soviets moved forward, oblivious to the danger they were in. From where the platoon sat, Pulaski's first round would be an oblique, downward shot. Given that angle and the distance from the M-1A1 to the kill zone, the 120mm. armor-piercing fin-stabilized Sabot round would have no problem penetrating the T-80s. Pulaski whispered to his gunner, as if the Soviets could hear them, "Hey, Teddy, can ya see 'em?"

"Sure can. Do you suppose they can see us, Steve?"

"If they could see us, do ya think they'd be pissing away all that artillery on those dummy positions on the hill behind us? No, and they won't till we shoot. Then all hell'll break loose." Pulaski told his driver, "Billy, you better be awake down there. When I tell you to kick it in the ass, I don't want any of your dumb-ass excuses."

From the driver's compartment, Billy simply answered, "Yeah." He was nervous. As he sat there maintaining the engine at a steady idle, he sweated. Alone in the forward nose of the tank, he could see nothing, only the dirt of the protective berm that covered everything but the tank's sights. At least the three men in the turret, physically located in close proximity to each other, could draw comfort from that closeness. The driver had only steel, fuel cells and instruments to share his ordeal.

As they waited for the troop commander's order to fire, Pulaski issued his fire command to the crew. With his hand on the tank commander's override, he yelled out, "Gunner—Sabot. Two moving tanks. Left tank first."

The gunner, already tracking their intended targets, quickly reponded, "Identified."

The loader had little to do. There was already a round in the chamber. He armed the main gun and cleared the path of recoil, and his response of "Up" quickly followed the gunner's cry.

Now they waited. The gunner tracked his target. He waited, watched and sweated. The driver, keyed up, was ready to move the tank into its final firing position. The loader, hanging on to his guards, watched the breech, ready to spring up and feed another round into it as soon as the gun fired. Pulaski, still standing in the open hatch, looked down at the two men in the turret, checking to ensure they were ready. The impact of artillery just behind the lead Soviet tank drew Pulaski's attention to his front again. Seeing the enemy approaching the troop's kill zone, he lowered himself and prepared for battle.

The radio came to life as the platoon leader issued his orders. "All Hotel elements—this is Hotel Nine-five. Occupy firing positions."

On cue, Pulaski called out, "Driver, move forward. Gunner, take over."

The gunner bent over to his left and looked through the auxiliary sight, a simple telescope attached to the right side of the main gun, to watch for the tank's main gun to clear the dirt berm. He held the main-gun control handles. This would keep the fire control's stabilization system engaged and maintain the sight and the gun on target as the tank moved. The driver moved the gearshift lever from park to forward and hit the gas. The M-1A1 shot forward and began to rise, its gun automatically depressing. Once the gunner could see over the berm, he yelled out, "Driver, stop!"

No sooner had they moved into position and the gunner returned to his primary sight, than the platoon leader came over the net again, "All Hotel elements—this is Hotel Nine-five. Fire!"

Pulaski bellowed out, *"Fire!"*

The gunner, still tracking the target, hit the thumb switch on his right control handle, activating the laser range finder. A digital readout showing the distance between the M-1A1 and its target came up into view. The range readout looked right to the gunner. With the ready-to-fire indicator showing all was ready, he yelled, "On the waaay" to warn the crew he was firing and pulled the trigger on his control handle.

In an instant the tank bucked and was engulfed in a cloud of dust from the muzzle blast caused by the exit of the 120mm. projectile and propellant gases. Inside, the breech block moved back, opening automatically and spitting out the small base plate of the expended shell into a box hanging from the breech. The

smell of cordite mixed with those of sweat and oil. Without waiting, the loader opened the ammo storage door and hauled out the
next round. The dual screech of "Target!" from both the tank
commander and the gunner did not stop or slow him. There were
more Soviet tanks out there that needed to be destroyed.

From his position with the second-echelon battalion, Captain
Neboatov followed the battle as it was joined. The scene unfolding before him was a far cry from his first encounter with the
Americans in late June. Then it had been a walk in the park. He
had not even realized that they had penetrated the Americans'
main defensive positions.

Today, however, would be far different. Despite an impressive
thirty-minute Soviet artillery barrage, the Americans appeared to
be not only alive but quite unaffected. The Soviet first-echelon
battalions were still in columns of companies when American
artillery began to fall on them. At first the artillery fire fell behind
the companies. That error, however, was quickly corrected, with
telling effect. The rounds being used threw out many small
bomblets that hit the tops of the tanks and BMPs of the lead
battalion. Each bomblet had a tiny shaped charge that could penetrate the thin armor covering the tops of the vehicles. Every
volley of American artillery engulfed a large portion of the lead
battalions in a sudden cloud of black smoke and flame. As it
cleared, T-80 tanks and BMPs could be seen staggering out of line
or simply burning where they had been hit.

Neboatov saw multiple puffs of smoke and dust appear in the
distance to the front. Enemy tanks and antitank guided missiles
firing. He watched as near-misses threw great clouds of dirt up in
front of tanks and BMPs in the lead battalions. There were, however, few misses. Armor-piercing penetrators traveling a mile a
second impacted with a large, brilliant white spark when they hit
steel. Reactive armor on the T-80s detonated but did not deter
the depleted uranium penetrator as it literally pushed its way
into the tank it hit. As the penetrator did so, it also pushed a plug
of the tank's own armor, the same diameter as the penetrator,
into the interior of the tank. Both the plug of armor and the
penetrator, superheated by the rapid conversion of kinetic energy
into heat, ripped through everything in their path. Crewmen, on-
board ammunition, hydraulic lines and fuel cells were torn open.
Flammables were ignited. Propellants of stored main-gun rounds,

blowing up in the confined space of a tank with all hatches closed and locked down, rocked the tank with thunderous explosions. Sometimes the explosions tore the fifteen-ton turret from the hull and threw it into the air as if it were made of cardboard.

The pace of the advance did not quicken. As the lead battalions moved at what appeared to Neboatov to be a painfully slow pace, they left in their wake a trail of shattered and burning hulks quivering from the explosions of their own ammunition and cremating their crews. There was little doubt that Neboatov's company, part of the follow-on battalion, would be committed early that day. Watching the number of burning and disabled vehicles increase by the minute, he realized they would be needed even before they had cleared the American cavalry screen and hit the enemy's main defensive positions.

Ten Kilometers North of Qotbabad
0545 Hours, 1 August (0215 Hours, 1 August, GMT)

The paratroopers were slow to form up into squads and disperse. Too many stood on the drop zone waiting for someone to tell them what to do and where to go. Senior Lieutenant Ilvanich seemed to be everywhere that morning, directing men where to go, yelling at those too scared to react and using his boot to motivate the slow and reluctant. Junior Lieutenant Malovidov followed Ilvanich's lead as the two officers struggled to establish some semblance of order after a near-disastrous jump. Their efforts were assisted by the faint light thrown off by the burning wreckage of a transport plane brought down by American antiaircraft missiles.

As he ran from group to group, Ilvanich couldn't help but think how few of the men he knew. Losses sustained during two combat jumps, two major air assault operations, several raids and numerous patrols and ambushes had made serious inroads in the company's original complement. There were few men with the company that day who had jumped into Tabriz on 25 May. Replacements and men from units that had been disbanded may have brought the company up to full strength, but did not make a coherent, combat-capable unit. The new officers and men did not know one another or the old members of the company. The trust and confidence between leaders and those they led that resulted from countless hours of training were missing. The men new to the unit knew the basics of soldiering but had never worked together. Simple combat drills that used to be easily executed by Ilvanich's old platoon required twice the time to perform and all of Lieutenant Malovidov's efforts to make happen simply because they had not had enough time to practice.

Once the drop zone was clear and all the strays had been rounded up, Ilvanich paused to consider his next action. He pulled a rag from his pocket and wiped the sweat from his face as he surveyed the eerie scene before him. Discarded parachutes and cylindrical equipment containers littered the drop zone. The brightly burning wreckage of two transports were visible in the distance. The thought that the company's BMD personnel carriers were aboard them did nothing to brighten an already dark situation. Without them the paratroopers had little chance of forming an effective strongpoint astride the Americans' main supply route. Any combat unit that had tanks would have no problem blowing through them anytime they wanted. Around the drop zone he could see the heads of paratroopers pop up as they checked out their sector from the prone position. Well, we are as ready as we are ever going to be, he thought. Time to get out of here.

From out of the darkness Malovidov came running up, hunched over, carrying his AK assault rifle at the ready. Panting, he reported to Ilvanich. "All men are accounted for. Both of the other platoons report the same. We are ready to move out." Then, almost as an afterthought, he added, "Oh, yes, Captain Lvov has been found. He has a broken ankle. He is with 2nd Platoon right now and wishes to see you immediately."

Ilvanich didn't turn or look at the junior lieutenant. He stood there and pulled out his canteen, unscrewed the cap and took a short swallow of water. Finished, he turned to Malovidov. "I suppose it is time to go see our commander. Lead off, Comrade."

With that, Malovidov turned and began to run off at a trot, crouched over, until he noticed that Ilvanich was following at a walk, standing erect. Malovidov stopped, straightened up and waited for the senior lieutenant.

When they reached Lvov, he was lying on the ground and seemed to be embarrassed. Ilvanich saluted and reported, then stood with one hand on his hip and the other resting on the AK that dangled from his right shoulder while his commander babbled about how he had hit the ground wrong and had to crawl over to where the company had rallied. As he listened, Ilvanich thought, So, you can't run away this time, you worthless bastard. Now I get the chance to see what a good Party man is made of.

His thoughts and Lvov's story were interrupted by a radioman who came up to Ilvanich and, out of habit, handed the radio mike to him, saying that the battalion commander wanted to speak to the commander. Without thinking, Ilvanich took the mike, pressed the transmit button and began to speak, then stopped. Lvov was staring at him. Their eyes met. Without apology, Ilvanich held out the mike to his commander and said he had forgotten that the captain was with them. He intentionally held the mike several inches beyond Lvov's reach, forcing the captain to prop himself up and stretch to get it. When he had it, Ilvanich stepped back, saluted and told his commander he would prepare the company to move out. He did not wait for a return salute, which he knew he would not get, or permission to leave, which he didn't care whether he got or not. He simply pivoted and walked off, feeling Lvov's eyes burning their way through his back as he went into the gathering dawn.

Bandar Abbas
0935 Hours, 1 August (0605 Hours, 1 August, GMT)

Duncan marched down the line, checking weapons, equipment and the men. In the background dozens of Blackhawk helicopters were going through preflight checks and coming to life. How different, he thought as he compared the fully armed, well-equipped, well-fed soldiers before him and what he and his platoon had been like while they were escaping from Rafsanjan. Most of the men in his platoon were new to him, the result of amalgamating bits and pieces of other units.

The remnants of the units of the 12th Infantry Division had been merged into a single brigade. Though many were strangers, most of the men had three things in common. First, they had all had experiences similar to those Duncan and his men had gone through. As a result, the second thing they shared was a burning desire to avenge their friends and the honor of their unit. Finally, they were all fully trained and competent combat infantrymen.

Duncan and his lieutenant, a man who had fought at Pariz and Sa'idabad, drove their platoon hard in the short time they had been given to prepare for combat. No one complained. No one asked why. They knew. They had seen the face of battle and knew it well. The only problem that Duncan had to deal with was impatience. They were ready to go, *now.* They were all impatient to wreak vengeance on an enemy that had once seemed unstoppable.

Shortly after stand-to that morning, word came down that they were about to be given their opportunity. Duncan could barely contain his excitement as the platoon leader briefed them on their mission. They were going to deploy north by helicopter to contain and destroy a Soviet airborne unit that had been dropped a few hours before in the vicinity of Qotbabad. The lieutenant told them that the airhead straddled the main supply route to the north and had to be eliminated. He had accentuated the word "eliminated." When he had finished, he asked Duncan whether he had anything to add.

From the rear of the platoon, Duncan commented, "Well, I can't think of a better way to start the day. You people know the drill. Precombat inspection in twenty minutes. Now hit it."

There was no need to repeat the command. His men scattered to draw extra ammo, fill canteens and grab their rucksacks.

Five Kilometers North of Hajjiabad, Iran
1245 Hours, 1 August (0915 Hours, 1 August, GMT)

Throughout the morning the units of the U.S. 2nd Brigade monitored the progress of the battle between the lead Soviet motorized rifle division and the armored cavalry regiment. Once the main Soviet effort had been identified, the corps piled on with everything it could. Working in conjunction with one another, attack helicopters, artillery and Air Force close air support hammered exposed Soviet formations. Artillery, firing counterbattery fires, reduced the responsiveness and effectiveness of Soviet artillery. The ground units of the cavalry regiment in front of the attacking Soviet regiments gave way grudgingly, moving back one step at a time, maintaining contact and exacting a toll from the enemy. While the cavalry's victory cost them dearly, by the time they were ready to pass the battle off to the 2nd Brigade the Soviet first-echelon motorized rifle division was incapable of further offensive operations.

The battle moving toward the 3rd of the 4th Armor was well defined. Reports from the cavalry regiment, intelligence gained from electronic-warfare units and in-flight reports from Air Force pilots returning from strikes against the Soviets provided a clear picture of what was coming. That, some say, is half the battle. Now all the 3rd of the 4th had to do was destroy the enemy.

The Soviets also had their intelligence units gathering information. They knew what they were getting into and had a plan for dealing with it. MI-28 Havoc attack helicopters moved in advance of the attacking ground formations, seeking targets. Artillery units began to move forward in preparation for the attack in the main battle area. Electronic-warfare units swept through the FM radio spectrum searching for active frequencies, jamming, listening or directing artillery against the transmitter. With grim determination, the second-echelon motorized rifle division moved forward through the shattered remains of the first-echelon division and continued the attack.

The command net of the 3rd of the 4th Armor came alive with reports from the scout platoon. The Soviets were coming forward with two battalions deployed abreast. No doubt there was a third battalion close behind, the second-echelon battalion of the motorized rifle regiment. As with the battle of 9 July, the scouts began to call for artillery against the advancing enemy. The Soviets' artillery joined the fray, striking at suspected locations in advance of their attacking formations and laying down a smoke-screen to cover the move of the motorized rifle battalions and confuse the Americans. Unlike the 9 July battle, Soviet jamming and artillery fire appeared to be quite effective.

From his position, Major Dixon watched intently as the Soviets began to close on the first line of barriers. The defending battalion was deployed in a wide valley in the shape of a large W. Each of the companies formed a leg of the W and faced into one of two kill zones, while the scout platoon sat on a small hill at the center tip of the W. Team Alpha, which was tank heavy with one mech and two tank platoons, along with Team Charlie, mech heavy with one tank and two mech platoons, covered the western V of the W. Team Bravo, tank heavy, along with Team Delta, mech heavy, covered the eastern V of the W. If needed, one of the company teams in the center could swing in the opposite direction to assist its sister unit. The tank-heavy company teams on either flank could be used to counterattack if needed.

The leaders of the battalion had positioned themselves where they could control a portion of the battle. The battalion commander was with Team Delta in the east. Dixon was with Team Alpha in the west. The battalion XO was at the battalion TOC, where he would monitor the battle, ensure that reports were being submitted to Brigade, orchestrate fire support, request assistance from Brigade as required and be ready to assume command of the battalion if necessary.

Everyone assumed that the Soviets would send one of the lead battalions on either side of the hill where the scouts were located. Otherwise they would have to close up and go through the kill zones literally hub to hub. Two American companies working together would be more than enough to deal with a single motorized rifle battalion coming at them one at a time.

All seemed to be in order and progressing as the leadership of the 3rd of the 4th Armor had projected until the Soviets were three kilometers from the scout platoon's positions. For a moment, all Soviet artillery fire ceased. This was no surprise. It was assumed that it was being shifted to the next line of targets in advance of the oncoming attack. In the distance, all Dixon could see was smoke settling in the low areas. From where his tank sat he would be unable to see the Soviets until they entered the hollow of the V being covered by Alpha and Charlie. The battalion commander, on the other side of the battalion's sector, could see only the engagement zones to his immediate front. Only the scouts were able to see the enemy.

The resumption of artillery was sudden and shocking. The hill where the scouts were located was smothered with fire and dirty columns of sand, rock and smoke thrown up by explosions. To the east, Team Delta's positions were also enveloped by a massive artillery strike. Multiple-rocket launchers, Dixon thought. Either they know exactly where we are or they're damned lucky. As he watched the artillery continue to churn up the hill in the center and Team Delta's positions, he waited for reports. Nothing came over the net. Nothing to report yet. He waited.

Only slowly did it dawn upon Dixon that something was not right. He looked at his map at the point where he had marked the Soviets' last reported position. Making some quick calculations, he realized that if they had continued to advance at the same pace, the lead Soviet elements would be at the first antitank ditch. Yet there had been no reports. Even Team Bravo, which

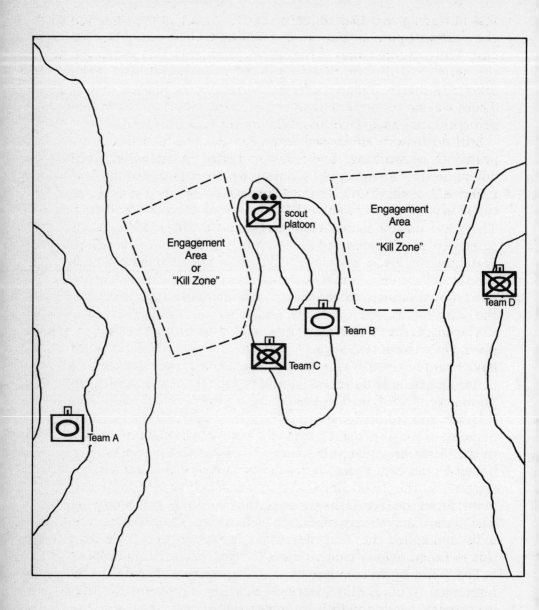

scout
platoon

Engagement
Area
or
"Kill Zone"

Engagement
Area
or
"Kill Zone"

Team D

Team B

Team C

Team A

DEFENSIVE POSITIONS
OF 3RD BATTALION, 4TH ARMOR

was not under fire, had not reported. The crack of tank fire and the *putt-putt-putt* of 25mm. cannon fire drifted over from the east. The two companies in the east were in contact! Dixon keyed the net to call the company commander of Team Bravo. "Echo Six-zero—this is Tango Two-two. What is your status? Over." There was no response. Dixon repeated the message. "Echo Six-zero—this is Tango Two-two. What is your status? Over."

Still no answer. He looked down and checked his radio. It appeared to be working. The firing increased in intensity. From where he was, Dixon could see nothing. Next he called the battalion XO at the TOC. "Tango Five-eight—this is Tango Two-two. Do you have contact with Echo Six-zero? Over." He waited. There was no response. Dixon panicked. He yelled to the loader to switch the squelch setting of the radio to the off position. Watching the loader do so, he listened for the rushing noise that should have come from the radio. Even with the squelch off, there was no noise. "Shit! Wilard, disconnect the antenna from the radio."

The loader looked at the major with a weird look, but complied. Once the antenna was disconnected, the squelch he should have heard before blared in his ear. The Soviets were using silent jamming on the battalion radio net, effectively blocking all communications without the people on the net knowing.

Dixon ordered the loader to reconnect the antenna. Turning to his remote box at his station, Dixon changed the radio frequency to the Team Bravo command net. The radio suddenly sprang to life as Dixon heard platoon leaders reporting status and enemy progress to the Team Bravo commander. He listened for a moment. From the reports, he gathered that the Soviets were moving past Team Bravo's positions, headed south. Dixon keyed the radio and called the Team Bravo commander. "Kilo Six-zero—this is Tango Two-two on your net. What is your status? Over."

The Team Bravo commander, in a fast and very excited voice, responded, "This is Kilo Six-zero. The better part of one battalion is currently passing right in front of us. Break. We're beating the shit out of him, but they keep rolling south. Break. I have negative contact with Tango Six-zero or Echo Six-zero. I think they've been overrun. Over."

That meant the battalion commander was probably gone. Dixon stood up in the turret and looked to the east. He could see nothing. He traversed the turret in that direction and looked through the thermal sight. At a range of four thousand meters he could make out the images of tracked vehicles headed south. The Soviets had broken through. Going back to the Team Bravo commander, he ordered him to use the alternate battalion-command frequency, since the primary was jammed. That done, he switched to the brigade-command frequency and contacted the battalion XO at the battalion TOC. He told him that the primary battalion frequency was being jammed, that Team Delta appeared to have been overrun and the Soviets were coming through. The XO told Dixon that he would have the TOC get everyone on the alternate frequency as soon as possible.

One at a time the units reported in, all except for Team Delta and the battalion commander. As soon as the battalion XO was on the net, Dixon had all units report their status. Neither team in the west with Dixon had been hit. At the last minute both Soviet battalions had gone into the eastern side of the W. Odds were that Team Delta *had* been overrun. Referring to his map that showed the graphics depicting the battalion's battle plan, Dixon recommended that both Alpha and Charlie counterattack from the west into the Soviets' flank while Team Bravo held in place. In the meantime, the XO at the TOC should get everything he could from Brigade to hit the Soviet forces that had broken through. With little time to think and no time to discuss the matter, the XO ordered Dixon to lead the counterattack. The XO would do his best to get everything Brigade would shake loose.

While the XO was coordinating for air strikes and attack helicopters on the brigade-command net, Dixon issued his orders over the battalion-command net. They would attack to the east, with both teams forming a wedge. Team Charlie would be in the north and Team Alpha in the south. Dixon would position himself in the center. When formed, the two companies would drive south of Team Bravo's positions and head for Team Delta's old positions. Once there, the two attacking teams would swing to face the north and the follow-on Soviet forces. Someone else would have to take care of the Soviet forces that had already broken through.

Dixon ordered his driver to back out of the position and waited until Team Alpha began to move past, then ordered the driver to follow the company commander's tank. As they moved into the valley, Dixon monitored Team Bravo's reports to the battalion TOC. One at a time Team Bravo was losing its vehicles. What

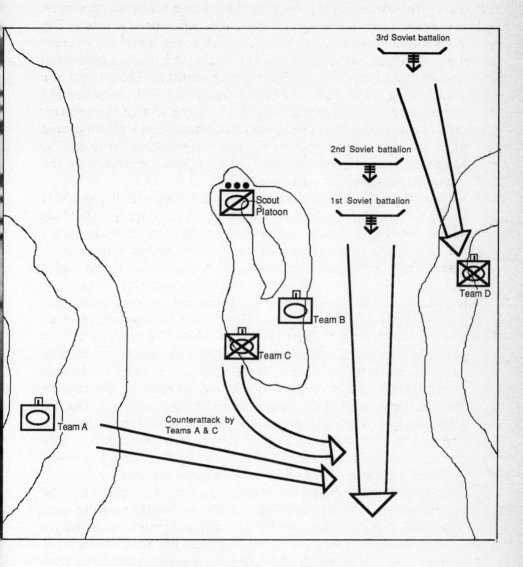

**SOVIET ATTACK, 1 AUGUST,
AND AMERICAN COUNTERATTACK**

effect they were having on the Soviets was not known. Whatever it was, it was insufficient to stop their movement south. A garbled and incomplete report from the mortar-platoon leader alerted the battalion XO to the fact that that platoon was being overrun. Attempts to regain contact with the mortar-platoon leader were cut short by the battalion forward air controller, who announced that friendly air was en route and would be on station in five minutes. The XO responded to this call, but his directions were cut short. Repeated attempts to regain contact with the XO or the TOC by Dixon and the Team Bravo commander failed. Absorbed in that effort, Dixon did not become aware until several minutes later that the counterattack was going astray.

What should have been a simple maneuver was not. As the teams moved into the valley that formed the western base of the W, they became intermingled. Team Charlie, wanting to avoid Team Bravo, came too far south before turning east. Team Alpha, cutting straight across the valley, ran head on into Team Charlie while it was still moving south. This situation was made worse by the fact that drivers in both the M-1 and the Bradley did not have thermal sights. The smoke lingering in the low areas they drove through made navigation and maintaining position difficult. Command and control were lost by Dixon and the team commanders. Then the quick death of the Team Alpha commander by an unknown assailant destroyed all hope of sorting that unit out. The counterattack rapidly degenerated into a cluster as tanks and Bradleys groped about in the smoke, searching for the enemy and the objective. Both were eventually found, but not in the manner that Dixon intended.

Instead of a sledgehammer hitting the Soviets in the flank, the two attacking teams collided with the enemy one or two vehicles at a time. The only thing that prevented complete disaster for the armored battalion was the fact that the Soviets were equally confused and muddled due to the firing into their flank from Team Bravo, obstacles that had not been cleared, scatterable mine fields that had been laid down by artillery, and their own artillery- and vehicle-generated smoke.

For the next twenty minutes a series of small battles erupted between vehicles lost on the valley floor of the eastern part of the W. The clusters of tanks and Bradleys rolled on toward Team Delta's position, cutting across the path of the Soviet vehicles attempting to move south. Most engagements were therefore flanking shots. In this kind of fight, tanks had the upper hand. Their main gun could defeat anyone and everyone they ran into. Their armor could defeat at least some of the weapons being used. Whenever a Bradley bumped into a T-80 and saw it first, the Bradley commander would fire his smoke grenades and back off into the nearest hole. This, however, was not always a good idea in the swirling melee on the valley floor. In more than one case, a Bradley backing up to avoid one T-80 tank backed into the sights of another unseen T-80 or BMP. The same happened to the Soviets.

Gunners, their eyes glued to their thermal sights, were normally the first to spot a target. Screams of "T-80—twelve o'clock!" or "Two BMPs dead ahead!" galvanized the rest of the crew. Tank and Bradley commanders had no time to think. It was simply a question of fight or flee. Normal crew duties and fire commands fell by the wayside as target reports from the gunners were followed by either "Driver, back up!" or "Fire!"

Unable to command or control anything, and knowing that he had no hope of doing either until he reached the positions where Delta had been, Dixon concentrated on fighting with his tank and surviving. Maxwell, his gunner, was quick to pick up targets. "Tank—twelve o'clock!"

In their excitement and the heat of the moment, the crew lost track of the fire commands. Hearing the target report from Maxwell, Wilard responded with "Up" as he armed the gun and cleared the path of recoil. Dixon, hanging on, yelled, "Fire!" even though he was unable to get his eye up to the sight.

Maxwell screamed, "On the way!" as he pulled the trigger. Firing and impact were almost simultaneous, due to the close range. Dixon, popping his head out of the open hatch at the moment Maxwell yelled, "Target!" watched the Soviet tank they had just engaged blow apart as their tank passed it. Maxwell's scream of "Two BMPs—twelve o'clock!" brought him back.

Wilard, knowing that HEAT was the preferred round for BMPs, but having already loaded a Sabot round, yelled out, "Sabot loaded!"

Since there wasn't time to unload the Sabot round, Dixon ordered, "Fire HEAT. Load Sabot."

Maxwell, responding without thinking, again yelled, "On the

way" and fired. His announcement of "Target!" was followed by the cry "HEAT indexed" as his hand reached up and switched the ammo-select lever from the Sabot position to the HEAT position.

Wilard, following through with Dixon's last order, loaded a HEAT round and announced, "HEAT loaded."

Again Dixon ordered fire. Again Maxwell fired and responded, "Target!" Dixon reached down, caught Wilard's arm as he was loading the next HEAT round and ordered him to load Sabot. Dixon did not want to run into a Soviet tank while they had HEAT in the tube. Sabot would take anything out, no sweat. HEAT was, at best, questionable when it came to the T-80 tank.

The battle fought by Dixon and his crew was repeated time and time again in other M-1s and Bradleys as they stumbled forward in the smoke toward the far ridge. Dixon could feel his heart pounding in his chest. He gasped for breath, almost hyperventilating in the effort. The air he breathed was corrupted with the acidic smell of chemically produced smoke, burning rubber, diesel and flesh, and burnt cordite from the firing of the tanks. Every stitch of his clothing was soaked with sweat. Questions without answers raced through Dixon's mind: How much longer can this last? How much longer can I last? Where in hell is everyone? The tank rolled on, unstopping and seemingly alone as the horror show continued.

As it climbed up onto the high ground where Team Delta's position had been, Dixon's tank came out from under the cloud of smoke—to be greeted by the sight of two BMPs off to the right. Dixon grabbed the override and began to issue a fire command, but stopped. The BMPs were not moving, just sitting there. It was obvious that they were destroyed. Letting go of the override, he turned his attention back to the direction they were moving in. Only the chance glimpse of movement through the corner of his eye alerted him to the fact that he had been wrong about the BMPs. Without further thought, he grabbed the override again and jerked it around, yelling his fire command, "Gunner, HEAT! Two BMPs!"

Wilard corrected him. "Sabot loaded." Maxwell followed with "Identified!"

Again without thinking, Dixon yelled, "Fire Sabot. Load HEAT!"

Once the gunner was on target and heard the loader yell, "Up," he ranged, screamed, "On the way" and fired. The Sabot flew over the BMP. In the confusion, Maxwell had not changed the ammo-select lever from HEAT, where it had been set for their last engagement, back to Sabot. Both Dixon and Maxwell knew what had happened.

Dixon repeated the order to load HEAT. Wilard responded with "HEAT up!" followed by Maxwell's cry of "HEAT indexed—on the way!" The second round hit dead center. Its jet stream entered the target's side, cutting through the BMP, which blew up in a shower of sparks and flame, the explosion of on-board ammunition literally ripping it apart.

A thud followed by a wave of heat across Dixon's back rushed into his partially opened hatch. He looked up to see that the second BMP had fired an AT-4 antitank guided missile at them. It had hit the side slope of the turret. There was, however, no visible effect within the turret. Dixon yelled, "Target—next BMP!"

The loader yelled out, "HEAT loaded!"

The gunner, eye glued to his sight, reached up and made sure the ammo-select switch was on HEAT. He didn't trust himself anymore and wanted to be sure. Maxwell announced, "HEAT indexed—identified!" to which Dixon yelled, "Fire HEAT!"

The gunner's "On the way" was followed by a second thud. As the tank recoiled from firing, Dixon turned to his left to see a third BMP sitting on the crest of the hill. When he heard the gunner yell, "Target," he grabbed the override, jerked the turret to the left and issued a new fire command without bothering to look back at the BMP just destroyed.

The BMP commander began to back down, firing his 30mm. cannon at Dixon in desperation. This did not deter Dixon, who continued to bring the turret around. Just as the gunner yelled out, "Identified!" the side and turret of the BMP was lit up by a rapid series of small explosions and sparks. Then the BMP blew up.

Dixon popped his head up out of the turret and looked to his rear to see who had killed the BMP. Two Bradleys, their barrels still smoking, were coming up fast behind Dixon's tank. Behind them came an M-1. For the briefest of moments, Dixon felt relief. He was drained, mentally and physically. His body shook from excitement and the effects of adrenaline. He looked at his watch.

Only twenty minutes had passed since he had given the order to move. We made it, he thought. At least some of us made it.

Not many, however, did.

Headquarters, 10th Corps, Qotbabad, Iran
1925 Hours, 1 August (1555 Hours, 1 August, GMT)

"The commitment of the second-echelon divisions by the Russian 17th Combined Arms Army into the 25th Armored Division's sector commenced shortly after twelve hundred hours. Penetrations along the FEBA were sealed off by local counterattacks and commitment of the division's reserve." Forty words organized into two sentences during the evening briefing to the corps commander summarized the battle that had consumed the 3rd of the 4th Armor. What had happened that day, however, was no longer of any concern to the corps except that it had set the stage for the next phase of the battle.

The real emphasis of the evening briefing was on the options available to the corps as a result of the day's fighting. These options were simple: the corps could remain on the defense and allow the Soviets to attack again; it could order the divisions to conduct local counterattacks to restore the original front line; or it could begin the corps counteroffensive. For several minutes, Lieutenant General Weir discussed all three options with the operations officer and the intelligence officer. He played the devil's advocate, attacking each option from various angles. There was no clear consensus on what was the best option. The operations officer preferred to limit the next day's operations to local counterattacks by the divisions. He felt that the situation was not sufficiently favorable for commencement of the corps counteroffensive. The intelligence officer was even more conservative. His people were still sifting through the glut of information, some of it contradictory, that they had received from various sources ranging from satellites to spot reports sent in by soldiers on the forward edge. He wanted more time to clarify Soviet dispositions and intentions.

In the end, however, only the corps commander's opinion mattered. As a commander, he and he alone was held responsible for the success or failure of his unit. For several minutes he sat staring at the map, slightly slouched down in his chair, his arms propped up on the table, the fingers of his hands intertwined.

When he had decided, he turned to his operations officer. "We attack. H-Hour will be twenty-one hundred hours tomorrow night." Standing up, he faced his assembled staff, "I'm tired of waiting for the Russians to decide what they're going to do and reacting to them. From here on in, we are going to make him react to us. Does anyone have any questions?"

No one answered.

"Good! Remember, think north!"

Chapter 20

*When you want to do battle, muster all your
forces, not neglecting any of them; a battalion sometimes decides a battle.*
—ARTHUR WELLESLEY,
DUKE OF WELLINGTON

North of Aliabad, Iran
1830 Hours, 2 August (1500 Hours, 2 August, GMT)

Ed Martain's eyes darted from his instruments to the ground
they were skimming along. His damaged F-15E shook and vi-
brated every time he attempted the simplest maneuver. Only by
reducing speed could he reduce the vibrations. But to do so only
meant that it would take them longer to make it back across the
forward line of their own troops. For better or worse, he pushed
his aircraft as far as he dared. In the backseat, Martain's wizzo sat
tight-lipped. Most of his equipment was malfunctioning or simply out. Whatever happened to him depended on Martain. There
was nothing he could do except check their six, or rear, and pray.

The mission, like most of the others, had been hastily planned
and came too soon after their last. At Bandar Abbas the ground
crews were literally falling over from exhaustion as they tried to
turn the squadron's aircraft around in preparation for the next
strike. Maintenance crews did their damnedest to keep a high
number of planes on line, but they were fighting a losing battle
as scheduled maintenance services, postponed too many times,
were finally beginning to take their toll. This, coupled with

losses to ground fire, had brought Martain's squadron down to seven operational aircraft. The squadron had been slated to be replaced and pulled back to Egypt for rest and recovery, but the latest Soviet offensive had caused that plan to be shelved.

The current mission had been going fairly well until they neared the target. Coming in at one hundred feet to hit a supply dump, the flight of two aircraft making the run found themselves flying over a Soviet recon unit sitting in a wadi. The lead plane got through before the ground fire reached a high level of intensity or effectiveness, but Martain, in the trail aircraft, was not nearly as lucky. His plane caught the full force of the Soviet ground fire, which knocked out the right engine, tore great holes out of the wings and the control surfaces and screwed up most of the electronics. Fortunately, just before he entered the worst of the fire Martain had dumped his entire load of bombs, exacting a large measure of revenge but doing little else. The punishing ground fire could not be avoided. That they were still airborne was nothing short of a miracle.

"Hang in there, Frank, we'll make it. If I gotta hold this thing together with my bare hands we'll make it." A sudden shudder shook the aircraft.

"I sure hope you do a better job holding on to this plane than you did holding on to that blonde back at Langley."

Martain was thankful for the wizzo's effort to relieve the tension. He looked down at his left leg for a moment. He had been hit. Some dumb Commie dogface, firing wildly, and probably with his eyes closed, had drilled him. The wound, in his upper thigh, was bleeding and painful. Martain hadn't bothered to tell his wizzo. Things were, after all, bad enough without heaping on more problems. Martain moved his leg slightly and was rewarded with a sharp pain that racked his entire body. Biting back the urge to scream, he answered his wizzo's taunt. "Thanks, pal. I really needed that vote of confidence. But I don't think you appreciate the situation. As I remember—"

His story was cut short by the wizzo's scream, *"Two boggies, five o'clock!"*

Martain cranked his neck around to the right and searched for the enemy. He caught a glimpse of them as one of them began a sharp dive in their direction. "Shit! No way in hell we're going to get away from them. Hang on and get ready to punch out." With that, Martain began to increase their speed and slowly turn away from their potential attackers.

The vibrations of the aircraft increased and were joined by a violent bucking. Martain could almost feel the frame pulling itself apart. The increased vibrations caused him a great blinding pain. He had no idea how long he could keep control. Ten seconds? Ten minutes? However long it took, he was hell-bent on pushing the plane and himself to the limit. The last thing he wanted to do was eject behind enemy lines. If he did, he had no doubt how it would end for him. With the wound he had, he wouldn't be able to escape or evade. Ejection as a last resort.

"What are they doing?"

His wizzo, body twisted and head bobbing from one side of the cockpit to the other, endeavored to keep track of their attackers. "I lost them. Can't see the bas— *There they are! Christ, they're right fucking on top of us!*"

Martain couldn't fight the urge to turn and look. If he was going to get spattered, he at least wanted to see the sonofabitch that did it. As he began to turn, the wizzo cried out again. "Oh my God, oh my God! They're ours! They're ours!"

Two French Mirage fighters nosed forward, taking up station on either side of the crippled F-15. The pilot of the Mirage on the left, sun visor up and oxygen mask hanging from his helmet, smiled and waved at Martain, then gave him a thumbs up, signaling that everything was all right, that they would escort him in. Martain relaxed, sweat still rolling down his face. Despite his pain, he forced a smile and waved back. Yeah, everything will be OK now. We got it made, we got it made.

Clearing his throat, he continued the story that had been cut short. "Like I was saying, Frank, I don't think you appreciate the situation back at Langley. There I was . . . "

North of Aliabad, Iran
1830 Hours, 2 August (1500 Hours, 2 August, GMT)

Slowly, and in a stupor, the young Soviet lieutenant made his way through the wadi that was littered with a maze of tangled and burning wreckage. Fifteen minutes before, that wreckage had been a reconnaissance battalion. In a flash it had been wiped away, smashed. Now it was nothing more than a collection of corpses and stunned survivors. Some of those survivors were attempting to save or help those who were wounded. Others, in shock or simply despondent as a result of the speed at which disaster had struck, sat or wandered about in a daze. Even the lieutenant, a platoon leader and a veteran of many fights who was accustomed to seeing death, was appalled at the magnitude of the disaster. That, and the fact that he was the senior surviving officer, was numbing to all who survived.

When he came to the place where, just before the attack, the battalion commander had gathered the company commanders to issue orders for that night's operation, he stopped and attempted to clear his head. His thoughts turned to the series of events that had led to the destruction of the unit. Despite the fact that everyone knew better, the battalion had set up in a wide wadi. While the wadi kept them below ground level and therefore hidden from sight except when someone passed directly overhead, the vehicles were packed in too closely. All was fine until two jet aircraft, American F-15s heavy with bombs and missiles, flying low and fast, began to approach the battalion's position. With the company commanders away from their units, some of the junior officers had ordered the aircraft engaged because the F-15s looked as if they were preparing to attack the battalion. The wild firing had damaged one of the F-15s, but not before they both released their bombs, resulting in catastrophe for the battalion.

Perhaps, the lieutenant thought, we can still carry on with the mission. In the vain hope of finding something that would tell him what their mission was, he began to search the charred remains of the bodies that had been the battalion's leadership. The stench of burned flesh and the sight of bodies ripped and burned beyond recognition, however, was too much for him. Wiping his hands on his tunic as he backed away from the corpses, he fought the urge to vomit. Whatever it was that the division had wanted from them, someone else would have to do it.

In his confusion, it never occurred to the lieutenant that perhaps Division did not know that the battalion was now combat ineffective and no longer executing its assigned mission.

Five Kilometers North of Aliabad, Iran
1945 Hours, 2 August (1615 Hours, 2 August, GMT)

Within forty hours of commencing an attack that had been so well planned and prepared, the commander of the 17th Combined

Arms Army found himself facing the same problems and grasping for the same solutions that the former commander of the 28th Combined Arms Army had faced. The waste of men and equipment was appalling. Two motorized rifle divisions were totally combat ineffective, reduced to less than 40 percent strength. The other two had sustained heavy losses in exchange for little gain and no clean breakthrough. Even the two tank divisions, held back to exploit the projected breakthrough, had suffered from American heavy bombers and attack helicopters. Faced with the prospect of losing the initiative and whatever advantages had been gained from the efforts of the motorized rifle divisions, the leadership of the 17th CAA decided to commit the two tank divisions. As a hedge against possible problems, they also requested permission to use chemical weapons.

The order that committed the 68th Tank Regiment to an attack beginning at 2130 hours on 2 August was received by the staff with an air of indifference. They had been through the drill many times before. The process and procedures needed to move the unit were almost rote. Major Vorishnov noted the lack of enthusiasm with which the commanders and the staff of the battalion conducted their preparation. Even he found it difficult to muster the necessary motivation.

Reports coming down from Regiment were less than favorable and revealed a situation ominously similar to what had prevailed during the failed attack in July. The 68th Tank Regiment was to be committed into a situation that was, at best, ambiguous. The attacking motorized rifle division that the regiment was to pass through was no longer capable of offensive action. It had punched a small gap through the enemy's main defensive belt but had been chewed up by incessant counterattacks and air attacks. Unable to penetrate any farther on its own, the division had faltered, stopped and finally held. To expedite the passage of the tank regiment through the stalled unit and steer it past pockets of enemy resistance, the recon battalion of that motorized rifle division would lead the tank regiment through the gap that had been created.

Vorishnov's mind began to wander as he sat and listened to the second officer present the assembled commanders the current enemy situation in the zone in which the regiment would attack. How many times, he thought, can we tempt death before it consumes us? Perhaps we will succeed this time. Perhaps we will perish. The differences between success and failure were no longer clear to Vorishnov. The fact that he was willing to accept either worried him.

Five Kilometers North of Tarom, Iran
2120 Hours, 2 August (1750 Hours, 2 August, GMT)

Ed Lewis paced back and forth in the battalion TOC, from the situation map hung from the TOC extensions at one end of the work area to the rear of the M-577 command-post carrier and back again. Master Sergeant Ken Mayfree, sitting at a field desk, was monitoring the radios and recording a summary of all transmissions in a duty log. Although Lewis could listen to the same radio transmissions over remote speakers located near the map, he preferred to stand in front of Mayfree and listen there. The major's nervous restlessness was contagious and annoying. Finally, while Lewis was standing in front of him, Mayfree looked his major in the eye and whispered, "Ed, if you don't sit down and cool it, I'm gonna break your kneecaps. You're makin' me nervous." Lewis looked at Mayfree with a blank look, mumbled an apology and went over to the situation map, where he sat down next to the speaker of the battalion radio net. He sat there for all of five minutes before he was up pacing again.

The 2nd Battalion of the 354th Mechanized Infantry had crossed the line of departure on time at 2100 hours as part of an attack to support the corps's main effort, also commencing at 2100 hours. The main attack, farther to the west, was being made by the 4th Armored Division and a British armored brigade. The 52nd Infantry Division, Mechanized, would follow. The 3rd Brigade's mission was to confuse the Soviets as to where the main effort was being delivered and pin as many enemy forces for as long as possible. Since 2100 hours the only reports received at the TOC of the 2nd of the 354th had been that the line of departure had been crossed by the scout platoon, followed by the two lead companies. Either the enemy had withdrawn or they were sucking the battalion into a fire sack. While the unopposed progress was welcome, everyone knew that it would not and could not last. The Soviets were out there, somewhere, waiting.

The battalion staff at the TOC was impatient. Every time the radio crackled to life, ears perked up and breath was held. Reports of negative contact did not bring sighs of relief, only heightened tension. Until something happened, there was nothing for the people at the TOC to do. Those staff officers with the command group, which was following the lead companies, were out there, moving forward, which at least gave them the sense of accomplishing something, doing something. The idle minds of the staff at the TOC, removed from the danger of battle, were fertile ground for nightmares and fear.

"Mike Four-four, this is Tango Three-two. Spot report. Over."

Lewis turned to the board where the radio call signs were posted. It was the scout-platoon leader calling the S-3.

"Tango Three-two, this is Mike Four-four. Send it. Over." The intell sergeant prepared to write the information down on a blank spot-report form. Lewis watched as Captain Norm Smithson, the assistant operations officer, stood near the map with grease pencil in hand, ready to mark the enemy locations sighted by the scouts.

"This is Tango Three-two. Six tanks moving south—correction, make that nine tanks moving south vicinity five two zero, seven seven five. They look like T-80s, but we cannot confirm. Continuing to observe. Over."

Lewis thought about that for a moment. Who else could they be? The thermal sights of the Bradley, great for seeing in the dark, did not always provide a good clear image. Vehicle recognition was, at times, difficult.

The battalion commander called Lewis. "Mike Six-eight, this is Mike One-six. Get with higher and find out if we have any friendlies stumblin' about in the dark to our front. Over."

Lewis acknowledged and picked up the hand mike for the brigade radio net. He was about to make the call when the scout-platoon leader came back with another report:

"Mike Four-four, this is Tango Three-two. Update on that last spot report. Eighteen T-80 tanks—I say again, T-80 tanks—moving south. Lead element now at five two zero, seven seven zero. We are assuming hasty defense vicinity checkpoint zero eight and preparing to engage. Request artillery and permission to engage. Over."

All eyes in the TOC were on Smithson as he moved the plastic symbol that represented the battalion's scout platoon and placed it on the map where checkpoint 08 was located. The intell sergeant took a red plastic armor-unit symbol imprinted with the number 18 and placed it where the scout-platoon leader had reported the enemy formation. The fire-support officer, hearing the request for fire, was already on his radio, talking to the artillery unit supporting the battalion.

After a moment, the S-3 called back to the scout-platoon leader, "Tango Three-two. This is Mike Four-four. Are you sure they're T-80s?"

The scout-platoon leader, without hesitation, replied, "Affirmative. If we wait another minute I can give you the bumper numbers of all twenty-five T-80 tanks."

Slightly disturbed by the wisecrack about the bumper numbers, the S-3 replied sharply, "Permission to engage. Break." Then, to Smithson, "Mike Nine-one, this is Mike Four-four. Get the redlegs on that target. Report to higher we are deploying to engage an enemy tank battalion attacking south. I will keep you advised. Over."

The waiting was over. The tension and stress of waiting was replaced by a flurry of frantic activity in the TOC. Calls went out to the brigade S-2 over the intell net, to the brigade S-3 over the brigade-command net and to artillery units. The S-3 began to issue orders to the company commanders over the battalion-command net, telling them where to deploy and how to orient their units. Lewis watched and listened to all that was happening. He made sure that all people who needed to be notified were and that the orders that were being put over the battalion-command net by the S-3 were written down and accurately posted on the situation map in the TOC. There was much activity but no confusion. They had done this before. The procedures the staff were now going through were no different from those they had used when conducting command-post exercises back in Tennessee. The difference this time, however, was that there were now real people out there. Real bullets were going to be fired, and real people were going to die. It was Lewis' job to see that everything was done to ensure that it would be the Soviets who did most of the dying.

Through the darkness the 3rd Battalion rolled. Vorishnov was concerned about their lack of coordination and of intelligence about what was to their front. Reports of enemy activity had been received on and off for the last hour at the regiment from its own recon elements operating somewhere to the 3rd Battalion's front. Vorishnov had hoped to go forward during the day and coordinate with the commander of the recon unit they were supposed to follow. He had wanted to get a feel for the terrain the battalion would cross as well as some information on enemy unit locations and mine fields. For security, however, additional recon had not been permitted. The division did not want to risk revealing when and where the tank regiments were going to be committed.

The failure in coordination now began to manifest itself. When the tank regiment reached the point where it was to link up with the recon battalion of the motorized rifle division, no one was there. Continued efforts to contact someone and effect a link-up failed. Falling behind schedule, the tank regiment was ordered forward without an escort. Ignorant of exact locations of both friendly and enemy forces, the 3rd Battalion, 68th Tank Regiment, plunged into the night and hoped for the best.

The sudden flashes on the battalion's flank therefore came as a surprise. In the darkness, they at first appeared to be artillery impacting at a distance. It took a moment for the tank commanders to grasp the true situation as flame from the rocket motors of antitank guided missiles closed on the battalion's tanks. The lead-company commander reported the missile attack while his tanks traversed their turrets in the direction of the oncoming missiles.

The impact of the missiles, the detonation of the reactive armor and, in two cases, secondary explosions lit up the night. Three more flashes from the opposite flank pulled everyone's attention in that direction. The battalion was in an ambush of some type. Intead of being greeted by the recon battalion of the forward motorized rifle division, it had run into the Americans. At least, Vorishnov hoped it was the Americans and not the recon battalion firing. How terrible, he thought, to have come all this way and be killed by our own people.

While the battalion commander issued orders to deploy into battle formation, Vorishnov reported the attack to Regiment. The regiment, tracking the battalion's progress, had concerns similar to Vorishnov's. Regiment wanted confirmation that it was the Americans doing the firing. Vorishnov replied that there was no time for that. Regardless of who they were, the battalion was attacking. The battle drill that it executed put into action the contact drill practiced many times by the battalion. The lead company deployed and turned to attack. The next company followed, ready to deploy and support the attack or bypass the lead company if it became too heavily involved. The third company also followed, ready to swing around and hit the enemy in the flank or the rear once the flanks were found. The battalion was committed.

Reports of the scout platoon's initial success were welcomed by all at the TOC. There had been a great deal of concern over the effectiveness of the Bradley's TOW missile against the T-80. Although not every hit was a kill, at least some Russians were dying. The scouts had the task of developing the situation as well as screening and buying time for the deployment of the remainder of the battalion. Lewis followed the orders being issued by the S-3 to the companies and watched as Smithson plotted the progress of the battalion. In another five minutes all the units would be in their assigned positions. The S-2 plotted the advance of the Soviets. The fire-support officer called out that artillery-fire missions were on the way.

Two of the battalion's own companies, reinforced with improved TOW vehicles, called ITVs, deployed on either side of the line of march they expected the Soviets to take. They formed a funnel that led into a tank company, a Kentucky National Guard unit, attached to the battalion. That company took up positions in the center, blocking the path of the onrushing Soviets. The fourth company of the battalion, held in the back of the center, stood ready to swing to either the left or the right, depending on how the Soviets reacted.

With nothing more to do for the moment, Lewis listened to the reports and watched Smithson and the S-2 plot the progress of the battle. The scouts continued to engage, drawing back slowly. Somehow the first report of a loss in the scout platoon passed unnoticed, until the number six listed as the number of operational Bradleys for the scouts was changed to a five. It's begun, Lewis thought, the dying has begun. That the same thought had not occurred to him when the destruction of Soviet tanks had been reported was not unusual. After all, the scouts were killing tanks; the crews of the T-80 tanks had no faces, no names. The men in the scout Bradleys, however, were very real to Lewis. They were people who lived in Memphis with him. They were the people he worked with, had gone to annual training with, dealt with on a daily basis. Sam Cane, a young teacher who taught Ed's youngest son, commanded one of the Bradleys in the scout platoon. Was Sam dead? Or was it Tim Wheaton, owner of the gas station just off the interstate exit, now a scout-squad leader? Was it his track that had been hit? The black grease-pencil figures on the chart next to the situation map translated into very real people. Real people whom Lewis knew.

Slowly the Soviets drew near. The scouts ceased fire and pulled away. Now the companies, in their hasty defensive positions, began to report sighting the Soviets and their readiness to engage. The tension began to build again. Everyone waited, the silence broken only by the traffic over the artillery-fire-control net as artillery lieutenants with the companies requested fires and submitted corrections after observing the impact of adjustment rounds. All waited for the batttle to be joined in earnest.

There was no doubt that the regiment had run into an American force of some size. The increasing tempo of artillery, and its accuracy, betrayed the fact that someone was watching and directing it upon the 3rd Battalion. Vorishnov, his head raised slightly out of the turret, saw no sign of more TOW-missile firings. That, however, was not comforting. It could only mean that the forward elements were finished and were pulling back to clear the way for the main body of the enemy force. Vorishnov wondered whether the Americans had been in defensive positions that were missed by the regimental recon or whether the battle developing was a bona fide meeting engagement in which the Americans now had the upper hand. The truth, however, did not matter at that moment. What did matter was that the battalion was again going into battle, regardless of how it had come about. Their orders were to find and fix the Americans. Once the situation had been developed, the tank battalion behind the 3rd would move to the left or the right to seek the Americans' flank. The quickest and most effective method of finding the enemy was to continue the attack. Once contact was reestablished, the battalion would turn and attack whoever did the firing.

The bright flash, the dazzling shower of sparks caused by the impact of a kinetic-energy round on a T-80, followed by the sharp crack of a tank cannon, told Vorishnov that they had found the enemy's main body. Just as the battalion began to reorient on the source of the tanks firing, it was hit by a wave of antitank guided missiles, artillery and artillery-delivered mines. In less than a minute, command and control vaporized as the attacking force was overwhelmed with superior firepower and with confusion.

Having nothing left to control but his tank, Vorishnov joined the battle. With his hatch buttoned up, he searched for a target. In his sight, the flash of an American tank firing caught his eye. "Target tank! Traverse left." The gunner turned his control handle and searched for the target. Vorishnov saw it first. The green image of a tank's turret was protruding above a mound, its gun pointed in another direction. "Target twelve o'clock. Fire!"

The gunner now saw what his commander saw, lined his sight on the center of the target, depressed the laser-range-finder button and waited for the system to input the data. When he was ready, he announced, "Firing!" and pulled the trigger.

The T-80 rolled on, its sights continuing to track the tank they had just engaged. In the distance a brilliant light cut through the obscuration kicked up by the firing of the gun. Vorishnov watched as a ball of fire rose into the black sky, casting long shadows on everything around. The American tank was dead.

Without waiting for its crew, the T-80's automatic loader was already preparing for the next engagement. The gun jerked into the loading position, slamming the breech open with a bang. The mechanical arm reached down and scooped up the next projectile and guided it into the breech. Finished, the arm reached down and scooped up the powder bag, ramming it home behind the projectile. As his gunner searched for targets, Vorishnov watched the loading of the main gun, careful to stay out of the mechanical arm's path. It's too slow, he thought, too terribly slow.

Targets were now plentiful. Less than four hundred meters to their front an American Bradley appeared out of nowhere. As Vorishnov prepared to engage, the reports of the follow-on battalion could be heard over the regimental command net. He was not concerned with those reports, however. The regimental battle was no longer his. His battle had degenerated to a one-on-one contest: his tank against whatever crossed its path.

"Mike Four-four, this is Oscar Six-eight. I have negative contact with my one six. I am assuming command. Over." The tank-company commander was dead. Lewis watched the situation board as he listened to the reports and the orders.

The S-3 responded without hesitation, "Oscar Six-eight, this is

Mike Four-four. I roger your last transmission. What is your current situation? Over."

"Mike Four-four, this is Oscar Six-eight. Five tanks and two Bradleys left that I know of. Enemy tanks are now passing to—" There was a break in the transmission, then a moment of silence while everyone waited for the XO of the tank company to continue. But he did not.

The S-3 tried to reestablish contact. "Oscar Six-eight, this is Mike Four-four. Say again all after enemy tanks passing. Over." There was no response. Odds were that the XO's tank had also been hit. God, Lewis thought, I don't even know that kid's name.

Reports were no longer clear, concise or, for the most part, even rendered. The battalion-command net was now cluttered by a series of short, incomplete radio calls between the battalion commander, the S-3 and the surviving company commanders. When both the battalion commander and the S-3 failed to reestablish contact with the tank-company commander, they tried to contact the mech-team commander on the western flank. That effort also failed. Assuming that both the company in the center and the one in the west were overrun, Alpha Company, the mech company in the rear, was ordered to swing to the left and cover that area. No doubt the enemy was attempting to blow through the battalion there.

That maneuver, completed in less than ten minutes, ran head on into the bypass effort of the follow-on Soviet battalion. The focus of the battle now shifted slightly to the west as Bradleys went to ground and disgorged their infantry, preparing to fight T-80s. Bravo Company, on the eastern side of the sector, was running out of targets. The battalion commander, seeing the same thing that Lewis did, ordered it to shift farther to the west, move behind Alpha Company and swing around to the north, heading off another Soviet bypass attempt. As with Alpha Company, Bravo ran into the Soviets in the dark as the battle continued to slide to the west.

Lewis watched and listened, wondering how much longer this could go on. Smithson, ever attentive to the reports, kept wiping off the grease-pencil numbers on the battalion status board and entering a new, lower number. Turning to the S-2, Lewis asked how much more the battalion could expect to encounter. The S-2 did not answer, merely shrugged his shoulders and shook his head. Lewis understood. No one, neither the people on the

ground nor the people in the TOC, could follow what was happening anymore. Whatever ability the battalion commander had
to influence the battle had been lost when the last company was
committed. It was now up to the tank and Bradley commanders.

As they listened to the calls and the fragmented reports, Smithson stepped back and looked at the status board for a moment,
then turned to Lewis. "Let's hope this was worth it."

Lewis did not answer. He watched the figures change, each loss
hitting him like a blow. No, it can't be, he thought. It isn't worth
it.

Fifteen Kilometers Northwest of Qotbabad
0435 Hours, 3 August (0105 Hours, 3 August, GMT)

The pilot of the AC-130 began to bring his huge aircraft to bear
on their target. Called Spectar, the AC-130 carried three 20mm.
miniguns and a 75mm. automatic cannon. It was the modern
version of Vietnam's "Puff the Magic Dragon," grown bigger,
more sophisticated and far deadlier. Slowly the pilot angled the
plane over until they were flying along a shallow bank to the left.
His eyes were on the projected sight to his left as he superim-
posed it over the target area. When he had done so, he held the
aircraft steady for a second, making sure that all was aligned and
correct before he announced his intent to fire.

From his position on the outer perimeter, Ilvanich listened to
the drone of the propeller-driven aircraft above, wondering what
it was doing and why it lingered so long over them. It sounded
like a transport preparing to drop paratroopers. That, however,
made no sense here. What was left of his regiment was already
surrounded and under continuous fire from artillery, mortars and
a steady stream of air strikes. Though no enemy ground attack
had been launched in hours, there was no doubt that that would
eventually happen, just as soon as the Americans had finished
pounding the regiment into pulp. Having had its supply line cut,
Ilvanich's regiment could no longer influence the battle, and the
Americans knew it. They were therefore in no rush to waste any
more manpower in eliminating the decimated Soviet regiment.
Firepower and air strikes would do the trick.

The air strikes were the regiment's greatest problem. The men
had no cover, other than hastily dug foxholes. At first, they had

been able to keep the enemy planes at a respectable distance with man-portable, shoulder-fired surface-to-air missiles. These, however, were rapidly used up, and the Americans were quick to sense this. By late afternoon American ground-attack aircraft called Thunderbolts lazily flew over their positions, attacking anything that moved or appeared to be worthy of attack. Ilvanich sat helpless as he watched the evil-looking aircraft swoop down and fire 30mm. explosive rounds at individual foxholes. It was this sight more than anything else that convinced him that this time all was lost.

A sudden sharp ripping sound jerked Ilvanich's attention back to the strange aircraft flying overhead. From one point in the sky three solid streams of tracers stabbed through the darkness. Like great evil fingers the tracers searched out positions on the far side of the regiment's perimeter. For a moment he thought the Americans were using some type of laser or energy beam. The endless chain of explosions, however, told him that the aircraft was firing conventional miniguns. Ilvanich stood up and watched, transfixed. Wherever the tracers touched the ground there was a maelstrom of explosions. It was as if God were reaching down with a giant hoe and methodically digging them out. Of all the instruments of death he had seen, this one was the most sinister and horrible.

Lieutenant Malovidov came running up from behind. *"What is that thing?"*

Without taking his eyes from the horror unfolding before him, Ilvanich replied in a hushed, resigned manner, "That, Comrade Lieutenant, is the angel of death heralding the beginning of the end."

Malovidov, angry at the response and anxious for a reasonable answer, came around to Ilvanich's front and shouted at the senior lieutenant, "Damn you! What do we do? I'm tired of your shit. Tell me, what do we *do?"*

Ilvanich looked at the junior lieutenant and thought, What does he expect? We have come to the end of the line. We die, you stupid bastard, that's what we do. That thought did not bother Ilvanich. He had been ready to die for a long time. In fact, after Tabriz and the firing squad, he had actively sought an honorable death in battle. Only death could cleanse his troubled soul and wipe away the images of blood spattered on the courtyard wall, images that were burned into his mind, images that visited him nightly. Death, however, eluded him. While he stood there, the circling aircraft stopped firing. Darkness and almost total silence returned to the battlefield as the American plane lumbered away to the south. Again death has cheated me, Ilvanich thought. There is little for me to do but continue.

Turning to Malovidov, he focused on the problem at hand. "No doubt, my friend, in a few moments the Americans are going to commence a heavy artillery bombardment, after which they will begin their long-awaited ground attacks."

"Can we hold them?"

"I have no intention of finding out, Lieutenant Malovidov. By the time they go over the top, I intend to be several kilometers away from here with as many men as we can get out."

In amazement. Malovidov asked, "We are leaving? We are running?"

"Yes, we are leaving. At least I am leaving with what is left of the company. Do you wish to stay and join your comrades over there?" Ilvanich pointed to the side of the perimeter that had been raked by the American aircraft.

"No, I'll go. But Lvov, what about Lvov?"

"We take the bastard with us."

"What if he refuses?"

Ilvanich smiled. "So much the better. He will die a hero's death as we break out. Come, it will be light soon and there is much we must do."

The sudden hail of small-arms fire caught Duncan and his men off guard. Instinctively they sought the protection that the bottom of their foxholes offered. After a few moments, the volume of fire began to drop. Duncan slowly raised his head and peered over the top. As he did so, the sound-powered phone leading from the platoon leader's foxhole buzzed. Duncan picked it up and yelled, "Duncan."

"What the hell are they doing?"

Duncan looked out of his foxhole again. The firing continued to subside. "I think they're getting ready to pull out, Lieutenant."

"They're attacking?"

"No, just trying to break contact." Then a thought struck Duncan. "Hey, Lieutenant, call the Old Man and tell him to let them out."

"*What*? You mean let them get away?"

"No, let them out in the open. Let the bastards get out of their holes and get them in the open where we can take them out. Beats the shit out of digging them from their holes."

The lieutenant thought about it for a moment before responding. "Yeah, that sounds good. Get the platoon ready to move while I talk to the CO."

Duncan gave his platoon leader a "Roger" and turned to Sergeant Hernandez. "Get ready to move out. We're going to go hunting Commies."

The breakout had been easy, too easy. Ilvanich, along with half a dozen men, were taking up the rear, watching to see whether they were being followed. Malovidov was in the lead, moving the company toward a rock-strewn ridge three kilometers to the west. Between the two lieutenants the remnants of the 3rd Company struggled to carry their wounded comrades and keep up with the point element. Of all the men, only Lvov had protested. Calling Ilvanich a traitor and a coward, he had demanded that they remain in place. A sergeant offered to silence the captain for good. Ilvanich, though tempted, ordered the sergeant to keep Lvov quiet but alive. The sergeant did so with great zeal, stuffing a dirty rag into the captain's mouth and binding him.

"Move it! Come on, let's go. Keep it moving." Duncan pushed and yelled and did everything but pick up and carry those who were dragging behind. Not that the men needed much urging. They were all as eager as he to get in front of the fleeing Russians and finish them. After a quick study, Duncan and his platoon leader had figured out that the only place the Russians could go was to the west, where a rocky ridge offered them protection and where they could hide during the day before they began their trek north. After having done the same thing for a month, Duncan knew what to look for. He was sure he was right. Now all they had to do was beat the Russians to the ridge and set up there, and they would have them in the open with no place to hide.

He stopped for a moment and looked to the east in the gathering light, then to the west. Less than a kilometer to go. A rifleman, panting and covered with sweat, came up behind him and paused. "Who told you to stop, soldier? Move your ass or Ivan will move it for ya."

The crack of small-arms fire and explosions of grenades at the front of the column startled Ilvanich. He turned and watched the company disperse and drop to the ground. Desperately the men scurried for whatever cover they could. There was not much. They were in the open, less than two hundred meters from the first line of rocks that would have meant safety. But those same rocks, instead of providing a hiding place for his men, concealed the enemy that was bringing effective fire down on them.

Dropping to his hands and knees, Ilvanich began to make his way forward. His path was blocked by men trying to dig in with their helmets and by the bodies of those caught in the first volley. When his movement drew fire, Ilvanich froze in place and hugged the ground. Although his face was pressed to the dirt, he could see one of his men crawl up behind the body of a fallen comrade, prop his rifle up over it and, using the body as cover, begin to return fire. The Americans soon located the soldier and began to concentrate their fire against him. Ilvanich listened in morbid fascination as bullets thudded into the body being used for cover. The soldier's lone stand lasted less than a minute. Ilvanich saw a stream of bullets from a machine gun climb up the body of the dead soldier and hit the live soldier in the face, sending him sprawling.

This is madness, Ilvanich thought. He looked around. There were dead and wounded everywhere. The moans and screams of the wounded were momentarily drowned out by a sudden burst of fire and the explosion of a grenade. Ilvanich decided there was nothing more to be gained from continuing the uneven contest. For a moment he considered grabbing his rifle and charging. He would at last be able to end his nightmares in a manner befitting a soldier. But he hesitated. If he got up and charged, his men would follow. And, like him, they would be cut down to no purpose. How easy it would be to end it now, he thought. I have wanted this. But not for them. I cannot do that to my men.

The sound of approaching helicopters in the distance finally convinced him the time had come. Reaching into his pocket, he pulled out a dirty white rag and stuck it into the muzzle of his AK. Yelling to his men to cease fire, he began to wave the white flag.

Duncan saw the flag as he sensed the slackening of return fire. For a moment, he wanted to ignore it. He wanted to continue firing. For the first time he and his men had the bastards pinned with nowhere to go. Finally he had the chance to avenge his old platoon leader and all those they had left in their smashed positions on that day long ago. This was his moment. He stopped firing, though, as did the rest of the platoon. Each man in his turn looked down at his enemy, now humbled and helpless. Whether it was out of mercy or a simple desire to stop the senseless killing, all firing stopped long before the platoon leader gave the order.

When all the men who could stand finally stood up, Ilvanich counted eleven men. A few others, including Junior Lieutenant Malovidov, were wounded and could not stand. As Ilvanich made his way forward, he saw Lvov, still strapped to the makeshift stretcher he had been carried on. He was alive. Ilvanich carefully moved over to the captain, watching the Americans as they approached. When he reached Lvov, he knelt down and looked into his commander's eyes.

"Well, Comrade Captain, we have come to the end of the line. At least you have." With that, Ilvanich reached down into his boot and pulled out a knife. "You will finally be able to give your father, the great Party man, the only thing that will make him proud of you, death in battle. Goodbye, you miserable bastard."

Duncan watched from his position as the Russians began to stand and throw down their weapons. He ordered the 1st Squad to gather the prisoners while the 2nd Squad swept the area and checked the wounded and the dead. He stayed with the 3rd Squad, covering the other two. As he did so, the actions of one of the Russians caught his attention. He watched as the man, obviously an officer, went over to a wounded man on a stretcher. The Russian bent, then knelt. For a moment, Duncan thought he was trying to help the man.

He was about to direct some men to help the Russian when he noticed a sudden glint of sunlight from a piece of metal the Russian pulled from his boot. The Russian then put it to the wounded man's throat. *The bastard's pulled a knife!* Without hesitation, Duncan brought his rifle up and fired a burst, hitting the Russian in the shoulder and knocking him backward. He watched for a moment until the Russian he had hit began to move. Two of Duncan's men ran over, grabbed the knife from the

Russian and made him stand up. Duncan cursed himself. Shit, the bastard was only wounded. The idea of killing one's wounded appalled Duncan. Animals, we're dealing with animals, he thought.

As the Americans marched Ilvanich off, he looked at Lvov, now being treated by an American medic. He shook his head. Lenin was right, he told himself. There is no God.

Chapter 21

Look at the infantryman's eyes and you can
tell how much war he has seen.

— BILL MAULDIN

The men began to stir and pick themselves up from the floor of the trench. Already they could feel the rumbling of the ground caused by the advancing enemy tanks. Had their ears not been ringing as a result of a fifteen-minute artillery barrage, they would have heard the tanks as well. Even as he shook off the dirt and the dust, Captain Neboatov called repeatedly to his outposts for reports, but got only static in return. Sensing that any further attempt was futile, he let the hand mike drop. The first enemy tank was yet to crest the hill before them, but Neboatov knew what the outcome would be. As the senior surviving officer and the acting battalion commander, he had little more than a company's worth of men and BMP fighting vehicles to hold a front that required a battalion by doctrine.

Psychologically, neither he nor his men were ready for the onslaught. For the first time since entering Iran, Neboatov's regiment was on the defense. A war, Neboatov knew, is not won by defending. But defend they had to. Stubborn resistance by the Americans, punctuated by numerous counterattacks, failure of the attack by Soviet second-echelon divisions and an inability to clear the American Air Force from the skies had crippled the 17th Combined Arms Army, robbing it of its offensive capability.

With great reluctance, the commander of the 17th CAA had ordered the remnants of the army's first-echelon divisions to assume a defensive posture while a frantic effort was made to gather up enough forces to continue the offensive. Neboatov's unit was part of that defense.

Neboatov had deployed his "battalion," the remnant of the 1st Battalion of the 381st Motorized Rifle Regiment, on the reverse slope of a ridge. By doing so, he reduced his fields of fire but prevented the enemy from hitting his positions directly. In addition, the enemy vehicles could be dealt with a few at a time as they crested the ridge. That was what Neboatov had planned and expected.

The appearance of British Challenger tanks, however, was unexpected. Having trained themselves so long for a confrontation with Americans and expecting to see the familiar form of the M-1 tank pop over the ridge, Neboatov and his men were momentarily transfixed as the first tanks of the 7th Royal Tank Regiment crested the hill, oriented themselves on the scene that greeted them on the far slope and began to charge forward. As a result, it was the British, not 381st MRR, that fired first. The impact of a high-explosive round on the BMP to Neboatov's rear sent him sprawling back onto the floor of the trench. He lay there for a moment, stunned.

Collecting his thoughts, he listened to the changing noise of battle. Tanks fired their main guns, and the chatter of machine guns and the pop of antitank guided missiles joined the cacophony. The earth about him shook. Neboatov rolled over and looked up as a Challenger, racing for the Soviet rear, rolled over his trench. He was showered with chunks of dirt and dust torn from the lip of the trench. When the tank was gone, Neboatov, still on his hands and knees, spat the dirt from his mouth and wiped his eyes with one hand.

Hesitantly, he got up and peered over the front edge of the trench. Enemy infantry had already dismounted, deployed, and were entering the trenches to his left. Small-arms fire and grenades could be heard close to where he was. Added to this was a noise that sounded like a wounded cat crying out in pain. Neboatov had read that Scottish troops always played their bagpipes when going into battle, but until that moment he had never believed anyone would do so on a twentieth-century battlefield. The strange, piercing music that cut through the other sounds seemed, to Neboatov, to be a death knell. The end was near.

In less than two minutes the battle had degenerated into hand-to-hand combat. Enemy tanks had bypassed him, destroying what was left of his BMPs. Whatever chance he had had of stopping the enemy was gone. As he watched, no longer able to influence the battle, Neboatov's emotions swung from despair to rage. With nothing else to do, he picked up his rifle, kicked the two soldiers lying at his feet on the floor of the trench and ordered them to follow. It would be a small and short counterattack. But at least they would try. That was all they could do. Try.

From the brigade commander's vehicle, Major Jones watched the 7th Royal Tank Regiment and the battalion of Scottish infantry roll through the Soviet positions and continue north. Though he still wished he were with the lead elements of the regiment, at least he had the rare satisfaction of seeing that all his efforts had finally borne fruit. Normally the staff officers, working well to the rear, in small groups under less than optimum conditions, never saw the end product of their work. They merely went from one task to the next, sometimes not fully understanding the full purpose of their labors.

Jones, using his role as a liaison officer to his advantage, made sure that he spent as much time with the 33rd Armored Regiment as was prudent. Today was one of those days when he had to be there. Nothing, nothing the corps staff or the Soviets could do, would have kept him away. History was being made that day, history that he was now part of. As he watched the battle and listened to its noise and to the reports coming in from the unit commanders, he thought of his father. For the first time in his life he felt that he was finally his father's equal, that he had earned his way in the Army, the regiment and his family.

Headquarters, 10th Corps, Qotbabad, Iran
1015 Hours, 3 August (0645 Hours, 3 August, GMT)

Lieutenant General Weir paced his office like a caged lion. Despite his best efforts, he could not contain his nervousness. Everything was going so well, it was unreal. The Soviet offensive, so long anticipated, had come and failed. The speed at which events were unfolding was far greater than anyone had expected or could have hoped for. The 25th Armored Division had absorbed the brunt of the Soviets' main effort, consisting of four Soviet divisions, while the 55th Mech Infantry Division had parried a supporting attack by one Soviet motorized rifle division. Though brutalized by two days of battle, the 25th Armored had held and given better than it had received. As a result of those efforts, the 16th Armored Division, reinforced by the 33rd Armored Brigade, and held back from the initial battles, had commenced the Allied counteroffensive. The 55th Infantry Division, suffering little during the defensive battles, had joined that offensive at dawn. Initial reports from both units were encouraging. The Soviet security zone and main defensive belts had been breached. All depended now on the outcome of a series of tank battles, then under way, between the attacking Allied forces and the Soviet reserves. If the outcome was favorable, the Soviets would have nothing left in Kerman Province capable of stopping the Allies.

Weir's main problems were the timing of follow-on operations and logistics. The 17th Airborne Division had been alerted to be prepared to make a combat jump with two brigades, one at Kerman and one at Rafsanjan, while holding its third in reserve. The drops would be made on order, timed to cut off the withdrawal of Soviet forces. If the paratroopers were dropped too late, they would bag nothing. By the same token, they must not be dropped too soon, lest the advancing ground forces be unable to reach them before the Soviets wore them down. The recent destruction of the Soviets' 285th Guards Airborne Regiment had served to remind everyone of that danger.

Resupplying the drive north was another problem. In the rush to prepare for the great expenditure of ammunition anticipated in the initial defensive battles, fuel had not been the highest priority. Now, with a breakthrough possible, every effort was being made to bring that valuable commodity into Iran and forward to the units. The last thing Weir intended to do was miss the chance of a lifetime because his tanks ran out of gas.

Weir stopped his pacing for a moment and looked at the small situation map in his office. He pondered the change of fortunes for the Allied forces. Well, old boy, he told himself, the Navy can put their boats away. A week ago I wouldn't have given Bob Horn a nickel for our chances. Now there'll be no evacuation by this Army. We are here to stay. All I need is a little time to grind those other people up a bit and get us some chips for our negotiators when they go to the table.

Moscow, USSR
0945 Hours, 3 August (0645 Hours, 3 August, GMT)

The officer from STAVKA finished briefing the Politburo on the current situation and left the room.

The eleven grim-faced men sat and considered what they had heard and what it meant. The 17th Combined Arms Army had failed to achieve a breakthrough and was, in fact, now being attacked. On the authority of the Front Commander, the 17th CAA had assumed a defensive posture. Most of the STAVKA briefing officer's answers to questions put to him by Politburo members had been prefaced by the caveat "It is hoped . . ."

The General Secretary looked at each member before he spoke. "It is time to open negotiations with the Americans. We have gained much and must ensure that it is not lost."

The Minister of Defense sat up, slapped his hand on the table and bellowed, "No! We must not give in. The army is still within striking distance. We must not stop now."

"We have tried twice, and failed twice," the General Secretary said. "This failure was far more costly. Why do you think we could succeed where we have already failed twice?"

Turning to look at the other members as he spoke, the Minister of Defense replied, "Comrades, we have not employed all weapons at our disposal. We must try again, this time with chemical weapons and, if necessary, tactical nuclear weapons. Quick surprise strikes will paralyze the Americans and allow us to drive to the strait, achieving our final goal."

All watched the General Secretary, waiting for his response, which was: "We have discussed this before. We decided on our goals and methods before we began this enterprise. I will not change them now. The political repercussions from employing either chemical or nuclear weapons would be far too great. Years of diplomatic efforts and achievements would be sacrificed for the gain of a few kilometers of dirt. The use of such weapons is not justified by the stated purpose of our intervention in Iran. No, we will not change the rules now. Besides, I do not trust the United States. You know their history, Comrades, as well as I do. Like a wounded animal, they will rise out of the ashes and seek revenge in a blind rage that will plunge us all into darkness. No, I will not lead our people into a holocaust as our fathers did. The Ministry of Foreign Affairs will immediately open negotiations as previously discussed."

The members of the Politburo sat there for several minutes. The Minister of Defense, seeking support or at least continuation of the discussion, looked toward each member in turn. As he did so, each man, in his turn, either turned away or cast his gaze down—except the last one, the Foreign Minister. In his eyes the Minister of Defense saw condemnation and unbridled hatred. Throughout the previous winter, when the plans for the invasion of Iran had been discussed, only the Foreign Minister had stood firmly against the idea. He had taken much abuse and placed himself in a very precarious position by resisting the will of the other members. The General Secretary, to sway the Politburo to stop the war, had just used the same words that the Foreign Minister had been condemned for using when he tried to prevent the war. Now, in his moment of triumph, the Foreign Minister, staring at the man who had been the architect of the disaster that they faced, took no pride in being vindicated. That little victory had been purchased at the expense of tens of thousands of dead and wounded.

Finally realizing he was defeated, the Minister of Defense went silent. There was no support for a continuation of the war. It had been decided. The battle would now be waged over a felt-covered table in a quiet room in Geneva.

Hajjiabad, Iran
1015 Hours, 3 August (0645 Hours, 3 August, GMT)

The figure walking between the rows of body bags was hardly recognizable as an officer, much less a major. He had no helmet or hat. His hair, stuck together by dirt and oil, was matted and ratty. The face was haggard, with sunken eyes framed by dark circles. Three days of stubble surrounded the expressionless mouth. The uniform matched the man. The tank crewman's coveralls were ripped, dirty and stained with oil, sweat and blood. The only equipment he wore was a pistol in a shoulder holster and a protective mask strapped to his hip. His boots showed spots where the black had been worn off. Major Dixon walked along the line of body bags slowly, looking. He stopped at each and bent down to peer at the name tag tied to the end of the bag. Not finding the one he wanted, he would go to the next, then the next, then the next, then the next.

The men of the graves-registrations detail paid him no heed. They had much to do and not much time. Bodies, already left in the sun for several days, were putrefying in the heat. As two men on the detail brought a body to the rear of their truck, they would stop while the sergeant in charge checked the name tag, looked on his list and made a check mark. The two men then went to the rear of the truck, where one counted as they swung the body bag back and forth until three was called off. In unison, the two men would swing the body onto the bed of the truck, where it made a loud thump as it hit.

When Dixon found the one he was looking for, he stopped. The tag had "NESBITT, JACK R. 176-35-8766" written on it. For a moment he looked at the bag, not knowing what to do now that he had found the body he was looking for. Leaning over, he began to pull down the zipper.

As soon as he did, Dixon was sorry. The stench that rose from the bag made him gag. He stopped, covered his mouth with one hand, then continued until the zipper was halfway down. He stopped again, then looked at the body. What he saw bore no resemblance to the man he had shared so many times with, good and bad. Dixon knew all there was worth knowing about the man in the bag. He knew his wife, his children, his dreams, his fears, his joys, his plans. Nesbitt had become a part of Dixon. He was more than a good sergeant, he was a friend. Now he was gone.

Slowly, carefully, Dixon closed the bag, then sat next to his friend. Unable to restrain himself, he began to cry. He buried his head in his dirty hands and cried without shame or restraint. So many men about him needed to be cried for, to be remembered. Good men, every one. So many.

The thumping drew his attention to the detail. Dixon raised his head and looked to see what was causing the thumping. He wiped his eyes of tears and watched for a moment. Suddenly, what the men of the graves-registrations detail were doing hit Dixon. He felt himself go cold and numb inside. Slowly, the numbness was replaced by a rage that began to build, a rage that overcame all restraint and logic. He rose mechanically and walked over to the truck, drawing his pistol as he went, his face frozen in a mask of hatred. Tears blurred his vision as he walked up to the sergeant, who paid no heed until he heard the click of the pistol's hammer being cocked.

Turning, the sergeant looked into the muzzle of a .45-caliber pistol being pointed into his face by a dirty major with tears in his eyes. *"Jesus! Are you fucking crazy!"*

In a low, emotionless voice, Dixon said, "These are my men. The next body thrown into the truck will be followed by yours."

All eyes turned to watch. The sergeant, visibly shaken, tried to reason with Dixon. "Sir, these guys, they're dead. I mean, they're dead, they can't feel nothing."

Dixon neither moved nor changed his tone. "These are my men, Sergeant. You will treat them with respect, or yours will be the next body on the truck."

The sergeant looked into Dixon's eyes. There was hate in those eyes. Hate that knew no bounds. "Yes, sir, we will be more careful, my men and I. Now please, sir, put down the gun?"

With the gun still pointed at the sergeant's head, Dixon slowly eased the hammer forward. Then he put the gun back into its holster and walked a few meters away, stopped, turned and stood there. For a moment, no one moved. Then, seeing that the major was not going anywhere, the sergeant ordered his men to continue loading. This time, they were careful to lay each body out on the bed of the truck. The major stayed throughout the afternoon watching until they were done. It was not until the last truck left that Dixon turned and walked away.

Geneva, Switzerland
0830 Hours, 6 August (0739 Hours, 6 August, GMT)

The two men and their assistants entered the room from doors at opposite sides. Each of them took his place at the table facing his counterpart. The Soviet ambassador opened his briefcase, pulled out a folder and arranged his notes. The American ambassador was handed a folder by one of his assistants.

The Russian began by reading a prepared statement. It declared that the Soviet Union protested the use of aggression by the United States to interfere with an internal matter that concerned the Soviet Union and the legitimate government of the People's Republic of Iran. For twenty-five minutes the Soviet ambassador enumerated, in chronological order starting with 6 June, what he described as the acts of aggression on the part of the United

States, as well as several alleged war crimes committed by U.S. forces in Iran and in international waters, all in violation of international accords and treaties. The Russian ended with a demand that all U.S. forces withdraw immediately and that the United States pay, through the United Nations, all war damages caused by "this imperialist war of aggression."

As the Soviet ambassador spoke, the American ambassador had fought back his anger. Throughout the entire harangue, he had sat there stony-faced, listening and waiting. Now, opening his folder, he read from a single sheet of paper:" 'The United States and her allies demand the immediate and unconditional withdrawal of all Soviet forces in Iran within thirty days. Upon completion of those withdrawals, a provisional government will be reestablished in Tehran under the supervision of the United Nations. Within six months a convention, again under UN supervision, composed of members elected by the Iranian people, will meet and draft a constitution for the establishment of a permanent Iranian government.' " With that, the American closed the folder and looked at the Russian.

The Russian, pounding his fist on the table, began to spout righteous indignation, accusing the American ambassador of unreasonable demands and not negotiating in good faith. He was about to read off another prepared speech when the American ambassador startled everyone in the room by rising, picking up his folder and turning to walk away. Flabbergasted, the Soviet ambassador asked why he was leaving. The American told him it was obvious that the Soviet Union was not interested in serious negotiations; the United States, therefore, intended "to seek resolution of the conflict through other means."

Convinced that the American was bluffing, the Russian let him walk out. He did not intend to show weakness by crawling to the Americans in order to negotiate. His orders had been to negotiate from a position of strength and to maintain the upper hand at all times. The Americans would be back. It was, after all, their way.

The Soviet ambassador's resolve gave out that evening when the staff at the consulate informed him that the American had left his hotel en route to the airport. In a hastily arranged meeting at the airport, the Soviet ambassador and the American ambassador worked out an agenda, drafted a cease-fire proposal and began serious negotiations.

Epilogue

Nothing but a battle lost can be half so melancholy as a battle won.
—ARTHUR WELLESLEY, DUKE OF WELLINGTON

Kilometer Marker 385 Along the Military Demarkation Line, Iran
0450 Hours, 5 October (0120 Hours, 5 October, GMT)

The BRDM armored car moved slowly as it entered the demilitarized zone. Major Vorishnov hated to enter the DMZ at any time, but especially at night. Lanes had been cleared through the mine fields, but that did not mean they stayed cleared. The Iranians had the habit of slipping into the DMZ at night and moving mines about. A week did not go by without a soldier dying in a supposedly cleared lane.

Entering the DMZ was strictly forbidden, especially with armored vehicles, but both sides did go in—to test each other's reactions and to find blind spots. Vorishnov would have preferred not to go in that night. One of his patrols, however, had gotten a BMP stuck while it was in the DMZ. Knowing the sensitivity of such violations, Vorishnov had decided to go in and personally supervise the recovery. He wanted to be out of there before dawn. Otherwise, there would be hell to pay.

Twenty-Five Kilometers South of Marker 385, Iran
0505 Hours, 5 October (0135 Hours, 5 October, GMT)

The young lieutenant, new to the unit, had been reluctant to wake the major. When reports about an unidentified vehicle arrived at the TOC, the lieutenant had decided not to bother the major until the vehicle was positively identified. Besides, the sergeant on duty told him that it was no big deal, that the Russians did that sort of thing "all the time." But when three additional vehicles were reported to have entered the DMZ, the lieutenant became nervous and sent a runner to wake Major Dixon and tell him of the violation.

Dixon stormed into the TOC, so enraged over not having been awakened immediately at the first report that he was unable to speak coherently. He chewed the lieutenant out, calling him everything he could think of. Then he turned on the sergeant on duty and chewed him out for being stupid enough to allow the lieutenant to do dumb things. When Dixon left for the DMZ at the head of a two-Bradley reaction section, he was still in a rage. It took the entire trip and the cold night air to subdue his anger.

Recovery of an armored vehicle is never easy. What looks so simple and commonsense in a book or during a demonstration is a major undertaking when attempted in the field, in darkness, by men tired, hungry and scared. Vorishnov, impatient to be out of the DMZ, stood behind the warrant officer, asking questions and rendering advice. The warrant officer, as tactfully as possible, informed the major that he had the situation in hand. Taking the hint, Vorishnov went back to his vehicle to wait. Leaning against the side of the armored car, he began to doze.

Night was giving way to predawn twilight when the commander of the BRDM shook Vorishnov and told him there was some kind of vehicle moving in the American half of the DMZ. Vorishnov climbed up onto the BRDM and peered in the direction the BRDM commander indicated, toward a slight rise south of the wire fence that marked the boundary between U.S.- and Soviet-occupied Iran.

Both men scanned the horizon until they detected a motionless antenna protruding over the rise. Evidently there was a patrol there, watching them. The antenna probably belonged to an armored vehicle. Vorishnov turned and looked at the progress of the recovery operation. It would still be some time before it was finished. With nothing better to do, he jumped down from the track and walked up to the wire fence, exercising great care as to where he stepped.

Once he was at the fence, Vorishnov stopped, folded his arms and stared at the point where they had seen the antenna. Perhaps he could cause the Americans to move or expose themselves. If both sides violated the DMZ, the Soviet violation could be explained as a reaction to the Americans' violation. It was worth a try.

"What the hell do you suppose he's up to?"

Dixon did not answer the scout-section sergeant immediately. Instead, he continued to watch the lone Soviet major standing at the wire, arms folded, staring toward the spot where they were. He couldn't imagine what the Russian was looking at. Rolling over from his stomach to his side, Dixon looked back at the Bradley to their rear. It was down low, its turret well below the rise. Their approach had been slow and quiet. There was nothing that could have given them away. Nothing, except the antenna. When Dixon saw the antenna sticking up instead of being tied down, he knew what the Russian had seen. Tapping the section sergeant on the shoulder, he pointed out the antenna. The sergeant mumbled an obscenity, then asked, "Now what?"

To the sergeant's surprise, Dixon stood up, looked in the direction of the Russian and said, "Now I go find out what he wants." With that, he began to walk toward the wire fence, being careful where he walked.

As he approached the fence, he could see the Russian watching him intently. Behind the Russian major the men working on the BMP stopped and stared. The Russian major was a big man, half a head taller than Dixon. Dixon did not let that bother him. He walked up to the fence and stopped, staring into the Russian's eyes.

For a moment, the two faced each other awkwardly. Each man had seen men of the other side, mostly prisoners of war. This was different. The man across the fence was not a beaten man. He was armed and he controlled other armed men. Not knowing what to do, and more from reflex than by intent, the two saluted each other.

Dixon spoke first. "In the name of the Allied forces, I must protest the unprovoked introduction of forces and armored vehicles into the demilitarized zone. This is in direct violation of the armistice agreement. I demand their immediate withdrawal."

Vorishnov, straight-faced, responded in English, "Our presence in the demilitarized zone is in response to your provocation. It is you who have violated the armistice."

Dixon looked from Vorishnov to where the Russian was looking—in the direction of the waiting scout sergeant and the concealed Bradley. Finally he said, "Perhaps we are both guilty of violating the treaty."

Vorishnov looked at the American and agreed. "Perhaps, but only a little."

Each man studied the man across the fence. Each knew what unit he faced across the DMZ and the role that that unit had played in the fighting. Each had seen much and knew that the man he faced had also. Both had seen too much.

It was Vorishnov who spoke first. "How long do you suppose this will last, Major?"

Dixon thought for a moment. "Hard to say. These things take time. In Korea, negotiations took years. We still have forces there in the DMZ."

Vorishnov sighed. "Yes, diplomats do not have the need to hurry. They do not have to face what we have to."

Dixon asked, "Do you suppose things would be different if they were here?"

"No, I suppose not. Besides, they are not of our kind. They could no more do what we must than we could do what they are ordered to do."

The Russian's reference to "our kind" was a revelation to Dixon. He had never looked upon a Russian in that light or thought there was a bond, a common ground, a similarity. As he considered that, it made sense. The Russian, like him, was a tanker, a veteran, a survivor.

A Russian soldier called out to Vorishnov. He turned and saw that the BMP was out of the ditch and beginning to move toward the BRDM. "It is time to leave now, Major. May your journey back be safe."

Dixon stepped back. "Yes. Be careful of the mines. We have a hell of a time keeping the Iranians from moving them about."

Vorishnov smiled for the first time. "You see, we share the same problems. Goodbye, Major."

With that, the two saluted, turned and walked back to their vehicles.

MILITARY ORGANIZATIONS
COMMAND RELATIONSHIP AND RELATIVE SIZES

<u>RED ARMY</u>

PERSONNEL

XXXX

| ARMY | (LARGE VARIATION, NO TWO ARMIES ARE ALIKE IN STRUCTURE AND SIZE) |

XX

| DIVISION | TANK : 11,470
MOTORIZED RIFLE : 12,695
AIRBORNE : 6,500 |

III

| REGIMENT | TANK (T-80) : 1,145
MOTORIZED RIFLE (BMP) : 2,225
AIRBORNE : 1,455 |

II

| BATTALION | TANK (T-80) : 165
MOTORIZED RIFLE (BMP) : 432
AIRBORNE : 312 |

I

| COMPANY | TANK (T-80) : 40
MOTORIZED RIFLE (BMP) : 93
AIRBORNE : 85 |

●●●

| PLATOON | TANK (T-80) : 12
MOTORIZED RIFLE (BMP) : 29
AIRBORNE : 23 |

●

| INF SQUAD/
TANK CREW | TANK (T-80) : 3
MOTORIZED RIFLE (BMP) : 9
AIRBORNE : 7 |

<u>U.S. ARMY</u>

PERSONNEL

XXX

| CORPS | (LARGE VARIATION, NO TWO CORPS ARE ALIKE IN STRUCTURE AND SIZE |

XX

| DIVISION | ARMORED : 17,304
MECHANIZED : 17,304
AIRBORNE : 11,674 |

X

| BRIGADE | ARMORED (2 TK, 1 INF) : 3,657
MECHANIZED (1 TK, 2 INF) : 3,968
AIRBORNE : 1,831 |

II

| BATTALION | ARMORED : 552
MECHANIZED : 844
AIRBORNE : 756 |

I

| COMPANY | ARMORED : 58
MECHANIZED : 107
AIRBORNE : 132 |

●●●

| PLATOON | ARMORED : 16
MECHANIZED : 31
AIRBORNE : 31 |

●

| INF SQUAD/
TANK CREW | TANK : 4
MECHANIZED : 9
AIRBORNE : 9 |

Glossary of Military Terms

A-10—The A-10 Thunderbolt, nicknamed the Warthog, is a ground-attack aircraft specially built for the U.S. Air Force to crack tanks. Armed with a 30mm. cannon capable of destroying tanks from above, the A-10 can also carry 8 tons of ammunition. It has a maximum speed of 423 mph and an operational range of 288 miles.

AH-64—The U.S. Army's current attack helicopter, named the Apache. Now being fielded, it is capable of carrying sixteen Hellfire antitank guided missiles or seventy-six 2.75-inch rockets. In addition, the helicopter is armed with a 30mm. cannon. It has a maximum speed of 192 mph and an operational range of 380 miles. A computer-driven fire-control system that includes thermal sights and a laser designator/tracker/range finder makes the AH-64 one of the most effective antitank weapons systems in the world.

AK—Avtomat-Kalashnikov assault rifle, the standard rifle of the Red Army. The original AK, the AK-47, fired a 7.62mm. round in either the semiautomatic or the full automatic mode. The rifle has a cyclic rate of fire of 600 rounds per minute but in reality can only fire 90 rounds, as the magazine holds either 30 or 40 rounds. Effective range of the AK-47 is 400 meters. The AKM was an improvement of the AK-47, a folding stock being the most noticeable feature. The current assault rifle of the Red Army, the AKS-74, which is based on the AK-47, fires a 5.45mm. round and has an effective range of 500 meters.

ATGM—Antitank guided missile.

AWACS—See **E-3 Sentry.**

Battalion—A military organization consisting of three to five companies, with personnel strength of 350 to 800 men.

Battle-Dress Uniform—Camouflaged fatigues worn by U.S. ground forces. Referred to as BDUs.

Blackhawk—See **UH-60 Blackhawk.**

BMD—The airborne version of the BMP-1 (See **BMP**).

BMP—A Red Army infantry-fighting vehicle introduced in the 1960s. It comes in two primary versions. The BMP-1, the original design, is armed with a 73mm. smooth-bore gun, a 7.62mm. machine gun and an AT-3 SAGER antitank guided missile. The BMP-2 is armed with a 30mm. gun, a 7.62mm. machine gun and an AT-5 SPANDEL antitank guided missile. Both vehicles have a crew of three and can carry eight infantrymen. The BMP is amphibious, weighs 11.3 tons and has a range of operations of 310 miles and a top speed of 34 mph. There are now several variations of this vehicle, including a reconnaissance version that has replaced the PT-76 light tank, and a command post.

Boggy—Air Force slang for an enemy aircraft.

Bradley—Name of the U.S. Army infantry-fighting vehicle. See **M-2**.

BRDM—The standard Soviet reconnaissance vehicle. This vehicle comes in two recon versions, the BRDM-1, now obsolete, and the BRDM-2. The BRDM-2 is armed with a 14.5mm. machine gun and a 7.62mm. machine gun; it weighs 6.9 tons, is fully amphibious, and has a top speed of 62 mph on land and 6.25 mph in the water, with a range of 400 miles.

Brigade—A flexible organization that consists of two to five combat maneuver battalions and various combat support and combat service support units such as engineers, air-defense artillery, military intelligence, supply, medical, maintenance, etc.

BTR-60—A Soviet eight-wheeled armored personnel carrier capable of carrying up to fourteen people. It weighs approximately 10 tons, is amphibious and is fielded in several versions, some of which have a small turret armed with a 14.5mm. and a 7.62mm. machine gun.

CAA—See **Combined Arms Army**.

C-5A Galaxy—The largest transport aircraft in the U.S. Air Force. It can carry 100 tons and all oversized cargo such as tanks, and has a range of 7500 miles.

CO—Short for "commanding officer."

Combined Arms Army—The Soviet equivalent of a U.S. Army corps in size and purpose. It has three or four motorized rifle divisions and one or two tank divisions, plus combat-support units such as artillery, rocket troops, air defense, attack helicopters and engineers, as well as supply and transportation units. The combined arms army is the main weapon of the Red Army at the operational level.

Company—A military organization that numbers from 50 to 180 personnel and is normally divided into platoons and/or sections.

Corps—In the U.S. Army, an organization comprising several combat divisions, independent combat brigades, armored cavalry regiments, and combat-support units such as artillery, rocket troops, air defense, attack helicopter and engineers, as well as supply and transportation units. It is a flexible organization that can be added to or have units taken from it, depending on the corps's missions. The corps is commanded by a lieutenant general and can number from 50,000 to over 100,000 men.

CP (Command Post)—The center where commanders and their operations and intelligence staff, along with special staff officers, plan, monitor and control the battle.

CQ—Short for "charge of quarters." This is a noncommissioned officer who is put on duty at company level during nonduty hours. He is responsible for the maintenance of unit rules and regulations and is the point of contact for receiving and passing important information at the company.

Division—A major military organization that consists of brigades and/or regiments and can have a personnel strength as low as 6,500 men or as high as 20,000 depending on the type.

Dragon—The M-47, currently the medium-range wire-guided antitank guided missile, with a maximum range of 1,000 meters, used by both the U.S. Army and the U.S. Marine Corps. The system consists of a tracker, which contains all the optics and the command guidance system, and the missile, which comes in a fiberglass tube that is disposed of after the missile has been fired. The missile and the launcher together weigh 30 pounds.

E-3 Sentry—An airborne early-warning and control system (AWACS). The Sentry, equipped with state-of-the-art radar and sensors, provides a look-down view of all air activity over an extended area of operations. It is more than a simple information-gatherer; the personnel aboard control the conduct of air operations, directing friendly fighters against hostile aircraft.

F-15 Eagle—An air-superiority fighter. Introduced in late 1974, the F-15, along with the F-16, is the mainstay of the U.S. Air Force today and for the foreseeable future. The A and C models are single-seater fighters, the B and C models are two-seater trainers, and the E model, now entering service, is a two-seater ground-attack plane. The F-15 weighs 12.7 tons empty and can carry a variety of stores weighing up to 8 tons in the A and C models and 12 tons in the E model. (The B-17 heavy bomber of World War II had a maximum bomb load of 10 tons.) In addition to bombs, the F-15 can carry four Sparrow and four Sidewinder air-to-air missiles and has a 20mm. gun with 920 rounds for air-to-air combat. Maximum speed at 36,000 feet and carrying only four Sparrows is 1,653 mph, or two and a half times the speed of sound. It is capable of flying as high as 65,000 feet.

Frigate—A small naval ship used as an escort and for submarine-hunting. It can carry a variety of offensive weapons, including a 5-inch gun, torpedoes, surface-to-surface antiship missiles, surface-to-air antiaircraft missiles, antisubmarine rockets, and a helicopter used in antisubmarine warfare (ASW) operations. It can also carry various defenses against missile attacks, including antimissile missiles, rapid-fire guns, and electronic and mechanical spoofing devices designed to confuse the incoming missile's guidance system. A typical frigate weighs approximately 3,000 tons.

G-1, etc.—See **S-1**, etc.

HEAT—High-explosive antitank. A HEAT round is a round that has a shaped charge in its warhead. Upon impact and detonation, the shaped charge forms a jet stream of molten-metal particles traveling at extreme high speeds. This jet stream literally displaces the molecules of an armored vehicle's armor and forces its way into the interior of the vehicle, where it comes into contact with flammable material such as on-board fuel and ammo—and, of course, with the crew. Reactive armor, now in use in several armies around the world, is meant to defeat HEAT rounds by preventing the jet stream of the HEAT round from forming.

Hummer—The M-998 high-mobility multipurpose wheeled vehicle (HMMWV). This is the replacement for the World War II–era one-quarter-ton truck or jeep.

KGB—The security force of the USSR, reaching into every aspect of Soviet life and into the affairs of all nations. The KGB comprises many services and organizations. Besides intelligence, it includes border security forces, battalions of paramilitary troops for internal security, and political officers attached to military units; and it mans and runs the State's prison-camp system for political prisoners. The head of the KGB is one of the three most powerful men in the Soviet Union.

LAV-25—A wheeled light armored vehicle (hence LAV), in use with the U.S. Marine Corps. It weighs slightly under 10 tons and has a top speed of 63 mph and a range of over 400 miles. Armament includes a 25mm. cannon, the same as that used by the M-2 Bradley, and a 7.62mm. machine gun mounted coaxially with the 25mm. cannon.

LAW—Light antitank weapon. The current LAW in use with the U.S. Army is the 66mm. M72A2 that fires an antitank rocket from a disposable tube and has an effective range of 355 meters. The M72 is being replaced by the AT-4, built by Honeywell and based on the Swedish LAW. The AT-4 weighs 14.6 pounds, fires an 84mm. antitank rocket from a disposable launcher and has an effective range of 500 meters.

LTVP-7—An armored amphibious assault vehicle used by the U.S. Marine Corps. It weighs 26 tons and has top speeds of 39 mph on land and 8.5 mph in the water. Capable of carrying up to twenty-five troops, it is armed with a .50-caliber machine gun.

M-1 and M-1A1—The current main battle tank of the U.S. Army. Type-classified in 1981, the M-1 is in the field in two versions: the M-1, which is armed with a 105mm. rifled main gun, and the M-1A1, which is armed with a 120mm. smooth-bore gun. The two versions have similar characteristics, which include secondary armament of a .50-caliber machine gun at the commander's station and a 7.62mm. machine gun mounted coaxially with the main gun. The tank weighs

61 tons and has a maximum speed of 45 mph and a range of 275 miles. The M-1 is the first U.S. tank to be protected by special armor, sometimes referred to as Chobham armor.

M-2—The current U.S. Army infantry-fighting vehicle, called the Bradley. The Bradley is armed with a twin-tube TOW-missile launcher, a 25mm. gun, and a 7.62mm. machine gun mounted coaxially with the 25mm. gun. It has a crew of three and can carry six infantrymen, each of whom has a firing port and a periscope from which he can fire a special port weapon. The M-2 weighs 25 tons, has a top speed of 41 mph, is amphibious and has a range of 300 miles.

M-3—The reconnaissance version of the M-2 Bradley, found in scout platoons and armored cavalry units. Its characteristics and performance are the same as the infantry version.

M-8—The standard Soviet troop-carrying helicopter.

M-16—The standard rifle of U.S. ground-combat forces. It fires a 5.56mm. round, either semiautomatic or full automatic, and is gas operated, magazine fed and air-cooled. The M-16A2, now being fielded, eliminates the automatic mode and fires a three-round burst instead and has several other improvements, including a heavier barrel that allows greater accuracy at longer ranges.

M-577—A fully armored and tracked command-post carrier. Used by battalion staffs and above for their command post, or tactical operations center (See **TOC**).

Mechanized—Term used in the U.S. Army when referring to infantry units equipped with armored personnel carriers or infantry-fighting vehicles. In the Red Army, these units are referred to as motorized rifle units.

MILES—Short for "multiple integrated laser engagement system." The system uses eye-safe lasers mounted on all weapons and sensors attached to all personnel and equipment. The lasers and sensors are set at different frequencies that only allow a "kill" to be achieved in training by weapons capable of inflicting a "kill" in reality. For example, an M-16 rifle MILES laser can "kill" an exposed soldier but not a tank.

Mine Roller/Plow—Devices attached to the front of tanks and designed to detonate antitank mines without damaging the tank pushing the device. In this way, a path can be cleared through a mine field even when covered by fire from defending units.

Motorized Rifle—Term used in the Red Army when referring to infantry units equipped with armored personnel carriers or infantry-fighting vehicles. In the U.S. Army, these are referred to as mechanized units.

NATO—Acronym for the North Atlantic Treaty Organization, which includes Norway, Denmark, the Federal Republic of Germany, the

Netherlands, Belgium, Luxembourg, France, Italy, Great Britain, Spain, Portugal, Canada and the United States.

NCO—Short for "noncommissioned officer"—a sergeant.

OPFOR—Short for "opposing force," a term used to describe the enemy during maneuver training exercises.

Orders Group—Selected commanders and staff officers who receive the mission/operations order from their higher headquarters. These people, in turn, with assistance from the rest of the unit's staff, will produce the necessary orders at their level to accomplish the mission assigned to them.

Overwatch—A term applied to a tactical method of movement in which part of a unit remains stationary, watching for enemy activity, while another part moves forward. It is the task of the overwatch element to engage any enemy forces that threaten the element in motion.

Platoon—A military organization that consists of as few as 9 men and 3 tanks in the case of a Soviet tank platoon or as many as 50 men in some U.S. platoons.

Point Element—A small group of soldiers or vehicles that moves well in advance of the main body of troops. This element is responsible for ensuring that the route is clear and navigable. Should the point element be ambushed, the main body will not be involved, provided the point was out far enough.

Reactive Armor—Not really armor in the conventional sense, reactive armor consists of numerous small metal boxes arranged on a tank's exterior and filled with explosives. If a HEAT round (See **HEAT**) hits this, the explosive in the reactive armor detonates and, without damaging the tank, prevents the jet stream of the HEAT round from forming.

Regiment—A military organization similar to a brigade but more rigid in its organization. It usually consists of one type of unit, such as an infantry regiment or an armor regiment. All battalions within a regiment carry the same regimental number.

RO-RO Ships—Cargo ships designed to allow for wheeled and tracked vehicles to be driven on and off. This eliminates the need for cranes and fully operational port facilities at the point of debarkation.

Round-out Unit—The current U.S. Army force structure does not allow the Army to have enough personnel on active duty to fill all authorized slots in active units. Some active-duty units are missing entire subordinate units. National Guard and Reserve units therefore are identified to fill out those active-duty units that are short when necessary. These Guard and Reserve units are referred to as round-out units.

RRF (Ready Reserve Fleet)—Civilian-owned merchant ships that are on short-notice recall by the U.S. Navy for use in transporting supplies and equipment in the event of mobilization or war.

S-1, etc.—The "S" stands for "staff" in battalion- and brigade-sized units in the U.S. Army. The S-1 is responsible for personnel matters, the S-2 is the intelligence officer, the S-3 is operations, plans and training, and the S-4 is supply and maintenance. At division and corps level, the "S" is replaced with a "G," which stands for "general staff." When more than one service is involved, as in a joint Army and Navy operation, staffs use "J," for "joint staff."

Sabot—The word is French, meaning "shoe." In the U.S. Army, it is short for "fin-stabilized armor-piercing discarding sabot," which is the primary armor-defeating round used by tanks. A Sabot is a kinetic-energy round that literally punches its way through the armor of the targeted tank. Though the round is fired from a large-caliber gun, the actual penetrator, made of depleted uranium or a tungsten/nickel alloy, is small, being only a fraction of the gun's bore diameter. This penetrator is seated in a base that equals the diameter of the gun tube and keeps the gases produced by the propellant behind the round. This base plate is the shoe, or Sabot. After the penetrator leaves the gun tube, the base plate falls away.

SAW—Squad automatic rifle. The M249 SAW is a 5.56mm. light machine gun now replacing the M-60 machine gun. The weapon weighs 22 pounds with a full, 200-round magazine attached, and has a cyclic rate of fire of 700 rounds per minute.

Security Element—A force responsible for providing protection, security or early warning to a larger force.

Self-propelled Artillery—Field artillery that is mounted on a tracked vehicle and usually provides armored protection for the crew.

Squad—The smallest military organization, normally commanded by a sergeant and consisting of 9 to 12 men.

T-80—The current Red Army main battle tank. The T-80 has a three-man crew consisting of the tank commander, the gunner and the driver. An automatic loader eliminates the need for a human loader. The T-80 is armed with a 125mm. smooth-bore gun, a 12.7mm. machine gun at the commander's station and a 7.62mm. machine gun mounted coaxially with the main gun. The T-80 weighs 39.3 tons, has a top speed of 50 mph and a range of 310 miles and uses special armor as well as add-on reactive armor. The T-72 and the T-64, both of which are earlier versions of the T-80, are similar to it in appearance and have the same general performance data.

Thermal Sight—A sighting system that detects heat emissions and transforms them into an electronic image.

TOC—Tactical operations center. This is the command post where the operations and intelligence staff monitors and controls the battle, receives reports from subordinate units, sends reports to higher headquarters and develops operations orders and intelligence estimates based on information coming from higher and lower sources. Other elements, such as the artillery fire-support officer, or FSO, are normally part of the TOC.

TOE—Pronounced T-O-E, not *toe*, it stands for "table of organization and equipment," a document that prescribes how much and what type of equipment and personnel a unit is supposed to have. A unit that has its full TOE has all assigned equipment and personnel. An MTOE is a modified TOE used in units whose mission requires special equipment.

TOW—Short for "tube-launched, optically tracked wire-guided." The TOW is the primary heavy antitank guided missile for both the U.S. Army and the U.S. Marine Corps. It has an effective range of 3,750 meters and can be fired from a variety of platforms ranging from a ground tripod to attack helicopters. Introduced in 1970, it has seen service in Vietnam and in the Middle East, where it was a decisive factor in the 1973 Arab–Israeli war.

Tracers—Ammunition containing a chemical substance that leaves a luminous trail when fired, enabling the firer to see whether his rounds are reaching the target. Machine gun ammunition is usually issued with one tracer round for every four rounds of ball ammunition. Large-caliber rounds for direct-fire weapons, 20mm. and above, normally have a tracer element on every round.

Traffic Regulator—Personnel in the Soviet Army who direct the flow of traffic. They are usually placed at critical points where convoys must turn, to ensure that the convoy turns in the proper direction or to sort out traffic jams.

Turret Defilade—A defensive posture assumed by a fighting vehicle that allows its personnel to view its assigned sector of responsibility without exposing the bulk of the vehicle.

UH-60 Blackhawk—A combat assault transport, or utility helicopter. This helicopter is currently replacing the Vietnam-era UH-1, or Huey. The Blackhawk has a crew of three and can carry eleven fully armed troops, six wounded in litters or four tons of cargo that can be sling-loaded. It has a maximum speed of 184 mph, a cruising speed of 167 mph and an operational range of 373 miles that includes a thirty-minute reserve.

Warthog—See **A-10**.

Watchcon Level—Level of military-intelligence activity used to indicate the amount and nature of intelligence that will be gathered. As the Watchcon level increases, more intelligence assets are used to gather information concerning a possible threat or to provide early warning.

Wizzo—An Air Force slang term used to refer to the radar/weapons-systems operator in the backseat of a dual-seater aircraft. Also called a backseater, 'gator, fightergator, guy-in-back, and ace of gauges.

XO—Short for "executive officer," the officer second in command of a unit. Sometimes the XO is referred to as a deputy commander, as in the Red Army.

ACKNOWLEDGMENTS

In putting this project together, I was assisted by a number of references and people. While it is not possible to name all the sources or people, I would like to acknowledge those books that were most useful and those people who were most helpful.

Those books that were invaluable, in order of priority, were:

Iran: A Country Study (DA PAM 550-68), fourth printing, edited by Richard F. Nyrop, published by the U.S. Government Printing Office.

U.S.–Soviet Military Balance, 1960–1980, by John M. Collins, published by McGraw-Hill Book Company.

Whirlwind, by James Clavell, published by William Morrow and Company, Inc.

Revolutionary Iran: Challenge and Response in the Middle East, by R.K. Ramazani, published by The John Hopkins University Press.

How to Make War, by James Dunnigan, published by William Morrow and Company, Inc.

The U.S. Rapid Deployment Forces, by David Eshel, published by Arco Publishing, Inc.

U.S.A.F.E.: A Primer of Modern Air Combat in Europe, by Michael Skinner, published by Presidio Press.

A number of people assisted in the effort by reading, editing and commenting on the rough drafts as well as providing technical assistance. I owe a great deal to them for their patience, their assistance and their willingness to give of their time. They include Tom Clancy, mentor; Jan Ciganick, good friend; William L. Nash, Lieutenant Colonel, Armor; David Hilliard, Major, Field Artillery; Mat Kriwanek, Major, Infantry; Don King, Major, Mississippi National Guard, Field Artillery; Kevin Grady, Major, U.S. Air Force; Joanne Moore, Major, U.S. Air Force; Mark Gumpf, Captain, Airborne Infantry.

Finally, I owe a great deal to my wife, Pat, for her encouragement and tolerance, and to my children for patience above and beyond the call of duty.

To all those who contributed and assisted in making this book a reality, thanks.

H. W. COYLE